Treman

A NOVEL

BY JOHN JOHNSON

Copyright © 2013 John Johnson
All rights reserved.

ISBN: 1484996577
ISBN-13: 9781484996577
Library of Congress Control Number: 2013909167
CreateSpace Independent Publishing Platform
North Charleston, South Carolina

Table of Contents

Dedication	v
Bulls Eye	1
The Prime	43
Getting to Know You	69
Confession	81
Palace City	107
Dew Drop Inn	119
The Palace	141
Too Close to Detect	165
A Closer Look	189
The Trap	211
The Decathlon Parade	231
Decathlon Day Two	245
Decathlon Day Three	259
Decathlon Day Four	273
Awards	293
More Evidence	307
The Japes	321
The Treman	333
Streak	349
The Battle	365

Dedication

The One to whom I dedicate this first book to is the greatest inspiration anyone could believe in. A Creator of thought and imagination whose encouragement is there for anyone who believes and can hear. He gave me the desire to share the mystery and path available for those who accept the challenge to seek the truth, the life, and the way..

CHAPTER ONE

Bulls Eye

The sun trickled through the branches as it rose over the sparsely covered hillside. It was the morning of the equinox, a day with an equal amount of daylight and darkness, in the last quarter of the autumn season. The third of the four moons, Henneh, a hazy pink moon, would begin to be visible, as Klue, the brilliant white moon, had hidden it for the last eleven and a half rotations of Amri-Farret. These two moons were the day moons, which turned across the pastel-blue firmament.

Fallen leaves lay in their fading colors of orange, red, and yellow. Some seemed to be alive as they rolled and skipped among themselves, almost as if they were chasing each other in a race to anywhere.

A curious squirrel, jumping from limb to limb, as if testing his ability to grab and release as he appeared to fly, checked the branches for a seed or acorn that had been delayed in falling to the ground.

The chill in the air was apparent. His coat was thicker than it had been for the summer months. And when a whistling feathered shaft grazed his front shoulder, it knocked both his and the arrow's flight off target.

A tuft of hair fell to the earth as the arrow continued its air travel toward the precise center of a tree. The thud of the tip hitting its secondary target triggered a mechanism that had gone unnoticed by the archer.

After glancing off the intended target, sight of the redirected thin beam had been lost.

And now being discouraged because of the loss of a meal and the arrow, the hunter headed off in a new direction. Reloading his bow with the next projectile from his quiver, he was totally unaware of the chain reaction that was taking place in the bark-covered treman tree.

Years and years before, the apparatus had ground its landing into the terrain and stood inactive until today. This was the day. That exact moment that could not have been duplicated. The chance was impossible. Only a precisely aimed hit to a button poised to start would reveal a form never to have been imagined—one that never should have been imagined.

The eager huntsman proceeded to head toward the western landscape, with his back to the rising sun and the wind brushing across his face. As the early-morning hunt was drawing to a close, he directed his feet back to the south, where the cabin had been warmed by the kindled fire he'd started before he had left for the pursuit of food. He'd have to rely on the hind legs of the hare he'd gotten yesterday and a canned jar of yellow beans he'd canned from his garden. He put the aged pot on the woodstove and poured half the jar of beans into the pan. Then he added the meat from the rabbit as the water from the bean juice began to heat. Adding two split pieces of wood from the wood box to the fire, he closed the door and felt the tap on his shoulder.

"Dad, did you get something?" Maddy excitedly looked over his father's arm to see what was in the cooking pot.

"I just about had a fatted-up red squirrel to put in there. But just as I shot my favorite arrow, he jumped to the next limb of that old tree by the treman, on the downside of Dillon Hill. That treman is so thick with gnarled, twisted kindling; we could keep the stove going all winter. And that's where I think my arrow still is. Couldn't see if it went straight through or stuck in the tree."

"Well, that's not too bad, Dad. You know it's going to be Celemass soon, and that could give me an idea of what you need for a gift," said Maddy. He got a twinkle in his eye as he remembered how his dad had mentioned his favorite arrow, because it was the one he'd made for his father's birthday this summer.

His family had moved there from a city, Burton, in the county of Dreck, which was twenty-five miles south. Raised in the hills of Dillon County since he had been born, Maddy had learned quite a few things and some important survival tricks, such as how to shape willow shoots, the straight ones, into rods and how to attach the tips with a few drops of sap from a crackle tree out back. They had brought it with them and planted it when it was just a sprig itself.

In the fall a juice oozed out along the main trunk where the limbs attached. It was so sticky, you could hardly get it off your skin, but it did its job as an adhesive. And it kept those tips on the arrows. He'd been on the lookout for a few shed feathers he could split and fasten to the notched end of the arrow. So he had his mind spinning its wheels on the next project. As he stretched his arms up and twirled them over his head, he noticed his father getting the bowls down and opening the drawer where the silverware was located. They had gotten the set from his mother's grandparents when they'd left the city; his mother's name was Cheraw.

"You know, Dad, if we both had a bow," Maddy started to say, "we'd have more things for those critters' eyes to look out for."

"We'd need more arrows too," Dad answered. Then he let out a chuckle, grabbed the handle of the pan, and brought it to the table.

He knew his dad hadn't meant that it was because he was a bad shot. He just knew Maddy was making the arrows. Two hunters meant more arrows. His father had been named Dray by Maddy's grandfather. He had a slim torso with legs that seemed to stretch for miles. Maddy, when he was younger, would have to take two steps to his father's one. His arms were strong like a steel worker who had worked for years in a refinery. He had a face that was stern, yet when he put on a smile, there was an understanding that could be seen to his heart. The times had been graceful to him, and he looked younger than his true age revealed.

After a nod of the head and a thank-you, they shared the morning meal and talked a little more about the chubby squirrel that was faster than he should have been.

"You'll have to take a walk out there and see if you can find that special present you made me. See if it landed on the other side of the treman or if it might be lying in the thickest part of the tree. I couldn't see it in all the undergrowth, but you might be able to wiggle into places I couldn't," his dad said, as he grinned at Maddy.

"Do you want me to clean up before I go and look?"

"No, you go ahead. I'll clean up." His dad had already put the dishes into the wash pan on the back side of the stove. "But be back before your Uncle Mel gets here after midday."

Uncle Mel was Dad's brother of sorts. He didn't really look like Dad, but he was burly and strong like him. They were best friends in school, and their parents helped each other break ground and plant their trees. Mel Dremel's parents had disappeared a couple years after they got to Dillon County and hadn't been heard from to this day. Dad's family just took Mel into their care until he was ready to live on the land they had readied.

The trees they had planted varied in shapes and sizes. Like the crackle tree, they each had their own special provision.

Maddy headed for the bottom side of Dillon Hill along the path that was evident enough to follow. Yet without knowing the lay of the terrain, you could easily enough find yourself wandering into the woods. He looked at the trees that had grown to their maturity. The ladlebalms and spikenards had been in their family for decades, maybe more. Continuing on, he passed the grove of ovanclaves, where they could gather its drippings for their lamps. Their fine hairs of sinewy threads would run into containers they placed under them, and the oily resin collected would burn for days. The hairs could be woven into wicks and could be ground into a powder after the season of resin was gathered. The powder was an igniter that could be mixed with the crackle-tree sap and stuck to the tips of the spikenard twigs. They were remarkable in design, but it was tedious putting all the parts together. They were a guaranteed copy of a match. It would light and burn for at least an hour before it would burn out.

As he came to the scencee trees, he found himself trying to remember the sweet smell they let off in the spring. This odor was a toxic scent that could do several things, from helping you sleep to giving you a super rush of adrenalin. It was all in the leaves. When the leaves first budded out in the spring, their first puff of fumes could be collected in a bag made from the ladlebalm sacks. These sacks were part of what formed when the ladlebalm went into dormancy for the winter. They were just now being shaped around the remaining balm fruit it produced. The fruit was delectable. You could use it only for a seasoning, as too much would make almost anyone break out in hives.

It was a tart, sweet fruit juice that, when put directly on your tongue, would make your eyes tear—and your mind want more. Actually, it was a narcotic in the right dosage. The sacks from the ladlebalm were like cloth, similar to the hairs found on the ovanclaves yet already spun into a sack shape. They resembled the cocoon that a monzi moth would spin around itself.

The monzi ate the leaves and gravitated around the scencee tree. The leaves of the scencee would then bloom into a purplish-orange broadleaf. They could be picked and used for patches on just about anything. The monzi moth changed colors with the scencee tree throughout the year and used the tree for camouflage. The monzi itself was an aphrodisiac. When you placed its wings over your eyes, you would experience and feel the thoughts of the closest thing to you—anything with a life force.

Its body skin could be peeled and placed over your nose and mouth to allow you to breathe in any situation, including underwater, in smoke, or in high altitudes.

In the fall the scencee leaves would turn to a pasty wax and could be molded into candles.

Maddy had always heard about their produce and knew a few of their uses but hadn't yet needed all they offered.

On his Uncle Mel's property, they had planted a couple of tremans. These trees had been around for what seemed like forever. They could only be planted after they dropped their seeds, which was once every forty-five years. And they had to be planted that same day. After more than fourteen turns of the spotted moon, they would become a tar that had not been found to do anything—anything but make a mess. The old treman had that tar so thick under it that nothing could grow through it. Nothing at all. The ancient treman down the hill had been there long before Maddy and his family knew there was a Dillon County. They didn't really know how long it had been there, but they had used it as a landmark for the corner of the four county lines.

On the upper side of the hill, to the northwest, was Clay County; to the northeast was Morgan County; to the southeast was Braden County; and to the southwest was Dillon County. There, right in the four corners of the counties, was the old treman tree. The seeds had been taken across the four counties as far as they could be taken in a day and planted. As far as anyone knew, they were only in range of the four counties conjoined corners.

As soon as Maddy turned that last curve in the path toward the hill, he saw it. How could you miss this treman? It was only the most memorable tree you'd ever seen, one for which painters would sit for hours with their easels and brushes and paint its grandeur. Maddy had spent many hours around that treman. He took his friends there and lay under its shade where there wasn't any tar.

Since his mom had passed on when he was fourteen, a year ago, he would run down and sit there, wondering if that ol' treman used to watch his mom walking down the path there. Lying on his back, on the hill, on what he thought was the line between Clay and Braden Counties, he'd watch as the wind seemed to go around the treman. There were days when he'd find himself talking to it, as if the treman were going to respond. He would even ask questions, as if the tree were a friend that would answer back.

BULLS EYE

Out of the few friends he had, one caught his attention. He knew what the business of the birds and the bees was all about but hadn't really gone any further than that. But something about Trace had him glancing her way when they were hanging out.

Trace Guthrie was the girl from Rood in Clay County. Rood was a little group that gathered just over the hill and down a little farther to the southwest. It was not what you would consider a town. There were different talents there, such as those who were able to shoe a horse and those who could drive a nail, but that was needed in almost every group in every county. The closest group found relative to Dillon County was about a mile farther east. The group was called Dellac. Out of the four connected counties around the old treman, there were other groups, such as the Elats group from Braden and the Thaed group in Morgan County.

Maddy would play a little game with their proper names, Trace and Maddy, and used their first letters to see what they would be like together—*M* and *T; MT*. Yes, he thought. I would be empty without Trace. Or just M.

They had been hanging around each other since they were much younger but could have counted on two hands the times they were alone together. Yet Maddy couldn't quite get his head around the connection. Did she think about him? Did she think less of him because his mom was gone? Or was there simply a different county thing going on?

Most counties had the same order they went by—rules and conditions stating that you had to buy and sell from a county that was connected to yours. So for the four counties—Dillon, Clay, Morgan, and Braden—there was an exception because they all connected at the treman and by whatever counties were on their other borderlines. The land wasn't laid out in perfect squares; there were lines that were designed by natural edges, such as rivers and mountains, along with straight geographical outlines. That is why the corners of the counties at the treman all shared part of the hill. Yet they did go by provision.

Their earth was called Amri-Farret, in the galaxy of Dregs. Dregs was the galaxy where the remains and residue of life forms found their alternative existence rather than just become a disappearing one.

In Dillon County there was a type of soil that grew almost every kind of tree known to exist. Clay County—thus its name—had soil that was hardened mud, which provided their county with the material to make pottery and blocks for building. Morgan County had a rolling grassy landscape, perfect for growing grains and feed, and raising livestock. Braden County had the minerals, such as rods of metals, which had been created by the turning of their earth, Amri-Farret, for thousands of eons. These rods could be melted down and molded into tools and instruments for building and gathering. There were different metals for different applications.

There was a peace ordinance for all counties so that if there were ever a wrongdoing, it was not tolerated. This ordinance had been around and was so simple to follow that there was no need for example. The ordinance was just never challenged.

BULLS EYE

The oldest person in the county would be the leader and spokesperson when there was a meeting of the minds. The eldest in Dillon County was a woman, Mantra Flagon, who had been there for decades. She was the granddaughter of one of the men who had helped draw and establish the county lines. The lineages of the elders are one of the responsibilities of the spokesperson for the county, and they kept the records of all who were born and how they tied together with their parents and their kin. She could have told you everything about her grandfather and father, even down to where Maddy had come from. When you moved there, as Dray and Mel's family had, you had to bring a recorded lineage from a minimum of four generations—a confirmed copy of the family's recorded ancestry.

The disappearance of Mel's parents had been a bit peculiar. There was a void left when Mel's parents disappeared, producing an unaccounted generation. They had recorded Mel in their lineage and the fact that his parents had taken claim to the land that Mel lived on now. The unique thing about Dillon County was that any time there were imported trees or transplanted trees, there had to be an exact diagram of where they were planted. Then they had to be registered with the leader of Dillon County—in this case, Mantra.

This was an element of the accurate ordinances in Dillon that everyone knew. Whenever there were newcomers to any county, the policies would be explained and clearly understood. There would not be debate about any issue, so that everyone knew what was what and who was who. The foundational system of all life had been a repeated cycle of knowing what would be done exactly and continually so the information could be passed on to any future generations.

This may have sounded utopian in fashion; more simply it was the way it was. And it always had worked. Always.

As he walked along the path, he was switching, with a stick he'd picked up by the ovanclave grove, at some of the tops of the drying flowers. As Maddy got closer to the treman tree's location, he noticed something was distorted. The unchanged treman was changing. A speeded-up swirl began to click and snap. Only the slightest breeze whispered through the air. The wind hadn't moved it before. That tree had seemed to have been resting for as long as Maddy had been studying it. It had added to its fullness and height, but those things weren't apparent to anyone who wasn't trying to notice. A few different drawings would reveal a change in the quantity of limbs and its tallness versus how it compared to sketches done in previous years. This was the only evidence that it changed from year to year, and that wasn't done every year.

There had been years where short periods of mists had been all that nourished the land around Dillon County, and in those years, the trees didn't change. Fortunately they still produced their leaves, sap, and sacks. There was a difference in size and the amounts that could be collected, even with little moisture, but other than that, who had that kind of interest? Who notices the minute things?

Now, as Maddy watched, the treman seemed to be coming alive. The clicking and snapping wasn't the branches breaking or falling off; the sound was coming from within the trunk. The movement wasn't a rapid burst of change; it was more like a series of slow-motion snapshots that could be thumbed through, showing the time-lapse changes. Without one being close and directly looking at the occurrence, this subtle transformation would have been unnoticed. Here this unsuspecting observer had unintentionally stumbled onto an event that would have been new even to Mantra's grandfather.

Maddy hadn't thought to fear what might be happening. His drawing closer to the treman was that of a curious kitten. He crept slowly up to the moving object, with the readiness to spring away should something go off too suddenly. He hadn't known fear, as there wasn't a concept of the action to panic. What was there to fear?

Carefulness wasn't just a second-nature reaction; it just was what everyone did. Taking chances and boldness wouldn't have described the society. Passive and acceptance were the motors that had carried the groups to the place where they were now.

Maddy's father had passed down the history lessons of the county, as far as he had the knowledge. But his family was an implant. The closest thing to knowing all of history would lie in the archives. They were kept in an organized vault at Mantra's. You relied on memorization and the teachings of the ancients and not only on the facts kept in the vault. If ever there was a question about the past, the crypt would be opened, and the answer to the question found. Even with Mantra's ability to remember jots and tittles of details, she wouldn't have known everything, especially everything that had transpired in the prerecorded time. And those logs and statutes were from those who had figured out that their times might solve a possible future question, not answer the indefinite.

Any stories or stretches of the imagination were only allowed with the clarification of just that. The storyteller had to begin the tale with a disclosure that what he or she were about to share was just a spurt of an imagination or just telling a story. The repetitive known facts became stories by their own resolve. The rarity of stories and their being fictional never held much water.

Maddy was experiencing a factual story, one that had the quality of capturing your attention. This was really going on, and his eyes and ears were piquing with new input.

It was an unexplainable mystery that he'd never heard anything about. Something had caught his attention in the moving pictures his eyes were recording. It must be a flash of the arrow his dad had shot. The glimpse of the flickering arrow as it bounced around on the route to the ground had him guessing there must be something on the tip, a wad of matter that made it fall the way it had. It hadn't just flown straight down; it had bumped as it fell. And unless the razor-sharp tip had broken off, it wouldn't have bounced off wood. It would have stuck.

Being jarred out of the mesmerizing spectacle he'd been watching, Maddy's sprang his feet into motion. He ran toward the base of the treman. Seeing part of the shaft on the slick, dark ground, he slid on his side, feet first, snatching the arrow with his right hand and shifting to his left. He used his left hand and arm to get his feet back under him. He thought about the games they would play and remembered the time he had done a similar slide into safety just before Ben had tagged him.

Running backward toward the path to home, Maddy had the arrow in hand, with a round object that looked like wood stuck to the tip. Still wanting to watch the event taking place, he never saw the dip and tripped, hitting his head on a rock-hard root from an ovanclave tree.

Maddy's eyes felt like daggers had been poked in them when he tried opening his eyelids. As he blinked and then tried to move his hands toward his eyes to rub them, he found it wasn't working. He could feel his arms and thought his fingers were wiggling, but he couldn't get them to move.

The sounds he heard were the voices of his dad and Uncle Mel. He heard the grinding sound of something being crushed with the pestle in the ceramic bowl.

They had gotten them from Trace's parents, after his mom was gone. Trace had brought them by, timidly offered them to Maddy, turned, and ran back outside. The ceramic bowl was brilliant purple clay that would have been dyed by the powder from the scencee leaves during their late-spring season. The grinder was that off-green color when the leaves began to change during the summer season.

Maddy was hoping he could see those colorful pieces of pottery, but his eyes couldn't open without stinging.

Calling out to his dad, Maddy started asking about his arrow. "Dad, where's your arrow? Why can't I see?" Then he asked, "What's going on with the treman?"

TREMAN

His dad came over with a moistened ladlebalm sack and wiped Maddy's eyes. "What arrow? And what's this about the treman?"

At this point Maddy started to see the shape of his dad and continued to ask, "Where is the arrow, Dad? Your arrow—the one I made for your birthday. I found it at the ol' treman." He tried to sit up, but again his arms would not cooperate. Then he asked, "What's going on with my arms? I can't get them to move."

"You got a pretty good knock on the noggin, and by the size of that knob on the back of your head, it's no wonder you are having trouble doing anything. When Mel and I came looking for you, it was getting on toward dark. We didn't think of much else other than to carry you back here and watch and see what might be going on."

Maddy could now see Mel in the background and asked, "Uncle Mel, did you notice the treman? You know what they are supposed to look like now."

"No, kid. I got pretty concerned about you first off, when we found you just lying there by the trail," he replied. "But I'm glad you seem to be coming around. Try to move your fingers again."

This attempt was successful. Maddy could make a motion with his fingers. What a relief to their minds—to Maddy's mind especially. If he could move them, maybe he'd begin to get feeling and motion back.

A few minutes went by, and Maddy began to tell his dad and Mel what had happened.

BULLS EYE

"When I got to the bend in the trail, just before you see the ol' treman, I hadn't thought much more than looking for your arrow. But when the turn put me in view of the treman, something looked different. That old tree was moving, just barely, but I could hear something too."

Mel stopped him and said, "Maddy, you know you're supposed to tell us that you're telling a story. Remember? You can't just start saying something like this without revealing it's just a story or an imagination."

"I'm not telling you a story!" Maddy exclaimed. "Not a fake story."

"Boy, that bump on the head must have knocked something loose," said Dray. "You'll be all right in a few hours. And in the morning, we'll see what your story is."

"But Dad…"

"That's enough for tonight, Maddy. Now get some rest, and we'll talk more in the morning."

Maddy tried to roll over and replay the sights and sounds he'd heard and seen, which were still very vivid in his mind. The bump on his head was pretty sore, though, and even with the excitement and wonder of his experience and trying to stay awake, he fell asleep.

The first noise of the morning woke him up. Dad was stirring the coals in the stove, getting it ready for the morning warm-up. After putting the wood in and shutting the fire door, he walked toward the entry, reaching up to grab his bow and quiver.

Maddy called out, "Dad, can I please come with you?"

"How's your head?" he replied.

Maddy hadn't thought about that yet. His mind had started thinking about the events of yesterday before he'd thought about any pain in his head. As he started to get up, things seemed just slightly fuzzy. But he wasn't going to admit that to his father or wait another second to get down to the last thing he remembered before tripping over that ovanclave root.

"I'm fine. Give me a minute to get ready?" he asked.

"One minute? What's the hurry? You usually like staying in bed until the fire gets going."

As he flew by his dad, he grabbed his jacket and opened the door. "Come on, Dad. Let's get there before the animals are all hidden for the day."

Maddy went ahead of his dad, turning toward the northwest trail. He wasn't hungry. He could not have cared less if ten rabbits and a hundred squirrels would have put bull's-eyes on their chests and screamed, "Shoot me," at his dad. He was on a mission. Nothing could stop his reason for being up and out of the cabin and his warm bed this morning.

When he rushed ahead of his dad, the hunter with a purpose, Maddy slowed down enough for his dad to be in sight. He didn't want to mess up the reason they were doing this hunt together. Even though Maddy had a completely different objective in his hunting manual, if his dad weren't there to witness it with him, it would be assumed to be another unbridled, unbelievable story.

The same time the squirrel had been jumping through the branches the morning before, out of nowhere it jumped from the ovanclave and bounded ahead of Maddy on the path, headed for the withering old tree by the treman.

The command from behind him was, "Hit the dirt!" Maddy's knees buckled, and to the ground he went. The whizzing sound of feathers whisking through the air went inches over his head. When he looked up from the puff of dust he'd created, the squirrel lay dead ten steps ahead of him. It was just one part of life that would pass along its energy into the circle of life.

It was a perfect shot. Maddy forgot his goal for a moment, as he considered whether he could have pulled that shot off. He was thinking about just how good a shot his dad was.

"What do you think now?" asked Dray.

"I think yesterday was practice for you and the squirrel. You just got better today from that practice."

Dad laughed and picked up the meal with the arrow in it. Wiping the tip off on his pants, he put the squirrel in the ladlebalm sack that was draped over his shoulder with the braided rope from the ovanclave's hairy thread.

"Look, Dad, the treman," said Maddy.

"Good thing we got that squirrel before he got to it today. It could have cost us another arrow," was the reply.

Maddy wasn't sure what he was expecting. He wasn't sure if there was anything to expect. He just knew he wanted to see what had changed from the last eyeshot he remembered before he had stepped into that hole that had caused him to lose his footing and trip.

Nothing!

Nothing had changed that he could tell. There was a spot where the bark had sheared off the undercoating and had a scaly-looking texture beneath. But that could have been there before his lights went out. The branches were what he'd last seen. There were no sounds and no more movement. His eyes were fixed to make sure.

Thoughts of what to say to Dad and how to explain what he was convinced he'd witnessed swirled in his mind. Then it clicked. The arrow was the missing clue. Find the arrow with that round thing on it. That will help tell a portion of yesterday's account.

Maddy ran back to the ovanclave root and dropped down to his knees again. He began to feel in the long grass for the missing clue. It couldn't have gone too far. He'd had a good hold of it when he'd started to retreat. The search broadened with no results. Then just as the thought came to question whether the experience was a story, there it was. The yellow-painted rings fixed his eyes, and reaching for the arrow, he wondered whether the object would still be on the end, stuck to the tip.

"Yes!" He let the joy escape from his vocal chords; he was joyful and cheered. Now he knew he hadn't imagined it all. This round wooden item was the key to it all. How right he had been.

Taking the tip out of it was no small feat. Even though it had glanced off the squirrel, it still had enough force to seat itself soundly in this peg. Just as his father got to him, it popped out. He quickly shoved it into his pocket and handed his dad the arrow.

"Here you go, Dad. Happy Celemass, a little bit early. Didn't have time to wrap it," he said as he smiled.

"I wondered what made you holler so loud. Well, let's head back. We'll prepare this meal and add the rest of those yellow beans with it for lunch."

Maddy couldn't wait to get home once there he jumped into his bed, and hid underneath the blankets.

"Are you going back to sleep, sleepyhead? I figured you got up too early," his dad remarked. "I'll get you up when lunch is done."

Lunch was the last thing on Maddy's mind. Who could think of eating when there was this piece of the treman in his fingers? He turned and rolled it in his hands. The feeling was back in his hands again, and the surface of this chunk, of what felt like knobby metal sandpaper, had piqued his senses. A section of the peg had a flattened, smooth area with grooves that looked like some kind of symbols. They had been etched by an engraving tool or pressed into the peg. Even though Maddy wasn't experienced in carving or etching, he'd seen items at bazaars and swap gatherings the counties would have once or twice a quarter.

These swapping events were a way to intermingle with the other groups and sample each other's handiwork. Bartering was the ideal. Almost any sort of currency was either a practical tool or a needed commodity.

Food and drink were exchanged, and inventive ideas were shared. When you were given an idea that would be of a benefit, the benefit was not salable but was freely shared. If it were able to be produced and become a ware, then bartering ensued.

TREMAN

Dad had found a way to stretch the hairs of his prey by soaking them in the scencee tree's summer leaf juice. After they soaked for a week, they could be stretched to four times their length and still maintain their strength. A couple years later, he had tried it with his own hair. The result was the same, except there was something different about human hair compared to that of the animals. It would swell up to the size of a thin rope and was able to be lengthened.

So for a few years, he had made articles out of the hair to trade for other articles the groups would bring for swapping. There were livestock and work animals also for trade. Those would bring quite a tradable option to the tables.

A ride animal was worth several times what livestock could be traded for. Mature rides would only increase in value, as they could do more procedures the older they got.

When Maddy's mom used to brush her hair and had hair tangle in her brush, his dad had taken the longest ones. After the soaking process, he made Maddy a rope he used for a bridle. That bridle had a set of reins and a strap that attached to the cinch on each side of the neck of the ride. It then looped along the sides of the body, providing footrests that continued to the split loop that went over and under the stub tail of the ride.

Dad had been able to trade ten of his longest ropes for a ride for Maddy when Maddy was seven. The ride was named Heaster. Heaster was a Gulf-bred animal, bred and raised by the Gulf of Hopelle. He was only five years old when Dad had traded for him. Now Heaster was thirteen. When he had turned eight years old, Maddy had found him floating in their water tank.

This was the first action they found he could do. Maddy had tried to get him out of the tank and ended up taking a bath with him. The harder he tried to get hold of Heaster, the more he'd float out of the water. Maddy was a little curious about this and jumped on Heaster's back to see if he could be ridden or not. Both found themselves high and dry. Heaster had floated himself out of the water with Maddy on him. They came to find out that Heaster wasn't just a floater ride; he could, being only eight, hold himself and a rider above water. Maddy only weighed a bit more than one stone then. For a ride to hold that much up, though, was more than most animals were normally capable of doing.

Dad asked, "Isn't it about time for the chores to get done? Heaster isn't going to get any more actions if you don't feed him something." That interrupted the inspection of the peg.

"All right, Dad. Thanks for the reminder," answered Maddy.

His ride, Heaster—it was time to go feed him. This was his time to spend part of the day with Heaster, and it went off with little to no interruption. His bond with his future carrier had grown pretty deep already. Heaster felt the bond blending closer each time he saw that pail of char sprouts heading his direction. The char sprouts were found along the banks of water.

There was a very small creek behind the cabin, which was where they got their drinking water. It had a small inlet, a reservoir that had pleasant, sloping banks that grew the sprouts like unwanted weeds in the garden. Good thing, too, as a ride didn't eat constantly, but when it ate, it ate a bunch.

The peg was still in Maddy's pocket when he was finishing his chores. While Heaster was finishing the last few sprouts in the pail, Maddy took the wedge out and began investigating it again.

The markings on that flattened side didn't look like anything he'd seen in the writings in the books of genealogy. They didn't look like anything he'd seen before. Whether he turned the object up, down, or around, the markings didn't disclose what they meant. One of the marks went deeper than the other four and was angled on each end. It was a little off center of the flat-sided peg. Of the other four markings, two connected at each of the ends of the deep mark, and where they connected was a diamond-shaped raised bump. It connected them to an overlay that resembled netting. His inquisitive mind thought long and hard about how he would bring this to his dad and what his reaction would be. If his dad didn't know what it was, who would?

He rubbed that swollen lump on his head and began to think about why the treman had stopped moving and making noise. Flashes of inspiration were snapping quicker and quicker as he replayed the events of yesterday. About to the place where he'd retrieved the arrow, it came to him. The movement stopped with the arrow falling.

He rapidly stared at the peg again and got it. This must have been what had stopped the motion. This must be the key.

BULLS EYE

Somehow, when the arrow fell out with the button, it shut down the episode he'd been watching.

Nightfall was coming sooner with the turning of their earth. Only about nine rotations of the moon with the greenish red spot were left for light now. It rotated within their view and spun as a timepiece, so they knew the seasons. The longest day of daytime light came in the spring, when the rays from their sun would reflect off two of the moons and kick off the growing season. The longest day was fourteen turns of the greenish spotted moon. The extra heat the moons' reflection produced would germinate any seeds a good deal faster than the single heat from the sun and one moon in the summer. The seasons were longer in the spring and really short through winter. Summer and fall varied a little, when the moisture clouds hung around. It was normal weather, though, and one couldn't assume it was going to be sunny or cloudy in summer or fall.

Winter never had a covering of the sky. Even though it was colder farther away from the sun, their winter moon, the preceding one, would pass enough of the sun's reflection to not allow wetness. There was an extremely rare day when the wet air would sparkle, and with a covering of crystal chards, the ground would look like a glass sea.

Maddy would try to sleep so he could wake up even before Dad in the morning. He needed to get back to the treman and see if he could find the place for this key. From the first glimpse he got of it falling, he would need a rope—a weighted, bent loop of metal Dad had by the barn that he could use for a grappling hook—and his climbing shoes.

TREMAN

For tonight, he would get a good amount of rest.

The mature treman was huge, and there were gnarly areas that you could hardly see through, let alone climb in. Looking up almost set his mind spinning. Being this close to the huge tree gave him the sense of being puny.

His climb began. From branch to branch, limb by limb, he placed the deep, treaded soles of his climbing shoes carefully with each step. He climbed upward. The stories of old, of that boy who climbed the crackle tree to the warlock's castle, trying to find that bronze harness that would make any ride invincible, kept Maddy on course—higher and closer to the place he'd seen the first flicker of the arrow. When he got close, his inspection intensified. He was trying to feel what he couldn't see, because the tree was only a half span in diameter now, making it possible to reach around it with his arms. His next step found him face-to-face with the notched void. It had the look of where a branch would have fallen out, and the shape was exactly like his key. The impressions were the mirror image of what Maddy held in his hand. The grooves in the peg were raised in the limb hole, and the buttons where the lines met with the four outer notches were set in. All that was left to do was to position it in place. Turning it so that the flat side went in first and the same oblong end was up, Maddy began pushing it in. When he felt it make contact, a click sounded.

The limb he was standing on straightened under his feet. Where a crook had been in the limb now was bent at a right angle upward. Then two rods shot out.

These were each two spans long where they had extended to the fullest point. The perch began to shorten into the main stalk. The rods now were becoming a trap and pinned Maddy to the tree. Above his head he watched another rod begin to form. The end of this rod came to a point that blinked with a sparkling of light.

Before he could move, the rod dove at his forehead. Just as the needle-sharp point touched his skin, Maddy awoke in a cold sweat.

It was only a dream. But what kind of vision was this? Was it a warning? Was this a foretelling of what could happen if the peg were replaced back into the void? There had been prophecies that the ancient ones had written as stories. They were all anyone had taken them to be, imagined stories for bedtime and campfire tales. He was thinking about one in particular that his friend Ben had told him.

They were gathering sticks from the ladlebalm for a fire, and Ben started telling the story his grandfather had told him about a shooting star that had blasted just past the second moon. When it hit their earth, it landed with a force that depressed it half in, half out. The tail split open, and an appendage grew out. Ben continued by saying that after a day it had become a tree that looked similar to the tremans already there. This treman lookalike had shriveled up the following day, and all but the split-open shell of the fallen star was gone. On the far south end of Dillon County, there was a fossilized fragment that the story was believed to be told about. Maddy had been there with Uncle Mel and his dad when they were trading with the group in the county to the south. He remembered walking by the location along the road. It was different and out of place, but this story had the evidence of the fossil fragment. Was or wasn't it a story? Maddy was confused now.

Maddy wasn't as eager to get to the treman as he had been the night before. Yet that sort of curiosity usually trumps common sense, which fortunately wasn't lacking for Maddy. His common sense told him to be ready to take the peg out if something like that were to really happen. And the divot where the arrow tip had stuck would just as easily be replaced with a knob he fashioned out of a piece of spikenard wood and pasted in with some crackle sap. Now he would have a key and some control of it.

He arrived at the treman, and this time the climb was about to become real. To reach the first bough that would hold him, Maddy had to use the rope and hook. Many of the lower branches had been taken off and used for heat when past winters were colder and the humidity hadn't been much. Other than being used for heat, there hadn't been any other real purpose for this treman, although it was a great shade tree and boundary marker. Ben and Maddy used to climb a lot when they were younger. The different trees in Dillon County gave them an advantage in climbing that the friends they had in Clay and Braden Counties didn't have. Maddy's first toss of the hook missed and came dropping back right at his head. He jumped aside, and it landed at his feet. The blackened ground showed a trivial nick where the hook had landed. Maddy picked it up again and pitched it underhanded. The hook found its spot. After a couple of tugs to ensure it would hold, his climb began.

The climb started to seem familiar. He wasn't sure if he was remembering the vision or all the times he had envisioned climbing that tree as he lay on his back in the grass. Either way his placement of the climbing shoes was sure, each move calculated.

He had climbed just past the point where the base ended and its main boughs started when there was a familiar voice crying out to him. It had a familiar sound. The problem was that where he'd climbed was adding distortion to things on the ground. As he struggled to find the sound he heard, it resounded again. This time he recognized the voice.

"What you doing up there, Maddy?" shouted Trace.

He almost fell out of the tree. What was she doing here? He replied, "Climbing!"

Trace continued, cupping her hands to direct her voice. "Why are you climbing the treman?"

He had not predicted this dilemma. This quest would have to wait. After all, how could he avoid making this heart-flutterer, the one bellowing at him, stop? Or way worse, have it go away?

"I'll be right down," he answered.

"No!" she responded. "Can I come up?"

Even with the tread of his climbing shoes, he was really close to falling out of the treman.

He would have to drop one end of the rope to her and pull her to the first climbing spot. What was he going to say to her? "By the way Trace, I found this key, and the treman was moving until it fell out and…"

He wanted her to know there was a gentleman somewhere inside him, so he answered, "I'll just come down. I want to talk to you, if you have time. Would that be OK?"

"OK," she said back.

Maddy hardly touched any bark coming down until he got to where he would have to drop. Of course he had to show off a little, so hanging down from the lowest bough, he let go and landed on his feet.

"What did you want to talk about?" she asked.

"Let's go sit down over there, on the uphill side, where the imaginary line of Clay and Braden meet," he suggested a bit timidly.

She grabbed his hand and began running to the spot he'd proposed, half dragging him along beside her. When they had gotten to the line, they plopped to their backsides on the ground and laughed.

"So?" was the question.

"Well, before you think I've gone loony," he said, reaching into his pocket, "what do you think this is?"

Maddy carefully handed her the peg, and as she took it, she looked into his eyes. She answered by saying, "Looks a little like those seeds the treman drops, or at least like the pictures and drawings I've seen."

Neither of them had physically held or seen a treman seed. They only lasted that short time before they'd turn to eosin tar, and their life experience hadn't experienced a seed-production year.

"Well, it could be, I guess," Maddy stated. "But whatever it is, I was trying to find a place somewhere to see if it fit in the treman. That's when you got here."

Trace said, "You were really up there."

"Almost to where I saw the arrow falling from," Maddy responded. "My dad shot at a squirrel yesterday, and his arrow missed the target and disappeared."

"How did that happen? Your dad never misses," she complimented him.

Being proud of his dad, he continued. "He got him today—shot it right out of the air," he said with just a touch of boasting.

"So now what are we to do?" Trace asked.

"Good question. Trace, I want to ask you something." Rolling his eyes and asking with carefulness, he said, "What do you think about me?"

With a flush of color that spread over her face, she replied with a cross-examining question herself. "You first?"

Now he'd done it. He had to tell her. This was a no-option moment. As he began to speak, Trace perked up on her arms, listening intently. "Well, I've been friends with you for as long as I can remember. And the day you brought that grinding bowl over, when Mom left, I pretty much locked in on you as being the new girl in my life," he continued. "Whenever we're together, I find it very hard not to get as much of you in my eyes as I can." Maddy's answer had come.

A silence! Oh, no! The "What have I done?" feeling, the silence you could cut with a knife came at Maddy's heart. He'd just opened his mouth and his heart to someone other than his father. All he had wanted to know was whether she'd thought he was odd or different because he didn't have a mom. He'd said far too much. Now this girl was holding his heart and not saying anything.

"All that, huh?" she replied. It was like releasing a breath that had been held forever.

Again silence. It was out there now. No rewinding or erasing it out of the air the statement had gone into.

"For now," the answer came from nowhere and amazed him.

Cocking her head to the side, she smiled. "That's a lot like how I would have answered."

There would never be silence again. The treman quest had vanished, as the swirling in his mind focused to this amazing picture in front of him. This was about the time when the young people would start isolating their possible mates. What a day this had become. It started out being a quest to answer the treman peg issue, and now Maddy was looking at what could be his future.

Words fell from their lips, as the conversation included past activities they had shared and how they made more sense now with the latest input. There, on the hillside, as they conversed, a bond was forming that only could happen where true feelings and caring would be.

By midday the discussion came back to their opening greeting. Maddy told Trace about the vision he'd had about replacing the peg, what he was planning to do, and why he had crackle-glued that handle to the key.

After the news of Maddy's vision, her concern came as she responded, "Should we see if your elder, Mantra, will let us look at the archives first?"

"Why shouldn't we? It's not like the relic of a treman is going to go anywhere soon," Maddy replied.

Passing by the scencee trees, they noticed one of the monzi moths had spun its wrapping cocoon. Maddy picked it and handed it to Trace, saying, "If you ever wonder what I really think about you, just try out the reading-thoughts method."

Taking it from his hand, she said, "I'll save it for later."

They got to Mantra's shortly before the seventh turn of the moon. A knock on her door had a delayed answer come from within. "Who's there?"

"It's Maddy, Dray Handle's son, and my friend Trace Guthrie, from Clay County, ma'am."

The door opened, and there Mantra stood, leaning with her cane in her right hand and a aged black book with orange, frayed edges in her left. It was one of the archive books. Maddy had tagged along one time when his dad had gone to ask Mantra a question about their property. When they went into her library area, Maddy remembered seeing a few books like this one on the shelves that encompassed the entire room. The shelves were oddly shaped and had been made from slabs of various types of wood; they had been cut and attached into larger upright slabs.

They were unique in that where the slabs would be shaped by the roughly cut thickness from the form of the tree, certain books would be placed on these protrusions to support the binding edge of the books. The walls were shelved to the ceiling and even over the entrance door to the room.

On the other end of the room, another door had been made from a solid block of wood. Maddy remembered the door and how the grain hadn't looked like any other grain of wood he'd seen before. In Dillon County, even with all the types of trees that were there, this wood was exclusive.

The blond latch was fashioned with a set bolt that was a light-gold color. The lift handle had a knob affixed to it that had been patterned after a leaf of the treman. The bar sat in a grooved slot. The hinge side had beefy straps of rod iron half a finger thick to hold the weight of the door.

"What are you young ones searching for?" she asked.

Maddy started, "We were wondering if there are drawings of—or any information about—the ol' treman on the county lines, the one that's in the corners of the four counties."

Mantra's face scrunched up. She tilted her head and said, "Something about that old treman has been intriguing me lately, too. Let's go and see. It is close to the time it makes seeds." She continued, "This is an anniversary of when the first sketch was done, back before my grandfather had started building this library, and even before the boundaries were established. A date they found on the sketch placed it twelve generations of treman seedtime ago or five hundred forty of our earth turns. The drawing was from all four sides. That's one of the reasons it became the corner marker of the four counties."

"Would it be possible to make a copy of it?" Maddy asked.

BULLS EYE

"As long as it is scribed on the copy that it is only a copy." Mantra was sure to add a serious gesture regarding the ordinances.

This would bring Trace's skills into action. She had been learning to draw and had a talent that would have her find her position in any group in the future. Talents and skills were important in that they gave direction to people's lives and their sense of worth.

No one's talent had been rejected for any reason. Trace had a gift. And they were about to see one of the earliest records of their counties' past.

Mantra was about to lift the latch when she turned and said, "This door was made from that treman's fourth generation of seedlings. Records show that the seed was planted next to Dray and Mel's parents' property line, and it was harvested in its second generation. One thing about those tremans—they grow almost as quickly as their seed needs to be planted. That's why they're intriguing to me. You don't see them grow. You could watch them for as long as your eyes could stay open, and you'd not see them move. But you shut your eyes, and there they are, almost fully grown."

Then Maddy said, "Like the monument down on the southern border and the story about it? What about the story that tells of the treman and its coming with that star?"

"We cannot say those stories are facts, Maddy, remember?" Again Mantra had to keep the rule.

Trace hadn't heard that story and set her mind to remember to ask Maddy about it later.

"Don't know how that happens because no one knows. No one has ever seen one move. They can draw their pictures, and no matter how long they spend or how detailed they are, from start to finish, the tree doesn't change. Yet if they were to come the next season, it could be different."

Maddy was bursting at the seams, wanting to tell Mantra he'd seen the treman move. But he didn't want to jeopardize his chance to get through the doorway.

Stepping into that room was like entering living history. The room felt alive with knowledge. Maddy sensed that, even without Mantra having opened anything in the archives, it was already in the air. All this new information was just ready to flood anyone's mind with more of an understanding. It felt like if you were to just think your question, the answer would be etched into your mind.

Mantra moved toward the corner of the room where the oldest drawings and scrolls were. These artifacts were from before the era of books. They were there long before Mantra and before her grandfather. Yet Mantra went straight to the earliest drawing of the treman. She knew its location precisely. There was a small table with two chairs in the middle of the room.

Anytime someone wanted to go into this room, he or she could not go alone. Two people had to enter it. That's why Mantra was more inspired to have Maddy and Trace there. It gave her access to the room also. The main reason was to ensure the records were replaced exactly as they had been before they were taken down and observed.

BULLS EYE

Mantra brought the drawing to the table and placed it on the table carefully. Even though it was on a parchment that had been preserved with the ladlebalm sap, this was truly prehistory and unexplained by anything other than its own existence. The artist wasn't known; only the date that the drawing had been done was on it.

Mantra opened a small drawer on her side of the table and lifted out a magnifying glass. Maddy watched as her intrigue of this parchment had her change from this ancient person into a younger-acting, very spirited person.

Her intensity was peaking to the degree that she didn't want to be waylaid by these youngsters' questions. She was filling her eyes with every line and curve.

Then Maddy saw it. Right there in the drawing's view from the east sat the peg. The artist hadn't missed one ridge of the gritty key. It hadn't changed. It was the only characteristic of the tree that hadn't changed. It wouldn't have been noticed as anything other than a knothole if you weren't aware of it. His eyes were being filled with possibilities, and his mind was racing.

What was this key? What did it mean? And why was it the only part of the treman that hadn't changed?

He couldn't hold back the question, and without thinking, he pointed to the spot and asked, "What's this, Mantra?" Her magnifier darted to the point to which Maddy had alerted her.

Her response was without knowledge. "I haven't noticed that spot before today, and I've inspected this with a fine-toothed comb. Guess it must have not been fine enough. What drew you to that spot?"

"I've been watching that tree for as long as I can remember, and I never saw that either," replied Maddy. "Do you have any idea of why it's there?"

"Well, I've heard stories about how certain seeds were a little different from the others, and my grandfather said there were seeds that made the treman trees more prominent. There were the stories that only one of the seeds was special. Stories—all these stories were just stories. And I tell you, even now as I say this, that these are stories. One of my favorites from my grandmother was a story about the special seed that hadn't grown overnight. Unlike the story of the crackle tree that grew to the warlock's castle in a day, this was about the treman tree seed. She told the story so well and it was so believable that it was hard to believe it was just a story."

Trace asked, "Who told her?"

"She said it had been passed down by her family for many generations," Mantra continued. "The special treman seed had come from another earth. Grandma called it a heaven. She said when it landed on our earth it was touched by a wonderful man who had spent his life studying how the love of heart could be explained. Once this man touched the seed, it gave him the answer. It was overwhelming to the man, and he dedicated the rest of his life to spreading this knowledge. The next part of the story had me snap back to reality. She said the treman seed and the man became inseparable, so much so that when the man passed, he wanted to be placed next to the seed in a specific spot he'd chosen. They placed the man and the seed in that spot. Forty-five years later, it began to grow, just as the treman we have here. There was never any evidence of change. No one noticed it becoming extraordinary. She said it grew and grew until the whole earth could have seen it. As it grew, unnoticed, it also was transforming within. The tree had become alive. The metamorphosis that was occurring inside the bark and branches was going on for generations. They had been shaped into particular and precise forms. There were ways that the wooden mass waved together like nothing a person had designed prior. It had moving and active parts, spindles, and shafts blending together into a living being that was not a design from our earth, other than the figure becoming like that of a recognizable being. It didn't have skin or flesh as we do, yet it was covered still. It didn't have bone or hair, yet it was becoming indestructible and hardening like the refining of metal. There was a driving force like that of fire. It was consumed in growth and, in motionless action, persisted without diminishing. It lived without notice, and even though it could be seen from afar, it was hidden—there but not there."

Trace piped in again. "That's it? End of story?"

"Oh, no!" said Mantra. "The best part came next. She said the Treman became like us."

"How?"

"Trace, this is a story," Maddy added.

"I know, but what a story." She asked Mantra then, "May I tell this story?"

"It is the same as any other story. You must forewarn that you are going to be telling a story." She continued, "When he became like us, it was done by the one part of the Treman that hadn't changed. She told of a place on the Treman where the kind man had placed his heart, the special part that remained of the man when the two parts had become one being. That's when Grandfather would pipe in and tell his snippet of the story. 'Just like we made your father, Grandma and I made him. The two of us made your dad.'"

"What happened to the Treman?" Trace was intent to ask.

"Well, she said he still is with us today." Mantra had a flicker of thoughts of her past and the stories by her grandparents, as she perceived that Maddy had been soaking the story up as much as Trace had. She turned to Maddy and offered him her hand. This ordinance was required. When an elder offered his or her hand, the one to whom it was offered must promise to seek the truth of a story and follow every bit of evidence to ensure it was either a story or fact. Mantra knew she had found the one who would pursue this story as she had tried to do and was still trying to do. Mantra knew there must have been something she may have missed that had brought these two young ones to her at this time.

Maddy took her hand and vowed to start his journey that she was on also.

Maddy and Trace thanked Mantra for her time and the story and asked if there was anything else she hadn't told them.

"Just one more thing for now," Mantra added. "A witness will add all the credibility you'll need to bring a story to life." She followed them to the door and bid them good seeking.

The light from the sun had gone to its evening resting place, and evening was upon them.

Maddy asked, "May I walk you home?"

Trace smiled. "Yes. Then you can tell me about that monument and the star."

BULLS EYE

As they started, he said, "Let's go by and let my dad know what we're doing. I don't want him wondering where I will be. It is a little hike to Rood, and the last time I didn't come home, he and Uncle Mel got pretty concerned and came looking for me."

The story, just as it is supposed to, became a teacher itself as they repeated it while walking to Rood.

That key in his pocket began to take on a whole new meaning. As he took it out and examined it some more, he couldn't help believe this was the key to the treman. He handed it to Trace, trusting that she was there to assist him to the end of this search.

After they got to Rood, they agreed to meet at the cornerstone treman in the morning. After an embrace, they said good night, and Maddy headed for home.

He looked into the starry sky and peered at the double moon, thinking there must be more. There must be more answers than what the books he had seen in Mantra's library offered.

He thought, What else? Where is there more about this story?

CHAPTER TWO

The Prime

The morning brought with it unusual moisture in the air. It was fog. Typically this was a springtime incidence, and even in that season, it was not a characteristic murkiness like this one.

Maddy heard his father stirring something in the pan on the stove. He asked what time it was, and Dray answered, "You tell me. The fog is thick enough for me to cut and throw in this pan for our morning meal. It must be about the second turn of the moon by now."

Maddy sprang out of the blankets and headed for the door.

"Whoa, slow down there, young man." His dad reached out and put his hand on his shoulder. "What's the hurry? It's not a fire. It's fog."

"I know, Dad, but I told Trace I would meet her by the treman this morning. I really don't want her waiting for me there alone."

With that certain grin on his face, he asked, "Do you think the haze is only here in Dillon County? She's probably at her group in Rood, frying up some steamy fried fog steaks—not frog steaks, *fog* steaks."

"But what if it's only here in Dillon County?" Maddy asked.

Maddy knew his father had seen things like this to know it wasn't an isolated incident. A covering this thick would have to be covering more than just here. The look on his face as he turned and looked at him revealed there was no further need of inquiry.

Dray then suggested, "Heaster still needs to eat, and he probably wants more than a fluff of mist to drink."

With that hurdle over, Maddy got right after the proposal. He went out to Heaster, having only his repetitive walk to the pen be his guide, as the pressed-down cloud was still very thick. Since he'd been able to float out of water, they had to adjust the ceiling of his confine with a few branches of the crackle and woven twine from the ladlebalm.

Heaster was anxious to see his companion, and the noises from his throat indicated to Maddy that he was excited to see him. The high, gruff growl could have been mistaken for a bad temperament if one was not familiar with the sound he'd made for the days and many turns of the spotted moon. As time had passed, their bond grew closer and deeper. The distinctive grunts and squeaks Heaster made were becoming a language between them.

Being hungry was an easy tone to recognize, and to hear the difference between wanting food or drink was in the

THE PRIME

degree of depth in the pitch. If things continued as they were with Heaster achieving levels of ability, and their connection, he might even start mimicking Maddy's words. An occasional ride normally started doing this at fifteen. He'd been grunting for three seasons, and what happened this morning would shock them all.

As Maddy opened the gate and set the water down for Heaster, he said, "There you go, bud."

Heaster lifted his head and mimicked back, "There you go, bud."

"Really?" Maddy said, as he dropped to his knees.

"Really," Heaster replied.

Maddy knew this was very early for a ride to do and wanted to see how far he could go with this. So he said, "Want to float with me?"

Heaster came back with, "Now!"

Shocked by the response of the new sounds he was hearing, Maddy swung his arms around Heaster's seal-skinned neck and asked, "Can you see in this fog?"

With a turn of his head, a look of uncertainty was returned. Heaster may have had more than a mimic response to the last question, but he hadn't seen a fog like this.

Maddy shrugged his shoulders and spent the morning with his ride, telling him the story about Trace and coming to the treman when he was starting to climb it. He also told him the story Mantra had told them about the treman seed and the man. The new set of ears he had to talk to was an uncontaminated freedom and opened up dialogue for Maddy.

It was about the time for his feeding, and he heard his dad yell out his name. Walking out into the yard, he saw that the thick haze had all but disappeared. Just a few spots around the trees and areas protected from direct air movement remained. Time had flown with the conversation he and his friend had shared. He ran to the cabin and sat down to eat with Dray.

"Dad! Guess what?" Maddy asked.

"Heaster had a pup." He smiled.

"Nope, but it has to do with him."

The shrugging of his shoulders was a gesture of not knowing, and he indicated with his fingers for his son to continue. "What?"

"Heaster repeated some of my words."

"Really?"

"And not only that—I thought I'd see if that was all he could do. I asked him if he'd want to float with me. And he grunted, 'Now.' "

"My, that is interesting." Dray knew that when a ride did what Heaster had been doing this early, he must be a primordial.

A prime could not be identified before it was seven. That's when its abilities would begin to develop. Primes would have advanced abilities. They would become breeders and, if they were extraordinary, could help their rider get a contract to eldership. Primes would live as long as their riders did. Their experiences could help the rider make decisions and keep records. Once they learned to communicate with their riders, they would recall anything they'd been told to repeat.

THE PRIME

Now, with this mimic and the floating episode at eight, the prime in Heaster would continue to increase quickly in everything a primordial could do.

Their skins were rutted, and the short hair was thick enough to protect from extreme temperatures, protecting him from both the heat and cold. The ability to float in air came from a mineral within their body makeup. It was a substance that was of the chemical helium in composition.

It wasn't like bone and muscle; it was a fleshy gas tissue that was solid when the ride would flex. Their four front legs were wing shaped, with a stubby, round pad for their soles. The rear two leg wings were for thrust or braking and didn't have the pads like the four it would stand on. The stub tail initiated the flex. When a rider was strapped in with his ride, the range of the tug pressure on the harness would relay how much flex was needed. This was a standard for work rides. Primes were smarter.

Not that a prime needed much direction. The connection between the rider and the prime could be nurtured so they could read each other as they rehearsed floating.

Floating wasn't familiar to Maddy, and he was going to have to train with Heaster to maneuver. Their watering trough experience hadn't given them much practice or skill. It had, however, been a link in their chain and reaction to one another.

Dray had gotten to sit on a ride only once at a trade gathering. He was much younger than Maddy was but never forgot the feeling. That's why when the opportunity presented itself to get Heaster; he wanted that encounter for his son. Now that he had a prime, things could change for his son and his career choice.

The typical ride became more or less a pack animal that was used for moving wares or a rider from place to place. A primordial was a great deal stronger and could float faster and higher than the common ride. It could carry both the rider and goods.

There were contests, for fun, that would go on at some of the gatherings, and the bigger the gathering, the more events. The meeting before spring planting was huge. It would be held in a different location every year, giving the groups an opportunity to show their produce and tradable items without the long-distance transportation issue.

There had been a contest to see what a ride could lift at one of these spring get-togethers. The weight lifted was ninety-two and a half stones—almost ten thousand pounds of weight. A stone was equivalent to a hundred pounds. For Heaster to lift Maddy when he was eight may have foretold what he'd be able to lift by the age of twenty.

Dray knew that feed was a key factor in size and how the ride would develop lift capability. Now that he knew Maddy had a connection with Heaster, he knew it would only benefit Maddy's chances for any goals he might pursue. He also knew it might be time for them to begin floating together. He wasn't an expert, but Mel had worked with rides for two winter seasons. So he certainly had more knowledge than Dray.

THE PRIME

After eating, Dray told Maddy he was going to go and talk to Mel about floating and was going to ask him if he would help them out.

Maddy saw a spark of excitement he hadn't seen for quite some time in his dad. Since Mom was gone, the sparks weren't happening very often. He hadn't stopped or even slowed down. A simple intimacy had been removed. Mel had become a companion to Dray, as Dray had put on the brother shoes for Mel. But friendship and brotherhood wasn't sparkle. Ignition came from the opposite gender.

It wasn't that Maddy wasn't excited about floating, getting on Heaster again, or learning how to float. He too had gotten that rush when Heaster floated with him over that livestock tank. His mind was heading in a connection direction. Maddy knew what he was going to do while his dad went to see Uncle Mel.

After a sendoff farewell, off they went. Dray put the harness on Heaster and headed for Mel's. This was an important day for them. Dray would get to share with his friend and brother what had just become a probability with few limitations for the prime. Dray took him out of the pen and led him away from his home base.

Maddy's day would be as important on the other end of the scale. It wasn't about balance. It was all about more. This new detail of his life had given wings to a fresh flash of lift-off. This could be his connection to a deeper relationship than friendship and family—his own personal family unit.

As he ran on the west side of their property, on the trail to the treman and just about at the ovanclave grove, he leaped over that root he'd hit his head on. He was reminded of the statement Mantra had made about no one ever seeing a treman tree move. The newest item in his pocket, the item he carried everywhere, was the game changer. He slowed his pace to a walk and reached in for the peg. When he got it out of his pocket, it had changed. The handle he had shaped to stick into the arrow-tip hole had turned into part of the piece. There were no seams or crackle glue where they had met. There was no evidence that there were different wooden pieces. It had absorbed the handle, and even the grain and texture had been altered to melt together.

A bit puzzled with the shape of the peg now, he had many new options scurrying in his mind. What had happened was the first and foremost. The stories that Maddy had been told were just stories. These stories had started to convert how he had been thinking before his visit with Mantra. Visions had been building and were taking on a new direction. Whenever he held the peg in his hand, the thoughts he would have were about the treman. They were spiritual in offering, like a calling to continue thinking about the drawing sensation he was having. That first time he discovered the details of the key, behind his blanket and in his bed, kept returning sporadically to his unintentional routines.

Physical contact with the essence of this item was having an effect on Maddy somehow. Now that he had seen the morphing of the handle, glue, and peg, his logic was putting pieces of this puzzle together at a quicker pace.

Could this have been what happened to the man and the Treman seed? This newfangled idea was playing a game of tug-of-war with everything he'd been told. The stories and the movement of the treman he'd personally witnessed were having a confusing effect on his young mind.

He wanted to talk to Trace about it so much. She had seen the peg and had a chance to examine it the day she found him climbing the tree. So if Maddy were to show it to her now, she'd have to believe and accept what Maddy had been experiencing with the visions he been having. He had to tell her.

But first he had to look at the treman again. Was anything different about it? Had it moved any more? The questions were racing in his thoughts.

As he turned the last bend and the trail to where the four counties came together, he saw several people gathered around the tree. Many of them had their cutting tools, axes, and saws with them.

Maddy moved to the tall grass and the thickets of brush along the path. He would try to listen to their conversation without being noticed. Mantra was there and seemed to be the head spokesperson.

"We're looking for this," she said, holding a copy of one of the drawings from the library in her hand. "It will look mostly like this, but it might have changed a little. It shows it being on the east side of the tree in this picture."

Maddy knew what she was looking for. Mantra had been on a mission, searching and following any leads about the treman most of her life also, and with the unintentional clue that Maddy had given her, her detective juices had been rekindled. The adamancy she was being inspired by was contagious. It was spreading to the group with her.

TREMAN

Maddy had been to see her very recently, and already she had a selected group there with her to seek out the new hint she had.

As Maddy watched from his hiding spot, they began throwing their ropes and gaffs at the lower boughs of the treman. They were leaping through the branches, preparing to cut any obstructions out of their way as they went.

Then Mantra shouted, "Now remember, no hurting anything. No cutting or marring. The tree must not change its appearance, or we'll be hiring an artist to keep the history of the tree intact."

Whenever there was a need for a sketch of the landscape or significant trees—those that had been transplanted or had their natural definition changed like the treman—a person from the closest city would need to have the change documented for the record. Then the adjusted drawing or building would be filed with the elder of the county for any future questions that may be brought into inquiry.

They were so intent on their search that they hadn't examined the change that had taken place that Maddy had witnessed. It seemed that the accuracy of what the tree was in the drawing and what was standing in their presence didn't matter. They were intent on finding the peg and the place Maddy had asked Mantra about, even though the knothole would be all they would find, if they found that.

Maddy wasn't sure exactly where the arrow and its object had fallen from. He stayed there, covered by the surrounding shrubbery for nearly three turns of the moon. After the search was halted, Mantra signaled for the regroup, and everyone

THE PRIME

who had come with her headed back to Dellac, unsuccessful for today.

When they were out of sight, Maddy reappeared from his covered seclusion. His inspection and recall of the last view he'd had mentally hadn't changed. But his search for the exact location for the gem in his pocket would have to wait.

With even more to share with Trace, he turned his feet toward Rood. The beaten path and hardened earth beneath his feet informed him he was getting close to Rood and Trace's home. When he got to the narrow road that would head to her place of abode, he remembered the times he had walked with her to that point. Her father was a bulky man who had gotten much of his physique from all the years of working with clay as he dug out and separated the best material for the blocks and bricks he would form. Their yard was littered with piles of wooden frames of various sizes and shapes that her father used for his trade. His name was Kendal Guthrie, and his wife's name was Beth. They had lived in Clay County and been introduced when they were young teens. Their marriage had been an unavoidable joining of flesh. Since both were from Clay County, one of the larger counties, there wasn't much documentation to be changed. If two people from different counties were to be joined, the lineages from both families would need to be filed in both home counties. That usually was a final note to one's connection to his or her prior county.

Maddy's parents had gotten very fortunate when they moved to Dillon County. Dray's great-grandparents had moved to Dillon as it was being surveyed. Dray's father moved there when the elders had died.

TREMAN

When he had met Cheraw, they had been working in a small factory in Burton, making steel shields for a dreg. This cart was designed to enclose a variety of materials and keep them safe from anything that might be contaminated. Dray had brought four of them for their family on the move from Burton. He had mostly used them for food storage and keeping wood dry when they would travel on any overnight or extended traveling venture. There were a number of dreg sizes, from those that could have held ten people to those that were easy enough to be used like a wheelbarrow.

The land was very unsettled back then. A survival state was the essential mindset. If you were frail or prone to sickness and disease, there may not have been much hope. That's what had taken Maddy's elder generation. An infection caused their lungs to collapse. They weren't aware of the scencee tree's swarm and the monzi moth's skin, which might have saved them. As with any early social order, experimentation had revealed new surroundings, and their unique creation was to be either useful or dangerous and best avoided.

Trace's dwelling was quite different from Maddy's dwelling. Even with exchanging building materials from other groups and counties, the convenient and available products usually were used to build a shelter. Their home was mostly adobe in substance. The walls and roof were solid and smooth. They had a rounded look that was a dome shape. The contour of the roof did not offer a place where the roof and walls met. They had used a certain type of clay for the walls that would support the roof and could be colored with dyes or would have a natural color, depending on where the clay was taken

THE PRIME

from. Mixing the sap and sticks from the crackle tree with the roof clay made it impervious to water. Shelters that had been abandoned across the county or that needed repair hadn't had the mixture of crackle sap. The roof edge had a lip formed for shedding away any rainfall from following the dome's roof edge to the foundation.

Kendal did not have a bad roof on his main dwelling or on any of his outbuildings. He was very good at his trade, and the evidence of having no cracks was proof.

When Maddy got to the front door and was about to knock, Trace opened it. Maddy thought about the discussion they'd had, and the old walls of uncomfortable, awkward mutterings were a thing of the past. There this girl stood, as excited to see him as he was to see her. Beth was on the kitchen side, stirring up a meal that had Maddy's nose acting as if it were a part of Heaster's floatable body. His head floated, swaying back and forth, at the smell that was filling his nostrils.

He didn't want to impose, knowing that food had been a little scarce at his place. His stomach had him offering a polite gesture of saying, "Mrs. Guthrie that smells amazing."

Trace followed up the comment with, "Would it be OK for Maddy to have a meal with us, Mom?"

"Sure. Just let me put in a few more sprouts," she said.

Having the peg from the treman in his pocket and seeing Trace with his eyes was interrupted by what now had developed into a way to his heart through his stomach.

Not wanting to seem too anxious, he said, "Not here to impose."

"Nonsense. It'll be a thank-you for walking her home the other night," Beth said.

"Thank you," he said. So many new things were going on in his life. His thoughts were swirling.

After they had eaten the meal, Maddy asked Kendal if it would be OK for Trace to go for a walk with him down to the old treman.

Kendal said, "Heard from a couple men at group this morning that they were called to the tree by the elders from all four counties. Mantra had initiated an inquiry to have any drawings or information about that old tree brought there by the other three elders. Our elder, Manfred, and two others went there first thing this morning."

Without offering his knowledge about why he thought they'd gone, Maddy asked, "Do you know what they were looking for?"

"Something about an unnoticed mark she found, I guess," Kendal continued. "Does your father need any clay works?"

"Not that I know of, sir." Maddy took Trace's hand and headed for the door. To stay away from additional comments, he switched the topic to his ride. "He might need something for my ride, Heaster, though. We might have a primordial. We might want some weights to get him stronger."

This was a two-fold answer. It would change the direction of the conversation, and it might put a check on the pro side of the pro-slash-con list for the qualifications to consider for Trace's future mate.

He had to leave immediately to avoid any other questioning. His story wasn't so much a story anymore, and he wanted to seek into what he had been shown so his report wouldn't be sketchy.

Out the door they went. He turned over his shoulder and said, "Thank you for the delicious meal, Mrs. Guthrie," as they ran out to the driveway.

Finally he could spill his heart and soul out to Trace. He could spill the beans, the milk, and the honey without her thinking he was crazy.

When they had gotten to the top of the hill and could see the treman, Maddy stopped and asked Trace if she wanted to sit down for a bit and look at the changed peg, which was now in his hand.

Maddy handed it to her and asked, "Does it look different to you, Trace?"

Trace examined it, turning it in her hands. "There is something. It looks like it's all one piece now."

Maddy wasn't overly surprised that she had noticed. They had both studied this one-of-a-kind item from all angles. Maddy had explained how he had put the handle in place of the arrow tip. It was still encouraging, as his heart was knitting with hers in an unspoken way. They were together in this, and that was cause for excitement.

As she handed it back to him, she raised her hand with it into the air, and while she was holding it up in the air, his hand touched hers. Together they held the peg, and an extremely loud cracking noise sounded. It sounded like when it would explode thunder during the rainy season.

They snapped their heads in the direction of the sound and found it to have come from the treman. From their vantage point on the hill, they could see a horizontal split at the broadened spot where the tree split in two at the upper main bough of the tree. Their shock turned to inquisitiveness as they looked into each other's questioning eyes. What should they do? And what had happened?

Maddy hadn't brought his climbing gear, and this crack was intensifying their curiosity.

"We'll meet here two turns before dark, OK?" Maddy proposed to Trace.

"Should I bring anything?" Trace asked.

"Just bring your irreplaceable self."

He hadn't wanted to ask Trace if she would walk with him all the way back to his place then back to the tree. He didn't think it would be safe for her to wait there alone. Things were out of the ordinary. Things had never been like this. How true that was.

Maddy was going to get there early and had changed into his climbing shoes again. He had brought a climbing harness, even though Trace wasn't feeble. He knew she wasn't weak like some of the other girls around. It was mostly for precaution and would give him a chance to help Trace into the bindings. She had been transforming into a beautiful young woman, and as innocent as he was, young guys will soon be men. He hadn't been looking at her as seriously as he had the last couple of days.

He had thought there had been a lot of wasted dreaming about her. Why would she ever have gone for him? Now that she seemed to have the same twinkling eyes as he did, his interest in the complete package had magnified.

THE PRIME

When he went by Heaster's pen, his thoughts gravitated toward his ride. If only Dray hadn't taken him to Uncle Mel's. His heart began to surge as he thought of that brief float they'd shared.

There was a sudden jolt of reaction as he heard his dad's voice. "Where are you going?"

He turned to see his father leading Heaster, who wasn't touching the ground. Like a balloon tied to a string, his ride was floating beside his dad. A twitch of his stub tail, and Heaster was heading in a beeline for him was a beeline headed right at him. His dad was desperately holding onto the reins. When the straps got taut, Heaster immediately headed upward. Dray's feet were coming off the ground when Maddy commanded to Heaster, "*Stay!*"

This was one of the first training words you would teach a ride. They had to learn that word and learn it well.

His tail relaxed, and slowly he floated to his round, padded feet.

"Wow, Dad, what did you and Uncle Mel do to him?" Maddy was overjoyed.

"I think it's more about you, son." Dray replied. "We were getting him to float pretty well. And he was repeating our commands back to us, but he didn't have the power in his lift until he saw you. You two will have to work together for a while—and soon—to see if there's more to him than we know."

Maddy brainstormed then asked, "Could I start right now? I was going to go back down by the treman for a while, and maybe Heaster could go with me?"

"Well, it is the present, and there is no time like that. First let's see how he is to get on, all right?" Dray had hardly finished speaking when his son came running.

Maddy barely touched Heaster's back and mounted his ride; he resembled a cowboy jumping onto the back of his horse. When his legs found his sides and he grabbed the reins, Heaster was in a ready position. After a very slight dip from Maddy's landing and a mild adjustment, an inhale, they were both heading upward. This ride and rider were the shoe fitting the foot like a glove does on the hand.

Dray said, "Make sure you are clear on your orders. When you want to go left, say the word, and right, say 'right.' To stop and float in place, say 'done' or 'stop.' He will stop floating in a direction and find a stationary position. Your Uncle Mel said those commands are universal, so every ride will follow them."

"What do I say to have him go?"

As soon as the word *go* came off Maddy's tongue, they were gone. Heaster was aware that Maddy hadn't floated, and he was getting to feel what the weight of his rider was all about. But Heaster was a primordial. They would soon be inseparable.

The connection between them was amazing. Commanding was a thing of the past. Their feelings for each other were enough that they were exchanging mind waves. When Maddy thought, *Right*, Heaster went right, and *Left*, left. *Up* was thrilling. No county-fair ride compared to the feeling they were having together.

Dray watched the two meld together in the air. They would be floating and then, like an arrow out of its bow, shooting across the sky. The height at which they were floating exceeded all his expectations. And for a moment, it was awe-inspiring. Then Dray came to.

They were high. If Maddy were to fall now, it would all be over. Dray cupped his hands and yelled, "Done!"

The team came to an abrupt halt. Dray called the order "Pen." The sails were still full, but the command took precedence. If not following orders was allowed, there could be terrible consequences.

The team was back by Heaster's cage, and Maddy dismounted. The air fizzled out of the balloon. The bubble had popped, but only for a moment. To finish the order, Heaster entered his stall, and as Maddy turned toward Dray, the understanding was clear.

"The obedience must be just as clear." Dray stood firm in his lesson.

"I've got it, Dad, and thank you for the advice! May we go now?"

"Yes." He added, "Be back before dark. And when you get home, make sure you brush him down well. Don't need him to be rode hard and put away wet."

All that was presently happening was all his inner most being was thinking. Ten days ago everything was normal. Now he was riding his ride and had a girl at his side and a quest in the middle of his path.

The word "Out!" and Heaster was floating by his side. It was so strange to have him off his feet. With a click of his fingers, they were both off the ground.

Maddy couldn't resist the desire to see the land from above. His first lift had been a concentrated attachment to

Heaster; this next float would bring a discovery to Maddy that he couldn't compare anything to.

Their union had come with patience. There always had been a silent relationship and bond that was more than just feeding and watering time. They were both young, and experience was being established every second they were together. Heaster had grown out of his skin, so to speak. His abilities were as natural as water flowing in a riverbed. Maddy remembered that Heaster had gone right past his feed trough. With a glancing scan of the countryside, they dove toward the riverbed. If they were going to keep this up, they would both need energy. Floating barely over the char sprouts, Heaster was biting them off, chewing and eating more than ever. The more he ate, the more he ate. After a few moments, Maddy said, "What about me?"

The response was, "Where?"

The meal he had shared with the Guthrie's was fading in the excitement. All he could think about were those fruit-sack cups on the ladlebalm. He'd need more than those, though. He didn't need any hives, just nourishment.

The flesh of the spikenard fruit, which hung at the tops of the trees, was a feast in itself. When he and Ben did their climbing, it was in the spikenards. They were squirrelly enough to climb up and get its crop. They produced fruit all year, and it could be eaten anytime. It resembled a pomegranate that fit in the hand. The fruit was inside, and the seeds were on the skin, covered by a clear blue casing. You could use the seed to bring down a fever and could increase body

THE PRIME

temperature with more seeds. Using them in the winter helped you resist the cold.

The flesh of the fruit was dry. When you sprinkled them with ladlebalm juice, from its fruit, it would create an explosive taste in your mouth that was always a treat.

As the thoughts of the treated fruit came to his mind, they were off. Heaster had a keen sense of smell, and the scencee trees were next to the spikenards. There would be no need to climb today.

When they got to the ladlebalms, Maddy picked one of the bags and opened it to get the fruit inside. They arrived at the spikenard grove and hovered above, picking the fruit not easily gathered by climbing. He put six or so nards—the fruit—in the sack. The upper branches also had a spike that was a handbreadth long. It protected the fruit from the drachma bird, which would eat the fruit before it had fully ripened. As the spikenard produced fruit all year, the drachmas had no need to migrate. If they weren't kept under control, they would ruin the harvest and prevent the fruit from ever getting ripe. To the advantage of the population, these birds were high in protein, and because they ate fruit, their meat also contained high levels of citrus and a vitamin that thwarted the cold symptoms of runny nose and coughing. The downside was that even though they were the size of a chicken, their bodies were slim and long, which made a shot from bow and arrow very difficult.

The spikes did make tremendously accurate darts that could be shot out of a blowgun made from jumbi cane stalks.

TREMAN

Almost every hunter started out using this weapon. It didn't have the carrying distance of a bow and arrow but was much more precise at close range.

Once the spike was picked off the branch, the fruit would not grow from that branch again, so being careful and not picking too many of the spikes were lessons learned early on.

With the ladlebalm sack full of nards, they floated in the direction of the ancient treman. While floating in gracefully to the ground, they could see Trace on her way down the hillside from Rood. Maddy hopped down, and Heaster landed, curling his feet under himself, lying on the grass, continuing his eating endeavor.

Maddy was filled with exuberance as he ran to meet Trace.

He lifted her off the ground when he got to her and twirled her around and around. The energy he had gotten from the Ladlebalm juice proved it was energizing his strength.

Trace wondered what had happened. His extra-energetic stride and the lift and twirl were evidence that something had changed. She hadn't noticed the floating duo, as she was paying attention to her descent down the hill. She spotted Heaster, unattended and not tied down. Maddy hadn't taken the time to explain what Dray was doing with Heaster when he told her father about the primordial. So he proceeded to introduce her to his freshly upgraded ride.

Heaster recognized Trace from the few times she had been to their cabin. Maddy had shown him off to his guy friends but hadn't formally introduced her to him. They had seen one another only from a distance.

THE PRIME

"Trace, this is my valiant steed, Heaster. Heaster, this is Trace Guthrie, our newest true friend."

Heaster reached out and bumped Trace's cheek with his and uttered a greeting, saying, "Greetings, Trace Guthrie."

Taken aback, she said, "He can mimic?"

"He can mimic very well," Maddy and Heaster answered in unison.

Making a motion of a pat on their heads, she said, "And so humble too."

Maddy had to tell her of his last turning of the moon. With every word she grew into their information and was about to ask for a ride when Heaster knelt by her side.

"I think he knows what you're thinking too," stated Maddy. "It's making me more interested in what he can do. He's practically changing and gaining knowledge and size moment to moment."

Maddy knelt to one knee so Trace could stand on his leg to get on without having to jump. Then, with a dominating launch from his legs, he landed behind Trace. Their flight was flawless; as Heaster took them around the treman three times then set his sights toward the riverbed again. He'd lifted them both with incredible ease. However, he was craving more char sprouts for energy.

Back at the river inlet again, Heaster touched down and unloaded his cargo. Trace and Maddy watched him walk into the inlet and curl his legs as the water deepened. He started to float there also. Now he could eat, expending little to any energy.

Maddy found a secluded spot where the sun was shining on the yellowing bank of ringed-leaf grass. They sat in the warmth of the midday sun. Without any wind blowing, the sun still created a slight heat. The ring-leaf grass gave them a cushioned, dry area to sit and the warmth the sun was giving them made for a moment of disconnect from the actual season they were in.

Maddy's day had been consumed by its events. His head was full of memories: all the stories that Mr. Guthrie had told, being together with Trace for more than one time today, watching his ride floating without restraints, not even counting all the trifle things, and now having Trace sitting here with him so they could enjoy it together.

Trace moved her hand into his, and they sat there watching the sun just begin to duck under the horizon.

The two moons, Harac and Cam, started reflecting the red sun as it was no longer in sight. Harac had deep green splotches on a lime background. Cam was the turquoise moon that turned on its axis fast enough that you could watch it move. It would be just enough time for Heaster to get Trace to her home and Maddy back before dark. As the green and turquoise moons reflected the red sun's rays, an ultraviolet ember prism of light beamed across the shadowed landscape.

Maddy called out, "Come!" and Heaster was kneeling at his side. Heaster stretched the ride to Trace's driveway to give them all the time together he could. When they arrived, Maddy jumped down and lifted Trace to the ground. He wanted that short fragment of the day to last forever. As her feet touched the ground, she said, "You had me feeling like you were a ride, the way you floated me off Heaster." Her lips shaped a kiss, and she blew it through the air at Maddy.

THE PRIME

She then ran to her door. She turned as she reached it and said with the slightest reservation, "See you tomorrow?"

With a leg swing, he answered, "How couldn't I?" His ride turned and flew.

He knew rides could move, but this prime had the game in his game bag. When the turn was directed toward home, the stub flexed, and in a blur, they were by the pen.

Maddy talked with Heaster while he brushed his coat. There wasn't really a sweat to brush off; it was more of a cool-down to relax the contraction in the prime's body. If he didn't relax, he would hover through the night, and any time off the ground used energy.

Dray looked out and saw Maddy wiping and brushing Heaster and knew he had gotten home safely. He'd put the treman on the back burner for today. How much more could a day hold in store?

When the cool-down was over, two worn-out, resting bodies lay together in the stall. Both had had a full day of pushing their bodies to the limit, and it was time for rest. What was better than to share this memory in their dreams until the next adventure of the new day began?

CHAPTER THREE

Getting to Know You

In the darkness, Maddy lay curled next to his companion. His eyes were darting side to side, and his breathing grew deeper and more rapid. It was evident that he was dreaming. In his subconscious dream state, another vision was becoming so real that the sights and sounds brought him to a position of believing he was really there. He was on Heaster. They were moving through the stars. Their speed was making streaks of light out of the luminary dots in the heavens. Turning to see where he'd been, he watched as his planet quickly went from a round sphere to a tiny dot then disappeared. He was not only seeing streaks of light but also the many large chunks of jagged rock whizzing by. Some just missed them by a couple of arm lengths. The rate of speed slowed as a planet came into view on their right side. To their left side, another planet appeared, similar to the one on their right. Although the planets were practically twins in shape and size, their colors were as different as night and day. The right planet had a pale, creamy color with a rippled ring on each end. The left was dark green, with deep blues and light blues woven together. Defined lines were between the green and blues. The blues were not as easily divided, as they blended in a different way along the deep green masses.

Heaster had slowed down and was brushing his head by Maddy's, directing his face to see a speck on the creamy planet. He continued more fervently to turn his head when his eyes opened to his ride, nudging him awake. Maddy could see a questioning look in his eyes that had him ask, "Were you seeing it too?"

With a nod the confirmation was yes.

"Should we go and see what Trace is up to?" As the request came out of his mouth, Heaster was moving in reply.

First they would sail in the direction of the river's inlet for an energy boost. While strapping the harness on him, he noticed that he had to let the strap out five notches to get it on him. Climbing onto his back, he felt his legs were stretched wider than they had been the day earlier. His prime was growing and not slowly. This was an overnight increase in mass. Reaching the inlet, Heaster relaxed his stub tail and slowly floated to the bank where Maddy jumped off with the ladle-balm sack in hand. He'd have his breakfast of spikenard fruit while Heaster filled up on sprouts. When they'd eaten their fill, it was a leap to his ride and back toward his cabin. The sensation of lifting off the ground still made him flutter on the inside as they rose to be level with the tops of the trees. Maddy wanted to tell his father what he was going to do.

GETTING TO KNOW YOU

Back at the cabin, Dray was outside splitting a few blocks of firewood, stacking them next to the chopping stump as he chopped. When the shadow of their image passed between him and the morning sun, his head turned to see Heaster and Maddy coming in for a landing.

"Morning, son. Heaster went for a morning ride already?" was his opening phrase.

In unison they answered, "Yes."

Maddy added, "And we rode down to the inlet by the river to finish some breakfast." He looked at Heaster, letting him know he was doing the talking for now.

Dray smiled. "He's growing, huh? He looks almost twice as big as he was yesterday."

"I know. I sure am glad he's able to go to the char patch. He's eating a lot more now and carrying enough sprouts for him would keep me busy all morning. Dad, I wanted to ask you if you've ever heard anything about any other planets out in the Bliss? Are there any facts or stories you've not told me about?"

Dray answered with a question. "What causes a question like that?"

Maddy wasn't sure how to answer his dad. The last tale he had started telling Uncle Mel and his dad ended with storytelling correction 101. "I was just wondering. Hard to believe there isn't something out there in the Bliss besides us. I mean, what does the story about that monument and the story about that pod that is south of us mean, anyway? Where did those come from?"

Dray cleared his throat and started, "There was a story I had heard when I was young, back in Burton, about things that had landed on our earth long before your great-grandfather was around. That pod has its story. But the things that landed here were nothing like what we have here on Amri-Farret. They have them, I'm told, in a vault or enclosure on the other side of our earth. I'd forgotten about telling you that story. I suppose now is as good a time as ever to tell you about it. And for the record, this is a story, Maddy. I have never seen this crypt or the collection of these items. The palace, or the control center, that I told you about, where the copies of all records from all counties and groups are kept, is where they have these items stored—supposedly. Again this is what I can only pass on as a story. The palace is off limits to anyone when the elders go there. They meet there the third week of the session between winter and spring. That's when any updates to lineages and changes in the geography are brought to be filed for the complete compilation of all the earth. Again, Maddy, this is an update and a repeat of what you already know with the additional information of the bits and pieces they have in the palace there. They say you can visit the palace, but I never have. So I don't know about any paperwork or documents you'd need if you could visit it."

"Is there any more to the story of what these things are, Dad?"

"I don't recall ever hearing details or descriptions of the objects, only that they were kept at the palace and were in a vault there. I recall there were supposed to be seven pieces."

Maddy's mission had just expanded. He would he have to look for the missing link in understanding what had happened to the treman, and he now had foreign objects that should be public knowledge added to his detection list. "So, Dad, is it OK if I go on a float with Heaster now?"

"Sure, and bring Trace around if you get a break from your busy schedule." Then he added, "Maddy, you are on the edge of manhood, and I know we have had the talk about the joining of two into one, but there also is the privilege you gain when you turned thirteen. When you have any questions that cannot be answered by handed-down generational knowledge, you have the freedom to seek the elder's mind bank."

"About that, Dad…I sort of already activated that liberty. Trace and I went to Mantra and asked about the treman." Maddy was feeling uneasy that he hadn't mentioned it to Dray until now.

"What haven't I told you about the treman that you would need to ask Mantra about?"

"I'll talk to you about it when I get home, OK? Trace might have been waiting for a while already."

"Go ahead. We'll talk later. Greet her for me."

"That will be a sure thing, Dad."

As he got to Heaster, the dip and welcome were like clockwork. He leaped off the chopping block and landed on his back, and up they went again. Their connection had such unity, even a flowing assimilation. The more they floated, the smoother their moves became.

Maddy had put the peg in a knitted sack spun from the threads of the ovanclave tree. With the melding of the handle and peg, Maddy had thought it best to keep the article in a sack to segregate it from any bit of contact, no matter what could touch it. He'd put it in the ladlebalm rucksack along with a couple more nards he had picked. He would offer one to Trace when he got to her place. For now their flight was a thing of beauty. The swaying between the rolling landscape of trees, small valleys, and rock-faced walls hadn't had the same effect as walking had on this adolescent floater. It was incredible. The movement through the air caused the breeze he was feeling on his face to cool him. As they sped up, a friction reaction changed the cool air into a lukewarm sensation.

Heaster's neck also acted as an airfoil that split the main forces of wind, deflecting them along his trim, lined body. The faster they went, the more friction, and the more friction, the more heat. Heat was an accepted adaptation with the early part of winter cooling down the surroundings.

The extended trip was over, and they drifted toward Trace. She was out in her yard eagerly getting her daily chores done. As they came closer, Trace waved so her position would be known. Maddy would have to be blind not to pick her out of the backdrop. Once on the ground, Maddy slid off and motioned for her to come to him.

She motioned with her head that she would be going to ask for permission. She would give her parents information of her intended outing.

The sun was providing warmth as the three of them lifted off. It was just past the middle of the day, and they were on their way to what had been a priority just a few days ago.

Then the treman came into view. The sensation in the air was that it was anticipating their arrival. When they landed at its base, a pulsating invitation seemed to draw them in. To be patient was becoming more difficult. As they slipped off Heaster's

GETTING TO KNOW YOU

back and took the blanket off him to spread on the ground for their unplanned picnic together, Maddy swung the backpack around and untied the opening. As he reached in to get the nards, he brushed by the packaged key. The lump in Maddy's rucksack had been changing again. And without a choice to be made, a surging desire made him take hold of the key and bring it out. Trace momentarily looked at what he had pulled out, and it was enough to put an inquisitive look on her face. It wasn't the same as what she had last seen. It was altered somehow. Maddy recognized the change immediately. The sack wasn't wrapped around the peg anymore; it had turned into a thin skin that still left the rounded face with the etching there. He was concerned, and his expression had changed also. He knew he had put the peg in the ladlebalm sack. Trace wasn't as concerned because she hadn't known about the sack. She was just attentive at the latest look it had taken on.

He remarked as he looked for reassurance. "This is unlike it was when I showed it to you the last time, isn't it, Trace?" He wasn't sure what to make of the transfiguration, but pieces were starting to go together.

Henneh was in full sight, unhidden at all by Klue. The brightness of the Klue moon was all that faded Henneh's shape and projection. It had taken its place in the day sky and offered a new beauty that Maddy and Trace would have been too young to see the last time it appeared. Henneh would follow Klue for most of the winter then begin to be drawn back to its hibernated position for more than a decade.

As they stared up into the clear sky, they interrupted each other. Simultaneously they started. "Do you think...?" After a small smile and a glance into each other's eyes, they both gestured for the other to continue. Then they burst out laughing.

"All right, Trace. Ladies first."

Trace began the question again. "Do you think we are the only ones who have such a beautiful sight to see? I mean, is there anyone else on Amri-Farret, who can see this?"

"My question is an extension of yours and yet is the same at the same time." Maddy hesitated for a moment then added, "Anyone? Or anywhere?"

These thoughts of these two young minds were no different from the inquisitive inspirations of thought that most of their former relatives would have had. Questioning life, how it had come to be, and whether there were other untouched, unanswerable, uncertainties was a very normal action. But facts and stories had their places. That had been nonnegotiable.

Maddy's lips couldn't be sealed any longer. "Trace, my Dad told me there are some objects at the palace that were found many years ago. He was clear that this was a story he had heard and didn't have any personal experience as to it being factual. But there is something about this peg, the story about the Treman that Mantra told us, and the bits and pieces at the palace that are overwhelming me."

Heaster's attention was cued in. In sync with Trace, he blurted, "Are we going to the palace?"

"I don't want to invite you to do something you don't want to do," responded Maddy.

"Should we go right now or get an early start in the morning?" Trace asked.

GETTING TO KNOW YOU

As the question wafted through the air, both heads and all eyes were directed at Maddy. He was the one with the decision to make. They could tag along, free from that later possible judgment. The initial proposal came from Maddy. And unless Trace wanted to get permission or relay to her parents what she wanted to do, the answer was perceptible.

"Then we'll leave at first light." Maddy didn't want to take all the blame and certainly wouldn't want to offend Trace's parents.

Their questions about what they may encounter on their anticipated journey were endless.

How long it would take? Where they would go first? And would they be received at the palace? Klue was sinking into the horizon, and the hazy pink of Henneh had gotten less blurred. Her shape came into focus, as her light, more pure and without the distraction of the light of Klue, took center stage.

It was time to get Trace home. They climbed up Heaster's tack and harness as their ascent and movement turned to the northwest. A slight contraction of muscle, and the trio flew quickly. They descended to Trace's front door within a few moments.

Maddy jumped down and again gave Trace a hand in getting down. She was as agile and capable as Maddy but didn't refuse his help. "I'll wait for you to get your answer from your folks." He was letting Trace know he'd be anxiously waiting to see her one more time before he left.

"Be right back, Maddy." She left to talk to her parents.

It seemed like he'd hardly turned to Heaster when she came back out. "I will see you at first light then?"

"First glimpse of Klue, or a shot of light from the sun, and we'll be here."

"See you then. Bye, Heaster."

A gruff of sound and "Bye" echoed back to her. She watched and couldn't help wonder if this might become a common sight, yet temporary location, to see Maddy leaving.

Maddy thought—the words were never vocalized—"Way up." His excitement passed on to his ride, and encouraged by their connection, up they went.

Their ascension was more gradual than their horizontal movement. Still, within a few blinks of the eyes, they were looking at their earth's character as never before. Only a couple drawings had revealed anything close to the physical spectacle they were sharing. Maddy had seen illustrations of his earth from his teachings and records in history books, but this…this was beyond that. He watched as the moons were fixed in orbit, with only Cam giving sign of movement. He could see all four moons from here. They were hanging at that place where daylight was transitioning into nightfall.

Trace had asked how long it would take to get to the palace. Maddy hesitated to answer only because he wanted to share that journey with Trace. He could have gone there and back right now if he had wanted to. That would soon be found not to be the case.

GETTING TO KNOW YOU

With Maddy focusing on the cabin, they moved downward. Heaster sensed it was time to get some rest.

At the cabin, Maddy took the tack off Heaster and brushed him down. Lifting and descending weren't as tasking as flexing. So for tonight, the wipe-down and cool-down were less timely. They both said, "Rest well," and their relaxation commenced.

Maddy opened the door to find Dray putting a couple of crackle blocks of firewood in the stove. They lived up to their names in that respect. As they burned through the night, the snapping and crackling of the fire had a familiar and calming effect for resting.

"Dad," Maddy started, "would it be wrong to ask to go to see the palace?"

"Suppose it's time for you to level with me, Maddy?"

"Yes, it is, Dad."

"Well? What's got you wanting to go halfway round the world?"

"I'm not sure of that myself. But there are a lot of pieces of my life causing questions. Like Mantra's story of the Treman, your possible facts of the items they have in the palace, Trace, and Heaster's being able to float…now."

"OK. OK. Let's find a place to begin." Using his calming voice, Dray took hold of the spewing of Maddy's relief valve.

"Heaster and his abilities themselves have been life changing. And girls can cause a man's heart to throw lot of questions around his mind. But why do you have all the fascination with the palace?"

CHAPTER FOUR

Confession

Maddy reached into his backpack and pulled out the peg. "I guess this is where it all started. That day I went to look for your arrow, the one I found by the treman, and you and Uncle Mel found me knocked out by the ovanclave grove…well, when I found your arrow, this was stuck to the tip of it."

He was going to hand it to his father when Dray exclaimed, "Wait! Don't move, Maddy!"

He rushed to the cupboard and took out an iron dish. "Put that thing on this. Now, Maddy!"

"What is it, Dad?"

"You'll find out soon enough. Go on with your story. I want every detail."

"Why do you believe this now? When I tried telling you and Uncle Mel before, you stopped me and told me to make sure and start with the story declaration."

"Facts aren't stories, Maddy. Please, I need to know everything completely."

"I was watching the treman, and it was moving. And I caught a flicker of your arrow falling to the ground."

"The treman was really moving? Not just a strong wind?"

"Yes. But only until I saw the arrow fall. I hadn't noticed it stopped moving until I was walking backward with the arrow in my hand. I wanted to get your arrow and get away to watch again. That's when I tripped and hit my head on the ovanclave root."

"So this was connected to the arrow until we went there in the morning?"

"Yes, and when I found your arrow, I pulled the peg off and put it in my pocket—"

"You hadn't touched it before that—the peg, I mean?" Dray asked.

"Not that I know of, Dad. What's going on?"

"What was the next thing that happened?"

"Well, then we came home. I started to examine it and saw these markings."

Maddy went to pick up the key, and his dad stopped him. "No, Maddy. I need to know more first. What did you do then?"

"I took the peg and went back to the treman to see if I could climb up and…oh, I forgot. That night before I went back, I had a dream about the treman. It kind of scared me."

"Why?"

"I was climbing the treman to put the peg back into the spot it came from, and the treman grew around me, pulling me into the trunk. Then this branch above me became a sharp, pointed arrow that was headed for my forehead when I woke up."

"Do you remember anything else about the dream?"

"Not really. It was a pretty short dream."

"Is there anything else?"

"When I was climbing the treman, just about to where I thought the peg might go, Trace got there, and I came down to talk with her."

"Has she seen the peg?"

"I let her hold it after I handed it to her, so that would be a 'yes.'"

"Has anyone else touched it?"

"Dad, you're kind of freaking me out. What's going on?"

"This is what it looked like when you pulled the arrow out?"

"No. When I went back to climb the treman, the dream had me think I should have some way of stopping any unwanted action, so I whittled a piece of spikenard wood and used some crackle sap to stick it in the arrow hole. I thought it could be a handle to use the key for a switch. Then, when I saw that the pieces had all morphed into one, I thought I shouldn't have it touch anything else, so I put it in a ladlebalm thread sack. Then that made it look like this."

"Did Mantra see it?" Dray's questions were leading in design.

"All I wanted to ask her was about the past drawings of the treman. And after the story she told us about the treman, I opted not to show it to her. She got really excited, though, about the knotty spot I asked her about in the drawing. That's what started the inquiry and the search for the spot on the treman on the four corners. She and a few others were there looking for it, I think."

"I'm not sure where to begin with this, Maddy."

"How about starting from the beginning?"

"That peg *is* a key—the key to the whole history that was before the history we have. I never thought it was fact. I believed the story could have bearing and that it was important. It was just hard to move it to the fact side of our life. Many elders have searched the archives for something that may have shown us what was before our tradition of passing on facts. Keeping the stories alive and accurate, in case a story could be proven to be factual, was an option for parents to pass on or not. When your mother was with us, she was the storyteller, and I dropped the ball on continuing to tell some of them to you. Certain stories have been found to be accurate and true with the passing of time. The story of the Treman that Mantra told you may hold a little more water now that this peg could plug a few holes."

"What holes does this fill?"

"The story says that the man and the seed became one, and this peg has definitely become one with the other tree parts that it touched," Dray continued. "There are hundreds of sketches of the treman, but no one knew what this key looked like or how it would be able to be removed. So when Mantra had a specific new spot to investigate, she couldn't leave that alone. The search for this key has been dismissed, mainly because it wasn't found for so long."

CONFESSION

"Why did you want me to put it in that dish?" asked Maddy.

"Here is another part of the story. The Treman that kind man had become and the place he had put his heart is said to be the *key*, the key that could answer any questions about anything."

"Dad?" Maddy grew more curious.

"Yes, Maddy?"

"I hope you didn't kill the Treman with your perfect shot to his heart."

"I believe we have time to explain that later. But I think your trip to the palace had better wait for a while."

Maddy was perplexed. He wanted to be with Trace and do a float with her, a long-distance float. And now he'd have to put the ride on standby.

The next morning, after tossing and turning most of the night, Maddy hopped out of bed and went over to the stove. The cabin had cooled, and the instant warmth the stove provided drew him there like a magnet. Dray had thrown in a couple of wood slabs that had just started popping and were beginning to heat the iron outer shell. It was warm enough to touch but not hot enough to burn the skin. Dray was sitting at the table, looking at this object in the iron dish. He turned the dish and studied the recent, newfangled item it held. As he lifted his eyes to see his son behind the component, it blurred and became lucid. Just about invisible but still there.

From his vantage point, all Maddy saw was the unchanged key.

" 'Morning, Dad."

" 'Morning, son."

"I told Trace I'd be there at first light. Is it OK to go see her before we do whatever it is we're going to do?"

"Sure. When you get back, we'll make some decisions."

Outside, Heaster was ready to don his gear. Maddy led him to the barn and got his harness on him. As he led him there, he talked about the things his dad had told him and how their trip to the palace was on hold.

They got to Trace's just before Harac had disappeared for the day, its sphere reflecting a fragment of the rays from the red sun as it set then faded out of sight. Klue rose, and his influence shed enough light for the grays and darkened shapes to be converted into piles of pallets and clay pots.

Trace was done with her duties and ran to the stoop to get her knapsack. When she got to the duo, she sensed a drop in enthusiasm that had been there the past evening.

"Are you OK, Maddy?" she asked.

"How could a guy be less than that after seeing the best thing there is the first light of day? But I want to let you know why I'm a little disappointed. Dad and I had a talk last night—"

"Is something wrong?"

"Oh, no. Quite the opposite, I hope. You can tell your parents that we're going to our place instead."

"Be right back." She scampered off then reappeared from the domed house.

Maddy explained what Dray had shared with him about the treman and the key. When they got back to the cabin, they gave Heaster more char sprouts then went inside.

CONFESSION

The cabin was empty. Dray was gone, and the dish that had been on the table was not there anymore.

Maddy stepped out of the doorway and shouted, "Dad, are you out here?" No reply.

He was getting a bit anxious when he suggested that they take an aerial inspection. With a call to Heaster, his steed was at his side. "The more eyes the better, don't you think, Trace?"

They got on Heaster, and they started to lift off when Dray called out from the path from the river, "I'm right here. I didn't think you'd get there and back this quickly. He sure is getting fast with his thrust, that prime."

"Dad, where's the key?" Maddy asked with urgency in his voice.

"I put it in the footlocker to keep it out of sight." They all walked into the house together, and Dray went to the locker and brought the saucer back to the table. "There will be a lot of fuss made about this key, so we'd better talk about what we're going to say and who we're going to say it to."

"Why 'who'?" asked Trace.

"Good to have you ask, Trace, seeing that you two have both touched the key. I wanted to tell you another part of the story when we were all here. The key was said to have been a one-person connection. The man who connected with the seed and became the Treman was alone on his trek. But Maddy, a couple of things have been revealed to me and connected some loose ends about your Uncle Mel's parents and possibly your mom. When there is no other explanation for an occurrence, even to presume isn't acceptable, and in storytelling, the norm is to ensure the listeners of a fable know that it is a story. So when there is no factual evidence and there is no solution to an incident, you don't tell a story you think might have happened. Rather we have accepted waiting and having time expose the truth, or we dispense with discussion about what happened."

"So what is this about Mom?" Maddy had gotten extra curious as to where his father was leading the discussion.

"First Mel's parents," he began. "When they had been in Dillon County for two years, they had been planting and recording their transplanting of the trees they had brought with them from Burton County. It was the year the treman dropped its seed. So the day they had to plant the seeds was the day they were gone. No one has any clues as to where they would have or could have gone. Mel was spending the night with your grandparents and me, and when we walked to his dwelling the next afternoon, we couldn't find them. We had known they were going to be planting the seed and went to the spot we thought they might be. All that was there was a small piece of frazzled bark and an indentation, the outline of what most tremans look like at their base, in the ground by it. There was a plot map a few steps away, where they had been recording their plantings. But that spot on their map wasn't marked with anything."

"What happened to the map?" Maddy inquired.

"It's in the part of those archives at Mantra's," Dray, picking up again, said, "where parts of evidences and occurrences are filed. There wasn't any proof of what happened, and odder things than that have taken place, so it was put in a file and is still there now."

CONFESSION

Maddy was intent on hearing more about his mother. "What does this have to do with Mom? And why haven't you mentioned anything until now about what happened to them?"

"Maddy, you know that answer. I couldn't assume. What's in my mind right now is bordering on the edge of saying or not saying what I am. It is materializing with this key. If I hadn't seen it with my own eyes, there would be no more adages."

"And Mom?" Maddy channeled the question to Dray.

"Maddy, the reason we didn't have a burial for your mom was because she vanished in a similar way. Not that I found a hole and a plot map, but the love I had for your mother went as deep as beyond the farthest star. I knew she didn't just packed up and leave us. Our love was pure." Dray's eyes flushed out a huge teardrop. "She used to sit with you, for turn after turn of Cam, telling you about our lineage and the stories you still laugh about. I am perplexed as to how well you remember those details and who was who. There was no way she'd leave you. She loved you. Existence was nothing to her but a story, had she not been able to hold you, her reality, in her arms."

"So what do you think happened to her?" Trace had gotten hooked into the splendor and sincerity of what Dray had been saying and had to ask.

"That's where I need to draw the line between story and fact. I'm not sure yet, but this new detail may be the light for us to see that the fact, that part of the puzzle, still has a missing piece."

"I believe one of those pieces is that it's time for a bite to eat." Mel entered with a sack over his shoulder and his shaft and flinger in his hand. He had heard the last part of the conversation about pieces.

Maddy's heart stuttered, as the climax of input about his mother and that flinger Uncle Mel had let him throw brought confusion and a shake of the head to him.

The sleek, native shaft, with painted waves of color and a scoop made of a carved scencee knot on its throwing end, had caused envy for Maddy when he would watch his dad shoot his arrows at a target. Mel would place the flinger in the scoop and hurl it with crushing force, many times exploding the arrows to pieces. It was a knockout weapon. The blunt, hardened end was perfect for taking game, which had skins they could use for several useful purposes. It wouldn't poke any holes in the pelts, but it had the force necessary to accomplish its task. It had the shape of a giant teardrop that would have been lengthened from one tip to the blunt-ended bludgeon.

Dray asked what was in the sack, and Mel poured out two drachma birds and half a dozen nards. "They were swooping around our spikenards, and one made the mistake of landing while I knocked the other down as it was trying to fly away with a nard. You could say I got two nards with one stone—a bit of fruit to go on a plate with my meat, so let's eat."

Their lack of enthusiasm had Mel ask, "Don't feel like fresh sliced drachma breast, sautéed in spikenard juice?"

Still there was no reaction.

Then Dray slid the bowled dish, with the key, in Mel's direction.

"What is that?"

CONFESSION

Mel was about to pick it up when Dray stopped him and said, "It's a gift."

"For me? You shouldn't have."

"For all of us." Dray asked Mel if he remembered the story Dray's mother had told him about the Treman. He and Dray would sit for hours and listen to her bring their past experiences and family outings into a vivid chronicle they would relive, again and again, to help with retaining those memories. Exact repetition could remain accurate, without adding false color. The tones could be elevated and changed with expression, bringing newness to a tale, and Dray's mother had that gift.

When the Treman story had been recalled from his childhood, a sudden flash of feeling twirling Mel to lightheadedness. He remembered his parents and their disappearance and those evenings Cheraw would tell of the past, of relations, and especially the stories. A baffled expression came to his face as the images of his parents brought both sad and joyful facial expressions to his conscious.

Turning the dish this way and then that, he looked up and asked, "Do you know if it is the right gift?" The story he had remembered was the story of the treman seed that had been planted and wasn't so wonderful. It wasn't Cheraw who had told it. It was a man from the group from Braden who had been exchanging wares with Mel and had told of a seed they had planted just before it turned to tar goop. When it had been covered by earth, it surged out of the hole and had skewed the planter. No one had seen it surge, but the planter was almost split in two. They found him the next day, lying by the tree, and the tree had grown to be almost as high as most dwellings in the land. Or so the story he remembered went.

"This isn't a seed, Mel. It's believed it is a key." Dray told Mel all that they had for facts and started to lay out a plan of what they were going to do next.

"They both touched it?" Mel asked. "And they are unchanged?"

"We were just going to try a couple tests when you walked in with dinner," Dray answered. "We could see if anything between them clicks while we eat."

Maddy piped in. "What are you two talking about?"

"If you two both touched that thing, it's most likely you will share something." Maddy's Dad suggested they get the meal going and then administer a couple tests. This new topic of their sharing something got Maddy doing a playback in his mind of their times together. Trace was blushing. She already knew something was going on. Whether it was the key wasn't that important. Their feelings for each other were those of two people who had just opened a box of love at the same time, and they knew the package was from and for each other.

Sitting down to eat the food they had prepared, with the key still in the dish, they asked a couple questions.

Dray started with, "How does it feel to float?"

In unison both Trace and Maddy started responding word for word. "It is amazing!"

"Dray, is that a test?" Mel countered with his own question. "What's your favorite color?"

CONFESSION

This was a great question, as Dray knew what Maddy would say. Maddy said, "Green!"

Trace followed Maddy and said, "Blue."

"OK, now both of you reach out and touch the key." Dray urged them to go ahead and do it. When they had both touched it, Mel asked the question again. "What's your favorite color?"

Together they looked at each other and said, "Purple!"

They were going to remove their fingertips from the key, but it wasn't as easy as it was to put them on it. Maddy tried pulling, and Trace tugged against him. Their fingers were attaching themselves with a stronger bond, just as Dray and Mel both threw their arms around them and pulled them off it.

The key had forced their favorite colors into a nontypical blend of them both that made them of the same mind, and it had absorbed part of something they didn't know.

They glanced at one another. And then Dray said, "I guess we know."

"Know what?" Maddy asked.

"We know you two will be more than friends from now on." Dray and Mel excused themselves and stepped outside to talk.

That left the two younger ones to exchange puzzled looks and opened their floodgate of questioning toward each other.

"Are you all right?" Maddy was first to speak.

"Are you?" Trace returned, hoping he would give the answer she wanted to hear.

"A big yes!" Maddy could tell they would never forget this moment they had shared.

"Did you see what I did when we were touching that key?" Trace had to know.

Maddy moved his head up and down and said, "Where was that place? I haven't seen anything like it."

Reentering the cabin, Mel and Dray said to Trace and Maddy, "We should go to Mantra's."

They were all in. Whatever they could find out about what they were experiencing, they were all for it. And the sooner the better.

"Let's go." Maddy and Trace again were together on their answer.

But Maddy had a standoffish reserve in his mind. He'd been the one to find this thing, and now he was being dragged around, almost as if he had a ring in his nose. He kept that in the farthest corner of his mind. He would think about debating questioning his father's decision.

Dray had a pair of metal tongs he used to reach into the firebox. He pinched the key with them and put it back in Maddy's rucksack.

"Dad, can Trace and I float Heaster over there?"

Tossing Maddy the pack, he said, "You might as well carry this with you there."

The thought Maddy had put in the back of his mind was just erased. His dad wasn't the type to steal thunder. He surely wasn't going to start with his son.

Maddy was smiling as he and Trace mounted Heaster and lifted off toward Mantra's.

Dray and Mel became small dots as the team rose above the trees. Mantra's was off to the northeast. Maddy was itching to see the treman and knew he could get to their destination before the men would, even with a speedy detour. Heaster sensed the thought. He turned his head northwest, and they were soon circling the treman.

The daylight was getting away, as the pink Henneh moon was in full sight, gleaming just behind Klue. The drift around the treman made Henneh look as if it were hanging in the tree, like an ornament on their Celemass tree.

When they were in line behind the treman, with the moon on the opposite side, the moon became two bulges on each side of the torso of the treman, as if they were two pink eyes watching them ring the tree. Had it been dark or even a tad more toward evening, the image would have been creepy.

It was time to get to Mantra's. Their conversation still revolved around the event they shared at the kitchen table and what they had seen in their thoughts that the men hadn't.

They were at Mantra's just as Mel and Dray arrived. Maddy left the rope of the knapsack looped over the riding horn as they slid down and all walked to her door.

Barely had their knocking started when the door opened. Mantra had a revived "get" in her giddyup, as she ushered them in and directed them toward the parlor. The latest discovery still had her excited and had renewed her search engine.

She went on and on. "We haven't found anything yet, but we haven't given up." She kept repeating the sentence aloud and under her breath. "How about it? Have you young ones found anything more? Any more clues we can move to the factual side?"

TREMAN

Maddy hadn't expected to cause such a spark. He was just there earlier to see if he could find the placement for the peg. Mantra was as excited as a monzi moth fluttering around the scencee and its blossoms. She could hardly stand still, scurrying from a pile of file folders she had on her buffet to another stack of papers on her desk. She was shuffling through them as if she were in search of a secret passage, line, or etching she hadn't read correctly.

Dray asked, "Could we look at the plot map of Mel's folks, the one they found after they disappeared?"

The puzzled look and the curiosity on Mantra's face could have pried out the deepest, hidden secret. And then she asked it. "You think that has something to do with the knothole in the landmark treman?"

Deception wasn't going to rear its ugly head. After all, a piece of their puzzle was still missing. They wouldn't want to start telling stories, especially to their elder. So Mel responded, "I wanted to see where those trees were and how many got planted that day. I was going to harvest one for firewood. It's getting colder every day, you know."

Part of recordkeeping was to keep a balanced account of how many trees could be planted and how many might be taken and for what purpose.

Mantra headed for the treman slab door. As she flipped open the latch and pulled the enormous door open, the room hadn't gotten any smaller. As thrilling as it was see something for the first time, this vast space, filled with so much history, still had Maddy and Trace in awe. It hadn't diminished in size from their first visit; it had grown. Their former quest had

CONFESSION

opened their eyes to just how much was in there and to the table where the drawings were laid out. Maddy focused on the drawings of the knothole shape and had missed the shelf after shelf and row upon row of information.

This entry took on a whole volume of visions. Mantra had gone into an opposing storeroom. Over the lintel was a plaque with the word maps on it. Under the word *maps* was a series of etchings and notches in three separate groupings.

Questions began to fill his mind. The middle grouping of notches looked very similar to the face of Maddy's key. As he drew a mental picture of the other groupings, he was interrupted by Mantra reeling back into the main room.

While they were paging through the plots, Maddy motioned to Trace to come look at the wooden plate over the doorway. Her talent for drawing was about to be required again.

"Do you think you could get a good enough mental picture of these other two markings to be able to draw them after we leave?" His question was asked with just enough volume for Trace to hear.

She nodded and focused on the etchings on the plaque.

"What are you two looking at?" Mantra asked, as she had noticed them staring at the placard.

Maddy returned her question with his own. "What are those markings under the word *maps?*"

"My grandfather said they found that one grouping, on the left, on the lumber they used to make this door." She pointed to the entrance. "They needed a sign over the map room, so they used the piece of wood for that. The others are just stamps copied from other lumber that had the same shape."

"So there have been only three of these markings?" asked Trace.

"Oh, no!" Mantra left the two men to continue their search and walked over to her two eager-to-learn students. "Almost every treman has been found to have one of these etched areas somewhere in its makeup. Its wood is perfect for making lumber, and because it has such a wide girth, it makes great tables and doors, without the need to glue pieces together. That's when they can find these markings. It doesn't happen that every treman has exposed this marking, as it could be within a slab that is cut from its wood." She turned to the table, "So if you harvest one of those treman trees and you find one of these marks, be sure to bring the piece of wood that you find it on. I keep those pictures or the actual pieces back here." She pointed to another smaller room. The doorway wasn't noticeable when you were standing by the table. It was just around one end of a huge bookcase. Over its doorway was another carved sign that read, TREMAN MARKINGS.

Maddy walked to the entrance and saw that the room was crowded. There was still room for more, but even with an orderly filing system, without knowing the categorization, determining where to start would be complicated. As he stepped across the threshold, Mantra stopped him and asked if he had any—and she clarified, any—wooden objects in his pockets or anything made from any other tree.

She offered an example. "I had a pen I had gotten from my grandmother, whose shell was fashioned out of a piece of a treman wood. I had brought it in there to make a listing of the new pieces that had been brought in to take to the yearly

CONFESSION

meeting. I set it on a shelf and went to retrieve a cup of water, and when I came back into the room, all that was on the shelf was the inner workings of the pen. The shell was gone, and I never did find it. If stealing were even a possibility, that would have been the closest I would have ever been to experiencing it. I still remember what it looked like but never found out where it went."

Maddy thought he might have an idea to propose to her. Then she added, "There have been other things that visitors have brought with them—carved wooden jewelry and buttons—that vanished too. One I recall vividly. A young man, about your age, Maddy, went in to look at the room's articles. He was wearing a whistle made out of a piece of wood. It was hanging around his neck by a leather string. He told me later he had lost his whistle and asked to see if it had fallen off in there. We never found it either. So that's just something I let everyone know before they go into that room. Wooden things might be lost forever in there."

Maddy knew his key was hanging on Heaster's riding harness horn. He did a quick once-over of his belongings and garments and went in.

There were piles of boards and stacks of blocks with the designs on them, categorized by the years they were brought in and where they had been found. As Maddy looked at the positions of these markings, he saw that they were, as Mantra suggested, from all over the tree. As he read where they were found and the dates, their details covered several generations, from only the county of Dillon. This had Maddy wondering if there were any other rooms or records like this.

"Mantra, I know I should know this, but are there any other records or artifacts anywhere else about the tremans?"

"That's a very good question, Maddy." She had a slightly puzzled look as she answered. "As far as I know, this is the only place they are kept. Even if a treman seed leaves the county, those who take them are required to file any and all changes with me, well, and this office, about anything that has happened or changed in the tree's appearance. If they are harvested, anything about the trees is supposed to come back here. That's because we have the originals of the treman. Of course the palace has all the information also, but we are supposed to have any and all physical evidence here."

"So everything should be here about everything?" Dray hadn't been taught this either and wanted the knowledge for any future information he would pass on as facts.

"As far as I know, that is all." Mantra responded.

Mel had been digging for what they had said they were there for, when "Here it is!" came from the direction of the table.

Turning, they saw him standing with the plot map of the day his parents were planting the tremans. They asked to have a copy to see how much they had changed or if there were any changes they could bring back to Mantra. She made a copy, stamped it with her "copy" stamp, and handed it to Mel.

"If there is anything different, let me know. We're going to go to the meeting at the palace soon, and when you have something to bring to the meeting, it's an even better reason to go."

CONFESSION

Mel answered her. "Sure will, Mantra, and thank you for the copy."

The four of them left Mantra's on a newly directed path that was zeroed in on the grove of tremans at Mel's.

Maddy and Trace lifted off with Heaster, and Mel and Dray followed on foot. The copy of the plot had been given to the airborne team so they could look at the area from above.

When Heaster had gotten to the grove, his hovering mode gave the passengers on his back a solid, unmoving positioning to look at the map and the grove. The tremans that had been planted were not there. The original plan hadn't included any of the trees that had been harvested. But there was a change they needed to show the men.

"Down," came from Maddy's lips, and Heaster began his descent.

This change wasn't going to be only for Mel's benefit. It was going to open a box of unanswered questions that hadn't been asked because they related to Mel. They had never been seen.

When Uncle Mel and Dray arrived, the aerial team showed them by pointing to a spot on the copy.

The trees that had been harvested were always banded with an iron band around the base of the trunk where the treman would be cut down. The band would be for marking and future evidence of where the tremans had been. There was a consistency about the banding and harvesting of the tremans. Their base was usually the same size, and the iron band that was made in Braden County had a metalworks shop that made all the rings. The pattern rarely would change, as the time to take a treman for produce was after the tree had gotten to its completed size. That's when the wood would offer its best lumber and would be useful for firewood. Taken too early, the grain of the wood would be worthless because the crisscross grain meant that sawing and splitting was virtually impossible. This fact had been found out many years before. So waiting for the exact time took patience and an understanding of the tremans background.

"This one isn't there!" the two were exclaiming as they handed Mel the map.

Mel compared the first plotted plant, looking from the paper to the actual landscape then back again. "That's the one…" His voice cracked. "…where they found that depression in the ground."

"No, Mel. Not there." Maddy again pointed to the place right next to the spot the last drawing had offered. "Right here!"

Dray peered over Mel's shoulder, and while he held up the map's copy, they saw where the gap in the plantings came into sight.

"It's as plain as day from above," Maddy shared.

The form of a question had been set in motion on their faces. "Maybe it hadn't grown?" Mel started.

Dray added, "Could have been an error. Maybe they put a mark where they were going to plant one and decided not to?"

"All we know about treman seed, and this is your response?" Maddy knew enough about treman seed that he knew that never happened. "When you plant it, it grows. Sure, you have to plant them quick, but if they are put in the ground, they grow. And, as for making a mistake, Dad, that doesn't happen when it comes to recordkeeping."

All four walked to the place where they discovered the void.

"Could this be right?" Mel reasoned. "So what do we do now, Dray? This spot doesn't have any sign of a ring, and I never took down a tree here without following procedure."

"There is no doubt that this spot was planted with a seed, agreed?" The question implicated uncertainty when Dray spoke the words.

All three, including Heaster, replied, "Agreed."

"Then we need more facts." Dray was sensing a connection to this spot that he felt might lead him to his own unanswered questions. "And to get more facts, we need to find out everything we can about these tremans."

Maddy moved into the conversation and opened with a request. "So does that mean it's time to go to the palace?"

"It's time for all the answers we can get, and if that is where we'll find them, then, yes, it is time to go. The only problem is we cannot all go. And even though you are old enough, Maddy, the expedition you're heading into may get controversial. There are those who want the facts before they stir the kettle. They might not allow any inspection without a reason to continue any action. There have been many conflicts quenched and averted by not poking the beehive just to see what might happen."

Maddy had set his face like a flint. "Dad, what if Trace and I went? I know we'd have to talk to her parents, but if they agree, would you mind?"

"You've never been there, Maddy." Dray wanted his son to expect and be ready for a few curveballs. "You check with them again about going now, and when you find out, let us know what your plans are. We'll work out the details then."

Just as they headed for Heaster, Maddy turned to Trace and asked, "You do still want to go, right?"

With her hand in his, she urged him onto Heaster and followed him on with his assistance.

Trace said "They will both be home now, and I never unpacked from the other day. Anything else I need to say? Look at that—you have me making up poetry."

Maddy touched the harness to Heaster's neck. He turned to Dray and said, "Be right back."

A flash of light sparkled as they burst out of sight. It would have fit into a "be right back" timeframe had it not taken a few extra moments to bid farewell to Trace's folks. Heaster's speed was increasing with each float, and Maddy and his connection were molding them into one as they flew. Even Trace and her pack blended with them as they took to the air.

Back at the cabin, Dray had been packing a few things for Maddy. He'd taken copies of his birth records, some food, gear, and his bow and quiver, along with a few arrows. He was going to wait for Celemass to give Maddy his bow and arrow set, but this was a special enough time to give it to him, as they may be gone for a while.

CONFESSION

As the trio arrived at the cabin, they packed and adjusted the positioning of their load for their trip. When Dray came from the cabin with his early Celemass gift for Maddy, the appreciation in their unspoken reaction made a tear come to Trace's eye. A gift like this was very special and had taken some eluding and craftiness to finish so Maddy would not know what his father was doing. With a longer-than-normal hug, the father-son team bid each other farewell.

Dray turned to Trace and said, "Get your eyes full. There will be things that you never will have seen out there. Could you make sure Maddy keeps his eye on the goal? This quest will teach you a lot about each other, and when both of your heads are together, it will keep your wits about you."

"It'll be my pleasure, Mr. Handle."

"Be safe, and keep your eyes on the eastern horizon. Being up in the air will give you an advantage over any weather changes headed at you." Dray finished his good-bye with "I love you, son!"

"Love you too, Dad."

They watched Dray shrink as they rose above the trees. They waved with excitement yet had a reservation because they knew they were going places unknown to them.

CHAPTER FIVE

Palace City

They were experiencing so many new and exciting things together that the ride didn't take too long for their first part of their trip. They were going to make a few stops to bask in their childlike wonder of the amazing discoveries they beheld. There was such excitement and time filled with finger pointing and soaking up the newness that their journey had an adolescent dating aura about it. In most ways they were out on an unchaperoned date, except for Heaster, who was all in with them on this venture.

"How long will we have to wait for an audience with the elders?" Trace was curious to know what her escort knew about the palace.

"First things first, Trace. Not that you could get any more beautiful, but we'll stop when we get close to the palace to get our good duds on. Then we'll have to find a stable for Heaster and find out where we can stay if we don't get in to see the elders right away."

Trace wrapped her arms around Maddy even tighter and said, "Sure am happy that you know what to do."

"Well, you've given me a lot of confidence. To have such a pretty lady riding with me isn't much less than dreaming. What do you think, Heaster?"

"If I knew what dreaming was, it would probably be something like the feeling I have giving you both a ride on my back."

All three of them burst into laughter.

When Maddy raised his hand to steer the prime into a clearing, the maneuver drifted so in cue with Maddy that no words needed to be exchanged.

"You made a perfect landing again, Heaster. Thank you, my worthy steed!" Maddy had taken on a role play to entertain Trace. "Your hand, my lady?"

As he reached out his hand to her, she had daintily landed her hand in his and said, "Thank you, kind sir. Your mount was so very controlled on his landing that I thought I was landing on a fluffy white cloud."

Trace smiled and slid to her landing. Maddy's strong, young arms gently brought her to her feet, her toes touching his.

"You are so beautiful, Trace." Maddy's face started to flush with hue. "Should we rest here tonight then get an early start at first light?"

Trace was caught in the role of make-believe yet resourceful enough to have her answer be true and intended. "But of course, my prince."

Maddy gathered a few twigs and some dry, fine meadow grass and bound them together in a bundle of kindling. He took out one of his handmade matches and clashed it against the striker he had taken from his pocket. This wasn't Maddy's first fire, and in his heart, he was hoping it would be just one of thousands he would share with Trace. The spikenard and crackle sap burned fast and hot to ignite the kindling Maddy had placed in a ring of small stones. He added a few larger sticks, and the fire offered both illumination and heat. Getting off Heaster had taken away their heated seat, and the warmth of the fire was a welcomed pleasure. After spreading out a blanket, the adolescents huddled next to each other for added warmth. Maddy reached around Trace to get his pack then laid her head on his shoulder.

"I'm not really hungry, Maddy."

Their union was growing stronger. He was going to get them a nard to share for the evening's meal, and she had sensed it.

"Maybe in a little bit," she continued.

"Once the fire dies down, right?"

Her eyes met his, and they moved their faces slowly together. Just as they felt their breath on each other's lips, Heaster piped in. "Do you two mind if I go on a graze?"

The wonderful moment would be delayed. "Go ahead, boy. Eat enough to get us to the palace early."

Maddy turned his attention back to Trace. "I knew he'd be getting hungry. He's been eating and growing like crazy recently. And he's getting so strong. I wonder how fast he can go. It hasn't been seven rotation years since I would have been almost too much for him to float with."

His words were landing in the air, as he felt Trace's head, heavy on his arm. She had fallen asleep. He carefully laid her head down on the blanket and reached for the pack. He was going to get a snack, enough to chase the growling sounds in his belly away. He covered her with the other blanket roll and reached in for the nard. Maddy sorted through the cluster of nards for a smaller one, just enough so it might hit the empty void in his stomach.

He bit the fiber off, and now that it was in his mouth, it had the sweetness of honey nectar and the filling of a fiber cake. He laid his head back and gazed into the darkening sky. His eyes slowly closed as he turned one last time to see this angel by his side.

Sleep was uninterrupted in this clearing, which was so far from anything but the sounds of the night air around them. And sleep they did.

Maddy's face was warming as he opened his eyes to see that Heaster had his nose just inches from his face, exhaling a verdant, humid smell of char sprouts. A chewing sound came from his mouth.

"Eating breakfast without us?"

Maddy sat up and looked toward Trace. Her face loomed of beauty. With the look of a flower having the morning dew misted on its petals, she was so alive yet still in a state of rest—a perfect picture Maddy would not soon forget.

As he touched her hand, her eyes opened. "Where were we?" She was chary as she looked to him.

PALACE CITY

"We were in my thoughts of how perfect you are in the morning. You looked like a flower lying there, just ready to open those petals to a new day. Would you like a little fruit for breakfast?" He handed her a nard he had been cutting into slices. His hand was dripping with the juice from the fruity mass in his extended hand.

Remembering their joisting theatrical production from the night before, she said, "Why, it is like the nectars of heaven you offer me, sir."

Maddy's smile wasn't containable. His face lit up as the smile turned to passion. He recalled the story his mother had told him from the ancient tablets about the man who offered the banned fruit of knowledge to his wife. The love he must have had for her was as unbridled as what Maddy was feeling for Trace. Even knowing what was forbidden, his emotions were on the edge of losing their self-control.

"That was one of my favorite stories of love too." Trace was peering into Maddy's thoughts. She took the prepared meal and said, "Good thing that's not what we're doing," as their smiles made the moment carefree.

"I was thinking maybe we could do an exploration of Palace City from above to get somewhat familiar with the layout of the city. Things will look different once we're inside the gates."

Trace nodded. "That sounds like an added benefit to our traveling schedule. I'm so glad you want to make a few memories with this trip."

"Your pleasure, my dear lady!" Maddy turned to Heaster. "Ready to go, steed?"

"Ready."

Once they reloaded all their belongings in their proper positions and tied them down, it was time to set course. Heaster's ascent brought the capital city into sight. The fields where crops and agriculture would be done stretched out across the countryside before you entered the funnel of the wooded area. There were two vast forests with a sort of tree that wasn't like any in their home territory. It funneled visitors in and out of the city. An open, marshy field just as you passed through the woodland spread out from both sides of the roadway. Then the stream, which got its water from the mountain's snowcaps, was behind the city.

The stone bridge you would pass over was wide enough for ten ox carts to cross it abreast. From the distance, they could see a vast covering of dwelling places, and deeper, in the center of the city, the living centers expanded upward. These living centers each would provide living areas for several people. High-rise apartment houses were larger than any structures these adolescent travelers had ever seen. There was nothing they had to compare them to. All the fresh sights and terrain were becoming their sustenance.

Maddy nudged Heaster slightly, with a squeeze of his legs, to have them go even higher.

An outer wall surrounded the city. It was oval shaped, with the back side tucked up to the base of a deep-green mountain range, and a gateway on each side large enough to get smaller traffic carts and wagons through. They were closed, most of the time, as a protective barrier on each side. They were for bringing the stones and slabs of rock from the quarry that were sculpted and formed into building materials and artistries.

The main opening, with its archway, had the words Palace City embedded into the curved arch. The streets were in a circular pattern, with seven streets coming out from the middle of the conurbation. Four of the streets came from the entrance of the palace, and the other three were spaced equally around the rear side of the palace walls.

Beyond the wall and the courtyard, the visions they had dulled as they saw the magnificent palace.

The main entrance gate that opened into the courtyard of the palace was enormous. It lifted to the sides and upward from an attached pivot point at the top center of the two huge doors. There was a rack and pinion gearing that swung the doors out of a groove about a handbreadth wide. As the doors rose, a solid plate rose from below to fill the gap where the doors were. When in the closed position, the doors fit into the groove, and when they needed to be shut, the doors closed quickly. The pins were a full span across the radius and were equally fit into the wall's giant shaped stones and polished to a glaze. The stones were holding the door's weight with an arched arrangement that tied together into the walls on both sides of the doors.

Their questions again filled the air. How had they built such an outstanding palace? Where had they gotten all the equipment and materials to make it stand so majestically?

Just as Maddy and Trace were soaring above this massive fortress, twelve identically dressed guards, on their rides, surrounded them. The rides were all the same size and color and had obviously had years of formation and floating training. Their flight was a performance to watch, as they, without command, flew in precise arrangement.

The riders' silvery uniforms were made with an armor cladding for shielding in the event they were attacked. In their right hands was a lance, stout and slightly pointed; in their left hands was a shield. The head of the lance had a profound, polished gray tip that would pierce or supply a blow to any opponent, depending on the strike area or the opponent's protection. The defensive shield fit into a metal channel on the leathery saddle. On the polished shield was an emblem of a lion's head, its mouth locked in a roaring pose.

The rides also were wearing armor across their chests, and their harnesses were linked, etched oval rings of chain, fashioned with footholds and odd-shaped rings for holding weapons Maddy hadn't heard of or seen before. The footholds were the stirrups for the rider to lock himself into a solid striking pose.

The guards had split into two groups of six and surrounded Maddy and his crew.

Drem, the closest one to them, was on a bit of a larger ride and spoke out. "Are you friend or foe? And what is your intent?"

Maddy quickly responded, "Friend! And we're here to seek audience with the elders."

Drem then said, "Follow me."

There was no objection or rebellion allowed with his voice of authority, and Heaster wouldn't need coaxing. He set himself in alignment with the leader, Drem, and followed as if he'd been in training for years. The other eleven riders split, five to each side, and one closed off the tail of the formation.

PALACE CITY

Maddy and Trace were puzzled as to why they were being escorted. The planet had always been so peaceful, but these riders weren't playing around. There was a genuine concern in their actions, and their response to this innocent citizens' flight wasn't making sense.

Questioning was stifled until their escort had delivered them into an open arena to an awaiting panel of authority.

After a minor inspection of their baggage and gear, Drem turned to the board, giving a nod of permission. Then, rejoining his ride, he and the other guards rose above the wall and turned in an arrangement of an arrow, heading toward the main wall of the city.

The three elders were seated under a cream canvas awning that had orange and yellow stripes. They were seated at a finely made table in high-backed chairs that were padded with scarlet cushioned seats and backs. On the table were papers, documents, writing tools, and three colors of inkwell basins with stamps and stamp pads.

Beckoning them to come closer was the middle person, Rogar Stoge, a man with grizzled sideburns and a pair of spectacles. To Rogar's right sat an older man, Eon Moen, who had had a twin brother, Mitch, who had passed away. To Rogar's left was a middle-aged woman, Audrey Kent.

After introductions and titles were given, the three welcomed them to Palace City.

Rogar, being the chief inquiring officer, asked, "Where do you stem from, and do you have your records?"

After shuffling through his pack, Maddy handed over his birth record and county citizenship copies. As he offered them to Rogar, he was directed to give them to Audrey Kent. Trace retrieved hers and handed them to the woman.

Eon Moen scrunched up his face in confusion and asked, "What do you young ones need to see the elders for? You have been to your own county's elder, correct?"

"Yes we have, sir." Maddy wanted to respect this elderly man, even with the charbroiled hardness written on his face.

The indication was clear that without getting past this trio, they'd be headed home, tails tucked and unanswered questions in their empty sacks.

"We were hoping to get more information, and actual firsthand evidence, of any unknown knowledge for our schooling." Maddy continued, "Will we be able to go inside?"

Rogar studied the face and peered deeply into Maddy's eyes, looking for any sign of deception. His heart softened when Trace offered, "This is such an honor to be brought before you for permission."

There was no secret spy mission here. It was just a couple of country youths searching for information and knowledge. Many adolescents wouldn't have been as interested in knowledge of history and artifacts as they saw Maddy and Trace were.

"We'll set you up for first thing in the morning." Rogar reached for the proper papers and the stamp, then pounded the stamp pad with green ink and then the papers, one for each of the visitors.

Maddy wasn't able to bridle his question of what the other two colors of ink were for. Eon said, "The blue is for the elders when they come in; the red is when you're denied."

Rogar then asked where they were planning to spend the night and what they were going to do with Heaster. He offered them a couple of brochures for inns with rooms and lodging for their ride.

Audrey saw their attire and their plain, honest earnestness and added, "My sister Emma and her husband have a nice bungalow attached to their home, on the east side of the city. They are fair and can work out a way for you and your ride to stay with them at a reasonable rate. Here is their address. How long are you planning to stay?"

Their response was simultaneous. "For as long as we can. Thank you."

The ears of the three had twisted their heads, as they answered in unison. A touch of a new alerted interest came to their faces. Had their ears caught it, or was this a coincidence?

"Do we come here in the morning then?" Trace asked.

"You'll go to the entry." Rogar pointed to a pavilion through an opening in the wall of the arena they were in. "An officer will check you in and stamp your papers as visitors, and you'll be given directions and maps of the palace."

"Thanks again."

Maddy had let Trace answer alone this time then said, "Yes. Thank you."

They got back on Heaster and lifted off. While they were rising, Maddy asked Audrey, "Will your sister have any food we can barter for?"

"Plenty," she said.

CHAPTER SIX

Dew Drop Inn

As they rose above the wall, Maddy looked back at the trio and saw them in an intense discussion. He wondered if they were talking about the way that their answers were in harmony or if it was about Heaster being bigger than the rides the guards were riding.

Maddy asked Trace if she had caught their look when they said "Thank you" in unison

There was a lot to take in and even more that may have been missed.

Trace was looking at the address on the card Audrey had handed them. "Sure isn't like when Ben or Javen tell us how to get to their place, huh?"

"It's a little bit different when they have street names and numbers instead of going past the big treman to the split in the path that heads toward the right and following it to the rock face with the moss at its base." They laughed together and headed to the east side of the city.

They didn't see many other rides, other than the regular-size ones. Those were for hauling and transport, but only one ride larger than Heaster may have been a prime.

The address brought them to a quaint little three-story dwelling. There was an area in the back with a stable, a landing, and stalls. A small eating place was in the front, where a couple of people were eating uniquely colored food. A placard on the wall above the front seating area had the words of the establishment fashioned into an arch.

Dew Drop Inn! It seemed to be a bit more than what they would be able to afford, but Maddy dismounted and walked through the open area, which was covered with a woven branch roof and made with what looked like the trees in the forest outside the city walls. The thick, burly leaves were folded together to form something that repelled water and still provided shade. There were about fifteen small tables under the roofed section. As he reached for the door to the inner rooms, it flew open, narrowly missing Maddy's face. He was able to get a hold of the door and get out of the way of its inadvertent assailant.

It was a woman with her hair partially in a bun, and a misted forehead that was just about to bead into sweat drops had a few strands of blonde hair falling along her face. She was carrying a tray with two platters of steaming food and passed by in a rush. There was enough time to catch Maddy with her green eyes as she threw a thank-you in his direction.

If this was Audrey's sister, they were definitely not identical twins. He looked at her facial features to see whether there was any resemblance at all and thought maybe the nose was similar. Other than that, this woman was a worker and possibly overworked. She was fit and trim from the speed with which she motored around the restaurant.

He waited, holding the door for her as she returned and beckoned him inside with her.

"Here for a room and a stall?" Emma was in her niche. "And you'd be in search of a job?"

Maddy was impressed and simply nodded his head.

She said, "Martin is in the kitchen, and we'll be getting our midday rush soon. You can go and talk with him." Emma veered off to a smaller room, where there were six more finely built tables. She placed the tray on a table in front of the order window. Two of the tables had guests, and the others were half covered with refuse and dirtied dishes from previous customers.

Maddy peeked through the serving window just as a plate of food landed on the counter. He was startled and began to retreat. All he had glimpsed was the top of a head with wavy black hair and a hand placing the plate on the surface.

He said, "Martin?"

And a round-faced man popped up from the other side. His face had "jolly" written all over it. He asked, "May I help you?"

"That would be a pretty-much-with-everything 'yes,' sir," Maddy answered. "But I'd like to offer you some help in return, if we could."

"We?"

"Yes, sir. I'm Maddy Handle from Dillon County, which happens to be on the other side of the earth, and I'm with my girlfriend, Trace Guthrie from Clay County, also from the other side of the earth."

"Your girlfriend, huh?" Martin was being his jolly self.

Maddy's face flushed.

"What can you do?"

"I'll try anything. But I've been cleaning my ride's stall for years. So I could take care of your stables for you."

"What about your girlfriend?" Marty knew there was more there than what his guest was revealing.

"Well, she is awful pretty. Maybe she could help with orders or waiting on your customers."

"So she *is* your girlfriend!" Martin spouted out a short barrel laugh. "Can you start now?"

"Yes, sir…Mister Martin, sir. I…I…mean…Mister…"

" 'Martin' is fine. Or 'Marty.' Emma just calls me 'Martin' when we get a little too busy. I suppose your ride will need a stall too?"

"That would be great, Mr. Marty." Maddy shook his head and Marty's hand, trying to get his newest acquaintance's name right.

"Well, go get her and bring her back here for your next task." Marty got back to business as he turned to the flat-iron stovetop and flipped a couple filets of meat.

Maddy got back to Trace and told her what had transpired. She was a bit apprehensive about waiting on tables, but she knew how to serve. "Let's do this," she said.

DEW DROP INN

Heaster lifted off and sailed to the back of the business, landing near the stable. There was fresh straw and plenty of char sprouts, just like at home, for now. With Heaster's appetite being what it had been, he'd be comfortable right there. After getting him settled, Trace and Maddy came in the back door, where the tack room was, and proceeded down a hall toward the kitchen. They followed the luscious smell of food that drew them through a sizeable doorway to their employer.

"If this all goes well, we'll get you kids fed up before the evening rush comes in. OK with you? You weren't kidding, Maddy, about…Trace, is it?" Martin offered Trace a handshake.

"Yes, sir. Trace Guthrie." She shyly shook his hand back.

Martin crinkled his nose and said, " 'Marty' is fine. There's an apron over there and an order pad on that shelf. Go ahead and get them, and go tell Emma you're ready. Her bark is pretty small, and she doesn't bite— only when we get busy." He laughed again.

Maddy asked if he should start on the tables or get right to the stables.

"Tables or stables? I think I'll call you 'Maddy Table Stables.' If you want to impress Emma, you could get to those tables first. That will give her a chance to figure out your need-of-a-room dilemma sooner."

The next couple of hours flew with the hustle and bustle of a feeding frenzy. The patrons who came to Marty and Emma's food and inn varied from the ritzy and well dressed to the meekly plain-clothed regulars and those who were in search of a room and lodging.

Emma treated everyone the same. It was obvious that whoever came there to eat knew what to expect—great food. Both Trace and Maddy, as best they could, were trying to be as useful as quickly as they could. They wanted to pick up the order of Emma's routine, shuffling patrons in and out and having them leave with their needs met.

Many knew exactly what they wanted to eat, so that made it easy to take orders and let Marty know what to fix them. They were regulars, who knew what they liked and were easy to manage and serve.

The food began to fill Maddy and Trace's eyes to the hilt, but their stomachs were telling a different story. The platters of main courses brought both a deeper hunger and an encouragement of expectation, as the spikenard fruit they had eaten for breakfast hadn't filled them to the brim. When any of the lodgers arrived, Emma would get them signed in and escort them to their rooms. That day there were only two other rooms rented. Maddy and Trace found that there were ten rooms available for rent, and only four were rented out so far.

The rooms were small, with enough room to stretch out and be comfortable. In the main room were a modest matching couch and chair and a counter with a sink and a cabinet, with a mirror on the upper cabinet door over the vanity. A bedroom, separated by a handcrafted wooden door, had an acceptably sized bed with two dressers for its guests. The shower and bathroom provided just that and not much more. Everything was neat, clean, and convenient. Each room was simply set up to be used and reset from one guest to the next.

The main room had one sizeable window with plush, thick curtains that would close out almost any daylight one might want to keep out for resting and for privacy.

By midafternoon, the guests had settled down to one older couple. The bags they'd carried in gave away the shopping sessions they had been on.

Marty was still organizing his kitchen for the next group who would soon be trickling in. That group would become a rage of business. He placed platefuls of round, white, sliced beggas and a generous strap of meat on two platters and called his wearied help to eat. "Maddy…Trace…time to eat." He'd fancied the edges with green-and-purple leaves that could have been a meal in themselves.

Their ears had heard the call. Had the taste not been as exquisite as it was, the two travelers would have swallowed down their meal in record time. But this was far too good to gulp down.

The beggas were tender and bursting with flavorful juices that had soaked up the oil and flavors Marty had cooked them in. Each bite made their salivary glands water in their mouths. The meat was some sort of fowl Maddy hadn't tasted before. It melted like warm butter and had a hint of honey as it turned on his tongue's taste buds. Nothing was wasted or left on their plates. They had worked up quite an appetite and not to finish this meal could have insulted even them.

When they had finished, and after they had retrieved their packs from the stables, Emma was going to bring them to their room. She had offered to help carry anything she could when she saw Heaster.

"That's an unbridled powerhouse of a ride you have there, Maddy." Emma was being literal, as Maddy had taken off Heaster's harness and reins. "Has he ever competed?"

He knew from the county fair he had been to that Emma was wondering if Heaster had ever been in a challenge of lift strength. "Not yet."

Marty walked in, wiping his hands on a towel and moving closer to the prime. "Sure is a big one." His hand swept down Heaster's neck, and he patted his shoulder. "He hasn't experienced a competition anywhere? He's got more mass around his chest than any ride I've ever seen. When he breathes, the natural swelling that his neck does is quite notable."

"You sound like you know a little about rides, Marty." Maddy could tell that comments like that wouldn't have been noticed by most of the people he knew.

"Not only rides, my boy, but prime rides. A few years ago, I had a prime I competed with. 'Brawn' was his name. He could lift more than any prime he went up against. I got him from a place called…let me see…Choppelle or Hopelle or something like that."

"The Gulf of Hopelle? Is that where you mean?" Maddy asked.

"That's it. I floated there with my father and picked him out of a litter of pups. Turned out he was from a lineage of a strain of rides that had been being cultured into a hybrid stallion. The thing was, though, as with any ride, there was no way of knowing if you got a prime or at least not until they were a few years old."

DEW DROP INN

"That's where we got Heaster from, the Gulf. He's just recently been exploding in size. Hope it's OK that he's eating so much."

Marty wasn't as concerned about the feed as he was about the prize that had just floated into his stable. "You know, Maddy, there is a decathlon completion going on in a couple weeks. This weekend and into next week, they'll be preparing the arena and accepting applicants for the meet. It's for rides, work animals, and a few young primes. Everyone will know he's a prime, but with him being so young and still growing, they'd let him try it."

"I'd like that." Maddy's thoughts connected with Heaster, who looked around at his rider. A blink of his eyes confirmed he was willing.

"There is a trophy and, depending on how many enter, quite a bag of coins. Winner takes all."

"There's a fee of only twenty shekels of silver to enter," Emma threw in.

"Twenty shekels?" Maddy's hopes sank, as that might as well have been a million to him. "I guess maybe next time. We never really expected to be here very long, and what you've offered us with room and board is overwhelmingly more than we were planning on. We thought we'd be stretched out on a blanket in the meadow outside the walls for a day or so. We never knew there were even walls here, nor did we know how extensive Palace City was."

The couple looked at each other and Emma asked, "Would you stay here that long? Or are you expected home?" The cogs in her thinking cap were turning as she felt her assistants had earned their keep today. She knew that, as the festivities drew closer, there would be even more business coming their way. Help was not always as effective or eager to work as these two were. The prime would be an additional bonus, for getting provisions, hauling firewood, or even providing transportation for her guests.

"We really don't have that much to go on. My dad sent us here with a little, but most of our planning for food and shelter was whatever came naturally—"

Emma cut Maddy short. "You drive a hard bargain, young man. What if we were to lend you some assistance? We might be able to work out a deal. You've already helped us get past the last rush. Let's see what this evening brings."

Their generosity was an unfamiliar experience for Maddy. His way of living was bartering, meaning it would be even or fair. When you got a deal or a bonus, it usually came without intent.

Emma motioned for them to follow her. To the left of the hallway that led to the kitchen was a cubbyhole. As she rolled back a sliding door, it opened to a narrow landing that went up a steep, slender stairway. It had been closed off for a while; the steps were coated with a fine layer of dust.

"Come on up." She escorted them to the crest of the stairs. At the top the hallway turned to the right and broadened into a charming little bungalow. The furniture was randomly placed around the room and covered with sheets of cloth. Maddy's mother would have been able to make him several shirts out of what was being used for a protective barrier from dust.

A couple of rectangular windows, just low enough to see through if he stood on his toes, gave the room enough light to see. A set of stacked beds was in a corner. Each bed had a pillow-shaped mattress that looked to be made from feathers.

"You'll have to haul water up here, but there is a sink and basin over in the corner behind that wall. You won't mind sleeping in the same room, will you?"

Emma was expecting that they were already confirmed guests, boarders, and help.

"No, ma'am," they answered without delay and in harmony.

"Good. Then take a few moments to get you familiar with the room, and we'll join you downstairs for the dinner crowd."

Emma excused herself, taking off and removing and folding a couple of sheets from the furniture. She tucked them under her arm and straightened chair on her way out. Trace and Maddy stood there in awe at what had just transpired.

"You can have the top bunk if you'd like." Maddy wanted to be as hospitable as he could, yet he was as shocked as Trace by their circumstances.

"Oh, no! You choose." She had hoped he hadn't known she was thinking about their sleeping arrangements. This wouldn't be a night out under the stars in the middle of a field. This was a room together, with only a nook and a wall to divide anything they did.

"That's OK, Trace. We can use a couple of these sheets to partition off a place to dress and use the bathing spot."

He had known what she had thought. Her face took its turn in turning a blushed pink.

"You choose, my lady." Performing a genuflection and an arm swing, he offered her the choice of beds.

Trace walked over and set her things on the lower bunk. "We can see how this works, and we can get this place swept up and how we'd like it after dinner."

"That is a great plan, Trace." Maddy was glad to take the top bunk; it would be like home. He threw his pack and his things on the bunk and headed for the hall.

"Maddy?" Trace had reserve in her voice. "Is any of this going too fast for you?"

"When I'm with you, Trace, everything goes too fast, especially the time I get to look at you." Maddy smiled with assurance that everything would be all right. "Be right down."

Trace wrapped the clean apron around her waist and tied it in the back as she left. "See you soon."

"Even Heaster couldn't keep me from that."

Maddy dumped the contents of the sack onto the puffy mattress. The object of the journey dropped onto his clothes. It was still there. The key hadn't changed at all from when they had left Dillon County. That would be the best place for it for now. He tucked it into a corner at the bottom of the sack and hung the backpack over the post on the bunks.

When he got to the kitchen, he wanted to make sure that both Emma and Marty knew about their scheduled visit to the palace in the morning. It happened that they were both filling up a tub with cut legumes that they were peeling with a rotary peeler. Emma had sent Trace up to clean a room that had been used the night before. She would change the bedding, fluff the pillows, and clean any mess that was below the standard that Emma had. She had shown her what one of the rooms that hadn't been used looked like and also where the cleaning supplies and clean bedding were.

"Marty and Emma, I need to tell you one of the reasons we came here. Emma, we went to get permission to get a pass into the palace, and that's where we met your sister. We've got an appointment for first thing in the morning. I hope that will still be OK. I don't want to miss the timetable. They might reject us from any further visits if we do."

"It is still early in the week, so the main rush is a light breakfast we serve to our overnight guests. Then it will be pretty slow until the lunch crowd starts getting here. That should work out best for both of us," Marty remarked.

"Thank you so much. It shouldn't take long. If we're going to be here for a while, we could always go again another day."

"You might want me to drop you off there. I don't know if I'd parade your prime around the palace, and I certainly wouldn't leave him unattended. Not because he'd be taken—it's just that some primes can get a bit aggressive trying to show their prominence and standing."

"I think Heaster would be OK with you riding him." Maddy was confident that this round-faced, cheerful friend had his best interests in mind.

The crowd came with a surge when the evening shadows appeared. Like animals out of their dens, they came seeking food for their nighttime slumber. Trace had reentered the dining area and was taking orders as if she had been doing this job for years. Several guests asked her where she stemmed from and how long she'd been working there. Her outgoing personality and countenance were a refreshing twist for the regulars, who knew she was new there.

What Trace hadn't known was that the wealthier guests would slip her a gratuity for her service. The lifestyle here was so much more open and carefree than the bondages of the country life's reserve.

The tables then to the stables were Maddy's order of priority. When the tables were clear and the dishes replaced, he would tend to any guests who needed to stable their rides. A few more rides came out into the night air. Maddy had a chance to peek out and see Harac and Cam chase across the night skyline. Cam at times was being obstructed by Harac as it rotated in an almost visible motion. At times a darker movement of the rides would move in their outlines. There was circling, lifting, and lowering as couples out for an evening date, those giving way to a hectic workday or those taking a relaxing evening out in the calm cool air, came for a tremendous meal delivered to their table. The awning seating vicinity had taken on a completely different atmosphere after the sun dipped below the horizon.

There hadn't been time to think about the workday in a slow or dragging way. The tables were cleared and were finally empty. The awning curtains dropped as the lights dimmed.

The heavy pots clattered as they were washed and put in their places in the kitchen. Marty was finishing wiping down the service window's sill when Maddy came in from the stables. "All bedded down and cleaned up, Marty. Will you still be able to drop Trace and me off in the morning?"

"Sure thing. What time did you need to be there?"

"Mr. Stoge said first thing. I guess I didn't see when they open those doors for the appointments." Maddy felt a bit embarrassed. "Do you know?"

"Be ready at first sign of daylight. That will get me back here in time to start flipping eggs. Do you need a wakeup call?"

Maddy still hadn't gotten how accommodating these two were. "That would be very much appreciated. Thank you, Marty."

Still able to produce a big smile, Marty bantered, "Are you going to check to see if your girlfriend is done with her duties yet, Table Stable?"

"Good idea." Maddy grinned back and headed for the inside dining room.

Trace was folding up her apron after taking the coins from its pouch and pocketing her tips.

Emma had seen her and said, "You earned them tonight, Trace. Thanks for the great help. If you'd like a snack to take to your room, it's on the house."

The night had fallen. With their early start the next day and the long but exciting full afternoon of helping at the inn, they were tired enough that landing on their pillows was going to feel incredible.

When they climbed the narrow stairs to their quarters, even their usual gabbing and chatter was hindered. It was time for sleep, with another fresh day to follow. Maddy made a hop-jump to the top bunk and flopped to his backside. He watched as Trace made her way to the partition. She came from behind the wall, after changing into a nightgown.

She sat on the featherbed then brought her feet onto its receptive, cool detention.

The light went from dim to out. "Good night," echoed in their ears.

In the dimly lit room, a bell that had been concealed in a corner began to move with the help of a string strung through the wall. It started with a short jingle then had a bit more intensity, ringing a bit louder. Maddy hopped down and reached the bell in time to muffle its clanging before it got annoying. A returned tug on the string communicated the wakeup call had been successful.

Maddy walked back to the bunks and reached to wake Trace. He stopped for an instant to look at this angel on the feather pad. Her imaginary wings may have well been the provider for the feathers that filled her pillow.

"Good morning, cherub." Maddy used the advantage of his thoughts to share his view of the sleeping, featherless angel.

Her eyes flittered open. "Prince, is that you?" Maddy wasn't absolutely sure if she was awake enough to role play or if she had been in a dreaming state. "It is you, Prince Maddy. Have the servants prepared our breakfast so soon?"

Now it was clear. "Why, yes, my princess. Whites from the golden goose, whipped to a perfect cloud consistency."

"Well let's 'do drop inn' on them." Their laughter broke aloud as Trace stood and gave Maddy a morning hug. "It felt like I slept on a cloud in heaven, and now I awaken to Prince Charming. Do I know where we are?"

"I'll go and check on Heaster while you change." Maddy practically drifted on air as he descended the stairs.

There was evidence that life had been going on for a while as Maddy's nose filled with the odor of cooking. In his nostrils, the smell reminded him of his dad making breakfast back at their cabin, and it sent his memories in motion. Maddy hadn't intended to stay for a lifetime and still had the treman issue strumming his thoughts, but he thought, Dad will understand, as he relaxed and continued getting ready.

"Thought I'd get you kids something to go on—an advance." Marty's kindness could be gotten used to. "It should be ready after you check on Heaster. Does he communicate with you yet?"

"When we don't know what the other is thinking, we speak to each other." Maddy let Marty know their connection had been made.

"It wouldn't hurt you to fill him in on our plans. You may be the only one sure that he'll be able to lift us all."

"We'll soon find out. We'll need to get some sort of an idea of what he can do."

Maddy scurried to the stable to see Heaster. "'Morning, boy! How'd you sleep?"

When he got to the stall, he saw that his companion had grown overnight. His sides had swelled and were touching the boards of the stanchion walls.

"How do we get you out of there, Heaster?"

The prime straightened his legs and shoved himself in reverse. His fur scraped the frame of the stall, causing the hairs to bristle out then lay back into place as he emerged from the pen.

"Good thing Dad made this harness adjustable. Thing is, we're only three notches away from all there is for alteration."

Heaster took the comment as a compliment and nudged his rider. "The char sprouts were incredibly tender and juicy."

Maddy looked in on the empty trough. "All of them?"

"That's all there were." Heaster replied.

"The man whose food you've eaten, Marty, thought you might be better off here while Trace and I are at the palace this morning. So we were wondering if you'd be able to lift us all, deliver us to the front gate, and then have Marty be your rider. Are you feeling pretty strong this morning?" Heaster started filling his chest cavity and coming off the stable floor.

"They are letting us stay here without cost. And there is a competition in a couple weeks. They offered to pay the entry fee for us. When we get back after lunch, we'll set up a workout routine for you. Marty thinks you have potential." Maddy reached for Heaster's cheek and scratched his sleek fur skin. "I know you do, Heaster."

"Are you ready for breakfast, Maddy?" Trace had looked into the stable as she walked by from the kitchen. "Marty said you were out here and that everything was ready."

"Be right there, Trace. I'm just finishing readjusting this harness." With a pat on Heaster's back, he said, "Be right back, boy."

The breakfast meal was delicious. When they were finished, the day was just breaking, and Emma shuffled them off. "I'll get this cleaned up, and Marty, I'll have the beggas boiling when you get back."

Marty gave her a peck on the check, and out to their carrier they went. "I know. You'll be right back." Her words held apprehension, as she knew this chance to ride a prime again would give way to too great a temptation. It had been years since he'd wrapped his stocky, short legs around a belly this big.

When Marty saw that Heaster's size had changed overnight, he asked if he could take a short ride after he let them off at their appointment at the palace. Maddy told Heaster and then agreed.

When they were all positioned on his back, the ease that came at liftoff was very impressive to Marty. "He didn't really move his tail at all to get us off the ground. When I asked about that short trip—well, do you mind if I try him at lift strength? We normally have our beggas delivered in a wagon, but they have them in crates just outside the east entrance. The gate is closed, so to get them here now is much farther for delivery than when you can go through the east gate. I could see if he could carry a crate back to the inn. All we'd have to do is lift them over the outer east wall."

"What do you think, Heaster?" Maddy thought a challenge might have him be at ease with Marty.

"We've got no attachments for the harness," Heaster replied.

"You can use the ones I kept from Brawn. We can swing by and get them from the tack room."

Outside the palace, when Maddy and Trace were getting down from Heaster, they noticed a few looks and glances thrown their way. An amber-haired, middle-aged woman made her way to the landing area and called out to Marty, "Will you be going back to your inn from here?"

"Yes, I will, Mary Ellen. Were you thinking about an earlier mealtime?" Marty answered, knowing she was a regular for a midmorning meal.

"I was." Mary Ellen was short with the chef, upset that he was acting as if he knew her that well. Then, after Marty's smile defeated her assumption, his hand held up two fingers.

"Only two tokens for a transport to the inn?" She felt silly that she had assumed any ill feelings for Marty.

"Only for you, Mary Ellen." He gave Maddy a wink with his puffy, swollen eye.

"May I help you up, ma'am?" Maddy moved in to assist her onto Heaster.

Honored to have a fine-looking young man offer to help her, she graciously said yes and used Maddy's leg to step up, offering his hand to balance and steady her climb. Marty sat her behind him and, with a nod of his head said, "Be back in three turns, Maddy."

"We'll be ready for you, Marty," Trace and Maddy replied together.

Up they went, with Mary Ellen holding onto her chauffeur and her satchel.

DEW DROP INN

"I see a way to bring Dad home some things he's been doing without, if people are that willing to pay for a lift." Maddy's words had already coincided with Trace's thoughts.

"Let's get to our half day at the palace," she said, starting to walk to the entrance.

CHAPTER SEVEN

The Palace

The archways of stonework told a story of precision workmanship. There were perfectly pieced-together cuts of marble and granite with pictures of different timeframes, from the past to recent history. The center archway over the entrance hall depicted a treman tree with a man's arms coming out of the trunk and a man's face with rays of light shooting out from the edges. From each hand there was a set of balances hanging from a finely cut pair of chains; the shaft was golden and made from a metal that could have come from Braden. The balances were scarlet red and polished to the point that they looked wet.

A female receptionist dressed in a red uniform checked their paperwork and documents. Once she approved, she took her green stamp and pounded each of their scheduled timecards. She then asked if there were any particular sectors they would like to tour.

Maddy asked about the seven unidentified pieces that he had heard had been found.

"They are in the 'unanswered' section. You will follow the main hall until you get to the seventh corridor, turn to the right, and follow that hall to a hanging sign that reads, UNEXPLAINABLE. The doorman will escort you to that museum's entry. Next!" She cut off any other questions, as she herded them into the palace's main entry hall.

Maddy had placed a day's provisions and their needed papers into his backpack. When the approved papers were handed back to them, Maddy tucked them in an outer pocket and swung the pack onto his back. "Ready?"

"Oh, Maddy! Look how beautiful it is." Trace was looking at the artistry.

That had been the easiest way to attempt to describe the splendor. Beautiful!

Stories were being organized to facilitate truth so they could be told in their future. How would they not exaggerate and still cling to the facts they were seeing?

The hallway floor was a sea of buffed crystal. As they walked on its surface, it appeared to be solid water over a bed of millions of burnt-yellow mirrors that turned to reflect light in every direction. With a closer inspection, one could see a pattern.

The ceilings were so high in the main hall that twenty men standing on each other's shoulders would be needed to touch them. Level upon level, five high, went upward. Stone railings and spindles protected the visitors from falling from the four upper levels. Each level had twenty-four rooms filled with thousands of years of history. A sign listed each room's contents, assisting visitors in narrowing down their searches. Years and significant happenings were listed on the signs that hung from the passage hall's ceiling.

The main hall's support pillars for the upper halls were sculpted beryl stone and had seating around the bases. Each pillar designated a corridor. The seventh one came and to the right was chosen. The corridors each ended with a T that connected them with a hall that ran parallel to the chief main hall.

As the woman in red had told them, a doorman was stationed at a desk halfway down each passageway. They had red uniforms, jackets with short tails, and ruffle-breasted shirts.

He met them with a polite, "May I be of assistance?"

Maddy asked for the 'unexplainable' room. That initiated an about-face, as the man said, "Follow me, please?"

They reached the doorway with the poster board suspended with no attached hangers. It dangled in midair. The doorman inserted a key into a locking device that unlocked solidly with the clunking sound on a metal strike plate. He opened the white-painted, round-topped, wooden door and stood to the side. "Let me know when you finish, please."

The door opened outward, and the doorman closed it behind them as they walked into the space. It was unusual in that there were very few items in the room. Along one side were the seven items that the story had referenced. Much to their amazement, they were not the shapes they had expected to see. Each piece sat on a pedestal and was encased in a clear round case. Inside the sphere a transparent rod with a flat, lucid plate held the piece in a showpiece position. The largest piece would have fit in Maddy's pack, and two of the smaller pieces could have been held in your hand together. The details hadn't been given simply because not many knew how to explain them factually.

The pieces had no connection to one another. There were no recognized conjoining edges or attachments, as a puzzle would have. Maddy spent quite a few minutes trying to see if there were any distinguishing markings or relationships to one another or to his key. Further study revealed that the domes were placed over the objects, blocking the only way to physically handle them.

Three of the seven pieces were cylindrical, and the four others were flattened, with various pins and shoots of metal that, although they were part of the piece, looked as though they had been fastened or fused at an accurate point. None of the pieces looked to have been disfigured, broken, or bent—as if there would have been a way for Maddy to know. The alloy wasn't anything Maddy had to compare it with. And the color wasn't like that of most metals used for tools and instruments. It was a lightly colored tan, and they all had that in common. Some of the parts had colored tubes of a ceramic or condensed matter and had a fine wire going through them that molded to the plates of metal.

Trace had been looking at a few of the other items, all in similar cases and presented in the same fashion. One in meticulous design had an uncountable amount of stringy, hair-like wires that stemmed out from a glob of tissue. It looked like a brain in size and shape.

THE PALACE

The room had lured them into its odd phenomena and strange items and had used more of their time than they had realized. By the time they would get back out to the landing pad, there wouldn't be much time left.

They pictured the seven pieces differently than what they had discovered. Trace had etched a drawing of them on the back of one of their appointment cards. Maddy knocked on the closed door. The knob turned, and the door opened.

"If we wanted to look at these again, would we need to specify it on a request to come again?" Maddy directed the question to the doorman.

"Any visits to the inside of the palace would need a reason for requesting a calling." "Thanks for now. Farewell." Said Maddy

Visiting all the vast amounts of archives would take years. There was one sign that caught their attention. It was in the second-story hallway. A sign that read TREMAN marked the entry to another room.

"Next time." Trace urged Maddy to keep their deadline with Marty.

"Just a quick look to see if that should be our requested option to visit." He took her hand, and they ran to the stairway connecting each level. The stairs were faced in the same upward direction, with one on each side of the main hall, allowing the visitors to go to the specific side they chose. Each landing had a director to show the way to certain rooms and would answer any questions it could.

"The treman room." Maddy already knew where he was going but wanted to give the usher his due.

"It is down the hall to your right, sir."

"Thank you," Maddy replied.

He rushed toward the door that the doorman had opened for the previous guests.

They heard someone say, "One group at a time, please." That slowed their pursuit.

Time wouldn't allow them to wait until these people might come out, but Maddy had gotten a glimpse inside that confirmed their next request, the Treman. The real thing from the story stood behind a protective barrier, as the door shut to any further assessment.

"Tomorrow, Maddy. We can get permission to come back tomorrow afternoon." Trace now took the lead. Hand in hand they hurried to the front entry. They ran to the three receptionists to set up another appointment.

Audrey recognized them immediately and asked, "Did you find my sister's?"

"Yes, ma'am." Trace answered. "They have been very accommodating and have given us the means to stay for a while. Could we get another appointment for tomorrow afternoon? There was so much to see, and there are things we'd like to be more exact in our facts about for future discussions and sharing information."

Rogar Stoge then took charge. "A certain request?"

"Yes, sir. The Treman room, please." Maddy was sure of his directive.

Eon scribbled a few words onto the document then handed it to Rogar. With a repeated action, the stamp slammed into the green inkpad then to the paper.

THE PALACE

"There you go, Mr. Handle and Miss Guthrie. Enjoy your endeavor." Rogar handed them their cards, impressed that this younger generation had such an interest in the history the palace held.

As they turned for the pad, a shadow brushed the path ahead of them. Glancing into the sky, they saw the newest team of floaters. Heaster's feet were put down to the pad; it was their pickup and delivery service.

Marty's jubilance fled from his face and in his voice, "Come on. Come on. There's so much to share." He reached out to give them a hand as they set their feet on the padded, broken-in, and innovative harness. Maddy sat back in the driver's seat, based close to Heaster's neck.

"You'll find it's the best place to sit when you're lifting weight." Marty was excited to get this team to work.

"Up!" The word sent them into an accelerated rise as Maddy felt Heaster react to his voice.

Onlookers turned their heads as the team shot up into the blue. The force with which they rose sent their stomachs to the lowest spot in their torsos. The pressure pressing them to his back pushed them tighter and tighter to him.

"OK, boy." Heaster's ears eagerly waited for his next movement change as he slowed without sending his passengers into space. "Let's get back to the inn." With a bending of his stumpy tail, they were propelling forward.

Marty started telling them about the maiden voyage they had gone on and the lift experiment. "Don't know what you'll be able to get him to do, but that crate of beggas didn't offer much of an obstacle. After I dropped Mary Ellen off at the inn,

I traded harnesses, putting Brawn's on him." He then spoke to Heaster, "Heaster, boy, you are a natural. He never gave it a second thought. He took right to it. I wanted to stay there and help the grower move his crates around, just to get him used to weightlifting, but as soon as we hooked up the harness to the crate strap, we were airborne. He balanced the load as he rose up then moved ahead without losing the center of balance. He's incredible. He was able to set the crate on that old rickety table in the stable corral without dropping it so hard that it would crush it. Four of the ten events of the decathlon he's got figured out, and we've just started!"

When they got to the inn and settled in the stable, Marty reached into his pocket and handed Maddy the two tokens that Mary Ellen had given him. "We can get you something to eat too, before the lunch rush."

In their day and a half of being in the city, they had received enough in coins to buy a pair of new shoes for of them. One token could buy most regularly used provisions, such as sugar, flour, or small items. A pair of shoes could be exchanged for five tokens. Back in their counties, coins and tokens were few and far between. Bartering had been such an everyday way to do business that coins became something to collect—not that they weren't going to use these coins. Here in the city, they used them on a regular basis.

The entry fee was a far cry away; it took twenty tokens to equal a shekel. But Heaster could play a part in raising the money for the contest. Maddy thought he could offset Heaster's feed by using his hauling ability to transport people.

THE PALACE

For now the lunch was ready for them to be fueled up for business at the inn. Emma had whipped a couple of beggas and mixed in some greens with them. A slice of pheasant breast was the meat portion, and she had freshly squeezed a glass of nectar from a tulles fruit. Tulles fruits were juicy year round. The peeling encased a fiber that seized the fruit in its pulp. They were squishy enough to hand-squeeze the juice out of, with the end opposite the stem able to be torn off, because its peeling was thinner at the tip. When they were fully ripe, they were deep green in color, and a lime color before they ripened. The juice would be the colors of the shell, letting the consumer know at what point it had been picked. They were the sweetest at the deepest green and a bit tart when lighter the color.

Mary Ellen had been sitting out in the awning room, reading a book she had brought with her. She had finished drinking her spurt, which was flavored with a pinch of honey crystal and a spoon of cream. "Emma, would Marty be able to get me back to the city center? The fare was well worth the fancy excursion that prime gave me this morning."

Emma had been setting out the silver and glasses for lunchtime. "What if our chauffeur takes you?" She motioned for Maddy to get Heaster ready to carry this patron to her destination.

"He is your driver?" Mary Ellen had a twinkle in her eye for what perked her interest in this handsome younger man.

"This is his expected, Trace. They may become recognizable faces around here." Emma was soon to nip any ideas Mary Ellen was stewing in her mind about Maddy.

Mary Ellen grimaced and shrugged. "Expected? That's not in the bag, Emma."

Maddy appeared overhead and came down to load his passenger. Mary Ellen reached out her hand, and Maddy pulled her up to sit behind him. "What a strong young man." She wasn't about to be undone easily, as she wrapped her arms tightly around Maddy's waist. "Ready if you are," she bantered.

Emma hurled a word of carefulness. "Maddy, you might check at the palace to see if there might be any other patrons that would like a ride back."

Mary Ellen was a fine-looking middle-aged lady who had gotten her wealth from her late husband's company. She had a reputation for enticing younger male escorts with her wallet. She lived in a penthouse suite along the main street of Palace City and owned the high-rise apartment building there.

"You could drop me on the roof at my building. There's an entrance to my penthouse suite there." She pointed to her high-rise as they flew above the downtown buildings.

"This is your building, ma'am?" Maddy was impressed.

"Would you like to come in and see it?"

"Maybe next time I can, ma'am. They'll need help at the inn, so I'd better be getting back."

"Please, Maddy. Just 'Mary Ellen.' You're not my employee." She lured her acquaintance relationship into a personal one.

"I'll help you down, ma'am." Maddy had slid off Heaster and supported her drop to the roof.

He climbed back on as quickly as he could and nodded to her as a gesture of 'Good day.'

THE PALACE

"Wait, Maddy." She had reached into her handbag and held out a silver shekel. "Day after tomorrow I usually have an early-afternoon luncheon at the inn. Could you pick me up about the third hour of the day?"

"It's only two tokens, ma'am. And I'll try to be here on time."

"It's 'Mary Ellen.' " She smiled. "And that is a tip for such a nice delivery."

"Thank you." Maddy touched the reins to Heaster's neck, and off they went.

"She's a bit assertive." Heaster hadn't spoken during their flight with Mary Ellen and had waited until she was out of hearing distance.

"*Assertive?* Where did you hear that word?" Maddy asked.

"Just paying attention to what I hear."

"Well, let's swing by the palace quickly and see if there are any clients."

"Dead ahead…sir." Heaster was picking up language skills effortlessly and heckled Maddy about what Mary Ellen had tried to ensnare him into.

"Oh, cut it out, my stallion. We'll be able to give someone a great deal, if he or she wants a ride. She paid enough to give ten people a ride."

"I don't think my back is big enough for that many," Heaster joked.

When the palace landing pad was in sight, they saw a younger couple waiting at the stop.

"Need a lift?" Maddy offered.

"How much is it? We just got here to Palace City and were looking for a place to eat. Only we don't know what the rates are or where we're going," the youthful man answered.

"You're in good fortune. Your first ride is on the house, and I know a great eating establishment."

"Really?" The lady joined the conversation.

"Yes, ma'am." Maddy helped them with their baggage and set them behind the saddle pad. "There are rooms to rent too, if you were looking. It's called the Dew Drop Inn, and the owners are amazing."

Maddy found out that they were there to watch the competition and had wanted to get to the city before it got too busy. They thought they could look around and visit the palace. Maddy didn't want to let them down by overemphasizing the palace and its grandeur but told them they would enjoy the structural designs, and it was a good thing they had a few days to explore it because of its vast area and amount of history.

They were from a southern county and had traveled there on foot. They had a darker complexion than Maddy did, and their hair was a shade of gray but not because they were old.

The man and his future wife, Jed and Jilly, raised racing turtles on his father's property. When he was attaching their luggage to the harnessing, Maddy had seen two of them in a cage that they had brought with them "After you eat and if you stay at the inn, Trace, my girl, and I would be honored to visit with you." Maddy thought that meeting more people would always be helpful.

"We'll see how that goes," Jed answered.

THE PALACE

When they got back to the inn, the newly developing team was scurrying with busyness. The dining areas were filled with chatter, and chatter meant delectable food. Maddy ushered his guests to a table still riddled with the last customer's clutter and began clearing the table, preparing it for Emma or Trace to wait on.

Trace got there first, and Maddy cordially introduced the couple to her. "Jed, Jilly, this is Trace Guthrie. She's the one I told you about on the way here."

As Emma was walking by, Maddy asked her if there were any rooms left to rent.

"Three left. How long will they be staying?"

"They're here for the competition."

"We should be able to accommodate you." Emma added, "We'll get you set up after lunch."

Jed began to see what Maddy had told him about the inn and Emma, and Marty, whom they were soon to meet.

Maddy finished clearing tables and had gone to check on Heaster and unload the couple's things. While he was taking the cage with the turtles in it, Jed came through the stable door and said, "Careful with those guys, Maddy. They move around in there so fast at times that they can jiggle the cage enough to open the door to get out. Seeing that this is a strange environment for them, they could take off."

"They're turtles!" Maddy had seen many turtles back in Dillon County along the creek and by the marsh, and none of them had set any land speed records he'd been familiar with.

"Race turtles, thank you." Jed wanted Maddy to get the full concept of what these guys could do. "We've been raising these hybrid turtles for many years at my father's factory. Their legs are longer than the typical turtle's. These guys have been trained not only to race but can be homing pigeons in their own fashion." Jed opened the cage and brought one of the turtles out. Instantly the turtle's legs grew longer, coming out of its shell.

"They love to run." Jed stroked the turtle's exposed head.

Maddy reached in to pat it when Jed turned it quickly away. "They are still snappers. But they'll get to know you soon enough."

The rush had ebbed to a trickle as Jilly came through the doorway next. Together they picked up their baggage and were off to settle in their room.

"Emma won't mind us having the turtles, will she?" Jilly asked.

"As long as they don't bite any of the other guests and they don't bark at the moon." Maddy wanted to break down any barriers of uncertainty with his offer of friendship.

"We'll keep their muzzles on them. They only howl at blue moons," Jed ribbed back.

Maddy had brought the bow and arrows that his father had sent with him out from the front of the stall where Heaster bedded down. He admired the workmanship his dad had put into the bow. The wood he had used was carved into a double curved shape with the string being made out of a substance that Maddy was able to recognize. It was the exact color of the harness he had, the color of his mother's hair. It had an engraving etched along one side that read, "May every arrow find its mark." A heart outline finalized the line of letters.

THE PALACE

He placed a target across the yard, against a bale of straw, and began sending arrows in flight. They burned into their intended location, on the mark, with precision.

Trace came out to ask if he was ready to get to their appointment at the palace. "Should we get going? I know Heaster's fast, but we do have only a few moments to get there."

Maddy replaced his archery equipment and leaped to Heaster's back, offering Trace his hand up. "I await your arrival, my lady," he said, continuing their role-play fun.

"Thank you, kind sir," she answered.

Their travel to the palace was swift, and when they arrived, there was a commotion going on. Drem was standing between two bantering men, as his ride, Josh, maneuvered himself into a defensive barrier.

"Keep it easy, gentlemen." Drem was being the pacifier of a heated argument. "Save it for the competition."

The two men shook their clothes back in order and brushed off the clash that had just gotten out of hand. Maddy saw Drem's control and maturity as he brought peace to the ensuing confrontation.

Drem noticed Heaster's decent to the landing area, taking note of how lightly he touched down. This prime was unique to him, and he'd been around enough rides to spot various strengths and weaknesses.

With their paperwork stamped, they reentered the palace. Their visit could be a bit longer, as Emma had given them leave from helping with the evening crowd, as long as they could be back to help clean up and reset for the morning breakfast crowd.

Their drawing card was waiting for them as they got to the door of the Treman room. The doorman opened the door, stepping to the side, as they went into the room. Maddy's pack shifted on his back with movement. The closer they moved toward the Treman, the more the rucksack churned.

The Treman was behind a glass barricade in a scene that made it look like it was planted in a forest. Imprinted on the face of the trunk was an opening that resembled all the treman profiles he had seen at Mantra's library. The inspection of the void gave Maddy the shudders. His mind raced to remembering his key's markings. He had fondled that key enough to know the marks were identical.

His heart leaped within his chest as his mother's stories echoed in his brain. The Treman of that story came from the union of a man and the seed—could this truly be?

A puzzle piece was missing from the stories he recalled. The key…there was nothing about a key. He turned his pack around and opened it to find the plug. When his hand made contact, a shock went through his whole body.

A vision played in his head in rapid order. The shock ignited a view of a mechanical wooden figure surveying a reaction taking place. There was a transformation, turning from flesh and bone to slates, and a pallid makeup of pieces of wooden and human parts. Flashes erupted of many ordeals and battles raging. Two of these creatures exchanged blows in an epic conflict. All of it funneled into torment and anguish of the scene before him.

Trace had seen the jolt that had surged through Maddy's body. "Are you all right? What happened?"

THE PALACE

"I'm not sure, Trace, but this key has everything to do with it." He held the object in his hand and lined it up between his eye and the hole in the Treman. "I believe it is—"

The article lit off his hand and attached like a magnet to steel to the glass divider. An alarm sounded, and the door's mechanism moved to the sound of an unlocking movement. Maddy pried and pulled the key off the glass as the door opened. He placed it in his pack again, and the doorman ordered, "Stand back!"

The two both stepped backward. "Yes, sir. We will, sir."

"What happened?" the guard asked.

"I touched the glass, I guess, and it set off the alarm." Maddy only disclosed what was necessary. "I didn't realize there was an alarm system or that you couldn't touch the glass."

The doorman pointed to a sign in the bottom corner of the obstruction. It said, Do Not Touch.

Their journey was becoming detective in nature. Discoveries and concealed answers were being revealed to this seeking duo, as their quest had an interesting way of playing out ahead of them. Although the next step was unclear to them, the enticing, need-to-know curiosity drew them back into what any good detective would do. They'd need answers, and answers came from questions. Those types of questions were easy to come by with their latest experience.

"Is there any location or person who has the facts about this Treman?" Maddy knew one thing the doorman didn't— what had happened just a few moments ago.

"Besides the books over there on the shelves, an oracle is embossed on a portion of a plaque in the 'unexplainable' room. The wordage on the plaque reads, 'To go where no one man has veered from to go where HE came from.'"

"Is it all right to spend a little more time in here?" Maddy needed to see those books.

"You can touch the books. Be sure to place them on this reading stand when you open them, to protect their bindings. But please stay clear of the display glass."

"Not a problem, sir." Maddy assured him. He was anxious to return to his quest.

The door closed again, and the duo turned their attention to the bookshelves. Scanning the details on the bindings to see what the books were titled, their eyes simultaneously locked onto a book titled, *The Flight*.

Maddy took the book to the reading stand and opened it to the introduction. It presented an option to "receive and believe" or "deny and doubt." The intrigue of the desire to believe was overpowering them to turn the pages. There were illustrations and chapters of images that took belief for them to accept. The images were of objects in midair, in an instant of captured time. Vessels were designed from treman wood. There were handmade items—from children's toys and folded-paper flight planes to what Maddy had seen in his vision episode touching the key.

As he read a section about how paper was made from the treman wood, it described in detail all the ingredients and amounts of each to make it. It explained how much farther and higher the paper planes would fly when they were made of treman-wood pulp.

THE PALACE

The pictures of the figures Maddy had seen had been sketched with incredible accuracy and resemblance compared to the recollection in his mind. The descriptions of these drawings only offered, "Artist and locations unknown." Where they had been found—and when—was indicated in several areas. He turned the page, and there it was—it was the exact vision. The drawing had come from…Dillon County!

Maddy pointed to the words DILLON COUNTY. It was said to have been found four hundred years ago this year. Neither of them had seen supporting data or teachings of these drawings. Still the answer evaded them. What was this flying object? They replaced the book and knocked on the door. The doorman opened it for them.

"Any more questions?" he asked.

"Is there a flying treman anywhere that you know of?" Maddy acted innocently childish.

"Those pictures and drawings are all I'm aware of," the doorman answered.

"Thank you. Do we have to be rescheduled to go back to the 'unexplainable' room?"

"Not if you don't mind waiting for an opening and the opportunity."

"Thanks again."

The time was passing quickly as they hurried to the hallway that would bring them to their destination. Fortune was with them, as no one was in the room or waiting. They showed the doorman their cards from their earlier visit. He opened the door for them, and just as the last doorman had said, in a nook opposite the seven pieces was the plaque.

The inscription was innate and practically crude in fashion. The clue was in the "he"; it was capitalized. To go where no one man has veered from to go where HE came from.

Was this the answer they had yearned for today? Would their quest become a deeper search? Who was "HE"?

The alarm sounded to announce that it was closing time. Another visit and more information were needed. Maddy and Trace made their way to the scheduling table again, and Audrey greeted them with, "Need more time?"

"Yes, ma'am," they said together.

"Do you have any specific location or time?" Eon prepared to scribble down their request.

"Is there an open option available? Not that we get privileged rights but rather that we can check out rooms that aren't being visited or to go to the palace for an extended amount of days." Maddy inquired

"We can authorize a two-week pass, if that would help."

"That would be great." Trace turned to Audrey and explained how busy Emma was and that they couldn't be sure of the times they might be able to get away.

The greeters exchanged nods, and Eon opened a drawer. He pulled out a stamp and a purple pad. After a double pounding, they were handed an authorized card with an extension of two weeks. It had "Dignitary" printed across the top.

"No more alarms, though, OK?" Rogar had already heard of the predicament they had been in.

THE PALACE

"It is so irresistible and awe-inspiring that you miss some things," Trace added. "We're sorry, but thank you for your understanding."

Heaster had been warding off a few children's pokes and prods with a snort of his nostrils. He welcomed their return. "Are we ready to go?"

"We may as well see if anyone needs a lift." Maddy scanned the crowded square.

"How about him?" Trace asked.

An apparent newcomer to town had a bag in hand and was looking left and right. He'd do.

"Compliments of the Dew Drop Inn. May we offer you a ride?" Maddy proposed a fare to the burly man.

With a softened facial scrunch, he answered, "Are there any rooms left there?"

"Yes, sir, and the best place for a meal too." Maddy reeled him in.

"I'm Carl Fine. And you are?"

"I'm Maddy Handle, and this is Trace Guthrie. Fine to meet you." Maddy was taking to this occupation like a comfortable old hat. It just fit.

When they got there, Carl stepped down, turned to Maddy, and handed him three tokens.

"Who's the owner?"

"Martin and Emma Dew are reason for the name 'Dew Drop Inn.' One of them should be around here soon."

Carl found his way to the check-in counter and rang the bell. Emma had been in the kitchen helping Marty prepare the evening's special. She caught Maddy giving her the thumbs-up signal, as he and Trace rose on Heaster and headed to the back of the inn.

"I'm here for a room. Are there still openings?" Carl asked.

"We're filling up fast. How long would you like to stay?" Emma readied her login pen.

"I'm part of the lifting contest during the competition. So I suppose until the day after it is over. Maddy said you have the best meals in town." Carl circled his hand around his midsection.

"You'd be a fine judge of that." She looked at the name in her registrar. "Carl." A welcome fit for a king and a comfortable and peaceful area put his mind at ease.

"What time is dinner?" Carl had his eye on the clock behind Emma.

"Whenever you're hungry," she answered.

"And the rooms are where?" Carl picked up his bag and was steered to his accommodations.

Maddy's coins were accumulating rapidly enough that he hoped to be able to pay for the entry fee himself. Their timeframe was dwindling, and his mind wandered to Mary Ellen. He didn't want to forget about a promising income in his attempt to raise the full amount of the wager himself. The trap had been cleverly hidden in the shekel she'd given him.

That night, the foursome—Jed, Jilly, Trace, and Maddy—decided to take a float to taste the evening activities of the Palace City life. The eyefuls of lights and the flare of nightlife gave them a broadened outlook of their trip. The stars and the moons were tremendous, but so many lights so

THE PALACE

close together would present a new stance and added depiction to their story.

There was a park on the west side of Palace City called Charm Park, most obviously due to the charming allure it offered, with the boardwalk and the flattened cobblestone paths that zigzagged throughout the entire park. The upkeep and gardening were exquisite, with picnic areas strewn in defined placement. It let couples have enough privacy to enjoy a romantic evening or was fit for an outing for the entire family. They had diverted part of the river into small canals with bridges and walkways that were ideal for young love and daytime exercise.

Each section had a hitch post for rides to be tied to, if there were rides or not. Heaster chose a spot next to the canal by a bridge. When the group had dismounted, he made his way to the stream and drank its clear, black, fresh water. Maddy spread out a blanket, and they sat together, talking of their travels they'd experienced.

"Is there a specific reason you're here?" Jed asked.

Maddy trusted them with their mission. "We found out there were seven pieces of an unexplainable matter here in the palace."

"Were they there?" Jilly asked.

"They were and more. Did you get your card stamped for a visit to the palace?"

"We're slated for first thing in the morning," Jed answered.

"We could all go together if you want." Trace was enjoying their new friends' company.

"But do you have an appointment?" Jilly was unaware of any extended passes that could be gotten.

Trace explained their knowledge of the two-week diplomat card they'd been given. "So is that a yes?"

Their reply was tied together. "Of course it is a yes."

Maddy looked at Trace and knew what she had detected. Jed and Jilly were connected, just as their lives were. It was an evident match, with the connection factor tied in.

Marty let them make a picnic basket of food so they could spend a couple of hours conversing about their lives and their families. As the night passed, they loaded up Heaster before proceeding back to the inn. The crispy night air brought the two couples into their companions' web of warmth. Trace was falling, and Maddy would be the increase to her fall. His heart beat stronger as she pressed into his back. The inn even had taken on a changed look from the night sky. Its quaintly lit ambiance set the mood for the end of their flight.

"I'd like to do this again, Maddy." Jed and Jilly were in unison as they left the pair of hearts on Heaster.

"We'd like that too," they answered.

At the stable stall, Trace excused herself, as she left Maddy to tend to unharnessing their ride. "What do you think, boy?"

"I think you forget how strong a connection we have."

Maddy brushed his insightful friend down and filled his manger with fresh char.

"Good night, boy."

"Good night, Maddy."

CHAPTER EIGHT

Too Close to Detect

The bell clanged twice, and Maddy turned to the edge of the top bunk and looked down to see Trace sleeping.

" 'Morning, Trace."

Maddy had left Sir Lancelot in his dream world this time.

Her eyes opened, and she raised her hands over her head and stretched. "Is it time to get going so soon?" she said, with a bit of envy about not being able to sleep in.

"Marty may have forgotten about our palace trip," he answered back. "I'll go see what's up. I need to get Heaster ready either way. See you soon."

As he was leaving, he gave Trace his hands to lift her out of her pillow bunk. Her feet touched the floor only long enough for her to jump up and wrap her arms and legs around Maddy to give him a hug good morning. "That's better," she said, giving him a peck on his cheek. "Now you may have a harder time forgetting me, until 'soon' is again."

Maddy's face beamed with a smile. "Trace…I've never had so much to look forward to."

Heaster's trough was empty when Maddy gave him a good-morning swat on his haunch. "Are you hungry yet?"

"That seems to be almost always lately." The prime had desire in his statement.

"I'm going to need to get a step for the stable besides the one we have out front for guests to get off you. I'm going to ask Marty if he minds if I take down this stanchion wall for more room for you too."

"That would be very nice." Heaster had all but done the task already, just by leaning against it during the night.

When Maddy got to the kitchen, Marty was sliding a spatula of beggas and eggs on one of two plates on his prep table.

"This is for you and Trace," he said, as he slid the second scoop onto the other plate. "I believe she is sitting out in the morning air under the awning."

"Thanks, Marty. You did remember that we were going to the palace with Jed and Jilly Ropel this morning?"

"Sure did. Shouldn't be too crazy this morning, but you never know with the tournament getting closer every day. Thanks for stirring up the business with Jed and Jilly and Carl. They've been good customers so far. You might want to see if Carl needs a ride downtown."

"I'll ask him. Thanks again for breakfast."

Maddy laid a pair of folded napkins over his arm and delivered the platters to the table where Trace was seated. His Sir Lancelot impression was ready. "Your breakfast, my Lady Trace. My, how much more beautiful you've gotten *so soon*."

TOO CLOSE TO DETECT

"A servant lad, are we?" Her experience with Maddy and their lord-and-lady routine was keeping her in a constantly joyous state.

"I am completely at your service, Lady Trace. May I join you?"

"What will the other servants think?" Trace teased back.

"I'm hoping they'll be getting the hint." Maddy's face changed to a more serious one.

"Are you flirting with me Table Stable Maddy?"

"More than flirting, Trace."

They were finishing their meal when Jed and Jilly came out of the inside dining room.

"What a delicious way to start a day," they chimed together.

Jed continued, "I think we're ready to go."

"I'll be right back. Marty wanted me to ask if Carl wanted a ride."

Maddy looked into the dining room and saw Carl wiping his face with his napkin. There was a mound of dishes stacked in front of him. "Do you need a lift anywhere, Carl?" he asked.

"That would be great. Hope that ride of yours ate his breakfast this morning. I couldn't quit with just three servings of those beggas and eggs. So he'll be getting put to a test."

Maddy hadn't thought about how they would all get on Heaster. Then a brainstorm of an idea came to him. He ran to the kitchen and asked Marty if he could empty the begga crate and fancy it up a bit to convert it into a carriage seat.

"That is a great idea." Marty saw a double benefit in that—one, it would bring extra customers, and two, it would give Heaster some great training. "There are some nicer ropes and tack in the far corner of the stable and a couple chairs in the lobby."

"That's going to test him all right."

"He's just getting warmed up, Maddy." Marty knew what primes were able to lift. This would be like a big bag of feathers, if he knew Heaster at all.

The harness had a ring on the underside of it where loads of weight were hung from. The crate already had a binding with a cam hook that Marty had used to bring it there the day he'd borrowed Heaster.

Maddy sat the two wing-arm padded chairs in the crate when Marty came carrying a red-linen spread they used for some of the bedding. "Take those chairs out quick, Maddy." Together they draped the spread over the top of the crate, forming a pocket inside to set the chairs in. Maddy replaced the chairs and fastened the rope strap to the four corners of the crate.

"Heaster," Maddy called out to his ride.

In short order they were cinched up and giving the improved carriage a test lift.

"I wanted to ask about the wall of the stanchion too, Marty."

"We'll see to that later. You'd better get going."

The ropes were added to the straps so that Heaster could land for the passengers who were on his back and still allow the crate to land first. As they came to the front of the inn, their travelers were wide-eyed as the crate landed softly and Heaster knelt to his belly.

TOO CLOSE TO DETECT

Maddy suggested that Jed and Jilly take the honor of the maiden voyage in the "carriage" so Carl could ride with Trace on Heaster's back. Marty hadn't missed with his understanding of primes. Heaster lifted off with a little grunt, just because of the most recent harness adjusting to his body, not from the weight of the load.

Carl asked if he could be dropped off at the track-and-field arena, so Maddy went there first. This arrival to the arena turned a few heads because it was an abnormal way of hauling people. Two passengers was a normal fare, but four and the chauffeur was reason to take notice.

Carl set a time to be picked up and handed Maddy his fee—three more tokens. Up they went, and their arrival at the palace landing pad also had gotten some attention. Maddy let Jed and Jilly out then helped Trace down. He took Heaster and the coach and moved them to a park-and-hitching area. "You are such a great prime." Maddy petted his neck and gave him a couple of taps. "We won't be long."

"Be right here." Heaster had enough slack in the rope to reach the edible vegetation. With food now being his first item of interest, he was fine with waiting there.

Maddy joined his party. They were already registered at the entrance.

"Where are you going?" Trace asked Jilly.

"Kind of a thought you would know what we would begin with. We wanted to see if they have started any records about our race turtles. They have a section of the palace for new inventions and creatures, so that's where we're going. What about you?"

"That would be a neat start for us too. Then we'll be going to see if there's a room about flying things," Trace answered.

"There's a section in the inventions area that's filled with diagrams and flying contraptions."

"We're off then?" All four spoke together.

The room was buzzing with other visitors. This huge area wasn't limited to one group at a time. It was filled with exhibit booths along its sides and at least fifteen different doorways to connected rooms off the great room.

The creatures they had penned up and in some in cages had been tamed and trained to be observed. Many were taxidermies from the years and years of genetic hybrids and specialty flora and fauna being blended into pets and work animals.

"We'll be over there." Maddy pointed to the multitude of flight objects, some hanging from the archways and others displayed on pedestals and stands.

Their inquisitive partners of detection barely noticed their leave, as they were soaking up their own discoveries.

"I don't see anything like what I saw in my vision when the key zapped me. But there are some mind-blowing apparatuses here. My curiosity is piquing, wondering whether there is any way into the Treman behind the glass wall."

"The alarms went off just by touching the glass, Maddy."

"I know, but there must be a way in there. Let's go and spy around up there a bit." Maddy's yearning to contact the Treman was growing intensely.

"I'll go tell Jilly where we went." Trace was being polite, hoping their friends would do the same for them.

TOO CLOSE TO DETECT

"Meet you there." He was on his way toward the Treman display room.

Maddy put his invisible detective garments on and his thinking cap. The doorman saw the diplomat card in his hand and asked if Maddy had any detailed questions for him.

"Do you ever add anything to the displays? And are there ways that the living ones are taken care of?" Maddy tried to be inquisitive without being obvious as to his intent.

"We have caretakers who water, feed, and give nutrients to the plants and animals. They come in after the palace is closed for the day. Why?"

"Well, I'm from Dillon County, and the tremans that are there are different from this one. I was wondering if there was any way to get a panoramic view of this one or even if you could touch the bark and—"

"My brother-in-law cares for the Treman on the odd weekend nights—a couple days from now actually. I could see if he would mind some company. If you're not afraid of getting your hands dirty and can be used to do some of his work, maybe you can help him out."

"That would be fantastic." Maddy's excitement was an encouraging sight to the doorman. He told Maddy to check with him the next day to see if he had gotten the OK from his brother-in-law.

Trace had walked to the plaque and was putting her deciphering skills to work. "To go where no one man has veered from to go where HE came from." It just wasn't making sense. Maddy joined her, and they studied it together for a while.

"Not even two heads are better than one on this riddle."

Maddy smiled. "Is that another riddle?"

"Let's get back to the jam and jelly. I mean, Jed and Jilly. It's getting close to lunchtime."

"The turtles here have nothing going on like ours." Trace and Maddy overheard their cohorts talking to each other as they walked closer.

"Greetings, friends." Jed was the first to see them coming. "Were you leaving?"

"Just wondering what your plans were," Maddy answered. "It's close to lunchtime, and we thought you might want to get a bit of food."

"We might come across something at one of the food booths this time. OK with you?"

"We're going to zip back to the inn and see what's going on there. We can come back later to give you a ride."

Handshakes and meeting times were exchanged as Maddy and Trace headed outside.

"Carl wanted us to pick him up, and Mary Ellen's pickup was at three, so we could combine them in a trip back to the inn." Maddy was hoping that Carl could be his distraction from Mary Ellen's advances. "Jed and Jilly were going to stay downtown until later anyway, right?"

"We could have the two of them ride in the coach if they'll fit. Carl is more than a full-size man." Trace was amazed at his size.

"But he's not very old," Maddy added with a cupid's grin.

Maddy was adjusting Heaster's strapping and the crate. He wanted to present Mary Ellen with a ride fit for a queen. A tap on his shoulder had him turn to face a man with a monocle in his right eye and a bristly, handlebar mustache. A fur-covered top hat banded at the rim with a bright red-and-blue silky ribbon topped off his orderly outfit.

"The name's Taylor, Tren Taylor," he said with a rolled tongue and a sophisticated voice. He extended his hand to Maddy. "What will you take for this dastardly creature?"

Without shaking his hand, and because of his insult to Heaster, he gave his answer. "He's not for sale!"

"Everything is for sale, my boy. How much will you take for him?" He reached into his chest pocket and retrieved his wallet. He began thumbing at a thick stack of bills, making sure Maddy could see them.

"Not this thing. He's much more than something you've got in there." Maddy stood his ground. Even though the paper that was in Tren Taylor's fingers wasn't familiar to him, paper currency was just that, paper. It had no value even if he were interested, because of whose fingers the paper was in.

His voice increased in volume and with intentional measure. "I offer fifty shekels!" He took out five of the papers from his folded carrier.

"I may look young, Mister, but I won't be insulted, and with respect to you, I say again that he's not for sale." Getting slightly frustrated, he turned back to attend to the rigging.

"Here is one hundred shekels!"

Maddy wasn't fazed, as he slowly turned to the older man. "Five hundred wouldn't do it. I will, however, ask my ride." Maddy beckoned for Heaster's ear and whispered into it.

Heaster turned and took a defensive stance. He moved his head to Tren's face and, after a couple of sniffs, belched a thunderous burp.

Tren's hat tumbled off his head, and the moist char breath dampened his mustache enough to droop it downward. Tren Taylor was humiliated. Replacing his wallet, he did an about-face, picking his hat from the ground and brushing it off. With a threatening tone, he said, "You are young, and this will not be the end of this." He pressed his way through the crowd of people that had gathered.

A couple had stepped up next to Maddy, asking for a taxi ride. "Can we afford to get a ride?"

They spoke loudly enough to ensure that the group of bystanders would hear.

"We'll go anywhere in the city for three tokens!" Maddy took the opportunity to kick off his recent business.

"A ride to the Dew Drop Inn, please?" The gentleman handed Maddy three tokens as he steered his wife to her seat in the box. Once they were seated, Maddy closed the protective arm of the opening and latched it into a locked position.

Questions were flying as Maddy helped Trace onto Heaster. "Is he fast?" "How far will you go out of the city?" "How much can he haul?" These were just a few of the questions as Heaster lifted off, taking the couple in the crate with him.

This was a deal for the couple. Any flying adventure usually was a five- to ten-token rate. Not only was this an adventure, but it also was a thrilling adventure. The pendulum they were in, hanging beneath their ride, would swing mildly as

Heaster changed direction. Carnival rides were connected to the ground and to a continuing pattern of travel. They went round and around or up and down. This definitely involved a risk factor and the thrill.

After dropping off their clients at the front of the inn, Maddy went to see if Marty was in need of help.

"Marty, do you know a man by the name of Tren Taylor?"

"I thought everyone knew him. Why?"

Maddy felt concern wash across his face. "Is he one of your customers?"

"Not too often. He can't resist the food, but the rest of it is beneath him."

Maddy disclosed the event in the yard of the palace.

"Now that would have been worth paying for." Marty belted into laughter. "He's one of the richest men in the city."

"What would he have needed with Heaster?" Maddy did not understand his offer.

"Not certain, but with the competition coming up, he may have thought this might be his winning ticket. He's not too keen on losing or being insulted. His ploy in the past has been to buy an animal for the competition then dispose of it if it doesn't win. He's not in the animal business. He's just in the trying-to-get-richer one."

"I hope I didn't make an enemy."

Marty caught Maddy's concerned look. "You just stay focused on the finish line. Has Heaster been adapting to the rigging and hauling?"

"It doesn't seem to give him any challenge at all," Maddy told him.

"Good! We'll slip in more weight a little at a time. That drape will cover the floor, where we can keep our secret about what we're up to hidden from the onlookers. He needs to be trained with a great deal of intensity the closer the meet comes."

"What'll we put in the floor?"

"You get that stanchion wall torn down and reinforce the floor of that crate. I'll take care of the weight. We need a pretty good-size veiled pocket for the weight. So make it strong. We wouldn't want the floor falling out from under your customers."

"That wouldn't be good, seeing that Mary Ellen is the next intended passenger."

"Better get to it. It's about an hour away."

Maddy attacked his instructions. Trace had put on her apron and was helping Emma with waiting tables. Maddy cleared a couple of them to get the chance to talk to Trace.

"You won't be doing this forever, Trace," he said with a hint of encouragement. "A princess shouldn't have to do servant work."

Trace's face lit up as she touched his dirty face. "Such a gallant prince, with such a dirty face. Maybe you should clean up a bit for your passengers? Not that you're not handsome, even with your soiled face."

"I think Mary Ellen needs to see me filthy."

"She'll be in the begga crate with Carl, right?"

"I'll be right back." Maddy touched her hand in good-bye.

Maddy lifted off with the couple he'd brought there from the palace. They were living in an apartment downtown, close to Mary Ellen's towering apartment. That was their destination, which worked right into Maddy's route.

The man handed Maddy three tokens and said, "That was the smoothest, softest ride and landing I've ever had. Is he going to be in the competition?"

"We're hoping to be, if we can raise the entry fee."

He reached into his coin bag and handed him a couple more tokens. "Consider it a tip and an investment. I believe he will do very well."

"Thank you, sir." Maddy accepted the offer. "And if you ever want another lift, I'll be at the inn."

Heaster lifted to the top of Mary Ellen's penthouse, to the landing pad, where he set the crate down without making a sound. His leg bent to give Maddy a stepping stool to the roof.

Maddy got to the door of the penthouse and knocked. He knocked again and received no response.

He turned around to go back to Heaster, when the door's peep window slid open.

"Is that you Maddy Handle?" she asked, looking at his back view.

"Yes, ma'am. I mean, Mary Ellen," he said, remembering her request.

"Come in here for a minute." There was no command in her voice, yet like a fox wondering why the coop door had been left open, there was a temptation to accept her luring appeal. The door unlatched and opened to Mary Ellen clad in a silk robe. The robe was loosely tied and made Maddy's cheeks begin to blush.

Snapping out of the trance he was feeling overtake him, he shook his head. "I have another customer I need to pick up at the track-and-field arena in ten minutes. Did you still want a ride?"

"It'll only take two moments." She turned and walked inside. The robe flowed behind her and waved like a silk flag in a light breeze.

Maddy was unaccustomed to these tactics of advances. Trace was the first girl he'd ever had a fluttering heart feeling about. The fluttering in his chest now wasn't like that at all. It was bordering on fear and thrill, which both could mean danger.

"I'd better not," was all Maddy could utter. Her poise of beauty was causing his forehead to moisten with sweat, and it was not that hot outside.

"Oh, you are a silly boy. I just wanted you to see this." She pointed to something behind a wall that led down the wide hall to a great room.

He relaxed with the notion that it wasn't her that she wanted him to see. He walked in and started down the hall when Mary Ellen said, "I'm sure you weren't born in a barn, Maddy. Close the door, please?"

He shoved the door closed and continued down the hallway to the green room. The ceiling had two oval half arches with white engravings and floral patterns of leaves and flowers and bracing that crossed evenly at its peak then continued to the opposing sill. The domed, clear window filled the space that would be magnificent to watch the stars from.

The tile was a marbled green stone so perfectly placed that there was no need for grouting. White pillars held the overhead window with two at each exit of the great room that led to other rooms and alcoves.

Clearing her throat she said, "The box, Maddy." Mary Ellen had gotten his attention back to her order of business.

"What is it?" The question brought him back to his guard.

It was wrapped in a shiny wrapping paper, with a blue ribbon finishing the wrap in a bow.

"It's for you. It is a gift—a gift from me to you, with no strings attached."

"But you don't know that I would need anything." Maddy knew that Celemass was getting close and gifts then were special, mostly with a purpose that met a need.

"Oh! Just open it," she urged.

To Maddy this truly did feel like Celemass. The wrapped gift was so big. What it was had him wanting to tear through the paper and find his treasure within the box. He carefully and hesitantly began to expose the container beneath the paper.

"I thought you were in a hurry," Mary Ellen prodded.

The box inside had a label that listed its contents. It was a specially designed harness with all the tack, buckles, hooks, and leathers.

He locked eyes with her. "I can't take this. It must have cost a small fortune. I won't be able to repay you."

"That is nonsense, Maddy. We know what your prime can do. There is no purchase agreement; it's a gift. You just win this silly competition."

"Are you for real?" Maddy knew lying was unacceptable and needed to know what she was intending.

"Of course I'm real." She exited to one of the rooms to dress.

Maddy opened the box. A white leather breastplate had the insignia made of a chrome-plated buckle with a letter, an *M*. The bold *M* had a framed *M* around the edges.

This was the no-strings attachment, Maddy thought, as he held the front of this strong, bound, and stitched leather. The craftsman who made this was gifted.

Mary Ellen returned dressed for the day trip, with a sun umbrella she used as a walking stick and an outfit Maddy thought looked ridiculous. It clung to her body, every inch of it, like a diving suit Maddy had seen swimmers use at the Gulf. It was bright red, and the parasol matched it.

"Ready?" Maddy questioned.

"Yes."

When she got to the pad, she saw the piece of equipment that was for carrying Maddy's clients. "I cannot ride in that," she let slip. Her true self-image emerged, as her disgust was evident.

"My other rider will be with you." He was scrambling for a way out of her riding with him on Heaster.

"He's not here now, so I will be riding with you on your prime." She had set her face.

Her forcefulness and determined decision had Maddy unable to change her mind.

They got in riding posture and lifted off. As they ascended, Mary Ellen caught Maddy around his ribs and squeezed in again.

Carl was waiting at the gate of the event field when they landed the crate. Then they touched down next to it. Mary Ellen cast an uninterested look at Carl when he asked, "Who's the dame?"

"This is Mary Ellen Moen. Mary Ellen, this is Carl Fine." Maddy introduced his intended match.

"A fine man and a dame," she mocked.

"Dinner's waiting!" Maddy's peacemaking skills were called on.

He got them seated in the crate, but Carl was so big that there wasn't much room for them to sit abreast. So Carl asked for permission to put his arm behind her.

"I just hope this prime can get off the ground." This was her way of allowing the option.

Maddy could hear a few exchanges of conversation as they headed toward the inn.

At touchdown the couple hatched out the fare when Maddy finalized the debate with his charge. "Free! No strings attached," he said as he went to the stable.

Marty had put metal plates by the enlarged stanchion. Maddy took the spread off the crate after taking the chairs out, opening the floor platform. The plates would fit with room around them. He got to the stack of plates and bent to pick one up. He didn't know what these things were made of that made them so heavy, but he could hardly move one of them, let alone lift it without help.

Marty came from the kitchen, wiping his hands and asking, "Need some help? These will give you an idea of the weights they use in the lift challenge. Each year changes as to how many the rides can lift, but the record is ten of these plates and four smaller ones."

"They must be a stone each." Maddy had guessed it.

"They are exactly that much. And there are twelve of them here."

"Twelve?"

"Brawn set the record. He didn't win the overall decathlon, but he could lift. We'll start him out with four or five to see how he does. Then we'll add as he gets used to it. The hardest adjustment for the primes is in their ability to hold their chests out to hold the breath they need to lift. Most can't tighten their chests muscles enough, and that means less breath. Less breath, less lift."

They put the five thin plates in the bottom of the crate, setting them in a balanced but secured manner.

"What do you think, Heaster?" Maddy felt his prime's thoughts.

"Looks like a flattened Carl." Heaster was confident he could lift them.

They clipped the hook on the crate's ropes, and Heaster started upward. A bellowing crackling sound came from the bottom of the box. And then up it all went. Heaster had done it. "Add more," he said.

"You'll get more with the chairs and customers. That crate is extra too, so we'll let you get used to that much for now." Marty knew how he'd trained Brawn. "Trust me, guys. I know what I'm doing. Our girls had been dealing the customers through the dining areas, so let's see if they need any help. Just up and down for a while, Heaster. Maddy will come and get you when it's time to get Jed and Jilly."

Maddy hadn't told Heaster or Marty about the gift from Mary Ellen yet. "Just think. When we enter this meet, lots of people will want to get their hands on you."

"We're inseparable, remember?" Heaster assured his life connection to Maddy. "See you in a bit, champ."

Maddy peeked into the dining room and saw his attempt at matchmaking might be working. Carl was eating while Mary Ellen was talking and adding hand gestures. Once in a while, Carl took a breath and would laugh at her behavior.

Trace came in carrying a tray filled with dirty dishes. Maddy intercepted her, taking the tray to the counter by the wash sink.

"How would you like a break?" His offer came with an outstretched hand.

"What do you have in mind?" She paused then said, "That would be amazing." Before Maddy could get the concept to her, she knew what he'd wanted to do.

"I know you've figured out that I was going to say, 'Just a walk.' " Maddy said it anyway.

"Not *just* a walk—but a walk with you. Where are we to go?"

"That you won't find out." He put the destination out of his thoughts.

They told Marty what they were going to do, saying they'd be back for the evening meal.

Maddy had seen a spot by the wall at the end of the road. It had a path that followed the wall toward the mountain.

When they got to the wall, there were hundreds, possibly even thousands, of images and paintings. There were people's art or signatures showing that they had been there. They all had meaning. Some were easily discerned, and others were deeper in implication.

The people who signed the barrier had come from all over the earth and put their marks on the wall. Where the wall tied to the mountain, a stream rushed under the wall, coming from the mountain's gorges. It rushed boiling from under the stone opening, foaming as it lulled into one of the city's channels. They sat along the manmade bank and dipped their feet in the cool water.

"How long has this wall been here?" Trace asked her escort.

"Good question. That's something to look for at the palace tomorrow." Maddy turned to see Trace's eyes looking deeply into his.

"This almost feels magical." She moved a little closer.

Maddy reached over and gave her forearm a tiny pinch. "Did you feel that? This is real. And for us to be in such a beautiful setting…" Maddy slowly moved his head toward Trace.

"That would be magical." She reacted with a move of her own.

As their lips came closer, their eyes stayed open. Every precious second was being captured for memory's sake. Suddenly an overhead sound came from the top of the wall and interrupted their kiss. A rumbling followed as a tremor shook the earth where they sat. Their first kiss ever had been delayed by this distraction.

TOO CLOSE TO DETECT

"Either that was going to result into an amazing lightshow of fireworks or there's an earthquake going on." Maddy composed himself and stood to see a vine growing its way over the wall. The sound had been a few smaller stones being knocked down, but that wasn't the reason for the movement of the land under their feet.

They moved back to the path and saw the thick vine retract from the wall. The subtle shimmy of the ground faded to stillness.

"We should get back to the inn," Trace suggested.

"We can come back with Heaster to see what is happening on the other side." Maddy had another thought going through his mind. His first was that he'd been interrupted, and second, his curiosity was piqued as to what caused the disturbance.

Their walk back was hurried. They held hands, and they gripped each other firmly. At the inn the evening flow of people came from the street, and people found their seats at any open tables. Maddy saw the night was going to be long, given the amount of people already there.

"I'd better get Jed and Jilly before we get swamped. I'll be right back." Maddy passed through the kitchen and told Marty what he was doing. "I should be back to help ahead of the rush."

"Will Mary Ellen need a ride back?" Marty was protecting one of his valued customers.

"It may take a bit longer. I'd forgotten about her. Sorry."

Maddy found that Heaster was still working the weight up then softly setting it down.

"We've got to go, boy." He unhooked the carriage. "We'll make better time without this."

They got to the front as Mary Ellen paced impatiently along the street.

"Sorry, Mary Ellen," he apologized.

Her eyes fluttered as she saw that she would be riding with Maddy on Heaster. "That's fine. Mr. Fine retired to his room. That leaves us alone for the trip home."

"I'll explain on our way." Maddy hoped to divert her advances with the story about what they'd seen—all but the almost kiss. He didn't want her to think anything about kissing.

"Do you mind if we take a more scenic route?" he asked, knowing the answer.

Mary Ellen wouldn't object to that. That would mean more time to spin her web. "I do not at all."

"Trace and I were walking by the pictured wall when a noise came from outside the wall. I thought we could see what it might have been from a better, heightened view."

Outside the wall, they saw a group of treman trees planted in a diamond shape and nothing else. There were no climbing vines on the wall and no activity of any sort.

"Looks like a nice place for a picnic in the middle of those tremans." Mary Ellen pointed at the largest treman at the water's edge.

"Know how long those have been there?" Maddy asked her.

"They have been there for quite some time. Micah and I would come out here, years ago, rest his soul, for a quiet time away from the hectic pace of the factory. They were there then."

TOO CLOSE TO DETECT

Something was not lining up for Maddy. What had made the rumbling noise was adding to his dilemma.

The landing pad received them as Heaster touched the surface. "There you go, Mary Ellen."

"Aren't you coming in to get your harness?" she said, losing her grip on him.

"Could we do it tomorrow? I still have a ride to get back to the inn, and I think they're really going to need extra help tonight," he answered.

"What time should I expect you?" She was trying not to act too hopeful.

"Does the morning work for you?" He was hoping she wouldn't have time to get too gussied up early in the day. She didn't come across as an early riser.

"Oh, that would be fine. Huh, there's that man's name again." She wagged her head and handed Maddy another shekel.

"Mary Ellen! That's more than—"

Cutting him off, she said, "About ten?" She was pushing her wakeup time ahead.

"That will be fine." He emphasized the "fine" to drive Carl's name home.

He was off with a salute to her and began steering toward the palace.

"Hope they're ready." Maddy didn't doubt his ride's speed, but he was beginning to feel the pressure of what being really busy was about.

"I'll get you there quick. Hold on!" his ride responded.

A concentrated burst of forward speed had them at the palace in seconds.

"That was really fast, Heaster." Maddy was being more impressed with every option Heaster was showing.

"With just you and me, this harness is nothing when 'go' is allowed."

They'd gotten there so quickly that Jed had turned away, not seeing them. When he turned back, they were there again.

"How'd you do that?" Jed asked.

"Guess he's pretty fast too." Maddy helped Jilly and Jed on, and back to the inn they went.

Maddy was earning his entry fee promptly, hoping not to have to borrow anything from the Dews.

The swarm of business, along with the smell of a mouth-watering aroma, whirled into the air around the inn. Jed and Jilly went to their room early, exhausted from the vast amount of information they had packed into their visit at the palace. "Should see if those turtles need anything," Jed exhaled at his expectant last task of the day.

"See you both tomorrow?" Maddy was enjoying their friend's fatigue, knowing that he wasn't alone.

Tables began to blur, from one to the next, with a steady stream of satisfied patrons. The night ended with a few needed alterations for the morning, and then Maddy hung his clothes on the bunk post and climbed into bed. It was cool and receiving, and he took enough time to notice Trace walk into the room.

"Are you as tired as I am?" they asked together. "Yes." Trace changed into her bed dress behind the makeshift wall.

"Good night, my lady!" Maddy passed into sleep, not hearing any reply.

CHAPTER NINE

A Closer Look

Ding! Ding! The bell was becoming less shocking as Maddy opened his eyes. Trace was moving to the wall to freshen up and prepare for the day.

"Beautiful already," Maddy said. "Just need to put on your royal gown."

She smiled as she disappeared around the corner. From the nook she asked, "What's happening today?"

"The doorman told me to ask whether his brother-in-law was going to let me get in to see the Treman up close." He replied with part of his plans and with less emphasis said, "And Mary Ellen gave me a gift that I'm not sure I should accept."

Trace's face came from out of the niche. "She gave you a gift? What kind of gift?"

"She's *old*!" Maddy nipped any jealous thought out of her mind. "She had a custom-designed harness made for Heaster. Between her and Tren Taylor, I'm not sure who's more persistent. He wanted to buy Heaster; she seems to want to buy me and wants the advertising rights too. She has a monogrammed double *M* on a buckle, like she's hoping I'll get her more business when they find out she's sponsoring me…I mean, us."

"Are you going to accept it?"

"It's really well made, and Brawn's harness is pretty old. I sort of already did. She's so tricky. But if you don't think I should, that will be the end of it. I hope Marty can assure me about Brawn's harness—"

Seeing Maddy tossing back and forth between accepting the harness for the competition and ceasing from any further jealous turmoil, Trace interjected, "She is old!"

They laughed as they finished getting ready for the day.

They pooled their tips, fare tokens, and coins together and came up with twelve shekels and seven tokens. Getting room and board from the Dews was helping their funds add up fast. It would have taken many passes of the sun to earn that much worth back at their homes in Dillon and Clay Counties.

At breakfast Maddy offered to pick up more guests for the breakfast meal then asked, "Marty, what are all the events in the decathlon?"

"I'll start with the main event, even though that's the last one they do. That's the lift. After they've gone through the gauntlet of burdensome and less important games and tests, they have the highest-ranked rides lift as much as they can, increasing the loads until they have the winner."

"Is that only for the finalists?"

A CLOSER LOOK

"Yes. The others vary. There's one for speed and getting from one point to another. Another is the fastest around the track for ten laps, an unmanned speed lap, an accuracy drop, a controlled setting down of sort of a crate, a maneuvering course with a load, a shooting test that tallies the score of the best of three arrows shot from their mount, speed of lift with a rider, and a joust." Marty looked at Maddy as he mentioned the last challenge.

"Did you say a joust?" He had heard it all right.

"We'll need to see if my armor will fit you." Marty had gone deeper into his revealing bag of information about the decathlon.

"What kind of armor?" Maddy was getting more and more concerned with each event Marty was enlightening him about, and now there was the joust and armor. He'd never even tried any on, let alone jousted with it.

"I have a practice javelin that you will need to get acquainted with."

"They aren't sharpened, are they?" Maddy's concern grew.

"Not the practice ones." Marty's answer also gave Maddy the truth about the real ones.

Maddy was about to throw in the towel when Marty let out a boisterous, roaring laugh. "They're blunt, but they still pack quite a wallop. I'm not sure how we'll train you for that event."

"I'd better get that weight added to the crate for Heaster. Is it all right if we go through the forest outside the city?" He'd heard there was a track nearby.

"Most of it. The west side has a path that weaves through the trees so he can learn to maneuver with the crate." Marty was trying to help in any way he could.

"He should do pretty well without a load. He's really fast too. I found that out after we left Mary Ellen's on the way to the palace."

"We have more than half the entry fee already, so we may not need to have you front us anything. Marty, Mary Ellen wants to give me a new harness. It's specially made out of the finest leather I've ever seen. I don't know whether I should accept it, though. I don't want to offend you in any way."

"She is a crafty one, but if she's willing to support you, that will be your decision." Marty had a slight reserve in his voice when he gave the hint as to her possible scheme.

"With that, I'd better get going. We have rides to give." Maddy strapped Brawn's work harness on his prime and hooked the crate to it. "Let's take a pass through this path in the outer forest. What do you say, boy?"

"Practice can only add to the skill level we'll need for the event." Heaster had been listening to the description of the different categories they'd be facing. "So when should we break that 'old woman's' gift in?"

"We'll haul a few people around after the maneuvering run. Then we will see what time it will be. I have to get to the palace to meet with that janitor, if the doorman has set it up. We should check that out first. To which I say, to the palace my fine steed."

A CLOSER LOOK

Maddy flashed his pass at the woman at the entrance to the fortress. She still needed to do her ritual stamping, and then he hastened to see what the doorman had done.

He had finished closing the door for a small group and was returning to his post. Maddy asked whether he'd been approved to tag along.

"His name is Shane Kield. He's a little shorter than I am and said he will meet you by the doors, along the wall, where the register table is. There is a 'service' sign over the doors. He'll meet you there at five, but if you're late, he won't be able to wait for you."

"I'll be there." Maddy was confident with his answer. He couldn't miss this opportunity.

Getting back outside where Heaster was waiting, he saw two people who wanted a pleasure trip.

"Five tokens for a tour of the city from above." He was hoping to be fair with his price.

"We heard it was three tokens for a trip anywhere in the city." The couple wanted the best offer they could get.

"That's for anywhere in the city, but you'll want a complete tour, which includes the outer forest. It is three for inside city limits and only two more for the extended ride."

He'd hooked them. The man placed the tokens in Maddy's hand and stepped into the basket with his mate. "Is the forest what we passed through on our way in?"

"Yes, but there is a trail through it that is simply to die for." He hoped he hadn't been taken literally, as this would be his first time there himself. But he was being paid to practice.

They set course for the outer-wall tour before the inner tour would end their sightseeing adventure.

The path was a maneuvering challenge for sure. The couple was swaying from side to side as Heaster handled the shifting weight below. His speed was steady, with little to no jolting or jarring movements. The path had pinned pointed changes in direction that followed the contour of small hills and rock ridges. There were wide curves and stunted straightaways that took abrupt right- and left-angle turns. The concealed crate came within finger widths of the path and would launch from the rise of a small hill coming back downward as Heaster traversed the weighted anchor slowly back to the lane.

The trees added a degree of difficulty, as the limbs of the broad-leafed boughs would threaten to snag the couple's coupe out of the air. Two narrow overpasses that were for pedestrians to cross the creek running through the forest presented the greatest testing. The crate wasn't able to cross by turning sideways. There was just enough room for it to go by. The second bridge had a protruded stone cap that sat on a pillar of stones, which widened and made the escape from their egress absolute. The ropes that hooked to Brawn's harness ring came together, leaving room for Heaster to lower the crate enough for the ropes to slice closely within.

"Up!" Maddy tested a response while Heaster had been concentrating on his last maneuver. Up they did go. The creaking of stretching ropes cinching down on the wooden slats at the bottom of the crate with the heaviness of the load pressing its substructure endured the climbing motion.

A CLOSER LOOK

The sway from turning to the eastern wall of the city was creating an extra force that constricted Heaster's chest. He inhaled, that increased more force in lift strength as the connected pieces of this flying company moved as one solid unit eastward.

Maddy had wanted another glimpse of the area over the wall where he and Trace had been interrupted the night before. The diamond shape he thought he remembered was now more a quadrangle. He spoke softly to his mount, requesting this snapshot view to be remembered for comparison to any future changes.

As they were about to pass the Dew Drop, Maddy dropped a food hint and asked them if they'd want a short break to eat before finishing their tour. They agreed, and Maddy set the crate at the curb, slid off Heaster, and opened the bar of their cage.

"Be back within the hour," he said, getting onto the seat pad and taking the reins up along Heaster's neck.

A voice called out as to whether he was going downtown from there, just as the crate disconnected from the street.

"Get in, sir." Maddy gave instruction for moving the bar and replacing it securely as the pair were seated and settled for the trip.

The downtown traffic of shoppers, various carts, and four-wheeled vehicles pulled by older rides that had been retired from flight scooted from shop to shop, loading and packing their purchases from the merchants' stores that lined the main street.

"That will do!" came from the carriage. Maddy chose a spot to set the crate down. A stairway rose to a second-level landing, and Maddy jumped to it so Heaster wouldn't have to block the flow of traffic. He ran down the stairs, skipping every other step to open the blocking bar and let his client out of the crate. The man handed him three tokens and tipped his hat in a thankful "Good day."

"Are you going to the palace?" A lady and her younger daughter, dressed in puffy dresses and lookalike bonnets, walked toward Maddy.

"We go anywhere in the city, ma'am, for three tokens." With a slightly puzzled yet accepting tilt of her head, she led her smaller twin to the chair, picking her up and patting her fluffed-up dress to her lap.

Maddy offered his hand to her gloved one and helped her to her seat. After locking the safety bar, he scurried up the stairway and jumped back onto Heaster.

"Hold on!" The mother positioned her personal safety arm in front of her daughter.

Up they went, slowly, so as to not frighten the first-time passenger. A squeal of joy came from her uncontrollably, and she said, "Wee!"

The palace was a short ride for the price Maddy had set, and it was before he realized the enjoyment his little first-timer would have.

When unloading he waved off the offer to pay, saying, "If this was her first time, there's no charge."

A CLOSER LOOK

The woman insisted on handing him four tokens, telling him that her daughter hadn't spoken in over a month. Her gratefulness was irreversible.

Maddy hadn't had such an exchanging of service for pay. He'd be careful not to open the door to greed. "Thank you, ma'am," he said, as he prepared his next passengers for their destination.

Passengers were abundant the whole day. When he would deliver his guests to their locations, there would be others to take their places.

One group in particular he transported had given Heaster a challenge—a family with four children, two of whom got on with Maddy and two who were held by the parents on their laps in the crate. They wanted a meal that was affordable, and the Dew Drop Inn was their most likely fulfillment. Maddy caught Marty's wink from the serving window of the kitchen. This had been his largest group, and the father gave him six tokens, one for each of his family.

It was approaching five in the afternoon, and Maddy knew he couldn't be late. Fortunately, his last riders were going close to the palace. He'd have to wait to go to Mary Ellen's until after his meeting with Shane.

He'd gotten Heaster settled by the outer area, where the trio of greeters was putting away their approval stamps and paperwork. Rogar walked over and asked questions about Heaster's lineage with a watchful eye as he patted him on his shoulder. "Fine animal you have here, Maddy."

"Thank you, sir. Will it be all right to leave him here for a few minutes? I know it's closing time, but Shane Kield is going to escort me through some of the background workings of the palace."

"Already learned everything about the forefront workings?" Eon asked.

Maddy knew there was no way to have covered all the information in the few visits he been there for.

"Not everything, sir. I just have a bit of a fascination about that Treman and how all the other foliage and plants are cared for. Dillon County was the only place I thought they grew because of the twenty-four-hour transplanting time. We noticed the four planted on the east side of the outer wall, along with the one inside."

"Those were brought here many years ago." Rogar had some knowledge he passed on. "They got here just under the gun. The 'story' is that one of the fastest primes ever raised had gotten the seeds here within minutes of time running out for them to be planted. Everything was prepared for their arrival, as they wanted to have a physical treman put on display here by Palace City. They'd tried one time within the walls, but the seeds wouldn't take hold and turned to the tarry goop. That's why they're outside. The one in the palace was just brought here after it had gone permanently dormant, long, long ago."

"So it's dead?"

"I should say not at all. It is just dormant. I would hate to think it would be dead. You must have read about its story. I've believed that story since I was knee-high to a knee-hopper."

A CLOSER LOOK

"There's Shane, Mr. Stoge. Thanks for your input." Maddy ran to the meeting spot and introduced himself. "I'm Maddy Handle from Dillon County."

"I have heard a few stories about that place. Is there any reason for wanting to get a closer look at the Treman?" This man was patient in his manner and had fair hair, with a uniform that had small pockets all around his waist and leggings. In those pockets were packets of powders with a few smaller garden tools he'd use to keep the plants groomed.

"It has intrigued me because of the stories our elder has told me about him, and seeing that he is here and that the treman from Dillon look a bit different, I wanted to get a look from all the way around." Maddy continued to be patient while Shane unlocked the door.

"Are you ready to go?"

"Yes, I am, sir."

They teamed up, and Shane took him to a staging room to get a uniform for him to wear. "There won't be so many questions this way. The other janitors and staff will think you're just the new guy. You'll have to leave your rucksack here in the locker room. Some of the displays are a little odd. You'll find that out shortly."

Maddy had so badly wanted to get his key closer to the Treman's notch to see if they were identical. He'd have to figure something else out.

The tour was incredible, and being on the other side of the glass brought a chill to Maddy as they entered the Treman exhibit. As soon as he touched the interior of the display, a flash went through his mind. A connection melded in his thoughts about the same conflict he'd seen earlier—the Treman and this other transforming figure resisting each other, battling with their exclusive weapons.

Maddy was able to see the back side of the Treman and up its trunk. There were scars in the bark and missing branches that looked to have been cut off. The blemishes had been placed on the side away from the spectators and were only visible from this vantage point.

Shane told Maddy not to get too close to the Treman and to really be careful where he stepped. "There are times when his roots get exposed. Don't know how, but they do, so I'll cover them over with soil and pat it down. It might be from watering the exhibit."

"How often do you come into this one?" Maddy was looking for another opportunity to get near the Treman.

"It's usually once a month, but we water the living plants once every week. We can just use the sprinkler system if anything looks like it needs it. It all depends on those things. Why are you so inquisitive about this?"

"The story about how he came to life has me probing to know if there could be any fact so I can prove it to be a truth. The story my mother told me used to have me lying in bed daydreaming about what would have happened, or not, to him. I guess that should have been my first question. Is this an image of the Treman story for history's sake or is this really the genuine article?"

"This has been here ever since I started. Guess I thought it was just a prototype for an imagery concept. The story that I heard was too farfetched to be real." Shane went back to finish watering the last couple of plants.

"Could I come back here next week?" Maddy had to lay this dilemma to rest once and for all.

"I believe the palace might not even be open because of the big competition and all. But if it is, I don't see why not. I'm scheduled for next weekend, and I could water this by hand."

"That would be fantastic!" Maddy took one more look at the notch to ensure he would be able to get close enough with the key. "Thanks, Shane. I could give your two kids a ride with my prime sometime if you don't mind, or I could even give your whole family a ride."

"You have a deal." They shook hands, and Shane continued on his routine customary checklist.

With the entire palace to attend to, and there only being a small weekend crew, a rotation was followed so that everyone was familiar with all the displays.

Maddy would be fortunate to have Shane working on this route next weekend also.

This next task of getting the peg in that room would be a challenge. But the uniform had plenty of pockets, offering places to put it. Maddy was just concerned with how it had been absorbing the things it was contacting.

Trace had been busy at the inn with the increasing clientele that came from the extra people in the city for the upcoming event. Maddy had dropped off a couple to eat at the café bar that was along the service-window wall. They served drinks of many flavors as well as appetizers, including a few light meals and sandwiches. Maddy told Trace he was going to get the harness from Mary Ellen, as he had a chance to take her aside to a niche and give her a kiss on her cheek.

"Practicing for the old lady?" Trace said with a smile.

"My lips are yours, my lady. They're solely and completely for you." Maddy took her hand and kissed it as well as he left.

Another group of three was by the makeshift converted carriage, waiting for a ride to a shop on the main street that was close to Mary Ellen's. It would work into Maddy's planned stop.

Maddy's humbleness and availability was receiving a good report. The word was spreading about this young man and his prime, who offered a great deal with his fare.

He'd gotten to Mary Ellen's rooftop and landed the weighted crate without making a sound.

Making his way to the glass-paneled door, he saw the box moved against the wall in the hallway. He knocked and patiently waited for his invitation to come in.

A few moments later, she came to the door with an outfit that made Maddy's eyes dart in his head. Trying not to notice, but never seeing what he was seeing, had him twisting and turning his head away, quickly glancing to her and away again. Her sheer covering was in no way modest and was causing Maddy to get very nervous. Thankfully she was wearing undergarments, but it only added to his embarrassment. She waved her hand and indicated the sheepish adolescent should come in. She turned, walking past the box and into the great room.

A CLOSER LOOK

"You are very late. Wasn't our appointment for ten?"

Being innocent was not going to help him work his way out of this situation, so he completely opened the unlocked door and headed straight for the harness box. His hands had taken hold of the handle, and he started backtracking, pulling the box across the hallway floor. A beautifully woven rug with tassels tied to either end was his undoing. The box caught the tassels and rolled in a lump of rug, stopping his sliding motion. The harness wasn't too heavy, but the box was making things very awkward to control.

As he bent down to fix the balled-up rug, her voice sounded. "Not even a hello?"

This was all a part of her deep plan. She stood there in a fuzzy blue robe that had covered his previous indulgence.

"Oh! No, ma'am. I wasn't going without doing that." Maddy was scrambling for a reasonable excuse for what looked like a robbery in progress. "I mean, Mary Ellen. I thought that maybe you were getting dressed, so I'd get the harness and the box loaded while you were covering…I mean dressing."

Her moves were precisely calculated. With each utterance came a sticky webbing of words. "You can get that shortly. There is something else for you in the parlor." She turned and walked back to the great room, taking a slight turn to a sitting room off to her left.

Maddy thought, "Said the spider to the fly." He said, "I really am picking up a passel of new customers and am getting close to having my entrance fee, so I should get going. Did you need to go anywhere?"

His words and question seemed to drop off his tongue, and he wasn't sure she'd heard him. "Mary Ellen?" He moved to one of the pillars holding the archway and went into the huge room, peeking around the columns to see where she'd gone.

"Back here, Maddy. Don't be so silly. I won't bite."

Maddy hadn't been afraid of much of anything until this circumstance arose. Now his heart was beating under his ribs. "What is it?" he asked, listening for her position.

"Come in here and see." Her comment was on the edge of what could have been an order.

His reflexes were coiled, and he was ready to spring in reaction as he heard where her voice had come from. He walked slowly to the room, where there were several ornately designed upholstered high-back chairs and a couple of lounge sofas. To his right a marble mantle crowned a fireplace that one could almost stand in, and to his left was a wall of windows. The drapes were all tied back. A ribbed, braided yellow rope tied them open, except for the one set that was closed.

"Where are you?" He didn't see her in the room.

"Out here." It sounded like it came from behind the heavy curtains.

Maddy was relaxing his reaction timing as he moved the curtains to the sides and walked through a paneled glass veranda door. He found himself on a patio with a phenomenal view of the main street. They were above the towering buildings below. A railing of giant stone spindles capped off with a flat stone top as wide as his arm was around the edge of the patio and curved along two sides of the exterior walls to allow a panoramic sight of the city.

"What is it?" he asked.

She took his hand and brought him to the railing. She placed her one hand on his lower back, and with the other, she lined up his eyes with her pointed finger, directing him toward the track-and-field area. "I can watch all the action from here if I want to." She was holding him closely as she spoke into his ear.

"Do you?" Maddy was going to turn this to his advantage if possible. If not, his legs were in ready-to-run mode. His question was to find out whether she was trying to get him to advertise for her or what exactly she might be planning.

"It depends on who is competing. I may have to go just to watch you this year." Her eyes presented an inquiring suggestion.

"I appreciate all you've done so far, Mary Ellen. Is there anything else I can do before I leave?"

"I love how you've been so accommodating to someone my age, and how you say my name. You are such a polite man." She intentionally suppressed any youthful adjective.

Without any thought, the words escaped his mouth with no intent other than to be complimentary. "You're not old!" She'd trapped him to say those words, and he never anticipated they would be misinterpreted.

"My! No! Thank you, Maddy." She took her prey, his arm in hers, back inside as they moved the drapes aside and reentered the parlor.

"Let me show you the rest of *my* palace." She had a locked elbow hold on his arm and drew him to the hallway, down to where the bedrooms and workout rooms were.

The legs halted and the heels dug in. "Maybe I could do that next time. I really need to get the harness loaded up and get back to the inn before the evening meal." He tried to untie himself from her grasp without showing fear. His assumption was correct about her advances so far. If what was happening was what he thought might be going to happen, he needed to escape right now.

"Could you give me a ride?" Her words suggested a double meaning. "There?"

She had succeeded for today. A seed was planted, and even though it was an insignificant seed of thought, it was enough. Mary Ellen was not unattractive. She was quite the opposite. She was in very good shape, and her beauty wasn't hidden beneath thick makeup. Most men would have been trapped by her web of seduction.

"Could you ride in the carriage? The harness will be on Heaster's back."

"That box will fit perfectly in the crate." She saw through his feeble attempt to sway her from sitting with him on the prime.

"I'll be securing the box until you change." Maddy knew he had lost this battle. He thought his best resolve was to continue to avoid her flirting.

"I won't be gone long," she replied.

The box did fit in the crate, as a hand fits to a glove. His last knot tied, she came dressed in a black silk shirt with

A CLOSER LOOK

buttons that was covered by a short leather jacket. The leggings were a deep emerald color that belled just over a pair of black knee-high boots. "I may not be going to the inn tonight. I'd like a tour along the main boulevard to check my options."

"That would be fine." Maddy felt stronger being with Heaster. "What other places have better food than the inn?"

"It's not always about better or worse. Sometimes different and untried is on the menu." The bait was being selected for her trap.

She did not need to hang on for support but wanted Maddy to feel her body next to his. Their float passed a number of established dining places, and Mary Ellen explained which ones were acceptable, where she'd been, and what was served. On the next street over was an old-world, old-style diner with an older crowd of patrons.

"Have you eaten?"

Maddy couldn't lie or even try to be deceitful. He was hungry. The aroma had a fragrance of a fiery, smoked meat. It was not discernible as to what kind of meat, but the platters he saw made his mouth begin to water. "No. But this looks expensive," he answered, knowing his fate.

"You never mind the price. This is fodder from an animal they ship here from Parnow. Wait until you taste this, Maddy. It'll become a frequent flight pattern."

"It won't take too long, will it?" He was succumbing to her bait. "I do need to get back to the inn."

"Most of what is on the menu just needs the sides on trays prepared. So it won't be long."

There was a small lot to the side where Maddy had his transport land. He felt obligated to escort her in, with a quick look back to give Heaster a wink. Next to the diner was a dry-goods store that Mary Ellen insisted on going to first. There were finely tailored shirts matched by jackets along most of one side of the front room. The opposite room was filled with rack after rack of colored leg covers.

"They do have a dress code there, so let me buy you an outfit to wear." Her offer was indicative. The last store-bought outfit he'd had was when he was a very young boy. Most of his clothing had been handmade from skins and cloth woven on looms by peddlers at swap meets. "Tailor-made" meant Mother or Father was the tailor. At times outgrown or used clothes could be traded or bought more cheaply. This made Palace City a melting pot of different customs and dress.

"I've never had a fancy outfit like this." Maddy relaxed, acting out a mother-son outing. She was almost old enough to be his mother.

With Mary Ellen's taste for clothing, Maddy got a little concerned that he might look silly. So he tried to find something more to his style. That just wouldn't happen in there. Everything was distinctive and high-end outerwear. His choice was made, and they waited a few minutes for a perfect sizing by a tailor to be completed.

Maddy changed into his garb and put his old clothes in a sack. He excused himself to run the bag to Heaster's baggage hooks.

"Don't we look frightful?" the steed remarked. "Who are you, anyway?"

A CLOSER LOOK

"She made me. She said if I don't wear this, we can't eat here." Maddy defended himself. "You want me to bring you anything?"

"I might just have to snack on some of these plants." He gestured at the flowers and potted arrangements in a landscaped garden between the lot and the building.

"Don't be obvious about it. You should leave them something." Maddy had a second to relax with his friend. "It isn't supposed to take long, so we should be back soon."

"Be careful, Maddy. She's hunting you."

"I just need you to help explain this to Trace. She knows she's 'old,' but she's still a woman."

"I'll be watching."

CHAPTER TEN

The Trap

Maddy got to the front check-in podium, where he found Mary Ellen getting a table for them. "We would like a table for two in a secluded booth, please."

"Right this way, ma'am, sir." The usher took them to an undersize corner table with a curved, cross-stitched leather booth. "Will this do?"

"This will be fine," she answered him.

There wasn't a way to sit across from her. The booth was deliberately made for two. As they took their seats, a waiter brought them each a glass for a beverage and asked what they would like. "We'd like a bottle of your best wine that will go with the evening's special meat being served."

"Yes, Ms. Moen." The waiter knew this customer from prior encounters. "The meat is from a young female drook, a breed raised in a valley beyond the Homer mountain ridge.

Very tender and having an exquisite taste. Might I suggest an Arbor wine?"

"That will be fine." She waved him away, turning to Maddy, who had his mouth partially open. "Hope you like this."

"Ms. Moen, this is too much. I am feeling inadequate to be here." Maddy began to feel her pressure again.

"It is Mary, Maddy. I am Mary Ellen. I used to come to this very table with my late husband every Friday night. Mitch loved their choice meats, so I hoped I haven't assumed you are a meat eater when you're not."

"No. I really like meat, but this is too much." He emphasized the "too much."

"Don't be silly, Maddy. I enjoy your company, and to have such a handsome escort is a bonus for me."

The waiter returned with the wine and poured a taste into Maddy's glass. He wasn't sure what to do, but with Mary Ellen's hint to taste it, he reluctantly did. Waiting for an answer, Maddy understood that he needed to respond. "Good?"

The waiter poured them each a glass and set the remainder of the bottle in a holder.

"Have you ever had wine before?" she asked, knowing what the answer would be.

"Not this way. My father had a bottle for Celemass once, before my mother was gone, and I tasted it then." Maddy felt more inexperienced as the evening progressed.

"Lift your glass with me, Maddy. Here's to winning." She toasted then took a drink.

THE TRAP

Maddy followed suit. The wine was smooth. It sparked his sweet taste buds, causing a warming effect as he swallowed. The taste of this wine wasn't what he'd remembered from the sip he'd taken with his father. The process that made it must have been much more involved to have the drink be so succulent. He wasn't aware of the effects it would cause because he'd never been under the influence of any significant amount of drink.

Mary Ellen continued to toast everything she could think of. Maddy was unaware of what this black widow was up to. By the time their meal arrived, Maddy's head had been affected.

The meat was all that it had been projected to be. It was tender enough to cut pieces off with his fork. It melted into his tongue with a force that caused him to savor what the drook had been fed. Juice from the white meat ran around inside his mouth, helping the minor chewing needed to swallow.

Mary Ellen was able to converse about a variety of subjects. She had many experiences and had traveled to several lands. As she talked, she encouraged Maddy to drink more of the bottle of mauve wine. His need had been met. He was filled, completely trying to proceed to the finish line of their time together.

"Are you ready, Mary Ellen?" he asked her, questioning why it hadn't seemed odd to call her that.

She motioned for the check and settled her account with the waiter. "Are you?" She was waiting to see how Maddy would react when he stood to his feet.

Clearly there was a lack of complete control of his body. "What was in that meat?" Maddy joked.

The seductress moved under Maddy's arm and laughed as they left the eatery, playing her partner off as her longtime eating mate. They got to Heaster, who had finished off more than was allotted to him because of the extra time Maddy was gone.

Mary Ellen didn't know about Maddy and Heaster's ability to converse. Heaster took advantage of that, knowing something wasn't right with Maddy. He stubbornly resisted taking any commands from her.

Maddy spoke to Heaster. "Let's get her home, boy." He would obey Maddy's command. Once on his back, they flew to her penthouse. The farther they went, the less Maddy spoke. At the landing, Mary Ellen helped Maddy off and took him into her apartment. Heaster still had the harness attached to the carriage and couldn't stop her.

Maddy's vision was blurred, and he didn't remember his surroundings when he awoke. He sat up in a bed. His clothing was out of place but still on him. The last image he could recall was the glass-paned door that led into the hallway of Mary Ellen's penthouse.

"Good morning, sleepyhead." Her voice crushed his heart in pain.

What had happened? "I have to go." He rolled out of the plush bedding, looking for his footwear at the side of the bed. He picked his shoes up and was rushing toward the bedroom door.

THE TRAP

"You might as well stay for breakfast. It's almost ready." She smiled.

"I've got to go—and now." Maddy still wasn't sure where he needed to go, but anywhere was good if it got him out of this situation. He chose the right way, going down the hall coming to the great room and then through the paneled door to the landing pad where Heaster was.

"I'm so sorry, Heaster. Get us out of here." He climbed on his back, putting his feet on one side and his head on the other.

The trip back to the inn was not far enough to clear his head and untangle the confusion of the previous night. He didn't and couldn't remember anything after that paneled door. Now he was about to face the firing squad of questions.

He took the time to unleash his ride, feed and water him, and brush him down. The whole time he was questioning himself. "What did I do?" Again and again the question came from his lips. He changed back into the clothes that were in the bag from the clothing store.

"Is this what shame feels like?" he thought, as he made his way to the kitchen and his first confrontation.

Marty was scooting around the heating irons, stirring and turning the foods that were cooking on them. " 'Morning, Table Stable!" he said, still in his consistently joyful manner.

" 'Morning," he answered.

"Not feeling good? You look a little tired around the eyes. Didn't get much sleep?" He was asking questions faster than Maddy could answer.

"Trace been down yet?" he asked.

"She's in the dining room, I believe." Marty was unaware of his overnight stay at Mary Ellen's.

"Thanks."

He walked into a commotion of order. Orders were being taken, and food was being delivered and eaten. Next week's activities, favored contestants, and their rides were the common subjects being discussed.

There she was—his beautiful, innocent Trace. He didn't see her any differently than he'd always felt about her, until it would be time to speak. Words would form, and then they'd disappear, as he couldn't explain what he didn't know. He could make excuses and then not know what they would be for.

There were definitive, never-again experiences that he did not know how to deal with or what to say about them.

Wine was done! That was a certainty. How people enjoyed feeling like this or why they'd want to possibly feel like this was beyond his understanding.

Emma walked by him at a quickened pace, saying, "The two end tables need clearing, and also I think there might be a couple who would like a ride to the main-street shops, based on what I heard them talk about."

The request got Maddy moving with some life. Then Trace saw him. Her one eye questioned what was going on as she raised her eyebrow.

As she came by him, he wanted to throw his arms around her and hold her, never to let her go. His patience won out. He would answer questions first before he'd try to explain the unexplainable.

THE TRAP

"Where were you last night?" The last question he wanted to hear was her first.

"Mary Ellen's." His chin sank downward toward his chest.

"The *old* one?" She made light of what she was hoping was nothing.

"Trace, I don't know where to start." Maddy wasn't holding back anything. His freedom depended on the truth being told. But he truly didn't know the whole truth. "Please wait until after the breakfast frenzy?"

That would have to do. They were extremely busy that morning. One pass of Henneh, the day moon, brought the rush to a slower pace of scattered customers.

The tables cleared and were prepared for the luncheon group. The lull of the midmorning provided Trace and Maddy with a moment alone.

Maddy thought their quarters would be the best place to explain what he did know, and when they got there, Trace noticed the new clothing on Maddy's bunk.

"What are these?" she asked as she took them and held them up as evidence.

"I'll get to that. Trace, I want to first say that I have been deceived. Mary Ellen took advantage of an innocent situation."

"Mary Ellen?" Trace wasn't sure she wanted to hear anything else. "It is just 'Mary Ellen' now?"

She started to leave when Maddy took her hand and said, "Ms. 'Old' Moen has to be the sneakiest woman on our planet. I haven't known anyone to be that way. Back home, truth was truth, and we both know that you don't consider a lie *ever*. I'd innocently gone there to pick up the gift she gave me. It all went downhill from there."

It wasn't about trust or truth. She wanted to know what had happened for him to stay the night there. She pierced deeply into his eyes and asked, "Did anything happen with her?"

"I don't know! Honest, Trace, I woke up in one of her bedrooms, and all I wanted to do was get back to you."

"You were in her bedroom and in her bed?" Her questions started to become increasingly agitated.

"Let me try this again." His head was still hazed from the night before. "She set a trap, and no matter how politely or soundly I tried to escape, she had all the exits locked."

"She locked you into her apartment?" Trace was beginning to shut her ears to what he was saying and only listen to what highlighted her assumptions.

"Trace, please, hear me out. After drinking that wine, I—"

"Maddy Handle, you need to stop! I think maybe we need to take a break. You're painting a pretty glum picture for me." She was leaving now, and Maddy wouldn't have a way to block her.

The tears in her eyes were too much for him as he saw her heart breaking. "Trace! Trace!" He followed her to the stairway, ready to grovel for another chance.

Her morning wasn't what she had ever hoped to have in her box of memories. She left Maddy standing at the top of the stairs and went out through the stables to go for a walk.

"Hey, boy." She stopped by Heaster and started petting his shoulder. Then she wrapped her arms around his neck and began to cry.

THE TRAP

"Whoa, Trace. What's going on?" The animal was comforting the person rather than the opposite. Heaster wasn't accustomed to crying but could feel her breaking heart against his neck.

Her voice broke between the words she spoke. "I never thought he'd do something like this to us."

"What did he do?" Faith in his companion wasn't going to be diminished by assumptions.

"He was with that old woman!" She increased her sobbing.

"It is true that he was with her, but we don't know how he was with her. When she helped Maddy into her apartment, he was barely able to stand, and if she hadn't been acting as a crutch, I don't think he could have. Maddy hasn't experienced drinking ever. I had to obey his command to take them to her penthouse to drop her off. Maddy had no intentions of staying with her. He really likes you, Trace. That I do know, and how the wine affected him was probably a very good thing. I believe he was victimized. Whatever happened wasn't his choice—of that I'm sure."

"What if he did do something?" Her trust was being built again, and hope was filling her heart.

"That woman—that old woman—wouldn't even be in Maddy's head if you trust him again." Heaster's words were making sense to her after her hearing about how influenced he was by the wine. Her thoughts changed toward Ms. Mary Ellen Moen.

She turned to see Maddy standing in the doorway of the stable. His "lost little boy" look covered his face and was showing every bit of an apology and regret for hurting her in any way. She ran to him, and they embraced. Maddy said repeatedly that this situation would never happen again. There, in the doorway of a stable, they gave each other their first kiss.

The emotions and trust were restored as their young lips pressed together. The connection was now unbreakable. They knew that nothing could have happened with that old woman. Their minds whirled with each other's thoughts. The link had coupled their chain together, and this chain would now withstand their expanse of life.

"Emma said there might be a couple that wanted a lift. Will you go with me if they do?"

"Right now I don't ever want to be away from you, Maddy. Yes, I would."

The couple that had eaten at the Dew Drop did want a ride, and with the weekend's busy shuttle service, Maddy had raised the entry cost. Trace gladly added her tips to his. They even had a bit left over to tuck away for another day.

The first day of the week began with a rigorous training cycle. Maddy and Trace worked for hours with Heaster, preparing him and Maddy for their challenges. There were several newcomers in their lives, as supporters attached and involved themselves, entertained by Maddy and his primordial.

The trio would give Marty and Emma help as they could, but Marty knew this was an imperative week for training.

The winding path of the outer forest and even the narrow exit of the overpass bridge couldn't defeat the accuracy of their flight. Speed was increased with sensitivity between ride and rider as the team became a fluid, moving unit. Their

THE TRAP

minds gelled in reactions to changing direction, with the unspoken commands becoming second nature.

The week blurred as the days blended together, bringing them to the day before the decathlon. This would be a day that reflected the practice and effort they'd put in.

Marty had been involved by establishing a diet plan for Heaster and Maddy. This night would be the last meal they shared together until the second day of the events. Marty said that to go in hungry was key advantage. A good night's sleep, and they would enter the gauntlet of the ten grueling challenges that lasted four days. The first day was to introduce the competitors and have a showing and parade, so that the audience could to see what kind of a competition it might be. The audience would make a few wagers on the side.

They pitted certain animals against others of similar size. This would help them get through the competitors more quickly, narrowing it down to the last few finalists. Quarterfinals and semifinals were held the first two days, with the final matches held on the fourth day. They would have victory awards along with the medals ceremony on the last evening. That kept more of people who came from farther distances to stay an additional night if they were to collect any awards and prize money they might win. Awards were given in the semifinals to those who would be third- and fourth-place finishers. Third place would be compensated with most of their entrance fee.

Scoring was done by percentages in each of the ten events. Longest, quickest, most accurate, and so on in each event would score a certain amount of points. The points were calculated to determine the finalists who ranked the highest in each of the ten events. They would go to the finals with a total of these points, which counted for one-third of their final score. The finalists would be determined there with the points they'd been given for performance and skill. Extra points were available in each event category for show. A memorable speed or lift done with flare or maneuvering could add points to a final tally.

Part of the fairness of the decathlon was that it would be new to all the competitors. No one would see the courses until they entered the arena during the parade of rides. The finals brought a changed course and different hurdles that would require even more skill than the semifinals.

Sleep had a way of evading newcomers to the challenges, with the adrenalin-fueled excitement going on over the upcoming performance and from being in front a huge crowd.

Maddy asked Trace to go for a walk with him, again, down to the wall of beauty. Hands interlocked they passed a numerous variety of art. One scene they'd missed on their earlier visit was of a couple standing by the wall, looking at a couple standing by the wall, looking at a couple standing by the wall, until it was small enough to be covered by a hand. In each depth, a tree with a heart shape carved into the trunk had a couple of engraved notches, suggesting that may they may have been the couple's initials. When Maddy looked closer, he saw that the notches changed in each deepening painting. The notches were those of a treman peg.

He wasn't expecting to go very far in the events with such little notice and practice. He said, "Trace, they look like us."

THE TRAP

They posed like the couple holding hands, with the woman having her head on the man's shoulder. They noticed they were standing by a tree that looked like the one in the wall.

A smile came to their faces when they added their image to the dimensional picture.

"You won't think any less of me if we are eliminated in the quarter- or semifinals, will you?" Maddy asked.

"Not now. My thoughts keep growing for you every day. So would I think less of you? Not possible."

Another kiss, and they continued their walk along the wall.

"I only want to know what you think about using the harness the 'old' one gave me. It's only for Heaster to wear, not to bring any attention to her at all. I just don't know if I should use it." Maddy wanted to rely on Brawn's old harness, but Mary Ellen's harness was brand new and still in the box.

"Have you even put it on Heaster?" she asked. "That would be the easy answer to that question."

"No. I haven't even tried it on him. Maybe it won't work for us. Keeping it simple would be less stressful." Maddy was thankful that Trace had suggested the fitting.

On their way back, they stopped once more at the multi-dimensional picture. On the wall above was a branch hanging down, its tip touching the heart etched into the tree of the picture. Maddy asked, "Did you see that there when we looked at this before?"

"No. I don't think so." Trace walked closer to the wall and was about to place her hand on the heart when Maddy experienced the flash in his head, like the one that showed him the same vision as the last one he had.

"Don't touch it!" He took Trace's hand again, and they left to go to the Dew Drop Inn.

"What happened?" She was confused because she hadn't felt anything when Maddy had.

"That same vision I had about the battle between the tremans flashed in my thoughts again." These visions were a part of Maddy that couldn't be shared.

"Why didn't I feel anything? Our connection is getting stronger, don't you think?" Trace had hoped to have that connection with her mate.

"One thing I do know, Trace, is that it doesn't feel right. So I'm glad you aren't sharing this. I don't want you to feel wrong ever."

The phrase they'd seen in the palace passed through his conscience again—"To go where no man has veered from to go where HE came from."

He'd passed it off with little attention as the night drew to a close.

The night moons, Cam and Harac, were chasing across the night sky when they walked back to the inn.

"I should try that harness on Heaster before morning. It could get hectic, trying to get him into it for the first time and get to the parade." Maddy was going to send Trace to their room and do the fitting himself.

"Trying to get rid of me, prince, to go on a maiden voyage without me?" Feeling like old times, Trace toyed with Maddy.

"Should we?" His tempting proposal wasn't hard to resist.

THE TRAP

"Get it a little bit broken in and have Heaster get used to it at the same time." There was common sense with what she was agreeing to. It would be a good idea.

They opened the box and arranged the straps and tack of the harness. In the darkened lighting, it seemed to glow, with its brilliant white leathers and shimmering silver catches, buckles, and hooks.

Maddy took an iron wedge that was next to the tool table, along with a short-handled sledgehammer, and placed the breastplate emblem on the anvil. He accurately put the sharp edge of the wedge at the center of the *M* and struck it with the hammer. Then he turned it a quarter turn and landed the hammer again.

"There. Now there is our logo." Maddy held the buckle up to Trace. It was a *T*. He had punched a *T* in the middle of the *M*. His thoughts went to the day when he'd thought how he'd be *MT*, empty, without her. "That was a silly thing I had go through my head, back in Dillon County, the day I was at the treman. I'd be empty without you."

Beneath the buckle's surface was an intricate mechanical device that Maddy was unaware was there. It was something Mary Ellen had her hand in when she had ordered the custom-made harness.

The new leathers were smooth against Heaster's coat. The hardness of never used, stiff leather wasn't an issue. The craftsmanship was revealed as they strapped and fastened the tacking on him.

"Take a big breath, boy." Maddy needed him to make any final adjustments that might hinder his breathing.

"Feels great, Maddy, but you two had better get on before I take that inhale." Heaster was feeling dressed to kill in his new gear.

The grips to aid mounting were amazing. The slight stretching of the harness creaked as they took position, making the sound of tightening leather being set. "Here we go."

"Take just an easy float, Heaster. Don't want you to get worn out for tomorrow."

The fit gave Heaster extra incentive. It brought encouragement and confidence to his future adventure.

Their evening flight took them high above the city. The lights and activity were acting together to bring a changed flow to the world below. The lamps and streetlights revealed the evening clothing was more outlandish, and the street venders had more of a flare to their advertising of goods.

They came closer to get more of a spectator's view as they circled the city, almost to the track-and-field arena, when they were aggressively confronted by the royal guard.

Drem led the confrontation on his ride. Josh's nose was aligned with Heaster's nose.

"Who goes there?" He commanded an answer.

Maddy responded with his and Trace's name, apologizing for whatever they had done wrong. "We were just out shaking off some of the anticipation of tomorrow. We meant no wrongdoing."

"No one is allowed to fly over the field. We who are in the competition aren't even allowed to go over the field. That's everyone you see here, Maddy Handle."

THE TRAP

The information Drem had let escape was dutifully noted. He now knew who some of the competitors were going to be. He also knew that Drem had done some investigating of his opponents or had heard about this newcomer and his ride, who were becoming well known around the city. He wasn't aware of who would be backing Drem. That would be revealed at the opening procession.

"We apologize again, sir, and we'll see you tomorrow." Maddy maintained his respect to the elder and steered his ride toward the inn.

Drem wasn't quite done with his intimidation and veered quickly in front of Maddy again. "We didn't say you were released. Did you forget—or are you too foolish to know—who we are? If you can rise faster than my lieutenant, then we'll let you leave."

Maddy now faced his first adversary. The intent was to belittle him. Maddy was not going to give way to that. He answered, "Doesn't the rulebook also say that anyone caught competing against any other participant will be disqualified?" Maddy had thankfully gone through the rulebook that he'd gotten when he'd registered to be in the decathlon. "That would make your lieutenant ineligible to compete."

His response was heard by the lieutenant, who was still awaiting Drem's orders. He could still order him to do his bidding, which would mean two challengers were out of his way.

"You just go home, boy." Drem added to his intimidation tactics.

"Yes, sir." Maddy was displaying amazing control of his temptation to show what Heaster could do and also show Drem he wasn't afraid of him.

They were released, and Trace pulled herself into his back. "You earned your last name, Maddy Handle. You handled that like a man I've been dreaming would be in my future."

All Maddy's pride was put back in check as his love returned into play.

Their float took them slowly and quietly back to the inn on a silent drift. Any time spent together now was deepening their connection to each other. Thoughts began to entwine about experiences and high points they'd shared. Maddy placed his hand on her hands, which were clinched in an arm lock around his waist.

"Is this what eternity could be like?" Trace asked her chosen guide.

She squeezed even tighter when the answer of "I hope so" passed her sense of hearing.

Heaster landed in the stable yard, where Maddy undid his bindings. "How'd it feel, boy? Any irritations or rub spots that hurt you?"

"None. The makers of this gear really knew what they were doing."

"Get some rest, Heaster. I think it'll be quite an intense day ahead of us." Maddy stroked his friend's neck. Then, with a tap on his side, he said, "Good night."

"I'm a little nervous about some of the events. The joust is the main one. I don't want you getting hurt."

THE TRAP

"You either. We will do fine." Maddy couldn't have fooled his companion, yet he had the same concerns he'd expressed. "You just get some rest."

CHAPTER ELEVEN

The Decathlon Parade

The day broke with a brilliant light that would be bright and warm.

As the bells chimed across the city, Maddy looked at the motionless bell on the wall, expecting that to be the sound to wake him from his slumber. The ringing from the town's square bell tower proclaimed a day of celebration. Jumping to the rug, he hoped he hadn't overslept.

Maddy used the crate, now without chairs, to bring his extra tack, armor, and a bushel barrel full of feed for Heaster. Other things Marty had recommended for emergency fixes were packed also. The harness had attached brackets and loops of chromed silver for tying down bundles and hanging his equipment from. There was a removable attachment that was adjustable for mounting many styles of bows, and a quiver rack for holding arrows.

It was time to get to the track, courses, and the obstacle arena.

Temporary stables for contestants were erected outside and to the right of the main coliseum.

Registrar officials were getting all the contestants and their rides a neck tag that had their names and their own special admission numbers. They checked to ensure the safety devises and that the minimum required equipment needed for each of the different events was present. The limit for what the gear could be was only minimally restricted. Having extras, such as thicker straps, was fine. In past events weak harnesses had caused deaths because they could break or malfunction and send their weights dropping onto officials or spectators below.

The lineup for the parade was being set in order according to the numbers and divisions of contestants. The heavyweight group was the last to show. As they had established that Heaster was a prime, although a young one, Maddy would be in that weight class. The march of contestants would begin exactly between dawn and high noon. The ninth hour came. Vying for position amid these heavy hitters, Maddy was thankful there was a numbering system. He had been assigned the number twelve.

As he walked Heaster along the line, he counted the labeled flags. "Ten, eleven—this is it, Heaster." It was the last numbered position.

"Wow! The lad can count." A man in ninth position was throwing an intimidation tactic at this first-timer. He was leading a wide prime whose legs were set out farther than

THE DECATHLON PARADE

Heaster's. A shade darker let Maddy know that this prime was close to twenty. The hairy fur along his mouth was long. He had been groomed with off-red, colored beads that were fastened with spacers to his whiskers. The prime was not unraveled by his rider's comment. He just continued to chew on a wad of cud in his jaws.

Drem was in the first ranking position. He was not wearing his guard uniform but attire that bore a family crest on his chest and one on the side of his right leg. His ride, Josh, was in a stance of attention. He was upright, with his neck stretched, having a finely painted spiral that ringed from a dot under his head down his entire neckline. The dot had the same crest as the emblem on Drem's breastplate. As the line would reveal, the obvious rides had been put in order of size and age.

Maddy had put on Marty's armor and was having a hard time keeping it from rolling off his shoulders. It was heavier than he'd thought it would be, now that he had to actually walk around in it. The leggings kept sliding down his thinner legs. Marty was stockier when he had competed. The armor was fitted for him. He knew this was going to be an additional battle between the armor and his body as he fought just to keep it in place.

The other teams were readied, and the riders walked to the right of their rides. A helmet was put on each harness horn and faced to the front with the lids closed. Many of the others carried a whip or thronging lash in their hands, so they did not hold their steed's bridles. Maddy had never whipped Heaster and quietly whispered to him, "What should I carry in my right hand?"

"Trace put a cloth napkin from the Dew Drop in your satchel. It has their banner on it. Wave that for Marty and Emma."

He pulled the leather string that cinched the top shut and stretched it open. It was a purple napkin with "DDINN" in the center. There was an embroidered "MT" with blue and green thread, with the *M* in blue and the *T* in green—their favorite colors on their melded color purple. Trace had done the embroidery during any breaks from her day's work and any free time in the evenings. It was beautifully scrolled on the tips of the letters and was large enough to see from a distance.

After looking at the art in his hands, Maddy took an arrow out of the quiver and poked it through one corner and out the top corner to make it a flag.

"How's that, boy?" A smile was forming, when the same voice of intimidation sounded.

"Surrendering already? Boy?" It was the intimidator on the huge ride.

"What does that mean? I've never heard that word before." Unbridled, the words flew out of Maddy's mouth.

"You will."

He had a naive appearance and unfitted armor but brushed his challenge aside. These men had been tested and were far from novices. At their level, this kid offered no threat to challenging their objectives.

The stadium had elevated rows of seating that encompassed the majority of where the events would take place. A few luxury-seating rows were placed in the best vantage

THE DECATHLON PARADE

points, so those patrons had a close vantage point to watch the events.

Their walk of display had begun. By the time Maddy entered the stadium's oval racetrack, the audience was cheering at peak levels. The enthusiasm built as the better-known and stronger challengers paraded around the track last. All the contenders had a chance to win the entire purse and top awards, but the chances were slim. The only reason they had placed Maddy in this heavy group was simply because Heaster was a prime. There were other brute hauling beasts that could carry tremendous loads but were missing the speed needed for the races. There also were smaller and very fast rides that had no lift strength.

Nothing had prepared Maddy for this experience. The crowd was cheering, and the rush filled his being. He turned his head, and the crowd's faces blurred because of the massive amount of people.

The uplifting cries and shouting relaxed him into what he was there for. The makeshift flag lifted into the air, and he waved it in full overhead circles. People he'd never met seemed to cheer even louder. As he came around the final curve, a distinctive voice pointed his eyes into the throng, and his ears waited for another clue as to where it was coming from.

"Maddy Handle! Maddy Handle!" He homed in on her. There was Trace, standing by Jed and Jilly, along with Carl, who was standing behind them. They were waving their arms and cheering along with the rest of the spectators.

It took more than an hour for all the groups to bear their colors and emblems. As they left the track, Maddy stopped short of stepping off, did an about-face, leaped onto Heaster, and floated in a tight, fast circle three times as he left, exciting the stadium. He caught up to the tail of the parade as the huge doors were closing behind them. The cheers escalated even through the doors, as Maddy's showboating had injected them with a last dose of applause.

Canvas tarps were hung from the partitions of each pen to separate the animals and keep any aggressive ones more passive. Maddy led Heaster into the pen and took his harness and gear off and hung it all up. Then he brushed him down. "I think we may have a few fans in the audience besides Trace, the Ropels, and Carl." Heaster had sensed an extra exuberance from the crowd with their exit display also.

"Did all that fanfare give you any extra strength?" Maddy was searching for unity.

"It did get harder to keep my feet to the ground, if that's what you are asking." Heaster was a pretty secluded country prime; this zealous crowd was an unknown to him.

His excitement had been in the joy he felt when Maddy came to the barn for their daily visits. This concentration of others having the joy could prove to be resourceful to him.

"You almost lost me with that triple when we left the track. This armor either has to be gone or adjusted somehow. I can't be falling off, doing our victory lap." Maddy laughed to his pal.

Drem walked by just as Maddy had spoken the words about the victory lap. He'd found out about the maneuver and how they had done their circles. "That move could have gotten you disqualified. No victory there. If you are penalized, victory is gone. They just send you home."

His tone couldn't be interpreted. Was he being helpful or threatening? "Is there anything else you want to help me with?" Maddy questioning the intention Drem was offering from the actions in his previous encounters. His asking for his help was his way of finding something out about this upright soldier man.

"Watching is a great way to get experience." His answer wasn't one that told Maddy where he stood. "See you in the ring."

"Thanks?" Maddy was confused.

Shortly after Drem had left, other visitors made an entrance. These two were a sight that didn't make things any clearer; Mary Ellen was being escorted by Tren Taylor.

Maddy put all he had in his arsenal in a defensive display. With this wave of assault Mary Ellen and Tren were showing that they were connected and had agreed on an arrangement.

"I see you chose to use the gift I gave you." Her investigation skills hadn't missed the play in this attempt to share the limelight, if there were to be one.

Tren had his own agenda of words. "Still going to dream that lumpy bag of animal is worth a hundred shekels? I'd offer you double what I did before, just to see him pull some plow around."

Words were forming in his mind, and his gander was piqued against Tren. The words filled his mouth, as he opened it to speak, but Trace spoke. "You have guests, Maddy? Stopping by to congratulate the winner, Mary Ellen?"

Not being easily put in her place, she replied with a touch of insult directed at Trace. "Just stopped to thank Maddy for wearing the harness I gave him. It would be such a shame to waste such an expensive gift."

Trace walked next to Maddy, tending to the straps that adjusted the armor as she tried to make a better fit. She was the one with the prize but knew Mary Ellen's wit had scored the point. Her thought was, "Cunning, maybe, but that's because you're so old."

"We could have fitted you with custom armor, Maddy." She broadcasted her wealth.

"You've done too much already, ma'am. I wouldn't want to overstep my bounds or requests."

The mousy, sneered voice of Tren pitched in. "You've already overstepped by entering this manly event. The only thing giving you any hope is that harness. They may give you a best-dressed ride award. It's about the only thing that could get that ugly windbag noticed."

Heaster wasn't going to take any more from Tren. His flat foot lifted then landed with what appear to be an accident, catching the edge of his water trough and hurling a bucketful of water onto Tren. His curled-up mustache hung again, dripping with water, to the sides of his mouth.

He raised his walking stick but lowered it quickly when Heaster caught his premeditated move. For an animal of Heaster's size to float at all was amazing, not to mention the damage his legs could do if he were to put any aggressive force into it.

THE DECATHLON PARADE

"Can we leave now, Mary Ellen?" He was showing a more feminine side than Maddy remembered in the square. "I must change before the first event this afternoon."

"Are Marty and Emma tending to their impoverished inn? It is so sad that they've invested so much time and effort and cannot be here to watch." Her parasol landed on her shoulder as she picked her way around the wet puddles of water and straw. "I'll be watching, Maddy. Let me know about the armor."

She avoided saying Trace's name intentionally, but Maddy had caught the "watching" word. And so he did as Drem had advised, by watching for experience. He'd be watching her closely. There was an oddity about her demeanor. Part of it was encouraging, but the other sensation was threatening.

"What was that all about?" Trace asked.

"Intimidation, maybe, or could have been jealousy, but atta boy, Heast. You put out half the duo's fire." He patted his companion and took Trace's hand. "So to what do I owe the honor of your presence, my lady?"

"I noticed your armor not being customized almost threw you off in your revelry, leg breaking, and curtain bow. Can we see if it will fit any better by adjusting your linkage?"

"It is just not made for me. Marty means well, but this armor would need a metalsmith to make it fit me."

They tried a few different minor tweaks and pulls, but to no benefit. It was awkward around the middle. When Maddy would turn his torso, the chest piece wouldn't turn with him. His arms made it move back and forth. With a lance in his hand, he wouldn't be able to both direct the javelin and avoid a blow to his shoulder. That event was later on in the decathlon anyway, so Maddy put it down for now.

"I see you found my kerchief?" She took the arrow with the skewed napkin on it.

"Thank you, Trace. I love it."

"Is that all?" Her inquisitive question brought a smile to his face again.

He knew her question was aimed to ask why he hadn't spoken those "I love you" words. "I love that you gave it to me, and not the old one."

Now her face lit up with a smile. "Surely, knight, there must be a love in your heart for a younger woman."

Maddy was growing ever closer to Trace. She in turn was deepening her feelings for him. The words were the audible confirmation of those feelings.

Carl came around the curtain. "Does that armor need some alteration?" He also had noticed what most of the audience had noticed about the armor.

"We just got done trying," Maddy offered.

"Let me see it." He took the chest armor into his arms and squeezed it. It was like a bear hug you may want to avoid if you valued your ribs. "Maybe we should put it on you to fit it?" He stopped momentarily to ease the tension that Maddy faced.

"I don't know if I'd want to wear it permanently." His face scrunched with the second attempt to constrict the armor.

"Here, try it now." This burly man looked like he could lift Heaster without his float reaction being used. He handed Maddy the chest portion.

THE DECATHLON PARADE

The section that he'd compressed brought the abdomen area closer to his skin, making the upper plating move with his waist. At the very least, now Maddy had some control of it.

"Thank you, Carl. It fits fine." Maddy's use of Carl's last name was fitting. He was a fine man.

"The lifters begin their competition brackets tomorrow. We won't be lifting what these boys will be, but if you want to see some strong people compete, we'll be there in the morning." He gave Heaster a couple thumps on his side. "Sounds empty, or are they hunger holes?"

"We'll feed him a bit in the morning for the energizer, but Marty advised that hungry steeds can lift more, and it doesn't slow their speed. That's our first meet. It's the speed race, where we will be racing from one point to the other. Then the second is the ten-lap speed race. We might have time to fit in watching you lifters."

"I'm heading back to the stands. These opening day ceremonies are pretty festive."

"Will you be staying here all four days?" Trace had mixed emotions about being there or alone back at the inn. The Dew Drop Inn would certainly be busy for the next three days. Tonight there would be a lights and fireworks display that Trace was hoping to attend with Maddy.

"You could stay here tonight, and I will give you a ride back to the inn after we compete. You can have the bunk they provided for us, and I'll lay with Heaster over there. Marty might close down for a few hours over the weekend, so he can come to the events too."

"You could come pick me up in the morning. I want you to get a good night's sleep so you'll be well rested for tomorrow, along with Heaster."

"You'll be OK here while Trace and I go to the festival of lights, won't you, Heaster?"

"I will if you give me a small handful of those sprouts for something to do."

"Make them last. Remember, hunger will be our friend in the race."

"You two have fun." He took the sprouts from Maddy.

The young couple made their way to the designated seating area for contestants and their crews. There were groups of three or four that helped each challenger get their riders and their rides ready.

"Maybe I should be here to help you get things ready?" Trace had made her choice as to whether she would stay at the coliseum or go back to the inn. They had fulfilled their obligations to Emma and Marty, so to help them with the busy times was a service for their new friends.

"I'll still take you back after the day is done." Maddy didn't need to have Trace stay in a makeshift bedroom stall intended for contestants. "But if you're willing to help us, that sounds great."

The shooting cylinders of lights spanned and crossed in the sky. The performers, acrobats, and the dancers moved around a center stage that had been set after the opening parade. Costumes with flashing reflectors of light drew attention. Cheers were echoing around the oval mass of spectators as they danced and showed that all their practice had paid off.

THE DECATHLON PARADE

The feats of landing and tumbling after leaping through the air and tossing each other from one to another with an additional flip in between was awe-inspiring for everyone. These two from halfway around the globe were amazed with all the activity they could fill their eyes with because these were things they'd never seen and things they may never see again.

The last few acts, with the fizzling light display, tapered off. The master of ceremonies announced the next day's opening events. An invitation was given to enjoy the sights, the patrons' different shops, and eating establishments around the city for those who had partially sponsored the competition. Booths set up just outside the arena were all open. Banners with the locations of goods and services were hung around the arena city. This had become the heart of Palace City for the next few days.

The palace stood in the background of the coliseum, the lights placed so that it showed a glowing marvel that was the heartbeat of the whole area. For now it would be in the shadow, but after the decathlon, it would become the chief reason the city existed, drawing people from everywhere on their earth, all days of the calendar year.

Maddy walked Trace back to get Heaster for the ride back to Marty and Emma's. As he held her hand tightly as the crowd funneled out, their shoulders bumped others as they were channeled through the entrances. When they arrived at the stalls, Heaster greeted them. "Evening endeavor?"

"We'll get Trace back to the inn and have to plan an early rising to get her back here first thing in the morning. Is that all right with you?"

"This stall is nice for a while, but any chance we can get out of it is better." Being penned after all this commotion and excitement of carrying passengers and practicing out in the forest had made Heaster used to the attention from Maddy.

"We'll be back just before first light, Trace, so not too much beauty sleep tonight. Each day you get more beautiful, and soon you may run out of ability to get any prettier." He set down, helping her off. "I will see you in the morning then, my lady?"

"Only if I don't get enough sleep. I wouldn't want you to be distracted tomorrow by all my beauty." Trace smiled at her attendant, Maddy, who was attending to her beck and call.

"Maybe you should get up earlier than you'd like. I never thought about how distracting you are for me."

With four small steps and a hop, Heaster and Maddy flew back to the arena.

CHAPTER TWELVE

Decathlon Day Two

The contestants' accommodations were assigned to ensure that each one was treated equally. If they needed to be contacted with event times or changes to their schedules, officials knew where they should be.

Shop owners' noise and the sounds of the other competitors getting things ready for the day's events woke Maddy from his short night's sleep. He had passed the night's hours by looking out at the night sky and had watched the moons crossing the horizon for most of the night. Then adrenalin and excitement had caused him to toss and turn. His mental preflight and reaction preparations kept running through his mind.

Times were posted for each event's categories and were placed by the entrances to the arena, the stables, staging areas, and on various vendors' stands. For the decathlon to flow smoothly, latecomers to the challenges would be ineligible. Being early to each event ensured that contestants' times and points would be counted and would allow time for them to reach their assigned positions.

Streetlights were still the main way to see as the sun was still hiding below the edge of the earth. Klue had just risen ahead of Henneh, and his brilliant white shine powered a touch of extra light as Henneh's soft pink poked the rim of her forehead behind him. Daylight would come quickly. Maddy took a quick survey of his events and the times they would be held from a schedule posted under the entrance lights. He'd have time to get Trace and get back before they began.

He threw a simple bridle on Heaster then hopped to his back. "Be careful not to overexert yourself; you'll want to reserve your strength for the first two races. Let's just do a warm-up float."

Maddy noticed one thing about Heaster's demeanor—as he grew into this prime age, he was able to control his talent better. Like a balloon gently rising into the air on a slight breeze, Heaster's motion was fluid, even as he changed direction.

His smiling princess was waiting for her knight in shining armor to make his entrance when Maddy appeared. When she saw him in his everyday clothes, bare back and all, her smile widened.

She watched Maddy, whom she hoped was her future, sitting on his steed and coming to whisk her away to Neverland—or to a land that never ended. He reached out his hand, and she used it to find her seat behind Maddy.

"It's a great day for victory, wouldn't you say, love?" Her daydreaming slipped from her lips. Their love was so fresh; hearing it spoken was still surprising.

DECATHLON DAY TWO

Maddy caught the "love" word between the frontlets. Feeling the same he wiped his eyes and said, "You must have gotten a ton of sleep, as beautiful as you are this morning."

Their days together were just beginning, and in a perfect way.

The arena was buzzing with activity when Trace and Maddy got back. The first event was being readied to begin. This competition had a dual scoring system. The fastest of each heat of six riders to get from the starting line to the finish line would receive a point, and the fastest time would receive two points.

This meant there were three points possible to be scored in this first competition. Maddy's heat was scheduled to follow the first race.

Drem was already in position, standing next to his prime and wiping down his neck and shoulders. The prime's sweat was enough to slick his fur smooth. When it was time, the other five racers positioned themselves according to their numbers. Drem mounted his ride and moved to the line beside them. A shot rang out to indicate the race's start, which caused a blur of movement heading for the finish tape. The shot had startled Heaster, causing him to jolt in reverse. As quickly as the race had begun, it was finished, and Drem broke the finish line's ribbon. Onlookers stood, cheering. Drem was one of the favorites of the city and was well known throughout it for his past performances and wins. In this event he had beaten the closest finisher by at least three lengths. He and his ride made a victory lap around the oval track, waving to the fans.

Within moments the next group had taken their places. Maddy was in the fourth lane. During the race from point A to point B a racer could not have any contact with any other racer. Touching another racer or ride would disqualify a contestant. Next to Maddy was a brute of a beast. The steed took up the full width of his own lane and some of the next one too. As they got to the starting line, Maddy spoke softly in Heaster's ear. "We need to get out of the blocks before this mammoth does, or we might touch him."

The announcers called for the contestants to be ready; the crowd fell silent; and the starting shot rang out again. This time Heaster was ready and didn't rear up; instead his stub tail set the team in motion. Maddy hadn't felt Heaster's power like that before the competition. The finish line's ribbon soon wrapped around Heaster's chest, and the audience was on its feet again, screaming with delight. A victory lap wasn't mandatory, but Maddy wouldn't have stopped Heaster from taking one even if he could have. To see the crowd cheering for them, these two young hicks from the other side of the world, would live in his memory forever.

When the first competition was over, the final results revealed Maddy at the top of the leader board for overall speed. Back at the inner corral, Drem sat down next to Maddy and said, "See anything, kid?" His face, still expressionless, wasn't telling Maddy the intention of his words.

"I saw us both win our heats," Maddy answered.

"The real victory comes when your name is at the top after all ten events. This is just where the games begin."

"Any more advice you have for me?" Maddy asked.

DECATHLON DAY TWO

"The ten laps aren't just about speed. There will be skirmishes for the winner's circle there."

"Um, thanks?" Maddy said, still not sure if the conversation was a challenge or simply friendly counsel.

Drem walked his prime out to the stable area. He'd noted Maddy and Heaster's speed and had experience knowing that even though the speed events made points, it could also make the winner haughty minded enough to relax and become careless.

Trace arrived after Drem left. She jumped over the fence to hug Maddy's neck. "To the victor the prize," she said.

"Isn't it 'To the victor the spoils'?" Maddy asked. He only wanted to keep the phrase in perspective.

"Are you saying I'm spoiled?" Trace asked, throwing him a mischievous look.

"Sweetly ripening," Maddy told her, as he covered his tail.

"I believe Carl's going to be lifting soon. Should we make our way over there and watch him?" she asked. Trace was restless and hyper because of Maddy's victory.

"Sure. Let's go. We don't do our ten laps until later. They want to kick off the decathlon with excitement and rouse the audience to stick around all day. Of course, for me, this day couldn't be boring." Maddy led Heaster to the other side of the corral, and they climbed up to the top rail to watch as these huge men attempted to lift far more than their own weight.

The heat of the sun was now taking the cool morning and patting its bottom away toward the next morning's start. The air was being warmed with the midday sunshine and by the body heat and exhalations created by the spectators.

This event was the stone lift. Carl stepped up to the mat and moved each stone from one pedestal to the next. The stones became increasingly heavier with each of the ten stones moved. Carl's earlier comment that the weight wouldn't be what the rides would lift now made Maddy wonder whether he and Heaster had been practicing with too little weight. These stones looked seriously heavy. Finally Carl had lifted them all. As the last stone landed on its stand, Maddy and Trace exploded with cheers for their friend. Carl nodded then headed off the mat.

The event's second round required the contestants to pull ropes attached to massive weight with the same scaling method they would use for the dead lift for the primes. The rope was attached to a scale to measure the contestants' pulling strength.

There were also two throwing events. Competitors were required to quickly throw sacks over a wall, and the second throw was to heave a round beam, attempting to land it on the higher of two adjacent pegs.

The final round was a dead lift. Contestants would hold a bar with chains attached to both ends. The chains linked through the mat and were connected to a scale that measured the maximum weight they could hold. The harder the lifters pulled, the more weight mediators added until the lifter had to let go.

The highest load scored the most points.

This would be Carl's event. He hadn't placed first in all the categories, but this round would be his moment to shine. Since he wasn't in first place overall, he had to lift more than anyone else close to his weight in order to win. Taking his stance he slowly bent down and wrapped his rosined fists around the bar's grip. Standing, he curved backward and lifted the bar higher and higher. The bar stopped at the peak height of his lift.

His fingers cinched more and more tightly around the bar that he'd lifted easily at first but now was becoming a torrent of excess burden. Pound after added pound then pulled the bar downward, and Carl had to strain to keep the bar in the lifted position. His muscles surged with energy, and he fought for every bit of holding power he had in his hands. His eyes closed while these flashing segments of time seemed to slow as he gave one final push of strength.

The people knew that the extra time meant more weight was being added to Carl's lift and began to murmur in low whispers that soon became clapping then increased to all-out cheering as he held on.

Carl strained, waiting for every second to pass. He'd blown the previous record away and was still holding fast. A couple of breaths of time, and the bar popped out of his hands.

He'd won. Maddy smiled, thinking maybe this year's winning circle would not be all local talent after all.

Maddy and Trace met Carl as he came down the steps and wrapped their arms around him with congratulations. His massive muscles were still pumped rock hard as the sweat began to ooze out of his body. They had known he was a big man, but they hadn't felt his strength this closely before.

"Why did you close your eyes, Carl?" Trace asked.

"I thought of the heart of the Treman and felt the strength he must have needed," Carl told her.

Their eyes locked, sharing a connection to the Treman that held another story for them in Carl's land. What he had to tell them might put an additional piece in the picture of the Treman puzzle.

When they got to the fence, Heaster asked for water. They took him to the stable and gave him a half bucket full. He downed it quickly and lifted his head. "More?" he asked.

"Pack animals and fawns drink a lot, but we're going to be doing the ten-lap race soon, and I don't want you too full of water. After the race you can drink yourself full, OK?"

Maddy handed him a few char sprouts and wiped his dripping face.

Many of the other categories were dwindling down during the first day of the events. Animals were being disqualified or losing their individual races, and several of the smaller rides simply didn't have what it took to get to the finals. Even so, the brackets gave the smaller rides hope to get to the final challenges at the very least. A steed's size wasn't an absolute guarantee that his name would be at the top of the placement list. Agility and charisma that may dazzle the crowd just enough to obtain those tiebreaking points were also factors to consider.

The afternoon's multilap event was getting organized. After Trace and Maddy had eaten some food from some of the vendors, they prepped Heaster for the race. Maddy noticed that Drem had wiped down his ride, making his fur sleeker, which would create less wind resistance. Marty had also suggested that getting into a wake of broken air would help save Heaster's energy for the last burst of power in the final lap and

DECATHLON DAY TWO

the home stretch. Maddy was racing against the eleven other competitors in his category. There wouldn't be anything for him to watch and learn. This would be an on-the-job training lesson. He'd timed Heaster doing ten laps in practice, but this race was against experienced riders who knew what to expect.

They had received their starting positions based on how they had finished their opening races. The six track lanes would be two riders deep. Those who had placed first, second, and third in the two short-distance heats were positioned in the front. The second row of six contained the remaining riders.

This meant Maddy was in the first inside lane with Drem next to him in the second track.

The announcers ordered them to be ready, and then the starting shot was fired. As if they were sent as a bullet out of the end of the starter pistol, Maddy and Drem surged ahead then were neck and neck. The inside track gave Maddy an advantage going into the initial curve, and he held the lead. Drem backed off just enough to fall into Heaster's air wake and ride it, just as Marty had suggested to Maddy.

Maddy let the reins out and nudged Heaster to change his speed into a jerking motion so that Drem couldn't take full advantage of Heaster's cutting through the air in the lead position. Suddenly a challenger made his way from the second row to the front as they came into the straightaway, cutting in front of both Drem and Maddy.

Five, six, and seven laps pressed the pack into a tighter group, which caused them to bump and jar together for each position. Only a couple of the racers had dropped back out of the main pack. The huge beast that was next to Maddy in his first race was lagging behind, along with a smaller prime and rider. The eighth lap started to take its toll on the lead rider, but as he slowed, he blocked Maddy's path. Drem was to his right, pinning him in and blocking Maddy's window of possibility to get around the leader. So far Drem had been honorable and avoided bumping and jarring into Maddy. But now that the ninth lap was almost complete, Maddy couldn't get out. As the tenth and final lap was flagged to begin, Drem made his move. Maddy watched as he touched his palms to his ride's neck and bolted past the lead rider. Maddy did likewise, touching Heaster's neck on the left side, and they swung around the right side of the lead team. He put both hands against the prime's neck. Maddy was catching Drem and leaving the group behind. Drem was still in the lead on the final curve before the home stretch and still held the lead by a prime's length.

"Got any more, boy?" Maddy asked Heaster, as he hoped to give him a final rush of power to catch Drem before the finish line. Drem's ride touched the ribbon first as they crossed the line. Heaster felt the broken ribbon touch his chest and punched upward, circling in a backspin and taking the ribbon into the air, then let it float down as the other riders blasted through it.

The applause was deafening. Heaster hadn't won, but his flare was the kick that might add a bonus point.

DECATHLON DAY TWO

Drem moved into an even position with Maddy, clapping his hands lightly, not to truly edify him but to give Maddy the credit due for their trick.

The name "Maddy Handle" was still in first place, with Drem in a close second.

A few smaller races were scheduled after the main ten-lap event to settle the audience again and control the crowd's rush to the exits.

Maddy waited as Trace made her way to the center circle where he was. The day was spent, and the excitement of the day would allow a better chance for a good night's sleep.

"Great job at the last flip, Maddy," she said. She'd been impressed by her adolescent team.

"That was all Heaster. It was all I could do just to keep my stomach from being tied in a knot. Must have been that prime in you, huh, boy?"

"Nice touch back at you, Maddy, for the neck connection. Never had that connect us before," Heaster replied.

"That was all Drem. He told me to keep my eyes open. When he did that to his prime, I thought maybe there was something there. Guess it worked."

Maddy then turned to Trace. "Thanks for the compliment. Are you ready for a nice meal back at the Dew Drop?"

"Sure am." This time both Heaster and Trace chimed in together.

"You two had better be careful; you might meld your minds together. It wouldn't hurt if you had to work together in one of these events, but I don't know how all three of us would know who was thinking what and to who," Maddy said and laughed as he finished.

The threesome flew back to the inn in time to order an evening meal. They were still trying to control their enthusiasm from the day's event.

"Marty, Emma, we're in first place," Maddy explained. He still couldn't completely contain himself with the news. "Thanks for the suggestion to be in this thing—it's an amazing experience."

They told them story after story about the day's occurrences.

"I wish you could have seen Carl…" Maddy looked up in surprise as Carl walked into the front hall, just after he had spoken his name.

"Too late to get a few orders of grub?" His growling voice gave the reason for the question. "Must have been the ideal food you serve here that helped me win the lifting event today. I saved my appetite for you."

"Having two winners at our hostelry sounds like a celebration to me," Marty said, whipping his towel over his shoulder and heading to the kitchen.

"I'll get the candlesticks out too," Emma said. She went to the bottom doors of the china cabinet and pulled out two beautiful holders. "These were my mother's. She got them from her grandmother. We'll light some wicks and eat together. Marty and I had a very busy day too—one of our busiest ever."

DECATHLON DAY TWO

Jed and Jilly came in carrying their turtle cage; their demeanor was unreadable. They were hiding something, but a flash of the ribbon on the cage's corner offered an explanation for their coming exuberance. "Nippy took first place in running the course in the turtle race!" Jilly exclaimed. They'd been trying to keep their joy hidden. "This will do wonders for our business."

As they were sharing their story, Marty came from the kitchen carrying a huge platter of food on a trolley cart. "Looks like I missed something. Do we have three celebrities in our midst? Hope I made enough food for the party." His expression of giving revealed why his small business was doing so well. "Let's eat."

Emma lit the candles and placed them on the tables they had moved to share the meal together. Had the food not been filling their mouths, there would've been even more conversation than there already was.

After the meal their many hands made light cleanup. The last few dishes were stacked together, and the tables were re-set with the placements for the next day's settings. Marty and Emma continued their food prep after the rest of the crew had gone to their respective rooms.

Maddy walked Trace to their bungalow, thanking her for being there to share this adventure with him.

In unison they said, "Would we have done any of this if we weren't here together?" Trying to stop their embrace would have taken bindings tied to pillars. They hugged each other tightly, sharing a brief moment of closeness.

"May I kiss you good night?" Maddy asked, hoping he wasn't stretching his boundaries too far.

"You truly are a prince, aren't you? Unless, of course, you are really a knight in oversize armor, either description is fitting, so the answer is yes," Trace said.

Maddy could have floated Heaster back to the arena after kissing Trace's lips. If there had been clouds, the "cloud nine" expression would have been understandable.

Heaster had filled his belly with food, and Maddy allowed him to drink water until he was full. The team was filled to the top of their throats with an eventful day. Relaxation would be sweet this night, a needed rest for the following day's schedule of events.

CHAPTER THIRTEEN

Decathlon Day Three

The lack of familiarity with the decathlon was a swirl so hectic that missing one's start times was a possibility. Having only two days to fit in all the required classes, challenges, and finals would prove to be a rigorous schedule, even for the seasoned veterans to keep.

Day broke with a horn blast. Maddy's eyes blinked into focus, and he knew by the light in the sky that he'd have to hustle to get Trace, which put added pressure on him. Untying Heaster, grabbing the bridle, and giving a *click-click* command from his cheek, he was back with Trace almost as fast as the giddyup had taken to order.

They were both strapping on leathers, double-checking the fittings, and inspecting the riggings for the accuracy drop, controlled landing, timed lifting speed, and shooting contests. These would be done before midday. Afternoon would be the unmanned lap, where Heaster would solo float the track while others set up the maneuvering course.

The first event was the accuracy drop. The center of the arena contained a stanchion wall that was shaped in a circle. An entrance and an exit gate were located on opposite sides, with a platform on a ladder tower, so that two perched officials could give the go-ahead when the participants' acceptable height had been reached. The seven rings in the middle of the stanchion represented a target. A span, the dimension of the crate Maddy had fashioned, was the size of the bull's-eye. Each rider would come into the ring and hook the metal plate to their belly rings. After that, once they'd been lifted to the predetermined point, they would align themselves to let the plate freefall as close to the mark as they could.

Each event offered a variety of points to score. The accuracy drop was a three-place scoring event. The three closest contestants scored points for their drops: three points for the closest, two for second, and one point for third.

The release device was triggered by the rider once he felt he was on target.

Maddy was imagining dropping nards onto the rocks back in Dillon and how overripe ones would burst into a spray of juices. He felt confident that he could make the small plate land on such a big target. But his confidence shriveled as Drem, the first contestant to make the drop, landed his plate inside the center ring. The participants' order, set by their numbered tags, remained the same throughout this day's challenges. Maddy would drop into his twelfth position.

DECATHLON DAY THREE

The contestants made drop after drop, and the plate was marked after each plummeted landing. Individually colored rings were placed around the plate to mark each player's landing point.

Finally it was Maddy's turn. He walked in with Heaster and reached down to grab the snap-ring hitch. The release catch needed to be set correctly, so that when he pulled the cord, it would unhook at the proper time. He realized this was a far cry from when he dropped nards from his hands.

Once the clasp was ready, Maddy mounted Heaster and lifted off. The officials raised a flag when he had reached the regulated height.

"We have one chance, boy. It didn't look this high from down there," Maddy said.

"We are in this together, Maddy. It looks right," Heaster told him.

Maddy took a deep breath and pulled the cord to release the plate. And it landed exactly the same distance from the pin, which was used to measure to the edge of the plate's ring, as Drem's had landed.

The contestants' dropping order was the tie-breaking decision. The first one to drop scored. Drem had taken first place.

There was chance involved. Being proficient could, but not for certain, bring the win. Maddy accepted his second two points gracefully.

The leader board still had Maddy in first place. They had given him a flare point for the finish of the ten-lap race. Six points for Maddy, five for Drem.

In the second round, a weighted crate had been moved into the walled circle. This would be used for the controlled landing. Riders would first have to circle the walled pen five times, lift the crate to the center, then place it on the same mark they used for the accuracy drop.

This could establish a decisive lead. Maddy knew Heaster was experienced in this, with all the fares they had taxied recently. Drem was not in the people-hauling business, but when he circled the wall, it was precise. His lift was remarkable, and his placement of the weighted crate was again inside the bull's-eye ring. It was not exactly on the marker pin, but it was a contender's mark.

Accuracy on the landing was the point gainer for all the riders. The circling and lift were judgment calls, but the landing was marked. Only Drem's mark was fully in the inside circle. Maddy was glad about this because he needed a boost in points. He knew that Drem would get two for certain. He had to get closer. When he entered the ring, he listened as the crowd quieted. Pressure began to build as he heard his beating heart. Once the box was attached, Maddy thought to Heaster, "Are we ready?"

"Got it," resounded in his mind.

The walled ring flowed by them, as their speed caused centrifugal force to lift the box outward. With the box almost touching the wall at spots, the fifth lap shot the team in an upward backflip trick as the box found the landing directly on the marker pin. For this event first place was his, with the total of three points. The crowd's cheers were thunderous now, sending silence fleeing.

DECATHLON DAY THREE

The next impediment was the lift speed. The two mediators were still suspended on the top of the tower, where they would clock the speed time from the ground to their location.

Maddy watched intently as each of his opponents attempted to fight for the first-place award. Their individual tactics were basically the same, and nothing had stood out to Maddy that could increase his lift propensity. Drem didn't do as well as a few of the others, and he had fallen to fifth place by the time Maddy took center stage. A competitor from another category had moved into their bracket, replacing a riding team that had been disqualified for not showing up.

This new competitor's lift speed was inspiring. Although he was a smaller rider, he had a lifting thrust that had taken him and his ride to the lead in this event. For Maddy to place would put a larger gap between Drem and himself. The smaller rider's longer neck was the key to his gaining the first-place standing

Lift speed could be gained by the exact timing of leg muscles and the downward flex force of the tail—not a difficult talent to achieve, unless there was a timer taking score. Lift was what these animals did naturally; speed took practice; and experience would reign.

The fans cheered loudly when they heard Maddy Handle's name called. Maddy prepared his stance, and the timer was set. The time wouldn't start until the contestant broke contact with the launch pad and ended when a ray of light at the imaginary finish line was touched, marking lift speed.

"Up!" Maddy's word commanded take off. He glued himself as close to Heaster's back as he could so they would move as one. They shot off the pad, and Heaster's timing was impeccable; his legs and tail flex were in perfect sync. They kicked up a puff of swirling dust, and it rolled around the pad in a small, oval cloud.

Nothing had shot upward so quickly that day as Maddy and Heaster. The three points went to Maddy, as his time smashed the others on the scoreboard. No fanfare was needed for extra points in this event; first place would do nicely.

As the activities going on around the center circle were being decided and points totaled, the ends of the wall were opened, splitting the single circle wall into two long walls. This would be where the arrow-shot-from-a-ride challenge would be held. The outer barriers would be used for the obstacle course.

To keep the arrows from ricocheting into the crowd, mediators raised a mesh net on the open end of the field of play. This would still allow spectators to see through it but protect them from any mishaps or missed targets.

The shooting contest came first. Nine arrows would be shot by each contestant, with three arrows shot from three different positions.

The first three were an in-line straight shot of three arrows at a shot board. Second were shots from a ride team that was floating at a moving target on a rail track. The last had the riding team shoot the three arrows at a stationary object. The most direct and accurate shooters, hitting their marks the most, would be awarded points for each hit that was made.

Drem took his position on his steed, which was standing on the ground. He shot right handed, leaning along his steed's

DECATHLON DAY THREE

neck. From that position all three shots hit the board. Maddy knew that Drem was abundant in experience. Archery was part of his training and procedure for being a palace guard.

He knew this could be where Drem would catch up with or pass him on the leader panel.

Several arrows found their ends stuck into the wooden board.

Maddy was able to use his handmade projectiles he'd gotten from his father. How Dray knew to make an extra arrow for him was astonishing. Maddy's quiver held ten arrows. He'd been using one for practice, and it was pretty beaten up from all the practice shots he had taken. So he would be able to use the remaining nine for the contest.

Maddy's first three arrows slapped the board; two were very close together, and the third was still in contention. The bows varied in their amount of curve and draw pull. Their weapons had miscellaneous designs and affixed carved trinkets, and feathers hung from the tips.

Cords of sinew and woven thread made up most of the draw strings. A couple of other bows were made out of a substance Maddy hadn't seen before. There was a shiny glaze painted on these curved works of artistry.

The moving target on the rail would be Maddy's toughest challenge. From the air he had hit what he was aiming for many times, but with a moving target, all he had was what Dray had taught him about leading the target enough for as long as the arrow's flight lasted to hit the mark.

"If your target is moving really fast, you need to lead it by quite a bit—and even more if there is any distance involved,"

Dray had said. The voice in his mind made Maddy remember how much he missed hearing his dad talk to him.

The orange feathers on the shafts tails of Drem's arrows had hit the board six out of six times, but they were not all the closest arrows to the hub of the center ring. Dray had used drachma tail feathers for tail stability that he'd dyed blue. There were only four of Drem's arrows counting in the first two portions of this event. Maddy would need to stick all three of his shots in this round closer for counted points.

Drem sailed back and forth, taking a shot with each pass in the last phase of this event.

Two hits were within inches of a direct strike. He could have counted eight points if he was the closest.

More and more tips sank into the soft wood, sending chips and slivers flying. Oddly these competitors had either practiced more or their nerves had settled with their six prior shots. The presented target looked more and more like a spiny tree sloth because so many sticks protruded at different angles. Several darts hit the meshed curtain, and many hit all around and along the path the target traveled. There were also hits that did not hit for points. Today, with nine possible points, that was not going to be the case for Maddy.

On Maddy's turn the target's center was still open. More than forty arrows had found their way to the round wooden plate, making an arrow's chances of glancing off a probability. Heaster was incredible, and even when he turned, his rider kept his balance. Maddy was able to stand on Heaster's back and let his arrows fly. The score, to this point, listed Drem with six points and Maddy with only

DECATHLON DAY THREE

two. Drem's last two arrows needed to be taken out of contention. The first shot slapped the hub and sank hard into its meat. Two shots were left. The second glanced off and rocketed into the air. It proceeded upward then turned sideways midflight before the tip sailed back down at the person who'd shot it.

After catching it out of the air then taking his last arrow out of his quiver, he placed them both on the string, pulling them back and sending them to the same spot together. One hit the end of Drem's orange-feathered tip, splitting it in two, and the other hit the hub.

Nothing compared to the roar that resounded. Maddy scored five points, if they were to count the arrow that split Drem's. They hadn't, giving him only four points, keeping the Maddy Handle name in the top position.

The buzz of questions spread his name around like a glob of honey dropped in a beehive.

"Who is he?" "Where's he from? "How old is he?"

All that remained for this day's competition was the maneuvering course. This course would be done without the riders being able to see the grid until they were brought to the starting line. It was time to get refreshed and fed up. The inn was their destination, far away from the hungry mob.

Trace had been able to be in the crew area where Maddy loaded her on. They soared above, leaving the people with their faces looking into the sky.

"What was the final score?" Maddy asked.

"Drem has eleven, and you have seventeen," she replied.

"I can't believe this, Trace. We're in this."

"Let's keep our grip on *this*. We don't want to get over confident," she said.

"I loved your last shot, Maddy." Heaster's input was a deserved tribute. "You did great, but this next feat may take some doing on my part."

"If you fail, we fail; we are in this together. I'd never send you to the droids, no matter what," Maddy told him.

"Let's chow down." With Heaster comment he knew that eating wouldn't affect his performance in the obstacle-weaving course.

Waiting for their food to be prepared, they shared the latest news of Maddy's score with Marty and Emma while they helped clear some tables.

The meal was delicious as usual. They finished by bringing their dishes to the kitchen, telling Marty they'd be back after the next race.

The float back was at a lower level than their float to the inn, since they would be disqualified if they could see the course over the arena walls. All riders were asked to wait in their stables until they were called to the on-deck circle. The on-deck circle maintained the theory of no delay in action and also prevented any late arrivals to the track.

To win this race, riders had to avoid contact with any of the obstacles, which had been strategically placed, and to have the best timed speed overall. The winner would receive a total of five points for finishing. If a contestant made contact with any barriers, the mediators would subtract a point for every one touched by either the team or the package they carried. Sensor alarms had been placed around anything close to the

DECATHLON DAY THREE

trail. Touching an obstacle would sound the alarm, which would keep track of the touches until the teams had crossed the finish line.

In the on-deck jetty area, the package would be hooked to the rides' harness rings just prior to them entering the course.

When Maddy was called to the prep area, he saw a large curtain blocking any possible way to see what was in store for them. Buzzers sounded, giving Maddy a clue to their sound and what he could expect on the course, so as not to be surprised if he were to touch something that could cause him to bump into something else.

"Slow and steady, Heaster. Having our connection here should make a difference here."

Following the horn that blew each time the finish line was crossed, the curtain was opened. This sight dazed Maddy. The arena had been transformed into an amazing labyrinth. Barricades could be seen ahead on the path, set before his eyes, with trees and projectiles placed so intentional dodging would be needed to avoid them. There was also a sensor that scanned the course to ensure that the teams would stay within a certain lift height and force the contestants to stay on the course and not just float over the obstacles.

The start sent Maddy on a brief straightaway that had only the undersize wall guarding the trail, but it was short-lived. The first curve required Maddy to swing the package enough to lift it over the bar that had been placed in their way. Silhouettes were cut out just larger than the size of the package and were located in four spots throughout the course. The rider would need to go over a wall while having the hanging pendulum make it through the void without touching them. The trails out in the forest had been great practice for Maddy and his cohort. Swaying and getting his crate through the bridge exit was a routine that was going to pay off.

The final run looked to be smooth sailing, when a shaft shot out from the left to block the path. Heaster's reaction had the lift they needed to clear the beam, but the package just nicked the pole. A blast of the alarm told them they couldn't traverse the course perfectly. They had avoided the stationary things, but this was a surprise. Just after the first pole, two others shot out. One came from their right and the other from the left. They had to duck beneath the last pole while keeping the package from touching the surface.

The track opened to the finish line, and Hester had a burst of power while surging toward it, getting best time they could.

The final horn blast stopped the time clock. There was a split decision between Drem and Maddy. Drem had not touched any obstacles but had finished behind Maddy's time. The officials deliberated, finally bringing their decision to the announcer.

As Maddy tried to be patient, his thoughts ran through the possible ways the score would affect the overall decathlon.

"In the decision of our obstacle-course main event, the judges have given five points to Drem Loaves, who finished the race second and touched no sensor, and four points to Maddy Handle, for the best time but for touching one obstacle."

DECATHLON DAY THREE

This made the score twenty-one points for Maddy, and sixteen points for Drem.

The last day held the real challenge—the joust.

Maddy was wrestling with how he could win this event over Drem, who was a seasoned veteran. Past years showed that he had won this event easily. He was favored to take top honors again this year.

But as of day three, Maddy held the lead.

After competing, Carl joined the setup crew. His strong stature was a welcomed support in moving the course pieces around. Maddy saw him lending a hand and asked whether he wanted to ride back to the inn for an evening meal with Trace and him. Carl accepted, joining them at the stable. Talk of the events superseded any topic that was brought up.

Conversation would always come back to the events. For Maddy being in the lead made the discussion pleasant rather than distasteful.

CHAPTER FOURTEEN

Decathlon Day Four

The next day there was a rush flowing through Maddy's heart as he awoke from a dream where he'd just been squaring off against Drem in the joust. They were moving toward each other at full speed, javelins aimed at the shoulder slot. As the blunt javelin tips found their marks, Maddy heard a throat clearing gruffly. It was Heaster, not grunting in his dream, but rather nudging him to awake.

Heaster knew what Maddy was dreaming about and had interrupted the ending. Of course the dream could be played out in real life if they met in the challenge. For now it was preparation time.

Mary Ellen appeared at the doorway of his temporary quarters. A knave-looking man carried a box that he set in front of Maddy.

"A gift for you, no strings attached," she said. "Open it. I can't wait to see how it fits."

Maddy knew her "no strings attached" really meant there were logging ropes tied to her advances and her gifts.

"I mustn't, ma'am." He wasn't sure how she would react. "Sorry, but you've been far to giving already."

"Oh, just open it, silly boy."

To pacify her he opened the box to find a suit of armor. Seeing it shaped to a T, and knowing it would fit him exactly, he closed the box just as Trace walked into the room. Seeing her adversary there, trying to buy Maddy's affections, stirred her heart into an almost uncontrollable state of revolt. Calmly she said, "Carl adjusted Maddy's suit just fine. You can leave now. Maddy needs to get ready."

A girl fighting for him was a nice gesture, but that suit of armor would give him a better advantage, especially against Drem.

"Could we buy it from you?" he sheepishly asked.

"You have fifty shekels?" she asked, letting them see her wealth by her bragging answer.

"No, ma'am."

"Then you'll lose on both ends of this box," she said, storming out and motioning to her knave servant to take up the box again.

"Is that what old persistence looks like?" Trace said, wanting to distract Maddy from chasing after the armor that could have been a good thing.

"It was like looking at me in a mirror. The chest was so shiny. I might have felt like a real knight with that on." His comments were not meant to make Trace feel bad or jealous.

DECATHLON DAY FOUR

"A knight has heart, and that, Maddy Handle, is what you have, even if you don't have armor to prove it. You don't need a mask."

"I might need one after Drem gets done with me. How did you get here?" Maddy asked, knowing he hadn't gone on his morning venture to get her.

"I couldn't sleep very well. I woke up in the middle of the night thinking of you alone here. So I got ready and helped Marty for a bit, getting some beggas peeled, and then hoped to get here before you would leave to pick me up."

"I think sleep is all you need to look stunning. This walking thing hasn't hurt that at all; if anything, walking makes your beauty stand out even more."

***

The minor jousters had drawn their matches and were already competing in the early morning.

A bracket chart had been filled out with names, drawn from a hat, for the competition's order. Minor jousters could advance when they won their competitions. Each jouster would move from a part of the early bracket to the advanced brackets when he won.

One loss sent a jouster to the losers' bracket, and the second loss put a jouster out of contention. Five points were given to the overall winner. Scoring was tallied with each jousting pass. After three passes the highest scorer would win and move ahead. The final match was between the last two who made it to the last bout of three passes.

Drem had knocked his first three challengers to the ground easily. He was dismounting them soundly from their rides. Maddy had not won any joust by knocking his opponents off. Instead he had won his first two jousts by scoring more points.

His third match pitted him against the huge ride and his owner. He knew that if he were to get hit by the force of the extra weight of the ride he could easily be knocked off his own ride for the total loss in the joust.

His strategy was to avoid being hit. That could only be done by causing the opponent to miss him by either hitting his shoulder first or by affecting his aim, using his javelin more accurately for both an offensive tool and a defensive guard.

The first two passes had Maddy hit the shoulder mark only once. His opposition had thankfully missed him twice. Their last pass at each other caused Maddy to land on the solid earth.

He'd been dismounted. He would now have to win every match to win the jousting competition.

Round after round sent animals to the stables and/or their riders to the ground. Maddy's final match in the losers' bracket was against a small man named River Bellow.

He was from Ranch River County. He wasn't very old but had an aim that could consistently put practice rings on the practice pole.

He'd won every meet in the earlier rounds. Drem may have even been challenged by him. His small ride, which he'd named Joe, had the look of a prime without the mass. He was connected to River much like Maddy and Heaster had their connection. The mini prime must have been a mutated prime. Rides weren't connectable to their riders the way primes and riders were.

Three passes let them each score a blow to their opponent's shoulder. They had tied. But Maddy had lost his first joust against the huge prime, which gave River the win.

Maddy and Heaster went to the stables, hanging their heads.

Trace met them. "What are you doing?" she asked.

"We lost." Maddy's answer along with his discouraged posture revealed that he was pretty down.

"What did you lose?" Trace asked.

"The jousts match."

"You're joshing, right? Maddy Handle, have you ever jousted before today?"

"No."

"I couldn't be happier with you. Not only did you win a couple matches and get to the final match in the lower bracket, but you also didn't get physically wounded. Did you see some of your competitors? They were *hurt!* Not just their pride. This is probably the best thing that could have happened. It'll get you back to reality."

"I guess," he said. His nose suddenly felt less bent out of place.

"So what do we do now?" Trace asked, trying to encourage Maddy to give a winner's response.

"Win the lift?" he said, still feeling the sting of the loss that had placed a question in his confidence.

"*Win the lift!*" she exclaimed. "No doubting allowed here. Now let's get this awesome animal of yours ready to go."

"I'd like to get my mind off this with some food. Could we take a lift back to the inn for a bite to eat? There are some fresher sprouts there for Heaster too. I want him to have as much advantage as he can summon for power," Maddy said.

The cheers continued in the distance for the winner of the joust, but not for them.

Drem had won. He and Maddy were now tied for the first time in the competition. The winner of the lift contest would be the overall champion.

The lift would begin right after noon. The inn was fairly quiet when they arrived there.

"Not many guests for lunch?" Trace directed her question to Emma.

"The early crowd has just given us this, a few stragglers, which is OK. You wouldn't want the pile of dishes waiting in the kitchen's overfilled sink basins."

"What would you say to a barter?" Maddy offered to help clean up the dishes for a meal. "That way you could come to the lift."

"You haven't seen the amount of dishes you're offering to do," Emma said. She raised an eyebrow at him with just enough hopefulness that he was being sincere with his offer. She smiled as he left Trace and her standing in the dining room.

"We wanted to go to the final lifting event of the decathlon. Marty has fond memories of his times with Brawn there.

DECATHLON DAY FOUR

Brings back the rush of when they won it. The bulk of hungry people stayed at the coliseum eating at the vendor booths, so they'll be there to get better seating to watch the lift."

"Do most of Palace City residents go to the lift event?"

"Yes, this is a major deal for the city. They'll close their shops early, like we may, to get there in time to watch the finalists lift. There are three rounds that eliminate the greater part of the rides. The weight they lift is amazing to watch, even the smaller competitors. The finalists then compete for the title. That's the place to be."

"Watching Carl was a thrilling time. He was amazing entertainment, especially if you haven't seen anything like that before."

"Don't want to let you down by talking this up, but you will be impressed," Emma said, as Marty and Maddy came in, carrying four platters of food. They contained a slab of sizzling drook, covered with a sautéed mound of beggas steaming with flavorings.

"Better get this down quick. .Wouldn't want to be late for the finals." Marty divulged his intention of going. "We'll have to drop the flaps around the awning and put the CLOSED sign up."

"We can all fit in the chariot we made. That way it'll be there to load all the equipment to bring back here when the day is through," Maddy said. He had brought it back to the inn for more room in his stable pad back at the decathlon.

"Don't want to take away any of Heaster's dominance in this lift," Marty said. He was aware of what this section of the decathlon was going to take.

"Just having you there will be encouragement enough for us, so delivering you there will be an extra support." Maddy had settled into a calm achievement mindset after talking with Trace. He'd already proven to be a force to be reckoned with, even without winning the all-around decathlon.

Back at the stables, Mary Ellen had set her deceptive, controlling act in motion. She had the harness maker put a device in the badge's chest plate of Heaster's harness that could be used to take the harness off easily. It was a mechanical release switch that could be triggered by a signal for simplicity in removing the harness. She wasn't going to be undone by a young girl, and certainly not Trace. Her plan was to dismiss the harness rigging when Maddy was in lift form. She needed to activate it by setting the release switch to remote mode, which she had done when they were all back at the inn.

When they had closed down shop, the foursome changed into their dress code and got to the stable. Maddy hadn't known that he would need the harness to carry the crate back and had left it back at the games.

"There's no way to bring the crate; the harness is back in our holding stall." Maddy wanted so badly for Marty and Emma to be there.

"Is it all right for him to wear Brawn's?" Marty offered.

"His practice harness will do to get us there. Heaster is used to it already too."

Marty moved to a chest that contained Brawn's show harness. He brought it out for Maddy to see. It was old school—a primitive and bulky harness at first glance—but it was very well made and strong.

DECATHLON DAY FOUR

"I would be honored if you would use this, Maddy."

"The honor would be all mine. Mary Ellen will probably be pretty upset, but she's older than this harness, so she'll get over it." Giving the Dew Drop Inn some advertising made it a win-win situation. Maddy had no idea what "upset" would be when her ambush was foiled.

With everything in place, they lifted off in the direction of the city's core.

When taking off, Heaster had turned to straighten the crate's bindings when a sharp piece of roofing material sliced partly through a strap on the harness. No one had noticed the cut in the strap. It still held together, but it was tearing with any extra pressure. Heaster swung into a setting approach when the strap tore through. The crate jerked, but the remaining straps held fast. They set down quickly, unharmed but slightly shaken from what could have been a disaster.

"Sorry, Marty. I really wanted to use this harness," Maddy said. He would have no choice but to use Mary Ellen's donation.

"One of the straps from Brawn's practice harness will fit here. You go get your preliminary lifts out of the way, and we'll get this changed out."

Drem had gotten through the first three lifts easily, along with the brute who had knocked Maddy off in the joust competition. Many contestants were dropping like flies. They couldn't get the lift needed or raise their loads above a set height to advance to the final meet.

Just as they finished strapping the harness on Heaster, Maddy heard them call his name.

"We'd better hurry." Maddy knew being late would disqualify him from the event.

"Go." The whole team answered, as they had their own duty—getting the strap changed.

Maddy and Heaster moved to the three heavy blocks when the crew attaching the loads waved them in.

The first block, the smallest, gave Heaster no challenge. Lifting the load to the required height and then resetting it to its base was simple. The second lift also looked to be as easy because of a little change in the outer size of the block.

The ropes tightened, and the density of the hunk surprised Heaster. He was handling it well, now knowing this was an eye opener that the third block's size would be immensely heavier yet.

Between each lift there was a brief break taken before the next lift attempt.

"Are you ready, Heaster?" Maddy asked. He had felt the harness tighten with the second lift and wanted to make sure they were both prepared for the next step on their way to the finals.

Heaster double winked at Maddy to let him know that he was.

When it was time, they attached the weight, and as Heaster moved upward, the leathers stretched as the unit came off the ground. As they reached the top of the lift, Mary Ellen pressed the button on her remote, activating the release.

Only one side let go. The T Maddy had stamped into the M of the emblem had malfunctioned the release. As the one strap came free, the crowd gasped, hoping they weren't going to witness a crewmember being crushed by the dropping weight.

Heaster still needed to lift the load a few more inches to qualify. "Hold on, Maddy," he said. With a reaction to the uneven pull on the harness, Heaster dropped so quickly that the naked eye could barely see the motion. He was floating upside down with the block on his stubby, round feet. This was unconventional, to say the least. Trace, Marty, and Emma had gotten to the pit crew area in time to hold their breath as they watched their team do something that had never been done.

Silence was held in place, as the move had grasped everyone's attention. Heads had turned to watch history being made. Something was happening that would become a story for the rest of time. Locking in on precise details was needed so as not to allow any personal input to glamorize the facts.

The weight rose above the required line, and the silence was broken. The only obstacle now was to set the load down again. In reverse action that had moved them into position for lift, as they came close to the ground, the team flipped, catching the unbalanced weight just as it sat on the landing pad. The block had almost missed the required box for advancement. The official raised his flag to signal a qualifying lift, and the crowd applauded again.

"Maddy, Maddy, Maddy," the crowd chanted.

"You are amazing, Heaster." Maddy knew who deserved the applause and whose name really should have been cheered.

They detached the hook, and Maddy made a lap around the racetrack. His eyes spotted Mary Ellen, who was still trying to press the release button, until she saw him catching her in the act. He sailed over her and unleashed the other front strap, dropping the whole harness at her feet.

Not everyone was aware of what had transpired. Mary Ellen and Maddy's connection was broken. Any future dealings were doubtful, and Maddy had handed her advertisement harness back into manipulative hands.

The finals were the main event. All the last-minute dealings, food needs, and distractions were being taken care of.

Brawn's harness was going to need approval, from the judges, that it was in lifting order, especially after the assumed accidental mishap they witnessed in their last lift. Maddy and Marty got it on Heaster, marching him to their booth. A thorough inspection got the stamp of approval.

Three finalists were announced to the audience.

"Maddy Handle, on his young prime, Heaster, who is a newcomer competing in the decathlon, stemming from Dillon County; our second finalist, Cleo Tusker, riding his twenty-eight-year-old prime, Brute, all the way from Decker County." The ovation grew with each finalist. Maddy thought how fitting the name Brute was for this huge prime.

"And our third and final qualifier, who is riding his steed, Josh, a fifteen-year-old prime, a member of our elite guard… our own Drem Loaves!!"

A standing ovation with a prolonged applause followed the announcer's tribute.

"Are you ready for the final lifting competition of the day?" the broadcaster asked, building the crowd into a roaring frenzy.

DECATHLON DAY FOUR

Cleo had placed last in overall points and would make his final lift first—not that Maddy needed any more pressure, being up against such a mammoth beast. Cleo's only hope was that Brute was getting older now, relying on his experience and size to confidently blow away any competition.

The event would be similar to the strongman's finals, where a scale measured the amount of lift capability. A hook and shackle attached to cables that went through the floor of the platform where the ride would begin their lift. It would be all about lift strength, no leg or tail flexes for speed. It was just pure lifting power.

The cables permitted the prime to get off the floor of the platform, which was suspended by staging above a four-sided, lighted measuring scale that gave the entire stadium visibility. The scale was connected to a machine that was anchored to the arena floor, and the machine gradually added weight against the prime's lift.

Brute took in his massive inhale deeply and lifted off. His mass stretched his harness, and then the weight held him fast. The scale's numbers flashed higher and higher then began to flash slower as the numbers started to be recognizable until they stopped completely and displayed a single number. To lock the scale at the heaviest weight, it needed to be held for three counts.

Brute had set the bar at 10,406 kilos. This was so intimidating to Maddy. He began to lose faith, hope, and confidence in all their hard work. That amount of lift strength could have lifted an entire home.

A few short weeks ago, Maddy was connecting with his prime for the first time. Now he was being challenged to do something he'd never seen. Local fairs had been baby food compared to this event, where a vast amount of meat was the meal.

When Drem won the joust event and tied with Maddy for first place, it wasn't enough to choose the order of who was up next. Maddy had held the lead. This event would break any possible tie.

Drem was preparing, and Maddy was putting Drem's advice to be observant in play. He watched as Drem slowly moved his hands together down the prime's neck and matched Josh's breathing. Having a look of a state of meditation, they moved as one being to the bearing area. The hook clasped with a loud clicking sound. Josh took one last deep inhale as they lifted upward. The cables were pulled taut, and the harness began making leather-stretching noises.

The peak of the lift blurred the scale's lights, which seemed they would never stop clicking higher, the thousands unit of measure was the only readable number, as eight, nine, ten passed. Eleven stopped the thousands place from changing; now the slowing hundreds place marked seven, then eight, then nine, and done.

The numbers in the last two places were still flickering… sixty, seventy, then to the last position, five, six, and seven. Finally they stopped—11,977. Three counts, and the flag marked a weight. The home team caused the citizens of Palace City to explode into acclamation.

DECATHLON DAY FOUR

Brawn's record would stand if no more was added. Four small clicks in the singles digits would have broken his record.

Drem had beaten the brute, even with his name and size.

Cleo and Brute would hold second place, and Drem and Josh moved into first.

Maddy felt a hand on his shoulder. A surge of supremacy moved through the touch into his body. All his hopelessness was leaving him as he turned to see his father. There Dray and Uncle Mel both stood in front of him.

Questions would follow, but the depth and intensity of his dad's arms were inescapable. Maddy hugged his dad tightly.

"How'd you get here? How did you find out we were even here? And how'd you get this guy to leave Dillon?" Maddy asked as he shifted his greeting to Uncle Mel.

"That'll be answered later. Seems you have a lift to win, with the name I see at the top of the scoreboard."

If Heaster could feel what Maddy was feeling right now, that record Brawn set would be history.

"Our last and final contestant for this year's event is… Maddy Handle," the announcer said. Two attendants waited for Maddy to put his prime over the lift area so they could attach the fastener.

With one jump he was on Heaster in an instant. "Do you see who's here, boy?"

"I smelled them," Heaster said, as he sensed their familiar smell.

The energy his dad had sent through him flowed together with Heaster. Maddy began stroking the sides of Heaster's neck and thought as he closed his eyes, "Breathe, boy. Breathe with me."

The snapping of the harness's clasp put every one of Maddy's senses on high alert.

"Up!" The word came that Heaster had needed to hear when his chest was filled to the maximum. And it came at the perfect time.

The cables were like overstretched piano strings, and the harness sank into Heaster's back. The lighted numbers spun, and each thousand number passed by. Eight, nine, ten, eleven.... The hundreds place still flashed higher numbers... eighty, ninety.... The thousands place changed to twelve. One hundred, two hundred—the clock was slowing to seventy, eighty, seven, eight, nine, until finally it stopped. The number read 12,290. The holding mark came from the entire crowd. "One, two, three!"

As the crowd counted to three and exploded into an uproar, the cables that had held the scale to the base machine snapped, shooting Maddy and Heaster upward. The clock tore through the platform, and its numbers faded as power left the lights.

Victory! The time for that lap had come.

Maddy circled the track and spiraled upward and outward over the crowd, the clock still dangling beneath him. Then they flew back to the platform, where the two attendants guided the clock back through the floor and unhooked the fastener.

Maddy swooped down to where Trace stood, waving her little hand-embroidered flag, and hoisted her into his

DECATHLON DAY FOUR

arms—the place he'd hoped she'd be forever. Together they made another lap before landing on the platform and waving their arms overhead to the people in the stands.

The presentation of awards and prizes would be held as the lights of day were fading away, which gave Maddy enough time to have a mini celebration with his family and loved ones.

"You'll never believe some of our stories, Dad," Maddy said. He was still amazed that his father was there. "You first, though. How did you get here?"

"We got a little worried. The last time you hadn't come home, you were lying out by that ole treman, face-up. Trace's family had faith in you, but week after week went by without any news. We mustered up enough to barter for a work ride that old Doc Blame had. He got us here, though, so that paid off. We had to trade our livestock, but that was fine. We didn't need anyone to watch or care for them." Dray's face expressed a mixed look of concern and joy after seeing Maddy was all right.

"When we got to the city, we heard about the decathlon. It only made sense you'd be here," Uncle Mel added. "If we were going to look anywhere, we thought this would be a great place to start."

"Never thought to see a name I'd recognize at the top of the chart, though," Dray said.

"How'd you find me in this crowd?"

"We just mentioned your name. It seems you've made quite a surname for yourself here in Palace City. They said you'd be down by the platform waiting to compete."

"It was miraculous, Dad. Heaster's something else. Thanks for getting him for me," Maddy said. He then introduced Marty, Emma, Carl, and the Ropels to Dray and Uncle Mel. They shared a couple of experiences about their traveling, their overnight stays in the lands between Dillon and Palace City, and their ride's speed not being very swift but good enough to get them there. Then they went back to Maddy's temporary stable room.

"Heaster was ready for everything. Couldn't believe how we've been syncing together during this decathlon."

"I'm ready for something to eat and drink too!" the prime piped in.

Everyone laughed.

"I'm serious," he said. He had exerted an extra amount of energy and was beginning to bend at the knees.

"What's going on, Dad?" Maddy hadn't seen his friend in this state of weakness before.

"He just needs some rest. After he gets something in him, he'll be fine. I think he's still growing. Sure got bigger in the last few weeks since we saw him last."

"That lift takes a massive amount of energy. Your dad is right. Rest and nourishment will get him back to the Heaster we know," Marty said. He remembered what Brawn had done after their own lifting day.

They had Heaster inhale just enough so that he floated slightly off the ground and then led him to the water trough, setting what was left of the sprouts beside it.

DECATHLON DAY FOUR

He drank the water and chewed on a few char sprouts then closed his eyes heavily and opened then closed them again.

"Just get some rest, Heaster," Maddy said. He saw Heaster's eyes and wanted to encourage him to get some sleep.

"You sure made us proud, son. You handled it like a Handle would," Dray said. He had missed his son, but he was relieved that Maddy not only had done well on his own but also had won a coveted victory at the competition.

"I believe you were the one who helped us get this one in the bag, Dad. You completely took us by surprise, showing up here in Palace City."

CHAPTER FIFTEEN

Awards

"We have met some wonderful people here," Trace said. She wanted to share her appreciation of talking to someone from home. "Wait until you meet Marty and Emma's food. Your tongues may never be the same."

"Marty?" Maddy looked at his newfound friend. "Sorry we broke Brawn's record."

"With you wearing his harness, knowing you, and being able to see it for myself, who could ask for a better way to see his record broken?" Marty smiled. He wasn't a man to hold a grudge; he was just too jolly for that. "The only thing better than all of this will be a party we can have back at the inn. Dray, Mel, we have a room at the inn you can stay in that opened up just before we came here. No charge either. Besides, Maddy's going to be paying for it all with his prize money."

His belly jiggled as a roar of laughter came out.

Maddy hadn't thought about winning any prize money; the trophy and awards were all he thought he might have a chance at.

"If you can wait until after the award ceremony, we'll get plenty of food when we get back," Emma said. "After all this, when people hear you were staying at our place, we may get more business than we can handle. We might even have to come up with some 'handle' for a food item."

Maddy made his way over to where his dad had stepped away. "Something wrong, Dad?"

Dray had been in a faraway place when his son interrupted his thoughts and brought him back to the reality of the stable. "Not sure if *wrong* is the right word. It can wait until after the awards, son. We can talk more back at Marty's inn."

The sun gave way to the rising moons. Harac and Cam made their way into the sky, with Cam playing his chasing game around Harac. Evening was upon them, and Heaster had gotten his needed rest. The emcee announced that it was time for all the contestants to line up in a parade formation.

Marty told Maddy that, as they had won the prime competition, he would be expected to be in full-dress armor and Heaster would be expected to wear a harness.

They quickly got dressed and found their places in the lineup.

The blast from six trumpeters focused the attention on the decathlon's latest participants.

This was the grand finale. The participants would make a final lap on the racetrack, and then they would proceed to a

AWARDS

position where they would wait for the winners' names and their events to be called.

Carl had stayed in the city to receive his award and prize. When they called his name with the lifting finalists, the applause doubled as they remembered his amazing feat of strength.

Time came to announce the prime division awards. "Cleo Tusk, third place in the heavyweight prime division." Cleo and Brute stepped to the platform to claim their award and prize.

"Second-place finalist in the overall decathlon, Drem Loaves, with his prime, Josh," the announcer said. The crowd's enthusiastic response was increasing. Drem floated to the platform, where he received his trophy and awards for the joust and the other individual events he had won.

The announcer's voice built with each of his next few words. "And this year's overall heavyweight prime and rider winners are Maddy Handle and his ride, Heaster."

With perfect control Maddy and Heaster floated toward the platform, performing a maneuver that thrilled the spectators—a triple full-circle loop—then landed by the awards table.

When they handed him his trophy, he held it toward Heaster then into the air. The final cheering was going to end too soon, but not before Maddy permanently locked this memory into his mind.

"We offer a thank-you to all this year's competitors and to the good people of Palace City for their hospitality and to the many great volunteers who made this decathlon one for the record books. We will be adjusting those records here at the palace. They will be open for your viewing tomorrow morning. Thank you again, and good night." The emcee nodded his head for the cue to close.

The light display at the closing ceremony put the opening display to shame. Explosions and fireworks lit up the sky over Palace City. The decathlon had come to a close. Only the cleaning crews and those breaking down the set were left with their tasks to complete.

It was time to get things back to the inn, and Heaster was back to full power. The crate would get most everything in one load, but what didn't get taken on the first trip would be attended to while Marty and Emma were preparing their celebration meal. There were no outside guests invited to the party other than those who were staying at the inn

The prize awarded to Maddy was staggering, by his account. The work he had done and the money he'd saved to raise the entry fee had just paid off thirty fold. Six hundred shekels would change their way of life.

Maddy's prize money would have required years of savings for Dray.

Maddy wanted to share this fortune with those who had helped him reach the goal. Conversation during the party was mostly about the final lifting event, but Marty had an announcement to make.

"Dray Handle, you have done a great job of raising this fine young man. He has helped Emma and me realize how people who are put in your path aren't always an obstacle you have to deal with or someone who passes by, but rather can be quite significant allies. A select few are even destined to become our friends. Maddy Handle, and you, Trace, we unite with you in that friendship. We thank you for letting us help you."

Their salute compelled Maddy to give one too. "You're the ones who helped us see that hard work and a smile are connected to success. So we thank you for your friendship and support as well."

The time had come to get some sleep. Trace retired to the attic room while Mel went to the room Emma had offered.

Dray and Maddy were spending their last few moments together in the hallway.

"Maddy, there is another reason Mel and I came to find you," Dray began.

Maddy saw concern on his father's face. "Is something wrong?"

"We're not sure if it's wrong, but it's about the treman on the corners of the counties."

"Has it changed any more?"

"How did you know it changed?"

"Remember when I was going to tell you about treman moving really slowly, but enough to see if you were really paying attention? You wouldn't let me finish because you said that a story needed to be indicated that it was a story before you told it. Well, I had a dream that night at the cabin about how the treman had changed into something not so nice. It was actually pretty scary."

"Mel and I went to look at the treman, and you're right about changing; it's very different. It was transforming all right—transforming into something terrible."

"Were there any limbs that were sharpened stakes?" Maddy's dream hadn't left his memory.

"The whole tree had them coming out of everywhere. It had a scaly appearance too—the bark, I mean. It was changing the entire outer look of a regular treman." Dray was drawing his son a picture as best he could.

"Did anyone else see it changing?" Maddy asked.

"I'm not sure about that, but Mantra had been there looking for that spot you'd shown her on the drawing. Don't know if she's been back. I wanted to see what you found, and what, if anything, was going on with the peg you have."

"Nothing had changed the last time I looked. Dad, Trace and I have been going to the palace, and I met one of the doormen's brothers-in-law there, Shane Kield. He's a caretaker and custodian. I got to get in to see the Treman they have on display. I couldn't bring the peg with me, but when we went into the display, to water and clean up the room, I saw a void in its trunk that looked to be the match for the key we have."

"A match how?" Dray's questions were being answered, but the answers were causing a need for more understanding.

"I studied that thing from every angle I could, and then realized I knew exactly what the raised carvings and notches looked like. I believe it matched that Treman's notches exactly. The size and depth seem right too."

"I'm not really making sense out of that coincidence other than the fact that they are both tremans." Dray hadn't studied the pegs like Maddy had at the library at Mantra's.

"There must be more to this. Shane said I could go with him again, but the decathlon has taken priority lately. We

AWARDS

wanted to take another tour sometime this week," Maddy said. He wanted his dad to know everything he did about the Treman.

"I wouldn't mind going to the palace while we're here. Mel hasn't been there either."

"You need to apply for an appointment, but I got to be friends with the palace welcome committee. Audrey Kent is Emma's sister too. Maybe we can get in there tomorrow."

"The sooner the better, I think, son." Dray's concerned expression hadn't changed since he began the conversation about the Treman. "We'll get at it at first light then?"

"We might want to get one of Marty's delicious begga-and-egg breakfasts to go on. They stick with you for a while, and they're tasty." Dray was beginning to realize how much his son appreciated Marty.

"Is anything going on with Trace and you?" Dray knew his son would be honorable with this young girl, but he still wanted to know what had been going on with their connection.

"I think she is the one, Dad." Maddy shut it off there. "Good night."

"Good night. It sure is great to see you that you both are OK. You are every father's hope for their sons to become." Dray walked to the room and quietly slipped in so as to not wake Mel.

Maddy was trying for the opposite by being a bit noisier as he got ready for bed. "I am awake, Maddy," Trace said. She'd wanted to see him too.

"I had a talk with my dad about the treman back home. He said there are odd things going on with it. Those four tremans that are outside the east wall, by the painted wall, are acting the same, I think." Maddy wanted to share everything he could with her, but he didn't want her to worry about anything.

"Weird. Did he mention anything else?"

"Asked about us," he added sheepishly.

"And?" Trace was twisting Maddy's arm to get him to speak from his heart.

"And I told him." Maddy watched her face flush as his statement made her feel embarrassed. "Not everything. Just that I thought you…"

Now the shoe was on the other foot.

"That I what?" Now it was Maddy's face changing color.

"That you were the one." Maddy looked at her eyes as he said "the one," hoping to see approval.

"Better be the only one, Maddy Handle. After your winning the decathlon and having all the winnings, there may be other girls who aren't old who are looking at you." Maddy could detect a touch of jealousy, but her blending it with her answer that she was the one made Maddy a believer of her being his.

"Think how much you'll be after we get old," he said. He knew her Mary Ellen comment was going to be a fun topic of conversation for years to come. "May I tell you something that will complete this day?"

"Only if we can say it together," she replied.

The next three words were spoken in perfect harmony. "I love you."

They shared a kiss then fell back onto the puffy featherbeds, which welcomed their bodies on what felt like clouds.

AWARDS

It was cool enough to lie awake, thinking about the last words they had spoken. The beds warmed them quickly enough to help put their minds into dream states as well.

Falling asleep was a wonderful but very short-lived event. The sounds, after the bell dinging, of kitchen noises, let them know Marty was at his station.

"Trace, was I dreaming, or did yesterday really happen?" he asked, rolling over the edge to look down at his dream. She was gone. His mind raced for a wide-awake mode. He shook his head to rattle his mind and eyes into clarity and then saw her come from behind the barrier. Her nightgown was a bit wrinkled from her having slept in it, but her face was as perky as her response.

"Your dream of yesterday has really come true." She moved to the bed where Maddy had been before he jumped to the floor. " 'Morning, Prince Handle."

"It is you, princess." Maddy reached out and pulled her close. "A dream would be to start this day how yesterday ended."

He moved to kiss her, but she placed her hand to his mouth. "My dream started when you said, 'I love you.' "

"It hasn't changed. I love you, Trace Guthrie, from Clay County. Is it kissing time now?" Maddy gently held her.

"What if you cause me to think I'm still sleeping? If you kiss me, I will think I'm dreaming still."

"Sweet dreams then," he said. He kissed her, and a day seemed to pass as they spun into a dream circle of thought.

A future path was laid before them—a home, a family—and suddenly they were inundated with a likeminded thought.

A screaming blur of stars flew by them, and they felt engulfed inside a compartment.

"What was that?" They spoke in sync, taking their lips apart.

"I don't know," Maddy said. "It felt like the same type of dream I had when I dreamed of the treman becoming that device. You thought it too?"

"Most definitely," she answered.

"Dad wanted to go to the palace first thing this morning. Do you think we could get the trio to stamp a card with the green stamp?" Maddy asked. Then he asked her to go with them.

"I think so. After they meet your admirable dad, and they know you won the overall decathlon, how could they deny us permission?" Trace made a good point.

"Let's get some breakfast. I'm hungry," Maddy said. He knew Dray probably would have gotten up already. "Early to rise" didn't always follow "early to bed" for Dray. Most of the time, rising early was just the way it was for Dray and Mel. The cracking open of a new day meant being the first one in line for breakfast. Maddy smiled when they got to the dining room and he realized he had assumed correctly. Dray and Mel were already discussing the day's plan of attack. Knowing what was ahead may have changed their plan.

" 'Morning, sleepyheads," Dray said. He stood and wrestled his hand through Maddy's hair. "You were absolutely right about Marty's breakfasts. When you two get filled up, we can get going."

AWARDS

Emma came in with a couple of dishes covered with Marty's handiwork. "These come with compliments from the chef. Welcome to a new day."

"May we tip the server?" Maddy asked. He still wasn't feeling normal with all the special treatment he'd been receiving and wanted to return the compliment at least.

"That's entirely up to you." Emma said. She sensed Maddy's feelings about being puffed up beyond his limits. "But all the honor is mine this morning."

Before he and Trace had come down, he had hand written a gift card that read, "For a free, two-day, two-person stay at the home of Maddy Handle in Dillon County. All expenses paid."

He handed it to Emma. "What's this?"

"A gift of appreciation," Maddy answered.

"How long is it good for?" Emma knew their business was growing and that time away may not be possible for a while.

"It's for whenever—whenever that is, just so long as it comes." Maddy hadn't realized he'd just made a joke, but the older three broke into laughter.

"Whenever that is…" Trace repeated so that Maddy could hear it again. His cheeks pulled the sides of his lips into a smile as he caught the pun.

They finished breakfast and went to the stables to get Heaster loaded up. There was no need for the extra weight in the crate now. Dray and Mel filled it while Trace and Maddy rode on Heaster.

When they landed near the welcoming committee, Rogar was the first to acknowledge and welcome Maddy there. "Mr. Maddy Handle, we were all pulling for you to win—or at least to give Drem some competition. He is the hometown favorite, but you've been helping get people interested in the palace again. Haven't had so many visitors until you started hauling all those guests here. What may we do for you?"

Maddy introduced his dad and uncle, Mel, and discussed getting them a diplomat pass.

As he was speaking, they got out two purple passes and stamped them. "There you go, gentlemen. Enjoy the palace. It's been waiting for you for a long time."

"Thank you again, Audrey, for recommending your sister's inn," Trace said. "We really enjoy them both."

"You're welcome. I'm happy to have been of assistance."

At the entrance the woman in the red uniform met them and stamped their diplomat cards, allowing their access into the palace.

Dray and Mel had the same faces that Maddy and Trace must have had when they walked in for the first time.

"The Treman." Maddy turned to the receptionist and asked, "How long has that been there?"

"Ever since they built the palace, it has tied most everything in Palace City into a balance."

"What do you mean by a 'balance'?" Maddy hadn't put the picture of the balances in the Treman's hand that were over the entrance together with the information in the Treman room.

"It explains it in the Treman room," she said. She was busy checking another group in as she answered.

AWARDS

Upon closer inspection, the scales would show the items in them to be seeds on one side and what looked like keys on the other.

Once inside they headed for the Treman display. The doorman, through whom Maddy had gotten to meet Shane, was at his post. Maddy asked if Shane was going to be doing another weekend cleaning tour so he could accompany him again. The doorman said yes and that he would try to set it up with Shane.

Rejoining the group, Maddy found that they were standing in front of the display, trying to get a better look at what he'd seen more plainly from inside the showcase. Mel was reading the phrase "To go where no one man has veered from to go where HE came from" aloud. Then he said, "I think I might know what this means."

"OK, Mel, share your visionary skills with us," Dray said. He hadn't known there were any clues remotely evident for Mel to decipher this message. The group knew of no explanation anywhere in the room for the saying.

"When I read it, something just made sense in my mind that it means that 'Together we look at the past to see the future.' Or that's what makes sense to me."

"Dad, Trace and I had a strange connection this morning. We both saw a picture of us being in a compartment, flying through the stars. We've been here looking at the things that have to do with the past—the Treman and those seven pieces—but what if this vision we saw is the future? If Uncle Mel is right about that saying, then there must be something more we need to find out about things that have happened with the Treman in the past," Maddy said.

"If there are any clues, they would have to be here. This palace is incredible. The only problem is, it would take weeks for us to get through just one floor—unless there is something with that peg that holds the key that will unlock this mystery for us. As far as history knows, things have been changing with the treman back home that have never happened before. That peg must be a part of that," Dray said, continuing to compile what he was learning.

"The doorman said he would talk with Shane about me going with him again this weekend," Maddy told his dad.

"Was there anything about the seven pieces you came here to see that made any sense out of this?" Mel asked.

"Not that we could tell. Maybe you could see something. They were definitely like nothing I've ever seen," Maddy said. He pointed toward the pieces' location.

"Where are they?" Dray was looking for the banner above the many entrances to the rooms.

"There in the 'unexplainable' room. That might be the next stop we need to take." Maddy was hoping they could see what an older person might see—something that they hadn't already.

CHAPTER SIXTEEN

More Evidence

As they walked to the room, Dray put his brain to work, recalling everything he'd been told about the pieces and the Treman. "Seeing all this coverage about the Treman that's here, on the walls, in the Treman room, and the things we saw at Mantra's—there has to be a connection with those pieces too."

"Have they got any idea how old they are?" Mel asked Maddy if there was any information about that in the "unexplainable" room or any of the books they'd seen.

"It's right up there. We'll have a greater chance of finding something with more of us looking." Outside the room Maddy led them to their next stop.

In the room they split up to cover more ground. Mel set his course for the pieces in the spheres. Dray went to the books about the history, and Trace and Maddy were looking at any stories that described them.

Book after book was brought to the bookstand, and pages turned as the four detectives searched for a missing link. Trace took the book that had "Dillon County" on its binding.

"Never thought much about our counties was very important in the history part of things," Trace added. "There is a section here about the pod that is south of you, the one that the story was about. It says that it was seen by over forty people when it fell from the sky, hitting earth. There's a note here that references other counties that had similar sightings. Port, Tinder, Denah, Rove, Mint, and Reign—that's the county where Burton is, right, Dray?"

"Yes. Get those county books, Maddy. Does it narrow it down to the pages about the falling pods?"

"In this one it's about in the middle—maybe that's where their accounts will be."

Maddy had brought all the books to the table, and they all took one, looking for the pod section.

"Here." They both had found an account about the pieces.

"The one in Rove says that another pod was seen hitting their county," Dray said, as he found the page.

Maddy confirmed, "Mint County has an account about where they found one of the seven pieces."

All seven county books offered pod stories. Each had witnesses and maps of accurate locations. The stories were passed down about what had happened at each location, but the pods had been marked only after the stories were checked out.

"The Denah County book states that there were two other pods they saw fall with the one they located in their county. They hadn't known their exact location of impact and never

MORE EVIDENCE

found any evidence that they even hit Amri-Ferret." Trace shared her findings.

"Does it say whether they were found in the other counties?" Maddy asked. "Those two extra pods—were they two of the seven, or are there two out there somewhere that haven't been found?"

Mel had been studying the pieces. "It's puzzling to me that they would have been sent in different pods, especially if they would fit together. Look at this."

The four gathered around the two pieces that Mel was pointing to. His mechanical visionary gift had picked out a possible connection. There was a place where the two pieces could possibly go together. It was a long shot, though, without taking them out of the cases to be sure.

The two pieces were completely different in shape, the grooves smooth on one, sharpened on the other. It may have been what researchers had missed. The connection between these two items didn't obviously look like they would go together.

"You might have something there, Mel." Dray could now see that a section did have a small flattened space that was identical to the other's shaped spot.

"What do we do now?" Trace was getting excited.

"Let's keep looking for any other records of the two pods that no one has found. There may be a story that was written about pods themselves." Dray was interested in what Mantra had passed to Maddy with the elder hand offering. Maddy had to follow any new findings about an unexplained identity that could be added to their knowledge.

"Found it!" Maddy held a book that was from a section about shooting stars. "Five hundred forty years ago, this time of year, there was a season of falling stars. It shows where twenty-nine of them were marked that hit the ground. It says there were hundreds of stars shooting above the planet and one that hit Henneh. The moon was red before the star hit it then turned the pink color it is now."

"How close are the places where the stars landed and were marked?" Dray took the book, mapping in his mind the distance from where they were. "Let's ask for a copy of this page."

Maddy asked the doorman to let them out and asked where they could get a copy made. He directed them to the office of inquiry, where, he said, they would have to have a notary come and make the copy, as the books couldn't leave the room with a visitor.

"I'll go," Maddy volunteered, and ran off in the direction he was given.

A few moments later, he returned with a woman carrying a copy machine under her arm. She had a case in her other hand that contained the proper stamps and validations to certify the copies were copies.

When she had finished, she handed them the copy then headed back to her office.

"This looks like we are going to be taking a trip." Maddy was rubbing his hands together. "When are we leaving?"

"One thing for sure is that we only have one copy. So no matter what, we go together." Dray was intrigued by the newly found clues. "Is the morning too soon?"

All agreed they'd leave after eating breakfast.

MORE EVIDENCE

"We need to take one more look at the treman trees on the east side of the picture wall before we settle in for the day." Maddy wanted his dad and uncle to see the wall anyway, so this would knock out two birds with one stone.

As they loaded up, Heaster nudged Maddy to look at who was coming their way. It was Tren Taylor, who was reaching into his coat pocket as he approached them.

"I'll make you my final offer!" He raised his wallet, which was in clear view of them all. It was bulging with currency. "I offer you an excessive one thousand shekels!"

Dray's head snapped around as Tren pulled out the offer from his wallet. This was more money than he had ever seen at one time. A thousand shekels would provide a comfortable living in Dillon. "What for?" he asked.

"My offer is directed at Mr. Handle." He sharpened his tongue, looking at Maddy.

"Speaking." Dray had his attention back.

"Perhaps I should be speaking to you. The father...uncle?" he asked, assuming Dray was related. "This lad clearly knows nothing about finance."

"Before you continue..." Dray's voice became stern. "...I am his father."

"Well, certainly you know this crude beast isn't worth that. This boy turned down more than he was worth before the contest. So I am willing to overlook his immaturity and offer him more...considering he did win."

Heaster snorted.

"Mr....?"

"Tren Taylor."

"Mr. Taylor, I'd like for you to leave now," Dray said, obviously struggling with self-control.

"Leave? Why...you are as immature as he is!" His squeak was shut off as Dray took hold of his tie.

"This is about honor, of which you clearly know nothing." Dray let him go. "You must know nothing about finance either. Maddy took home more than half of that in winnings. Your pocketbook isn't fat enough to make an offer for what he is worth. So please excuse yourself after you apologize to my son."

Heaster was getting a drink of water from the trough as Tren answered, "That won't be happening."

"What do you think about it, Heaster?" Dray gave a nod, and Heaster's mouth became a showerhead, covering Tren with a prime's throat and mouthful of water. "Would a crude beast know to do that on his own?"

Tren stood there dripping, along with his handful of money.

"Up!" came from Maddy after he and Trace were seated, with Dray and Mel in the crate.

"Right now, Heaster." Dray watched as His stubby tail lifted as he was relieved of yesterday's meal. "You got a direct hit!"

As they propelled forward, Uncle Mel furthered the insult. "Maybe he is a crude beast."

"We are on to the east wall, Heast," Maddy said, curious to see the juncture.

While they were floating over the wall, the positioning of the diamond-shaped treman had changed. One was moved to

MORE EVIDENCE

the middle, making a row of three with the single tree closest to the wall. "They were a diamond shape last time we saw them. I am certain." Maddy looked at Trace. "Right?"

"They were for sure," she answered.

They came to a rest outside the wall.

"Let me see that map of the locations of the star strikes." Dray looked at the map, believing he'd seen one of the locations out there. When he rolled it out, the one he'd seen close to the city wasn't on the east side. It was out by the park that Jed, Jilly, Trace, and Maddy had gone to for their outing.

"I remember now. That monument in the center of the park must have marked that spot. We could go there after we eat, or we could take a basket and do an evening picnic. You both would like it there. They've got groomed trails all through it," Maddy suggested.

"Sounds like a plan," Dray agreed.

They arrived at the inn as the after-dinner rush was finishing. They volunteered to help get the evening meal ready when the cleanup was done.

Maddy asked Marty if he could whip up a picnic basket comparable to the one they had taken with Jed and Jilly. A few minutes later, he came, carrying the basket and a cooler with beverages in it. "I think they might eat a bit more than Jilly does." He grinned as he handed Maddy the baskets.

Heaster had been gulping down partially chewed sprouts when Maddy came to the stable to hitch up the crate. "Sure am hungrier than I remember."

"Hopefully you won't look like Brute. He was too big. But we'd figure it out if you did."

They picked up the other three travelers and lifted off, heading outside the wall to the park. The monument was where Maddy had thought. Heaster landed them, as light as a feather landing on a bed, then lowered to the hitching-post area, where he began eating again.

They found a table to sit at close to the center.

Marty had a knack for food preparation. They ate to their fill, planning the next couple days' journey. Maddy walked to the memorial and read the plaque. This was a spot where a star had hit. More than five hundred years, and all the work to build the park would have surely unearthed something unusual. This spot could be checked off the list as a possible relic location—twenty-eight to go.

Back at the inn, they told Marty that they were planning an out-of-town venture and that they would try to be back for the weekend. "Could we use the crate? We'll all be able to go together that way."

"Under one condition—you get me another crate of beggas brought here. The busyness of the decathlon week burned through the whole last crate."

"Your wish is my command. Sure you don't want two? Heaster could haul them. Besides that, he has been eating up all your sprouts. Do you need any more of them?"

"Getting them delivered right to the storage stall is worth a few sprouts and bedding. Maybe when you come again. Look forward to seeing you when you get back." Marty's generosity was one of his obvious gifts.

Maddy delivered the begga crate and reloaded their baggage carrier with a few supplies. "When we get back here to

MORE EVIDENCE

check out the Treman display with Shane, depending on the outcome, it might be nice to spend Celemass back in Dillon. I'm sure Trace is missing her parents as well." Maddy had a dual purpose behind this suggestion—one, to see the treman changes at home, and two, to get a welcomed break away from this lifestyle. "That will be our probable goal anyway."

They had set a course that would explore the closest sites first. When the farewells were finished, the foursome, Heaster, and the work ride left Palace City—a course set without the certainty there would be anything in their bags at the end of the journey.

The first three sites came up bare—simple stone markers with brief explanations of what the sites were. The landing at the fourth gave them something. It was a rocky terrain that wasn't easily accessible on foot, a small mound surrounded by fairly mountainous walls. A stone marker proclaimed the tale of why the scene was marked there. A divot at the top of the mound would have been the impact bowl. It was not as small a disfigurement as the others they'd checked. They would have a bite to eat there at an area under a huge tree that was evidently very old, where they chose to set up their table. While Dray and Mel put the meal together, Maddy and Trace sat on a root that had been exposed from the years of soil being used for nutrients, as well as some erosion. They were discussing stories about past Celemass gatherings they'd experienced.

Maddy had picked up a stick that was lying by the root; he used it to poke at the ground, drawing stick characters and circles. One prodding action moved the dirt, exposing a shiny surface.

"What is that?" Trace had seen it as the reflection of light shot a beam at her eyes.

They looked down, not seeing anything because of the dirt recovering it.

"Right there in the dirt you just poked at." She got to her knees and moved the covering that had been hiding the object.

Maddy called to Dray, "Dad, come over here quick!"

They continued brushing away topsoil that had been wrapping this gift for ages. The case looked to be a cylinder with only half of the tube there. It was fairly long, with a large piece of a mechanical device inside the curved half of the large thin pipe. As they unearthed it, Mel saw places on it that might interconnect with the pieces at the palace.

"This has got to be another piece, with the exception that this must be a more important piece given its size and shape." Mel's comments were accepted by the rest. "What we do with this is the question. I don't know if there should be archeologists or excavators brought here to see if there is anything else."

Mel had a good point. There could be more at this landing than this item. There could be another piece buried anywhere, and without some sort of detection tool, they might be walking on other pieces without any hope of finding them.

As they inspected it, they found markings that could have been a language of words they didn't know.

The edge of the cylinder cut through the markings, offering the possibility that there was another half with more markings. The decision was made to bring the piece with them at least to the next marker.

MORE EVIDENCE

Their lunch was ablaze with "what ifs." What if this was another part? This would change everything. The stories of the seven pieces, the books holding only part of the story—this would make them void of all truth. What if there was another half? The questions continued as they lifted off to the next site.

There were three more sites they had planned to check out on their first day. Then the next seven sites would send them to an area they hoped the map was up to date with, as they were in a county inhabited by people who were rumored to be not too accepting of outsiders that stories told about people who were not too accepting of outsiders.

The next three they planned to see that day held little likelihood of their finding anything extra. They would have been found. The landscape was mostly flat and open. The only uncertainty was that any pieces could have been covered, like the last piece, with years of natural elements playing their part.

The night illustrated majesty. Only the cool air could add to the chill that the sky was presenting to them. They fell asleep watching the moons move through the background of stars—sparkling diamonds too far away to touch, yet they drew your hand to try.

The crackling embers faded into a simmering pool of coals covered by a gray dust of ash as the sun rose, casting long morning shadows that shortened with each inattentive look.

Rising early, Dray came in from a morning walk. "Is everyone awake?"

The response was delayed as Trace pulled her blanket up around her face to keep the fading morning chill from getting under her covering. "Soon," she and Maddy answered.

"You are missing the best part of the day," Dray went on. "The first part, the part you'll never see if you don't get up to see it."

Maddy sat up looking at the food being made for breakfast. Mel had joined Dray and was popping a piece here and there into his mouth as he cut the nards they had brought with them. "Haven't had these for a few days."

"If you stay in those blankets, your uncle might have them eaten before you get your chance at them."

They packed their sleeping gear into the crate and made their way to the unfolded table. The fruit tinged the back corners of their mouths with tart sweetness.

"Think we will have any trouble with the Japes?" Maddy had heard the story of the Japes, who had acted first then asked questions later.

A warrior that had been surviving in the desert battling the elements for each day's life they named Élan. Élan had mated with a beautiful woman from the south named Raych. Their descendants were nomads, wandering the desert at night in search of food and finding shelter during the day from the red sun's heat. The Jape females were always fair colored, so even a little sun would affect their bodies and could harm them if they weren't covered. The males were always a darker shade, making them better night hunters and tougher in the sun.

MORE EVIDENCE

"As long as we move in the daylight, we should be fine." Dray knew of them as well.

The first site and the second were both marked by a high, slender pyramid. The slate was set up higher, as the sands of the desert would blow around. If there had been anything at these two places, the sands would have swallowed them up. The third, fourth, fifth, and sixth markers weren't all just desert sands. The evidence at its best would have been hidden by time. It wasn't looking very hopeful that they would find what they found yesterday. When the seventh marker could be seen, it was set in an inlet, in front of a ridge of mountain rock. This vast inlet had appeared just off the edge of the desert sands. It was a safe place from the barren region of mostly sand they had been moving over for most of the day. This would be their overnight resting site. There was plenty of daylight left, but as the sun set behind the wall of the ridge, a shadow shaded the camp.

Their fire brought heat and better light as they searched for any possible clues. Maddy used a prod to break through the surface, hoping his last accidental find might be repeated. The light from the sun disappeared, leaving only the fire's blaze to see those things in its light. Stories of the day, and of the past, entertained the companions, who were keeping warm around the campfire.

CHAPTER SEVENTEEN

The Japes

A chilling screech stopped the sound of voices as they heard a whooshing sound that Maddy knew well. It was the sound Heaster made as he lifted quickly into the air.

Dray and Mel were on their feet; Trace was in Maddy's arms. "What was that?"

"That sounded like Heaster taking off, Dad. But what was that screech?" Maddy didn't trust the screaming sound to be a good thing. He was right.

There was movement where the rides had been standing. Terrible, unspeakable sounds reached Dray's ears, and he realized it was the stabbing and cutting of flesh.

The Japes! They had killed the work ride and were making quick work of quartering and dissecting it. Dray's crew had their bows drawn, with arrows ready to shoot. Facing the action, Dray walked toward the shadows. "Come out!" he commanded.

A dark figure moved into the firelight, holding a dripping cutting tool.

"That's close enough!" Dray ordered. "Who are you?"

"I am Javan, grandson of Élan."

His speech, though broken, was understandable.

"What have you done?" Dray was still unsure of his intent.

"We have found food for our whole group." Javan clearly felt no remorse for killing the animal. "Join us?"

Dray turned to his companions and slowly released the draw of his bowstring, putting away the arrow. "It might be a good time to join them."

As they gathered their belongings, Maddy could make out the figure of Heaster high in the sky. He thought, directing his energies toward him, "Stay close but not too close." He watched Heaster move up and down, knowing he'd gotten the message. Maddy hadn't uttered anything; this was the first distant connection they had, keeping his position secret, which for now would be to their advantage.

They followed Javan to the wall of the ridge, where another wall face covered an entrance into a huge cavern. As they entered the abyss, they heard chanting and sound of celebration. Further in a blazing fire was burning, and figures were jumping around it. It was a group of Japes. More than a hundred of them filled nooks and crags of the cave—young, old, male, female were all visible. There were a few still carrying in parts of the ride, bringing them to the fire and to various places within the large cracks of the cavern, which were simple individual dens. Activity was stirring them into a rabid frenzy, as food was now plentiful. Javan brought them to a very aged man. He sat, legs crossed, watching the goings-on.

"Élan," Javan said, introducing his grandfather, and then commanded, "Sit!"

He was now the one giving orders.

Maddy was experiencing a story that would last for the remainder of his days. His eyes were glued to the wrinkled old face, and he waited for any sound he would make.

As his eyes focused, he could see, from his seated position, a flashing from the fire behind Élan's headdress glancing off something in a shrine. It was a comparable match to the piece they had found by the tree root.

Maddy motioned for Dray to look at the shrine. Fortune had dealt a new hand. They had wrapped the other half in a blanket they'd left at camp. Maddy thought to Heaster, telling him to carry the crate out of sight. Whether his prime had gotten that thought was yet to be discovered.

Élan spoke. "You have given us a sacrifice. Eat with us. We welcome you to stay."

The Japes must have known that rides were edible, or they were just hungry. Maddy had never tasted one and asked Dray if he should go with Javan to get the things they'd taken out of the crate to share. He'd also be able to see if Heaster had moved the crate.

"Javan, we have more at our camp that we want to share." Maddy's mind was torn between trust and distrust as he offered. The Japes had just killed their animal without hesitation.

"We go now. Morning might be gone." His broken words came.

They departed together, leaving Trace with Mel and Dray.

At the camp the crate was gone. Maddy thought, "You're amazing, Heaster. Don't know how you did it, but you did it."

"No problem" flashed in his mind. It was Heaster.

They continued their conversation without Javan knowing. "Where are you?"

"Up!"

Maddy saw his silhouette on the ridge against the starry sky.

"We found another piece in the cave. Looks like the other side of the cylinder in the crate. Be in touch, and stay clear."

"I will do." Heaster knew the fate of the work ride and had no desire to end up the same way.

Javan helped carry the bags of food and extra clothing back to the group in the cave.

The beggas Marty had sent Maddy gave to Élan. "Maddy," he said, sharing his name, then said, "Dray, Mel, and Trace." He pointed to them as he was saying their names.

An elderly woman with a slight hunch in her shoulders came from a hollowed opening by the shrine. As she passed it, she nodded her head then turned to face them. Even age hadn't stolen her beauty.

"Raych!" Javan called, recognizing that his grandmother had come out of her room. He ran to her and helped her walk down to sit by Élan.

"Grandmother, they brought a sacrifice to feed us all." Javan still really considered the ride as a voluntary gift. "Maddy, Trace, Dray, and Mel," Javan continued.

THE JAPES

"Welcome. We have not had friends bring such a bounty before." Her speech was elegant, not broken like her grandson's. She spoke as a delegate from a high society. "Will you stay with us and be our guests?"

There was eeriness in her lingering on "guests." Things were beginning to seem strange. The relaxed atmosphere, in light of how the Japes had treated the ride, wasn't lining up.

Élan hadn't done anything more than invite their next meal into their abode. No feeling was given to them. There was no interest in why they were there or discussion as to why they would have brought them a "gift" that was of substantial worth.

The fire and celebration continued into the early morning.

Maddy had gone to look at the piece. Within the shrine the piece was surrounded by beads on strings. A few small bones were tied together alongside two skulls. As Maddy looked, Javan came to stand behind him.

"What are these?" Maddy asked, pointing to the skulls.

"My parents," he replied shortly.

"What happened to them?"

"Killed!" His word had a sprinkle of excitement as he spoke it.

"What about this?" Maddy reached out to touch the half cylinder.

Javan grabbed his arm. "No touch!"

"Why not?"

"They touch. They killed. Only Raych can touch. Not even Élan."

Maddy remembered Javan's warning. Was this why Trace was with them? He thought, Maybe only a woman could touch this piece.

The nocturnal Japes would sleep most of the day. Only a few of the younger ones wandered around in the morning. Daylight was their time to rest for their nighttime gathering. Eventually the young ones found places to shut down their energy, finding their furs and sleeping spots.

The ride hadn't been that good to eat, and as morning broke outside the cave, hunger kept some of Maddy's crew from sleep. Maddy tested his telepathy with Trace. "Can you hear me?"

Her head turned as she looked in his eyes. A slow blink answered his question.

"I think you are the only one that can touch that piece," he noted, still using his thoughts.

Maddy touched Dray's arm and woke Mel from his light doze.

"We're out of here," he whispered softly.

All agreed.

An exchange of a ride for a piece to their puzzle seemed to be a fair trade. Trace carefully took hold of the piece, avoiding making any noise. After she was holding it, they made their way to the cave's opening.

"Heaster, come! Bring the crate too." Maddy hadn't got the thought completely off when Heaster came into sight. He'd been waiting for any movement from their coming out of the darkened entrance. Heaster descended with the crate. They would all need to travel by Heaster's power. Maddy leaped to his back, reaching for Trace's hand as Dray and Mel got into the crate. The extra supplies were gone, which was a double-edged sword. They had nothing to provide them with food, but the crate was lighter now.

They lifted off, looking at the bloody spot where the ride had died. Their bows!

"Down!" Maddy hoped to get them then get out of there.

Dray jumped out of the crate before it had touched the ground, running to the weapons.

Bundling them under his arm, he was heading back when a crazed screaming came from the cave. The Japes were pouring out of the safe darkness, with no regard for the bright sunlight, leaping over the random rocks. Dray slipped, smashing his knees as he fell.

"Get up and away!" he yelled.

Mel shot over to him, taking his arm around his shoulder and assisting him back to the crate.

When Maddy saw them get in, he was already moving upward. Heaster was watching for the timing himself. The crate pulled off the ground just as one of the Japes soared from a rock, getting hold of the crate. The unexpected weight began to drop them as Heaster flexed an extra surge to his tail, lifting them back up.

The Jape was fighting to get to Mel and Dray. Mel used his strong hands to take the Jape by his forearms, forcing him to release his hold, and then Mel dropped him to the ground. He'd landed on another Jape, breaking his fall, which helped him survive the plummet.

When the team became a small dot in the blue, they looked for a place to set down. They wanted to regroup, check what they had for supplies, and get a better look at the pieces they had found on their expedition.

"Javan said that piece is what killed his folks, but how that happened, I don't know. I didn't want to put us in the same danger. Evidently you are able to handle it without being harmed, Trace. Maybe for general purposes we should stick to that plan." Maddy was still in disbelief over the past day's events.

Mel was tending to Dray's injured knee as Trace took her piece and set it by the other one Maddy had taken out of the wrapping.

There was no questioning the validity that these were part of the same unit. But just how they would fit together was still mystery—if they were all from the same part.

"How will we get these anywhere near the seven pieces they have at the palace?" Maddy posed the evident question. "And should we even try? There's no telling what this is or what it does. Why were these found now, when the other seven have been around forever? This also doesn't mean that there are no more pieces. What if there are more at the last sites that we have not even gone to yet?"

The questions were relevant. There were still thirteen of the twenty-nine markers that they hadn't seen. The seven pieces were logged as being found by the pods, and there were no pods by the markers they found these two pieces by. They decided to go back to Palace City with their finds. For now they needed to get Heaster some food, and they were hungry too.

THE JAPES

"Are you strong enough to carry us a little farther?" Maddy was standing by Heaster, knowing he was affected by the heat and lack of water. Without his getting water, his body would lose power more quickly. Food was his secondary need.

"We should get going." Dray could see that the prime was being pushed. The other ride had shared the load that Heaster now was carrying alone.

"We should be able to get across the desert sands by nightfall if we don't need to push him. We'll lighten the load of anything that will jeopardize his strength," Mel added.

He took the seats out of the crate and broke out a few of the boards that weren't needed for structure.

"We might want to bury them so we don't leave a trail the Japes can track." They followed Dray's suggestion and covered the evidence as best they could without using too much effort or time. Heaster was their life force. He would get the rest of the water they had.

They floated closer to the ground at first with an occasional uplift to see anything ahead that would offer them what they needed. The desert hadn't seemed so far across when they were seeking the markers. Now the heat seemed to be adding to the distance. Setting down would just delay them, sapping the vitality they needed to reach their goal.

One last view into the distance gave them hope. The peak of a land structure and then more formations came into sight. They had made it across. The map showed a lake just beyond the first crest. The landing was a bit rough as Heaster set them by the edge of the water and immediately dunked his head in.

Maddy unhooked the crate straps then jumped into the water, cooling himself off and drinking greedily.

The others followed. "I'll see what the woods have to offer us for food," Mel said, and took the bow and a couple of arrows into the trees.

"That was too close for comfort." Trace walked out of the water, wringing out her hair. "We had it pretty nice in the city. Food and water were never far away."

"We should be able to get there tomorrow. I don't want to miss the meeting time with Shane." Maddy's motivation was more passionate with this new evidence.

Mel came back with his shoulder bag bulging with food he'd found: wild berries, some roots, and a rabbit. This would curb their appetites.

"There must be some inlets for you to find food, Heaster." Maddy sent him off. "Don't forget where we are."

They had found their way to finish this day. Satisfied with the food and drink, they rested. The sleep they'd lost the night before made sleeping easy now. Small waves quietly rolled against the shore with the warm humid air filling their chests, relaxing their bodies into a peaceful rest.

The day brought with it a stronger breeze, across the water, causing larger waves. They slapped the shoreline in clapping repetition. Eyes opened to a grand sight—the sun was reflecting off the deeper water, sending a dancing light show to the smooth rock wall. The four watched a motion picture with naturally made effects.

Mel had taken the early shift of gathering more food for their full day's travel to the city.

THE JAPES

Dray was getting around with more agility, still bearing a limp but able to walk on his own feet.

Heaster had gotten his needs met, and the rest had him ready to haul everything again. Packed and loaded, they set off for their objective.

The new sights were amazing. Their journey had been a giant loop that was now ending as they saw the city come into view. A temporary dwelling place felt like they were coming home after a long, exhausting trip. The inn would bring those friends, food, and encouragement they had left only days before. The period away had seemed to extend time until the reality of past helped them see that it had been only four days.

They all got together in Dray's new room with the two pieces. The areas where the word markings were on both pieces lined up precisely. Trace held the first in place as they moved the second next to it. A shock snapped the pieces, causing her to jerk her hand away from them. They lay there rocking, as cords of lighted waves moved along the grooves on the inside of the curves.

"Maybe we need to wait until we see the other parts. Then we can see if there is any relationship between them, or if there is a specific place for the pieces, whether they are on the inside or the outside. Trace, could you sketch them from both sides so we can use the drawing when comparing these to the ones there?" Dray directed his question to her.

"Sure." She made a duplicate drawing of the halves, and then Maddy had to say, "This enough?"

"You are really good," Dray complimented her gift.

CHAPTER EIGHTEEN

The Treman

Maddy's appointment was later that day. He took the key with him as the others went to the "unexplainable" room. The sections might hold better clues now with the drawing to look at. They still weren't ready to reveal the mystery. This was their reason for not bringing the cylinder parts with them, as well as not being able to hide them in a backpack.

Mel held the picture Trace had drawn next to the domed covers protecting the pieces. The puzzle was taking form, as Mel could see places where they could fit together. The connections began to make sense as he studied everything.

"How will we ever get these all together?" Mel asked. Turning to Maddy he handed him the drawing.

"I'll ask Shane if they ever have to care for them in any way. That might be a way to try it."

Their tour for the day ended. They would take Heaster back to the inn until Maddy finished with Shane.

Maddy met Shane, greeting him with a handshake. "Is everything good to go?"

"Not sure what you are doing, wanting to come along and all, but you helped me get home less tired last time, so if you are ready, we are good to go." Shane was a mild man with a solid work ethic.

In the locker room, Maddy put the key into the leg pocket of his overalls, concealing it from Shane. Anticipation mounted as they entered the display. Maddy inconspicuously made his way to the trunk of the Treman. The rounded hole drew his attention like one mesmerized in a gaze. As Shane turned to sweep a pile of dust into a dustpan, Maddy took the plug from his pocket and reached for the hole.

"*Life!*" That was all Maddy could say in explanation of what happened as the key slid into the slot, making a loud clicking noise.

Shane looked back as the hum that followed the startling click brought the question to his mouth. "What did you do?"

"I—" Maddy's answer was chopped short as he stepped back to where Shane was, still staring.

"We need to get out of here." His hand groped for the keys to open the door.

The tree that had been dormant, unchanged, and constant since he'd been working at the palace was transforming with a metamorphosis action right in his presence.

"They are never seen moving! What's happening?" Shane demanded.

THE TREMAN

Maddy could have offered a suggestion, but he was too busy memorizing the altering tree as it turned into a mechanical, living, moving Treman who was being soaked up into his memories. Both men were unable to react as the branches retracted into the trunk of the tree.

The husk of bark divided into symmetrical units that slid up as a matching cutout slid down to replace it. Scales like a fish's became a shield as three solid bands surfaced at three even intervals. These all spun while still attached to the tree trunk. Two were spinning in the same direction—the third, the opposite way. While the base drew into the bottom, the center section slowed in action. The smaller branches and leaves became a shroud covering the top section with a pinecone look. When the center section stopped, two distinct vertical slots appeared. They opened to reveal eyes that were the deepest green Maddy had ever seen. They blinked a few times as the center rotated a quarter turn left, then right. They looked like an animal's eyes except they opened sideways.

Both lids that opened and shut were thick but pliable, blinking randomly and individually.

Shane had gathered his composure enough to get the door open. He reached for Maddy's arm saying, "We are out of here."

The Treman spoke.

"Peace! Do not touch him." Five understandable words were spoken. The bass tone came from within. Then he uttered another word. "Please?"

They were the first people that had heard the Treman speak since the story of him began.

335

It was an assumed disconnection that had gone on for time, times, and a half of time that he had really lived and audibly spoken.

"Maddy Handle, will you step forward?" The figure was speaking directly to Maddy.

What was this? Maddy's question had distorted into many. The most obvious utterance fell out. "How do you know me?"

"I am the Treman, the one Mantra told you about."

"I have a thousand questions for you then." Maddy hadn't noticed that Shane had left.

"We may need to get out of here before your companion comes back with the whole world. You can ask all the questions you want when we're out." Treman sensed the urgency to leave.

"Out where?" As Maddy's question was asked, a protrusion came from the trunk—a round slab to stand on.

"Get on." Treman knew he would comply. "Are you ready?"

Another rod telescoped out for a handle to hold on to.

"For...?" Maddy held tightly to the shaft.

They rose higher and higher to a slanted glass roof that let sunlight in for the plants. When the tip of Treman was close to touching, another transforming action took the roof apart and redesigned it to a shape he could fit through.

The movement was not like Heaster lifting off. It was like that of a machine that had solid parts covered by a fleshy, firm rubber coating, more committed and rigid when it moved than how Heaster moved. The flight brought them to the top of the mountain behind the palace, where they landed and could see the whole city from above.

THE TREMAN

"Ever been here?" Treman knew this place. As he continued he transformed back into a tree. "The guards won't pay any attention to a tree."

"So how did you know me?" Maddy's barrage of questions had begun.

"The key absorbed some of your thoughts. They were good, Maddy."

"I thought the key was for the treman in the corner of the counties. It wasn't until Shane got me in to see your partially hidden side that I recognized the identical etchings you have."

"That isn't a good treman anymore, Maddy. For the key to be back in me—that means he's been set in play, he and his seed. So what happened? Don't leave out any details."

"Do you want me to start from the beginning?" Maddy wasn't sure where that was.

"All you know that I don't know from the connection we have." His understanding way had Maddy spilling out his life, finally getting to the peg removal.

"Dad was hunting and had shot an arrow that must have hit the peg. When I went to look for the arrow, I saw the treman moving, which isn't supposed to be possible. That's when I saw the arrow fall. I ran and picked it up, and it had the key stuck to the tip. He didn't move after the arrow fell out."

"He is still moving, just not as quickly. When your dad hit the peg, it activated the treman, and if the key had not come out, you might not be here." Calculations were clicking as he spoke.

TREMAN

"What does that mean?" Maddy wasn't sure how this beautiful tree he had known to be a landmark could be anything else.

"He will be turning darker and more evil every day. How long has it been?"

"But he always looked so warm, and I used to even talk with him—me and my mom. How could he be evil?" Maddy continued his inquiry of a not-guilty plea, appealing for the tree's innocence.

"My key stopped him from fulfilling his mission, making him just a passive treman."

"Mission?" Maddy listened to every word.

"There was a seed sent here from another heaven. It was sent here to destroy all living things. Thankfully my father stopped that, sending my seed."

"Mantra, our elder, said her grandmother told a story about that seed from another heaven. It was a good seed. That was a real truth?"

"That is where I came from." Treman went on, "However, that treman's first cycle of seed was used to produce tremans that would construct an army. Many of these seeds were not able to live, yet people continued to plant them, unaware of what they were creating. By the third cycle of seed, the treman was able to move like you saw me move. He declared war. Battles raged, and the treman grew in power."

Overhead an object passed. Maddy dove to the base of Treman. It was the elite guard, making their final pass over the city before nightfall.

THE TREMAN

One guard had fixed his eyes on a movement. Not knowing it was Maddy, he dove down for a closer look. A root that Treman engaged covered Maddy completely, hiding him from the guard's hovering inspection. He returned to the unit, reporting what he had done to Drem, who was back in his leadership position of the guard.

Drem looked down and recognized the out-of-place Treman. They persisted on their nightly check, when Drem ordered his second in command to take the squad back to the stables.

"I'll be there soon—one last lap around the palace." Dray added

"Yes, sir!" The lieutenant took the lead as they went back to their quarters.

Drem circled—but not the palace. He went back to see what the Treman was all about.

The root had retracted, allowing Maddy to talk with Treman again.

"I'll be!" Drem exclaimed when he spotted them. He had lifted above the cover that Treman had landed in, moving to a place to dismount. "You surely don't do normal visitor things, do you, boy?"

Maddy sensed that Treman was about to guard him and hastily said, "Friend!"

Drem's demeanor was sharp with the loss Maddy handed him, easily misread for aggression. He was as enthralled as Maddy was with Treman. He had heard the stories. Part of his desire to be in the elite was because of them. There were stories of battle that had intrigued many young men, and he was one of them.

"Is it true?" Drem turned to hear an answer from the tree.

"I am true." Treman started his change, when the alarms went off. They peered over the edge to see a commotion of people and action around the palace entrance.

"Is that about you?" Drem was putting together the pieces.

"I would say probably." Maddy told him what had happened in a quick review.

"Stay here. I'll take care of it." Drem got back on Josh, floating up and over the crest, then straight toward the middle of the gathering crowd.

In the distance the lights from the Dew Drop were visible. Maddy's eyes spotted a floating figure moving toward the palace. It was Heaster. Maddy wasn't sure who was riding him, but he knew his own ride.

"Come." The word and the thought were vocalized.

"Where are you? At the palace?" Heaster replied.

"Come by the crest, on the mountain behind the palace."

Heaster told Dray where they were going, as he was the rider Maddy wasn't sure about.

They saw Maddy standing by the tree when they got to the top. It had gotten darker, with only the night moons beginning to shed their dull light.

Dray asked, "What are you doing up here?" Unprepared for any voice other than his son's, Dray flinched when he heard the deep answer. "He is here with me." The voice reverberated through his body.

Dray saw no one as he faced the voice. "Who is... 'me'?"

THE TREMAN

Treman spoke again and said, "You have a good son, Dray Handle. I am Treman."

Dray backed into Heaster, who was looking at the tree himself. "Maddy, how are you doing this?"

"He's real, Dad. All the stories we have been passing down through our generations are real. I put the key in his void, and he came to life again. Treman is doing this."

In light of what Dray had for evidence, it was appearing that the Treman did indeed look like the one in the display. His son wouldn't be telling him a story without telling him it *was* a story. The last hint was that the tree was talking.

"All right, so what do we do now?" Dray needed answers.

"How long has it been since the arrow incident?" Treman asked, knowing there was a timeframe deadline they were dealing with that they knew nothing about.

"About five weeks ago—a day or so more," Maddy was trying to be specific.

"We need to know for sure. He will be able to fully transform on the forty-fifth day after he was activated."

"It was six weeks today." Dray had been counting the days from his hunt. "That was the day I shot at the squirrel and lost the arrow."

"Then we have three days to get prepared," Treman answered.

"Prepared for what? Celemass?" Maddy asked. The celebration of Celemass was in three days.

"It amazes even me how things work out." Treman's history held the answer to the statement. "We'll need to get back to the treman soon. If he's moving, we may be closer than we think."

"I was telling Maddy about the treman's change when we first got here. It hadn't moved but it was changing." Dray offered all the information he had.

"There's something else, Treman," Maddy added to their dilemma. "There are four tremans outside the east wall that are moving. We first saw them in a diamond formation, and that's changed. One was moved completely."

"That means it has begun," Treman stated.

Drem returned, advising them that they should stay put for the time being. "There is quite the turmoil going on at the palace. Everyone has been removed from the inside, causing some chaos in the courtyard."

"We need to go." Maddy asked Drem a straight-up question. "Are you with us or against us?"

"Hoped I was a good guy—you are the good guys, right?" Drem's answer told them he was in.

"You're right!"

"All right then! Who's the bad?" The stories had not uncovered everything there was to know, and Drem was about to get an updated lesson.

"Anyone could be anyone after the next three days," Treman cautioned as he passed on key information to his listeners. "If they get to the transforming stage, you won't know them without a specific way you cannot always see."

"Did I miss something?" Drem hadn't heard the explanation about the amount of time they were dealing with.

"We might have only three days to get things done." Maddy shared what Drem had missed.

THE TREMAN

"So what exactly can you do?" Drem wanted to know what strategies and weapons Treman had. His experience in defensive preparedness had taught him to get an inventory of what was available for use for both offensive and defensive strategy.

"To keep it short and simple for all of you, there are things I won't be able to explain right now."

His way of saying what he did say let them know he had many options.

"Clearly you are able to move. Is there any time? How far? What do you need to exist?" Drem was looking for weaknesses. Any training for battle began by looking for weakness. An aggressor's weaponry and skill were only as strong as his weakest link. He wanted to know where Treman's Achilles' heel was, if there was one.

"Weakness. Telling you—*that* would be weakness. It is there that you will find my strength." The riddle was not critical or integral to their mission for now.

Dray had been sizing up Treman. "How heavy are you?"

"How heavy is your brother?" he replied.

"I don't have a brother."

"You do now. What else would you like to know?" Treman was opening his book to them; all they needed to do was accept his words.

"What can you change into?" Dray's question was inspired by Treman's comment about not being able to know who was on their side because of the tremans' ability to change.

"More than what you see now!" Maddy had watched the transformation in the display.

"I ask because we need a way to get you back to Dillon without drawing attention to you."

"What would you like?" Treman was willing to put on a display.

"How about becoming a bookcase?" Maddy thought a wooden object would make sense.

"I could do books, on that subject." Transformation underway, Treman's form retracted and expanded. Moving parts were everywhere. The tree shape distorted itself into a smaller, compact stack of books that just as quickly turned into a man standing before them. His realness was unequal to any carving or model of a man's image. He was as real as Dray. The image was inviting, yet the metamorphosis they'd witnessed held them at bay.

"Don't be afraid. I am with you always." He walked over to Maddy and extended his hand to him. "Take my hand, Maddy."

When their hands touched, Maddy could feel things that he wanted more of. The hand was more than a feeling of flesh—in it there was motion that could be felt, of every living thing. Life itself stirred with every pulse. "That is how you'll know them. If you touch their being, the force will be the same."

"What makes you different from them?" Dray wanted the understanding Maddy had felt. He took the other hand, seeing Maddy's thoughts.

"That." Treman had taught them. "They won't do that. They will not show the life for another. They are about destruction."

THE TREMAN

Drem was hesitant as he approached them. He wanted any advantage he could for what lay ahead, so he took the hand that Maddy offered him. Dray's home and life flashed in his mind as Dray saw Drem's world also.

They released Treman and grabbed each other's forearms. "Brother."

A connection was confirmed of their unified basis. Their lives would be now destined to walk this next leg of their journey, knowing they were linked in a chain of future events.

Drem escorted them back to the inn. Using his authority, he indicated he was taking them back to ensure their safety, putting aside any questioning.

As they were floating there, Maddy, who rode with Treman on Heaster, asked him how long he could stay in a particular form. "I have so many questions to ask you."

"Everything depends on the circumstances. When there is no threat or danger, I stay in a form as long as I have need. As to all your questions, ask."

They set down at the inn. Dray walked in with Treman as Maddy got Heaster settled in the stables for the night. Drem would meet them in the morning. Maddy ran inside to find Trace and his dad talking in the hall. Treman stood motionless as they spoke of what they would do tomorrow.

"Your connection to him is strong," Treman said to Trace, as he sensed it when Maddy saw her. "That will be a benefit."

Trace hadn't been introduced yet and had no idea who was standing in her presence.

"Treman, this is Trace." Maddy introduced them.

TREMAN

Trace wouldn't need to have the rest of the proper introduction finished. She could only utter, "Nice to meet you." She took his hand and felt the surging motion like the rest had felt. "Wow! It is really nice to meet you! Really, really nice to meet you."

"You as well, Trace Guthrie." He had read her name from Maddy as well as her life touch.

"You know me?" Things were getting strange for Trace.

"I do now and am happy about it."

They went to Dray's room and discussed the next day agenda, if it were to come.

Treman sensed the cylinder parts. He moved to the corner where they had put them and picked them up. He was able to touch them both with no effect to his being.

"They don't hurt you? Either piece?" Maddy hadn't dared touch the half they had taken from the Japes. Watching Treman carry them to the table sparked his inquisitiveness. "Is it safe to touch?"

As he reached, the Treman said, "Not so quickly, my young friend."

"Do you know what this is?" Trace posed the next question.

"Not exactly." His makeup, which only resembled flesh, was immune to the items and allowed him to touch them. "It isn't from this planet. How did it come to be here?"

Maddy told him the story of how they'd gotten the items.

"They look like they could all be part of the same device." Mel was waiting for his mechanical input to help him with the understanding of them. "Trace's drawings that we took to the palace showed that these could very well be parts of one complete object."

"Let's get going. Waiting until morning might be an added delay. Time is passing."

"Treman, we are going to get some rest. We can leave first thing in the morning."

The planet wasn't so massive that it would take days to get to their cabin. Maddy had gotten to the city in two unhurried days. If they were to push Heaster's speed, they could shorten that time.

"We'll wait until daylight then?" Treman confirmed.

"Daylight" was their response.

Treman didn't sleep. Once the key turned him on, he would only be stopped by removing the key. That was his only weakness.

His power would be continually charged by any manner of light. Even total darkness wouldn't shut him down. The key was only for activating transformation. He had absorbed sights, sounds, and anything in contact with his body and conducted a reading. The display floor had been his contact to the outside. The stronger his power, the further he could read.

The pods were something he couldn't read. This cylinder was his night mission. He was testing any connection to see if he could read it.

Time was now critical. The trip needed to begin. Dray's mental alarm went off, opening his eyes to the early new day. Shortly after him Mel awoke.

"Good morning." The greeting was from the alert and ready Treman. "How long until we leave?"

"Food isn't a requirement for you?" Dray knew the answer before he asked. "Marty will have breakfast ready, and then we can leave."

Maddy and Trace were already eating when the three men came from their room carrying their baggage. The good-byes were finished with Maddy giving Marty an envelope, saying it was just a thank-you card. "See you after Celemass, maybe?"

"We could use your help if you're ever looking for something to do." Emma hugged Trace good-bye as they loaded the crate.

"Thank you so much for everything, Emma." Trace felt tears sting her eyes. "Be ready in case."

In the stable Treman took the form of a ride and carried Dray and Mel. Maddy would be with Trace and the crate.

"We need to see what the east wall is saying." Treman lifted off in that direction.

Following him, Maddy lifted off, waving good-bye to their friends as they stood in front of the Dew Drop waving back.

"Be ready in case of what? And where did that other prime come from?" Emma asked Marty, as if he would know the answer.

"Maybe the ride is for them to come back with? Possibly that other person that was here is letting them use his?"

"Then where is he, smarty-pants?" Emma took her notepad out and wrote down what Trace had said exactly.

CHAPTER NINETEEN

Streak

The tremans had shifted closer together, still in the same configuration but much closer.

"They'll be connected soon. When the treman gets to full power to transform, it will activate all the tremans that have been planted from his seed—all the bad ones anyway."

They were on their way to Dillon as fast as they could float forward. Maddy watched the transformed Treman do the same things his prime could do. He couldn't be a more distinguished ride. It was like looking at a mirror image of Heaster, only a different shade of color.

Over mountain ranges and territories they flew; some were familiar, as they remembered them from their trip to the city. Treman was heading as directly to Dillon as possible to cut their traveling time to its quick. They might be there by dark, barring any obstacles that could delay them.

TREMAN

Klue was higher in the sky in this season, with Henneh off to his left. The pink color had deepened, as the reddening sun sat on the horizon. From the air the familiar landscape of home was disappearing with the sun. The cabin was close now, as shadows became darker. A few more moments, and they would be there. It had gotten too murky to trust going to the treman tonight, even with Harac's lime light giving off its glow.

They would rest and venture out in the morning. Two days left until Celemass. Maddy was too tired to think about the gift giving or the treman. The good, the bad, and Trace were the thoughts that rock-a-byed him to slumber land.

He would take Trace to see her parents after they passed the treman.

A magnificent tree stood in the cabin's front yard—one unlike any tree that was in Dillon. On it were all manner of fruit globes; teardrop shapes and thin leaf wedges of fruit blended in with the surrounding foliage, with painted drops of many shades scattered throughout its small and large limbs and branches. Luscious, luring victuals tempted any eyes to consume them. It was Treman in all his grandeur. He seemed to be taking all the trees, and blending them together was as close as you could come to explaining the sight he was showing them. As the morning risers walked out of the cabin's door, they paused in awe.

Watching all the folding, turning, retracting, and flipping was as impressive as the full tree. Then the tree became a man that stood in its place.

STREAK

An inviting "Good morning" interrupted the show of awe they had watched as Treman welcomed them to a new day. "Are you fed?"

"That fruit looked good enough to eat," Maddy responded.

"Not my intention to tempt you." Treman turned with a wave of his arm to a table behind him. It was covered with food—not all discernible but there ready for consumption. "Enjoy."

They moved to the table, tasting the strange globs and recognizable food.

"Where did you find all this?" Trace touched her lips to protect any food from falling from her mouth as she asked.

"There is a bounty of options around us if you open your eyes to see them—and are taught about how they work together." He transformed again into a prime. "For now I will continue to use this form to avoid attention. Are we full?"

Maddy had gone to get Heaster, leading him into the open yard. "Will we need any weapons?"

"If your father can hit a key with his shooting ability, it might be wise to have bows with us."

"Had I known about the key's purpose, I wouldn't have shot an arrow within five hundred miles of that tree." Dray dropped his idea into the conversation.

The other treman was unlike what it was the last time Maddy had seen it—not because it was physically so different; it was the knowledge of what truly lay beneath its surface that changed it.

Their first glimpse of it had caused a reaction from Treman. His old adversary, who had been in the same state of dormancy as he had been, was now set in motion. Time had helped slow the conversion, but Treman knew that transformation would be possible, and at the same speed, he could change in only two days.

Maddy took Trace to her folks. The couple was elated to see their daughter home again and safe. "I may not be here for long. There is a problem that has arisen with the treman on the county lines."

She wanted to give her parents more facts and share her experiences of her traveling, but time was the new dictator.

Kendal told her, "Mantra has been busier than a bee around a honey jar. The treman has been changing. Almost every day she's been out comparing her drawings to the physical treman, writing in her sketchpad what she found in her day-to-day observations."

"Have you been there?" Maddy wanted to know how involved he was, if at all.

"I went down there and watched for four hours a couple of days ago, but like the story, you don't see them move. How those tremans know if anyone is watching is a mystery."

"My dad and Uncle Mel are there now. We were going to go back and take a look too."

"Would you like to come back for dinner, Maddy?" Beth was hoping for more time with her daughter.

"That could work. Are you ready, Trace?" Maddy didn't want to miss anything, so he hurried their good-byes.

When they made it to the treman, Maddy saw Dray climbing up the tree, while Mel was on the ground holding the other end of the rope Dray had tied around his waist.

STREAK

"What are you doing?" Maddy threw his question up at his dad. Heaster had landed by Treman, still in prime form, who was supervising the climb.

"It should be up a little higher and around the back side," Dray said.

"Have you seen Mantra here yet, Uncle Mel?"

"Is she supposed to be here?" Mel returned a question.

"Kendal said she's been tracking and documenting any changes with the treman almost every day," said Maddy.

As timing would have it, her name seemed to call her into existence. The little old woman came waddling up the molehill. They could make out her hat first as she climbed to the top before coming to where they were standing.

"You finally came back from your trip, Maddy Handle? Did you find out anything when you were there about the Treman and those pieces?" She glanced up at the treman and then back at Mel, who was holding the rope, then refocused on the treman. "Dray Handle, what are you doing up there?"

"Trying to find—"

"Where his arrow had hit the tree a while back," Maddy finished. His quick misdirection of the question gave her an answer without his lying. "What are you doing here?"

"This ol' treman has been changing. I've never seen anything like it. I've been looking through all the old manuscripts and information about tremans in the past, and there's nothing about this kind of changing." She was baffled but hadn't given up. "Just wanted to see what has changed today. The branches are odd. They are losing limbs—and not just this one. There are a couple of them over by your place, Mel, over by where your parents disappeared, that are changing too."

"Falling off?" Maddy knew what had happened with the Treman but was waiting to see if Mantra had the same thing happening.

"If they are, they aren't lying around anywhere; it's more like they're getting shorter," she said.

The treman was retracting. That happened right before the transformation.

Maddy took Treman aside, leading him over to where Heaster was. "What are we going to do? How do we stop this?"

"The same way it happened last time—"

Maddy interrupted him. "What do you mean by 'last time'? This has happened before?"

"No. When the treman was put into the dormant state, I went dormant as well." Treman was telling Maddy about how he had defeated this treman many years ago. "There was a battle shortly after the treman had budded with its second batch of seed."

Mantra saw their conversation. "Where did that prime come from, Maddy?"

"From Palace City recently. I won the decathlon when I was there."

"Well, good for you! Was he part of your winning?"

"Kind of." He stopped, not giving any more leads to further questions. Maybe she would know another story about the tremans. "Mantra, I need to tell you something about this treman."

"Go on." Her detective instinct was still seeking more about it.

The branch Dray was standing on pulled toward the tree. His hurt leg caused him to slip, and had Mel not been holding tight to the rope, he would have fallen. All attention was aimed at Dray as he hung suspended from the rope. Mel let him down to a lower limb. His balance on that perch was short-lived; the limb moved too, with everyone watching. They needed to get him to the ground. Mel was getting that done.

"This may be a treman in your grandmother's story that was left out. We found the Treman to be real. He was at the palace on display."

"I saw it." She'd seen the Treman during one of her elder meetings. "Of course that is a real display for the people to connect to the stories that have been told."

As she was talking, Treman began to transform. He took the form of the man and walked over to her. He slowly brought his hand to her. "Feel for yourself whether I am real."

"What sort of trickery is this?" Her fear was shaking her conscience of what she had witnessed. Her hand was about to correct the lack of trust. "Are you real?"

She took the hand, experiencing the fluid force of possibilities that those who had touched his hand had consummated. Her grandmother's face flashed to her frontal lobe, with memories of the story she had told her.

"There is a part I remember from another story. The other pod that brought the Treman seed to this planet—I thought it was just a story. She told me it was a story. I didn't know it was factual."

"What were they?" Maddy needed to hear this story.

"I don't want to say this is fact; it has always been a story to me. It is one that I chose not to tell because it seemed so far from being probable. She said there was a weapon that was sent here that the treman seed was sent to retrieve—a weapon that could do things that weren't so good. The second seed that came was evidently yours, the one the man had accepted. The problem came when the first seed wasn't able to fulfill its obligation until it had gone through its second season of seedtime.

"For ninety years the hatred built for our planet. Finally the season of seed came again. The first seeds grew close to the treman because no one had known what to do with this type of seed. The second batch of seeds was transported everywhere, as far as they could be taken before they turned to goop. Sounds like a story so far, doesn't it? The original treman was creating an army with his seeds. Had it not been for you stopping him, Treman, we might not be here to repeat history. She said that you gave your understanding to the man and that without his help you wouldn't have been able to do what you did. He had given you a reason, a reason to forfeit your life. There was a battle after the seeds had been planted. The treman transformed, and his seed took many lives, as those who planted the seeds were met with different ends. Some were killed when the treman exploded from a seed to fullness; others disappeared; and other seeds had no effect other than to become another tree. How have I forgotten the importance of this story? I thought it was only a story. I didn't know you were real."

"It's all right, Mantra. It not only is hard to believe—it is hard to accept it to be true." Treman gave her comfort in his words. "Here is where we are now. The treman is about to have another chance to fulfill his obligation. That mustn't happen."

"Will the same resolve work this time?" Mantra knew that what the story said had to happen.

"Everything is different this time. He won't be as vulnerable, and he only has a short time to complete the final step in his ability to change. That's what we were looking for. We need to find the place where his keyhole is." Treman was more concerned in this moment with Dray's findings. "Did you find anything, Dray?"

"I've been looking for that spot almost daily. Had men up there looking. Nothing is showing up." She showed them the picture Maddy had pointed out at her library, one with an odd knot that appeared to be a void in it. "It should be up higher than Dray was, but they've looked higher without finding it now. Can it move?"

"It isn't supposed to until he can transform. It could be that he's covered it for protection. Once he completes his programming, though, it will be exposed whenever he transforms. It has to be exposed in order for him to convert. It could be anywhere after he changes, but it's always on the outside." Treman showed them where his key was, on the side of his neck, by his hairline. "The next time I change shape, I can have it be somewhere else."

"Let's just cut it down!" Dray was getting impatient.

"Good thought, except that cannot be done with any tools you have. Once his key has been enacted, the wooden appearance is only appearance. It is harder than metal. Even trying to burn it wouldn't work."

"So it can't be cut down, burned, or stopped?" Trace asked.

"He can be weakened, but that will only last a short time. When he's weak his reaction time slows enough to get a shot at his keyhole. Weakness, I'm afraid, only comes from expelling energy. That will be dangerous. It will be a battle."

"Can we shut off all the light to make him weak?" Mel sought for a solution.

"That helps stop his recharging, but there is no way of covering him completely, as he is now. His power won't be depleted in the open. He is using energy, but it is replaced instantly by the light everywhere."

"We have tarps. Can we try?" Dray was desperate for anything to help.

"It'll need to be done quickly." Treman encouraged their attempt then put the idea into action. "Heaster, get me over the treman."

Heaster got over the tree with Treman on his back. Treman jumped off, transforming into a gigantic cover. As the edges touched the ground, the team all tried to jacket the boundaries with dirt and anything they could. The tar gunk on the ground under the treman was a hindrance to do a good enough job. The smaller thickets and brush stopped the covering from touching the bottom, thus letting light in.

STREAK

It hadn't worked. Treman resumed his figure as a man.

"What about digging it up?" Trace suggested. It proved to be a frustrating question. The ground was too solid and covered by the seed goop right under the tree.

Their options were disappearing, and so was their time. The retracted limbs were evidence that things were starting to escalate.

"What about all the pegs in the library—the ones found when other treman trees were harvested? Are they good for anything?" Mantra suggested.

"How many are there?" Treman saw hope. "If we can get him to absorb them, it may cause the real one to show itself."

"Get Mantra back to the library, Maddy. We'll keep looking. And hurry!" Dray shouted.

"But what about the records?" Mantra had spoken out of tradition. She quickly realized they needed whatever options they could think of to solve the problem that seemed hopeless.

Back at the library, other blocks were being placed. The treman door to the library was molding into the frame. They tried to get it open and failed.

"Do you have a good rope, Mantra? I'll have Heaster pull it open." Maddy went for the rope as Mantra struggled to get the latch loose. Maddy tied the rope to the handle and to Heaster's belly ring. "OK, boy. Pull!"

The door popped open. They went in to get the pegs from the treman markings room. As they walked into the room, some of the pegs were lit up. Their notches were dim, blinking, colored lights.

TREMAN

"We might want to keep these flashy ones separated from the others." Maddy wasn't sure what the plugs were doing, and not all were doing it.

They were able to get almost fifty, about half of each kind of peg, to take with them. As they got closer to the treman tree, more of the pegs started turning.

"I don't know what's happening to these, Treman, but more are lighting up all the time, especially when we got closer to you. The ones that changed on our way here are in this bag." Maddy handed Dray the bags.

"Are there good and bad pegs?" Dray asked.

"They are all keys, but some are from his personal treman seeds that were harvested. We don't want to put those on him. Hard to say what might happen."

As he opened the bags, a few of the keys acted as if they were magnets and the treman was metal. "Get them off! Quickly!" Maddy reacted as their attempt had gotten three of the ten that stuck fast to the trunk. "Take those others away. Watch to see if another keyhole shows itself. There were only seven that we couldn't get off, right? So if an eighth one comes out, that will be his."

"We keep calling him 'the treman tree.' Was there another name he went by?" Maddy had a point. Things could get confusing as to which tree was which.

"Streak. They called him Streak because of the way he fell from the heavens." Treman went on, "They all are given their markings, and that's how you tell them apart."

The keys had sped up the movement. Streak was almost there. "There! There it is!" Trace saw the keyed mark.

STREAK

"Dray, Mel, your bows!" Treman ordered as he took charge. "A direct hit should shut him down."

Trace was pointing to it, eyes locked on it, so as not to lose it among the others. The archers were ready to fire their darts. They would try to hit a moving target with an arrow. Skill and years of practice would now be put to the test as the pegs changed constantly. "The one to the left!" Trace practically screamed.

An arrow flew. Miss! Dray released, hitting just behind the slow-moving key. The arrows fell to the ground without marring the barky cover. Two more arrows were lying in their tray of the bow. A draw, and both arrows took to the air. Mel had aimed at the wrong plug but had hit it. Sparks flashed as the key and arrow fell to the base. Dray's arrow was off target again. Arrows kept falling to the ground, but four had hit the wrong keys, disabling them. Three remained. They only had two arrows left. Their aim had to be true.

"It's the middle one." Trace still kept her eyes on the original.

Mel drew back and shot.

He'd hit it. The sparks flew again. The last two keyholes were now both moving.

"I must have gotten mixed up!" Trace cried in alarm.

Dray drew his bow, moving the tip's aim from one key to the other, uncertain.

"Shoot, Dad!"

His shot hit. As the arrow fell with the fizzling plug, they all exhaled a sigh of relief.

It was all too soon.

TREMAN

As soon as the arrow landed, the tree began to morph. The last keyhole had evaded contact. They had missed the day of change. Streak was changing after years and years of being stationary. The base, where it met the footing, shed all clinging growths. Moss and fine particles of dust fell to the tar. Huge cracking sounds were emitted, and the ringed sections became visible. The rotation started at the rings. They watched the complete transformation in a hypnotic trance, except for Treman. He was changing as well.

"Heaster!" The trance was broken. Treman had become a prime again, calling for them to leave. "Get on! We have to get away!"

Mantra watched history come to life as they pushed her onto Treman. Trace, Dray, and Maddy were on Heaster while Mel had gotten on with Mantra. As they floated off, Maddy looked back to see an object hurling at them. "Down!" His command saved them from being hit by a driving lump of metal. It exploded over their heads, sending shrapnel flying everywhere.

"To Palace City!" Treman gave their destination as Maddy was about to ask. "The treman's connection to those at the city wall may have gotten to the four outside. They may be changing too. They may become one, or they might all be their own unit."

"Will they all have Streak's capabilities?" Dray hoped to hear a good report.

"They can move on their own, but he is the chief overseer. His orders will be followed to the death. These aren't simple trees anymore. If they all are separate units, we are at war with an army of could-be-anythings."

"Are we going to be able to tell them from anything else?" Mel demanded answers.

"By their keyway—that's it. The seed tremans will be easier to spot in the beginning because of their need to learn how things look and act. People are harder for them to copy because they can't stand them. We should get prepared. We may find carnage when we get there. The defensive plan is to guard the seven pieces at the palace. If Streak gets them, we won't do so well. Anything or anyone between him, and those pieces won't be tolerated."

"That is our defense? Be ready to be killed?" Trace wasn't keen on losing what she had just gained. Her life with Maddy was fresh, exciting, and newly started. This venture wasn't looking so appealing.

"Good always prevails, Trace." Maddy tried to shake the prominent thoughts that were battering against a secure door to his vault of hope.

They had just sailed through these airways. Even with the recognizable landscape, the trip was lengthening. They would reach Palace City the day before Celemass, the day of celebration of life and giving. And they would meet it with a looming cloud of death and taking in their wake.

Maddy lightened the heaviness with a question. "What were you going to get for me?" His over-the-shoulder request proposed a call for hope that Celemass would remain a good day.

"Get for you?" she asked.

"For Celemass. It's tomorrow."

"I don't know, Maddy." A moment of peace soothed her mind. "How about a surprise?"

"I'd like to give you tomorrow today, a day early." His desire to spend a lifetime with her was going quickly, yet his talk of tomorrow had brought her a glimmer of hope.

"Can I open it?" She was unfocused on the mission, as she hoped for tomorrow and what she had dreamt of most of her life. It was her dream to be with a wonderful man and some children in a warm, cozy home.

"After you get some sleep. We all need to get a couple of winks of rest. We have a big day tomorrow."

The subtle suggestion of his words worked to close Trace's eyes in sleep.

Maddy nudged Heaster to get alongside Treman. He pointed to his passengers on his back, showing their fatigue. He was tired, in addition to his other riders. Mantra was catching herself, as her head would drop jerkily forward in slumber. Mel was nodding off too.

"A few moments then." Treman floated to a clearing, landing by a narrow river. Heaster could get food and drink for the last bend of their journey. The shadows lengthened as a small fire lent their sleep warmth and peace.

CHAPTER TWENTY

The Battle

"We need to go." Dray shook Maddy's arm on his way to Mel. Trace had fallen asleep on Maddy's chest and woke to find his eyes looking into hers.

"Feel better?" He had gotten some sleep and was hoping Trace had as well.

"I was dreaming about a machine that could take us to a place far, far away. Four people could fit in it, and it went to places in a flash—like the cylinder, only much bigger. The shape opened, a few buttons were pushed, the hatch closed, a puff, a blast of energy, and gone."

"If we had one of those, we could get away from Streak and his minions." Maddy smiled then tried to recall the words that were already in Trace's ears. He'd reminded her of their situation. "Sorry, Trace. That sounds like an amazing machine."

As they loaded up again, the sun dropped to a sliver of a dome on the horizon. The next leg of their journey would be at night. They kept the bit of light behind them as the city was ahead of them. A few hours had passed when the city became visible as a glowing field; its lights were a beacon to follow the rest of the way.

The Dew Drop was the most logical place to go first, as it was close to the east wall and the four trees outside it. They dropped Trace off to tell Emma and Marty what had happened and the danger that would soon be at the door of the city.

Flying in at dark had prevented Drem and his guards from seeing them. They hadn't gone by the palace so as not to attract that kind of attention just yet. They wanted to see what the trees were doing first.

The action Streak had started had begun to move the tremans' branches and limbs in likeness to their commander. They had begun to change, but distance had delayed them.

"Dray, go with Maddy and get Drem. Tell him we're going to need his help. Mel and I will look for their keyholes. If we can find them, we'll try and disarm them."

"Be safe!" Maddy wasn't concerned about Treman. It was Mel that he was troubled about.

"Think he'll be on duty?" Maddy knew from the skills Drem showed at the contest that he would be an asset to their cause. His shooting skill and Josh's being a powerful prime would prove to be of value.

"That's why they are called 'the elite.' They are the city's finest riders. He'll be there."

Dray's words were confirmed, as in seconds they were surrounded by the guards.

THE BATTLE

"Drem, we need your help." The words were firm and stern.

This was what he lived for. "To what extent?"

"Everything you've got! The treman back on the county lines, called Streak, has transformed, and we believe he'll be coming for the seven pieces in the palace. They're part of some kind of weapon he was sent here to get. The story is fact, Drem. Not a made-up story!"

"Riders, get to the palace! Lieutenant, have four of the guards inside the 'unexplainable' room and the other two squads patrolling the outside of the palace. I'll be right there." His order sent them in formation toward the shining palace.

"Where's Treman?" Drem was again getting his chess pieces located and in position.

"He and Mel are at the east wall with the four tremans that are there," Dray informed Drem. "They are trying to shut them down."

"So there is a weak spot? How is it done?" This was Drem's chance to find the weakness.

"You need to hit their eyespot key. They will have it exposed somewhere. It is how they can change. It would have worked for Streak, but we missed his button when trying to stop him. I believe he may be a little ticked off. When we left Dillon to get back here to the stronghold of the palace, he hurled a sort of exploding rocket thing at us."

"How much of a window do we have?" Drem wanted time to set his defense into place.

"If he knows where to go, he could be here anytime. If he thinks the pieces are still strewn around the planet, we might have until daylight." Maddy knew they had taken a break on their way, and Streak might not have any reason to stop.

"You should go get Marty's armor on, friend." Drem had found an ally in this young competitor. "Hurling rockets sounds like quite a weapon in itself."

"Thanks, Drem. We'll be at the east wall if you need us." Now Maddy knew where Drem stood for sure.

"We'll get together in about an hour to go over our strategy," Drem said as he started to leave. "Come to the palace."

"Dad, I need to tell you something," Maddy blurted out. "I got really knocked out by some wine one night a while back, and this older woman—"

Dray stopped him. "Did you learn anything?"

"That's what I was getting to." She was going to give me something—I think because she liked me, but I told her I couldn't take it. I think I'd like to take it now."

"Maddy Handle, what about Trace?" Dray was missing Maddy's point.

"It's armor, Dad. She had it specially made for me to use in the jousting event."

"Where might it be?" Dray's understanding was still possibly going to be stretched.

"Heaster, let's get to it." Maddy and Dray were on their way to the penthouse.

At the landing of Mary Ellen's high-rise, Maddy went to the door with Dray. The doorbell rang, sending a chill of the bad memory down his back. An eye peered out of the curtained side panel of the entrance door. It was Mary Ellen. She was in her normal dressy clothes. The door opened.

THE BATTLE

"Well, if it isn't Maddy Handle, and what, his bodyguard?" Her eyes inspected Dray, sensing she had a real man reflecting in them.

"Mary Ellen, this is my father, Dray Handle. Dad…Mary Ellen Moen. I'm here for two reasons."

"Let me guess—"

Mary Ellen's need to control everything was stopped when Maddy cut her off. "No time to guess. First, the city is in danger, and I wanted to warn you. The second is to ask you if you still have the armor. It looked like it would fit really well. I would be willing to buy it from you."

"Chivalry isn't dead after all." She didn't hold a grudge now that Maddy had brought her a warning about the danger. "You go in there and get it. It's in the hall where it was before."

"Thank you, ma'am." Dray tipped his hat to her.

"So that is where he learned all those manners from. Are you single?" Her eyes still hunted for any new prey.

Maddy returned carrying the armor. "We've got to go. I don't know how safe you'd be up here, Mary Ellen. You might want to find shelter closer to the ground. Thanks again."

They were back at the stable in an instant. Maddy was finishing putting on the armor as Trace came out. "No helmet? I wouldn't want my knight in shining armor to mess up his pretty little face." She got closer to where Maddy was standing behind the partition wall. "Wait, that isn't Marty's armor. Is that the old one's suit? Hope it doesn't have a switch that makes it fall off whenever she wants it to."

Maddy was about to explain. "Trace—"

"You look like an incredibly edible egg in there." Her desire to forbid Maddy the safety of Mary Ellen's gift was gone. "A prince in a knight's uniform would be a better description!"

"I…"

Dray came back from the kitchen.

"I'd better get going." He was about to leave his newly found reason to live hanging on his dad's interruption.

"You gonna tell her something, son?" His eyes told Maddy he accepted their relationship.

"I want to kiss you?" He was a little shocked that he'd offered to kiss Trace in his dad's presence but now would be obligated if Trace accepted his proposition. "If that's OK."

Trace moved to a perched position on her tiptoes, eyes closed, lips semipuckered.

He set down the helmet and took her arms gently in his hands and kissed her.

"Be right back." He took his helmet and, with Dray, lifted off and headed east. "Tallyho."

No treman in sight but the hunt was on.

Mel had made some torches and waited for their return. He sat by the tremans, watching their every move as best as the small fire he'd started would permit. Dray and Maddy floated in, setting down by the temporary campfire in the center of the four tremans.

"Won't the fire give light for powering them?" Maddy had remembered the speck of information Treman had shared about how they were charged by any light.

"Smart! We were trying to see if they would slip and show their mark. And we were hoping they would still stick

THE BATTLE

to the 'no movement while being watched' clause they have always followed—if the fire alerted them that they were being watched. Please put it out, Mel." Treman was happy to see Maddy was a quick learner.

Mel made a move toward the fire just as a flying shaft stuck deeply into his thigh. If he had not stood, it would have hit him in the chest. Dropping to the ground he held his leg where the pointed rod had almost come through the back side.

The fire was now an absolute disadvantage. Treman raised his changing arm, sending a casing that covered the fire and snuffed out the firelight.

Dray had gotten to Mel, pulling the object out of his leg while applying pressure as he wrapped his oozing wound. Another shaft was repelled by Maddy's shoulder guard and stabbed into one of the treman's trunks. It had punctured it. The stake had hit the mark, shutting down any further action of that treman. This hadn't gone unnoticed. They needed to get out of their range.

Whether by chance or pure fortune, one treman was down. With its means of transforming shut down, it was a vulnerable wooden object again. Fire had changed from a disadvantage to become an advantage again. "Light it up!" Treman took away the fire's shell.

Maddy took the outer ends of a couple burning firewood pieces, placing them at the base of the tree and setting it ablaze. On Heaster's harness, his early Celemass gift from Dray hung ready to be used. He ran to his ride, taking the bow and quiver into the darkness. The single front tree had been defeated. The three trees in a row remained. The fire from the tree was a disruption that caused an outer tree to reveal its mark. Maddy took aim and sent an arrow at the controlling device. It hit with a thump, dead on target—one more downed adversary.

Dray had taken Mel to a safer spot behind a rocky wall. He watched as his son was turning into a warrior, into a man.

A whistle to the prime brought Heaster to where they were.

Dray shifted his bow to shooting position again when Mel was settled.

Above the situation, Drem and Josh floated in with two of his guards. He had seen the fire and come to lend a hand or find out the reason for the flames. Their plan to meet and discuss any plans had been postponed. The battle had officially been initiated.

Mel was going to need medical attention. The dressing Dray had put on him was nothing more than a tourniquet that was soaked with blood.

A whistling sound, not from Dray, was heard as a rocket hit one of Drem's guards, exploding when it contacted his armor. The guard was knocked off the ride and fell to the inside of the wall. The prime had been hit by the explosion and was going down, fighting to stay afloat.

He had found them. It was Streak. The way that the tremans communicated had brought Streak to his offspring trees. The mechanics were deep within their makeup. All their actions were controlled by their key, which was the form of communication between them, the way they transformed, and

THE BATTLE

the only way to stop them. The design of what they could do all lay inside the key that came from the genetics of the seed. Each seed was like the seed of any other plant, with the same basic structure, parts, and processing, but not exactly the same in how it was able to change or perform.

As Streak flew into their midst, he rotated and then landed by the two remaining trees. He converted his vessel into a tree again and began communicating with the other two. His shape was like the first form that Treman had become in the display room at the palace—the three rotating round blocks. This would be the most difficult of all the treman tactics to figure out. Who was who? Streak had almost every characteristic that Treman had: the same rings, the blocks, and the ability to transform. How they would know Treman from the others was going to be essential.

A voice projected from Streak. "It's been a long time, Treman. Will you be joining us on our mission or choosing to be destroyed?" It was a cold and deep voice. In light of the fact that his previous choice had put them both in hundreds of years of bondage to stillness, the answer was expected.

"Not today, Streak." Treman's answer was firm and deliberate. "So do you have any stipulations or demands?"

"I demand you bow to me. These people will die if they try and stop me, and if you do not bow, you will die as well—only a much more tortuous death." Streak's words were penetrating.

"What do you want all that for?" Treman thought Streak's quest may have been altered with the passing of time. If the pieces were still his undertaking, they would be defended until the last beat of their hearts.

"Because of this prison I've been locked in. Today my freedom will not be taken away from me. As you see, I have an army this time around."

"Three of you are an army?"

"There are more than three of us." His form motioned toward the western night sky.

There, in the light of the night moons, an even line appeared. The line grew thicker and more pronounced. It was at least a hundred more tremans that Streak had picked up along his way—transferred seeds planted randomly across the land, now at his beck and call. The communication had given Streak the information the east-wall tremans had gathered from this area.

Dray and Mel took aim and hit the last two tremans' marks. They drooped as the keys fizzed out.

"*No!*" His blasted word shattered the air. Streak had just been antagonized by these people for the last time. "Now you die!"

He turned and fired a rocket at the place where Dray and Mel had been taking cover.

Maddy and Heaster watched as the area exploded, sending rock fragments, dirt, and flashing particles in all directions.

"*No!* Dad!" Maddy screamed as he watched the demolition destroy the vicinity his father was in. Any passiveness was gone as his next three words resounded. "Now *you* die!"

His quiver was being depleted of arrows as he fired one after the other at the wicked treman.

THE BATTLE

"Keep your tiny needles in your quiver, *boy*!" The ridicule in Streak's voice egged Maddy on to the point of no return.

Nothing Maddy shot at him had any effect. Arrows glanced off him like throwing toothpicks hitting a rock. One of Streak's appendages started shooting back the shafts that had hit Mel. They came at Maddy in secession faster than anything he'd ever seen shot from a bow.

"Up!" The command came. As he rose, so did the shafts that were being aimed at his movement. Rod after rod being shot missed, just behind his evading motion.

The other tremans would be here too soon. The time had come.

"Retreat! To the palace! Quickly!" Drem had taken charge.

As they fled to the palace, the line in the skyline became clearer, as the dark night gave way to the breaking of dawn.

Their flight was interrupted by Maddy's question. "Treman, my father and Mel? We cannot leave them there."

"I want vengeance as well, Maddy. But we are alive and need to live to fight another day." His words, though true, were not what Maddy wanted to hear. His dad and uncle were gone. They were retreating to the last line of defense, with a hundred more practically indestructible enemy tremans almost upon them.

"Practically!" This was the key word Maddy repeated. The keys were their weakness. They had a weakness.

"Practically what?" Drem wondered what Maddy had meant.

"I'll tell you inside," he replied.

375

Back inside the palace, the entrance doors were sealed. The structure was designed to withstand the adversities of time. A few rockets and shafts weren't going to buckle these walls. Huge square-shaped stones, in a bricked pattern, formed a fortress wall that held the beams, and the construction of the peaks was evidence of a monument for the ages.

"Your thoughts, Maddy?" Drem was about to see if his plans were coupled with this practical suggestion.

"*Practicality* is the word I should have used. It says we need to be practical—not fight his way. He wants us afraid, beaten, and running. What we need to do is invite him in."

"Invite him into the palace? That can't happen." Drem's duty was to keep the palace secure and protect it, not open the doors to defeat.

"Surrender!"

Maddy wasn't in his right mind. Letting him in and surrendering to such a destructive force as Streak wouldn't end in a happy land.

"He won't accept surrender. And he will be ready for any tricks." Treman knew that about his foe.

"One thing before I tell all—does he know what the pieces look like?" Maddy was making more sense now.

"He must." Treman realized where this was going. "I will become the pieces he's seeking."

"Practicality—we use the weapon he's seeking as our best weapon for our offense." Maddy had to put his plan into production swiftly.

THE BATTLE

"One question." Drem knew most of the art of war. "So Treman becomes the pieces, and how does that capture the flag?"

"It doesn't. It gets Treman in contact with him, and that's when his mark will be most evident. I believe that when Streak is shut down, all the others will be too."

"Another question." Drem wanted every detail explained. "How will Treman shut him down?"

"Oh, he won't. *You* will."

"I don't know what is in that melon of yours, kid, but in case you need to know this, I don't know what I'm going to do."

"Exactly!" That was Maddy's ace in the hole. No one else could know for now. "The rest we'll figure out later—that's all I have for you."

Maddy went to the "unexplainable" room with Treman to see the pieces, leaving Drem standing in a baffled state of mind.

"What are you thinking, Maddy?" Treman didn't have all the pieces put together himself.

"You give your life for his. You already showed us that you were willing to give up your life to keep Streak from taking everything." Maddy wasn't asking Treman to die again. He didn't know how or why he was suggesting his plan would work. He had felt it from deep within himself. "The two pieces that are at the inn—you'll become them in transformed mode. Then I'll take your key out. That way Streak won't know the pieces are you. He won't sense your life force."

TREMAN

"My key is in your hands?" Treman was aware of the need for trust.

"It was there before and it worked, didn't it?" Maddy still hadn't let on how the final blow would be given. "Truth is, you must trust me this time."

Pounding noises echoed from the enormous locked palace doors.

Maddy had Treman transform into the cylinder shape they had found on their star-strike mission and then removed his key. The absorbed tree parts that had been attached when Maddy was carrying it in his rucksack were gone. He held the heart of his latest comrade in his hand, with hope and some apprehensiveness. "This has to work, right?"

Inside an upper room, above the entrance, was a slot for viewing those who would be requesting entry—or in this case, to see those who were demanding it. A torrent of blows was being waged against the doors, shaking their mounts and hinged attachments but not able to move them out of the groove they were in at their base.

Maddy took the symbol of surrender, a white flag, and put it through the opening, waving it frantically to get attention. Streak was on the rear side of the onslaught, watching his army beat the doors, when he saw the flag.

"Stop!" came from within, and instantly the lesser tremans stopped their assault.

"Surrendering so easily?"

"We are ready to negotiate." Maddy started his negotiation. "Besides the bowing thing, what else is your desire?"

"To get what I was sent here to get! The weapon!"

THE BATTLE

"If we give you this weapon, will you leave—and leave the people of this city alone?"

"Why would I do that?" This massive aggressor had no reason for sparing anyone.

"So you could avoid the killing of innocent people. They have done nothing other than store your weapon in this place, keeping it from being lost." Maddy hoped to find some compassion, some gap in his layers of hardness.

"When you give me the weapon, I will leave. But Treman dies after he bows!"

"Back away from the entrance, and we will bring you the things you want."

The command was given. The tremans backed off, forming a gauntlet pathway to Streak. The giant doors were opened enough to let Maddy get through with the pieces. As he walked between the lines toward his enemy, Maddy looked at the opposition and its superiority. His antagonist was waiting at the end of the two parallel rows. When he reached the end, he set the pieces on the ground in front of him.

"What is this?" Streak demanded an answer.

Just the question Maddy had hoped for. Streak hadn't known about the pieces. He thought this weapon would be in one piece, not many.

"Is this a trick?" His order came with no rebellion allowed. "Put it together! Or the girl dies."

A gofer treman brought Trace from behind Streak's massive bulk. He had detained her at the inn on his way to the palace. This was not in Maddy's plan. He asked her if she was all right, as he saw there was a drop of blood on her lip. The battle had tweaked an unexpected event that would need to be adjusted to, without doubting or delay.

"I'm fine, but Maddy, you can't put it together—he'll kill us all anyway." Trace had experienced his rough, callous treatment enough to know he would do whatever he wanted anyway. She had been forced to tell Streak where they kept the weapon. She hadn't said anything about it being in pieces.

"This is your little companion, isn't it? I felt your connection the day you were standing on my limb and the day you floated around me with her riding that worthless prime." Streak was taunting Maddy beyond what he had ever felt.

Every ounce of Maddy shook with longing for vengeance.

This evil intruder that Maddy had admired for his majestic stand only days ago, while daydreaming on the hill and looking at him in awe, was now his utmost archenemy, taunting him by pushing his most guarded buttons. Repeatedly.

"You are the brilliant one here—you do it!" Maddy pushed the pieces closer to him with his foot.

Trace was mishandled some more, yanked around like a ragdoll.

"Are you certain you want to do that?" The evil in Streak's voice let Maddy know he wouldn't be kidding around for much longer. He wouldn't hesitate to have Trace torn apart.

"I don't know how! This is how they were found. If we had known they went together, wouldn't we have done that already?"

The truth in his voice must have been convincing, because after a pause Streak ordered, "Bring them to me!"

THE BATTLE

The time for his plan to be delivered was now. If Streak got the pieces together without transforming, the whole move would be headed for the scrap heap. Maddy moved them closer but still out of Streak's reach.

With a suspicion looming, the giant machine began rotating and adapting into a form that was capable of assembling the parts.

Maddy spotted his keyway. Now all he had to do was get to it with Treman's key.

"Where is Treman?" Streak had changed and was walking guardedly, approaching the cylinder.

"In the palace awaiting his fate." In his mind he spoke to Heaster. "Tell Drem I see it and to get ready to shoot Treman's key to me."

Heaster had heard; he waited for his next instructions after telling Drem to be ready.

The mechanical arms of Streak couldn't open the cylinder that was Treman.

"Maybe you need to be like us to get it open?" Maddy was now on the offensive.

"I will never be like you! Weak, scared, puny!" His character was inflexible as he continued trying to open the cylinder.

With the treman preoccupied, Maddy gave the mental directive: "Now!"

Heaster passed it on to Drem. The key, attached to the end of the arrow's tip, now flew at Maddy. If he missed it, the key would be destroyed, and hope for Treman would be lost.

With no rehearsal of catching an arrow out of the air, Maddy had one chance, only one shot.

Drem's aim was flawless. Maddy's eyes locked on the arrow, onto the life of Treman on the point of the thin shaft, as it came at him.

He took a half step to the side, moving his open hand in a roundhouse motion. Time slowed in motion, as everything was weighing on the catch. His hand closed, snatching the feathered end of the arrow, in real time, out of its flight. He was so close to missing yet found the perfect place for using the arrow as an extension of his arm. Two steps and a fencer's lunge forced the peg into Streak's showing keyhole.

Maddy gave a twist and detached the arrow from Treman's key. A shockwave of energy froze the machine that Streak had become, sending a burst of visible sound waves as he and all the tremans—still lined along the pathway to the entrance—became trees again. The transformation had left Streak planted in the center of the street.

They had stopped him. Any doubts or assumptions of defeat were gone. Trace ran to Maddy's arms, almost knocking him off his feet. The extra weight of the armor and his future life made his knees buckle.

The palace doors opened as Drem and Josh, along with Drem's guards and Heaster, came to where they stood in their embrace.

Maddy was overwhelmed. The relief of victory brought tears to his eyes; running down his cheeks were lines of wetness, as his thoughts went to his dad and Uncle Mel.

"What's wrong, Maddy?" Trace felt his loss as he spoke their names.

"Dad and Mel." He broke down even more.

THE BATTLE

The battle had come with a cost—not only his dad and uncle, but Treman had given his life as well. The two moves of defense that Maddy had missed had a huge price tag. Treman's decision hadn't been completely thought through; it couldn't have been or Streak might have figured out what Maddy was going to do. Maddy hadn't figured out how he would take Treman's plug out without reenacting the wicked rival.

A noise from where the cylinder was attracted their attention. The cylinder slowly grew into the form of the prior Treman in the exhibit. It also was in the center of the street. It looked so alive when it had completely changed. The seven pieces lay at its base.

"We should get the parts back inside." Drem had his guards pick the items up and return them to their room.

Maddy needed to go to the east wall. He called Heaster to him, boarded with Trace, and lifted off with Drem and Josh as they steered their way to the wall. In the light of day, the small smoking embers of the trees that had been burned were mostly piles of ash. The blast area was rubble, with no sign of the bodies. They set down; Maddy slid off and got his balance on the rocks turning beneath his feet. He stumbled forward, looking for anything that might not have been destroyed.

To his side an extruding boulder shadowed a mound of smaller rocks—and what looked like the tip of a shoe. It was his uncle's shoe. As Maddy rushed to the scene, tossing the undersize rocks away, the sound of a throat being cleared caused his head to snap up. He looked behind the boulder and found Dray leaning against a wall with Mel lying on his chest, held in his arms. They were alive! Dray had moved them to the safety of the boulder after firing their lethal shots. Streak had missed them, only scattering the debris across Mel's legs.

Mel was dug out; his injured leg was in dire need of care, but he was alive. Maddy's heart was revived. It hadn't been a total loss of his father, his uncle, and his friend. Getting Mel back inside the city walls, to a doctor Drem knew of, saved him from losing his leg.

Dray held his son, asking questions about what had happened. He was thankful for everything. Not only had they defeated the enemy within their gates, but they also had lived to tell about it. Their stories would be told for hundreds of generations. The young man from Dillon County had led the way to saving Palace City.

"What happened to Treman?" Dray asked the unavoidable question.

"I used him to save everyone. He gave his heart to me, and I used it to put Streak to death. I believe he knew what the ending was going to be. And he still gave me his life. He trusted me, Dad. He trusted *me*." Maddy again felt the loss as he recalled the special times they had shared in their brief time together.

"And as long as you don't forget, son...as long as you never forget what he gave you, you will have a reason to live. He gave you a chance to live." Dray knew the pain of loss but also knew the life of his son had given him a reason to live.

Cleanup was underway as they returned to the palace. The two rows of treman trees were a stark reminder for anyone who would visit the palace archives in the future. Streak was being carved down piece by piece, being in the vulnerable

THE BATTLE

state of a tree again. His branches, limbs, and trunk slowly piled up to be burned for a celebration on Celemass.

Maddy took charge of the demolition, looking for any sign of the key, but found nothing. This time the sacrifice Treman had paid was never going to be undone. The key was lost.

Celemass was an incredible affair in the city. The joyful tumult of the people rose in exuberance, and the high energy of giving was felt by everyone. Life had been given by Treman for a perfect example of what sacrifice truly means—to truly give your life for theirs.

Maddy had taken the two parts of the cylinder to the palace to be placed with the others. Trace carried one and Maddy the other. As they entered the room, the seven pieces, protected under their domed shields, started to shudder.

The two pieces they had brought into the room were set on a new display table. Maddy set his down, followed by Trace setting her half beside it. They joined together without their assistance. The plate, where the etched, coded words were sealed into one inscription, changed into words they were both able to read out loud together.

"TO GO WHERE NO ONE MAN HAS VEERED FROM TO GO WHERE HE CAME FROM."

Made in the USA
San Bernardino, CA
06 December 2013